The Amazing Marriage by George Meredith

George Meredith, OM, was born in Portsmouth, England on February 12th, 1828, a son and grandson of naval outfitters. His mother died when he was only five.

As a fourteen year old teenager he was sent to a Moravian School in Neuwied, Germany, staying there for two years.

After reading law he was articled as a solicitor, but quickly abandoned that career path for journalism and poetry. He collaborated with Edward Gryffydh Peacock, son of Thomas Love Peacock in publishing a privately circulated literary magazine, the Monthly Observer.

At age twenty-one he married Mary Ellen Nicolls, Edward Peacock's beautiful widowed sister, and mother of a child, on August 8th, 1849. Mary Ellen was twenty-eight. The marriage produced one child; Arthur (1853–1890).

Meredith collected his early writings, all previously published in periodicals, in an 1851 volume, Poems.

In 1856 he posed as the model for The Death of Chatterton, a well-known picture by the English Pre-Raphaelite painter Henry Wallis, which romantised the teenage Chatterton's demise.

Although Meredith received some publicity for this his wife received rather more attention from Wallis because of it. Mary Ellen ran off with Wallis in 1858, shortly before giving birth to a child that all assumed to be Wallis. Tragically she died three years later.

From that dreadful experience emerged a collection of sonnets entitled Modern Love in 1862 together with much of his first major novel; The Ordeal of Richard Feverel.

Meredith married Marie Vulliamy on September 20th, 1864 and they settled in Surrey. Together they had two children; William (born in 1865) and Mariette (born in 1874).

He continued writing novels and poetry, often inspired by nature. He had a keen understanding of comedy and his Essay on Comedy (1877) remains a reference work in the history of comic theory.

In The Egoist, published in 1879, he applies some of his theories of comedy in one of his most thoughtful and enduring novels.

During most of his career, he had difficulty crossing over from critical acclamation to popular success. It was only in 1885 that his first genuine commercial success appeared; Diana of the Crossways.

An artist's life throughout the ages, when not subsidised by a patron, is often difficult. Meredith found it no different. With an unreliable income stream he sought to bolster that with a job as a publisher's reader.

The company that gave him this lifeline was Chapman & Hall (an eminent publishing house who could include Charles Dickens, William Makepeace Thackeray, Elizabeth Barrett Browning and Anthony

Trollope on their roster). His advice to the company was very well received and made him influential in the world of letters.

To this influence he was able to add a circle of friends that included William and Dante Gabriel Rossetti, Algernon Charles Swinburne, Cotter Morison, Leslie Stephen, Robert Louis Stevenson, George Gissing and J. M. Barrie.

In 1868 Meredith was introduced to Thomas Hardy. Hardy had submitted his first novel, The Poor Man and the Lady. Meredith felt the book was too bitter a satire on the rich and told Hardy to put it aside as it was likely it would be savaged by reviewers and destroy his nascent career. Meredith had received the same reaction with The Ordeal of Richard Feverel. Although it had brought him success it was judged so shocking that Mudie's circulating library cancelled an order of 300 copies.

But these years, creatively, were very prolific and successful for Meredith. Novels and poems flowed from his pen including everything from The Adventures of Harry Richmond to Diana of the Crossways and many poetry volumes include The Lark Ascending (which later inspired the Vaughan Williams music)

In 1886, tragedy struck the Meredith household when his second wife, Marie Vulliamy, died of cancer.

Whilst his personal life was producing horrendous scars he was receiving many accolades. Oscar Wilde was a fan. In The Decay of Lying, (originally published in the January 1889 issue of The Nineteenth Century) he says of Meredith "Ah, Meredith! Who can define him? His style is chaos illumined by flashes of lightning".

In 1891 Meredith was even the subject of homage when Sir Arthur Conan Doyle in his Sherlock Holmes short story The Boscombe Valley Mystery, (published in the popular Strand magazine) when Sherlock Holmes turns to Watson during case discussions and says "And now let us talk about George Meredith, if you please, and we shall leave all minor matters until tomorrow."

Before his death, Meredith was honoured from many quarters: he succeeded Lord Tennyson as president of the Society of Authors; in 1905 he was appointed to the Order of Merit by King Edward VII.

George Meredith, aged 81, died at his home in Box Hill, Surrey on May 18th, 1909. He is buried in the cemetery at Dorking, Surrey.

Index of Contents

BOOK I

CHAPTER I

ENTER DAME GOSSIP AS CHORUS

Everybody has heard of the beautiful Countess of Cressett, who was one of the lights of this country at the time when crowned heads were running over Europe, crying out for charity's sake to be amused after their tiresome work of slaughter: and you know what a dread they have of moping. She was famous for her fun and high spirits besides her good looks, which you may judge of for yourself on a walk down most of our great noblemen's collections of pictures in England, where you will behold her as the goddess Diana fitting an arrow to a bow; and elsewhere an Amazon holding a spear; or a lady with dogs, in the costume of the day; and in one place she is a nymph, if not Diana herself, gazing at her naked feet before her attendants loosen her tunic for her to take the bath, and her hounds are pricking their ears, and you see antlers of a stag behind a block of stone. She was a wonderful swimmer, among other things, and one early morning, when she was a girl, she did really swim, they say, across the Shannon and back to win a bet for her brother Lord Levellier, the colonel of cavalry, who left an arm in Egypt, and changed his way of life to become a wizard, as the common people about his neighbourhood supposed, because he foretold the weather and had cures for aches and pains without a doctor's diploma. But we know now that he was only a mathematician and astronomer, all for inventing military engines. The brother and sister were great friends in their youth, when he had his right arm to defend her reputation with; and she would have done anything on earth to please him.

There is a picture of her in an immense flat white silk hat trimmed with pale blue, like a pavilion, the broadest brim ever seen, and she simply sits on a chair; and Venus the Queen of Beauty would have been extinguished under that hat, I am sure; and only to look at Countess Fanny's eye beneath the brim she has tipped ever so slightly in her artfulness makes the absurd thing graceful and suitable. Oh! she was a cunning one. But you must be on your guard against the scandalmongers and collectors of anecdotes, and worst of any, the critic, of our Galleries of Art; for she being in almost all of them (the principal painters of the day were on their knees for the favour of a sitting), they have to speak of her pretty frequently, and they season their dish, the coxcombs do, by hinting a knowledge of her history.

'Here we come to another portrait of the beautiful but, we fear, naughty Countess of Cressett.'

You are to imagine that they know everything, and they are so indulgent when they drop their blot on a lady's character.

They can boast of nothing more than having read Nymriey's Letters and Correspondence, published, fortunately for him, when he was no longer to be called to account below for his malicious insinuations, pretending to decency in initials and dashes: That man was a hater of women and the clergy. He was one of the horrid creatures who write with a wink at you, which sets the wicked part of us on fire: I have known it myself, and I own it to my shame; and if I happened to be ignorant of the history of Countess Fanny, I could not refute his wantonness. He has just the same benevolent leer for a bishop. Give me, if we are to make a choice, the beggar's breech for decency, I say: I like it vastly in preference to a Nymney, who leads you up to the curtain and agitates it, and bids you to retire on tiptoe. You cannot help being angry with the man for both reasons. But he is the writer society delights in, to show what it is composed of. A man brazen enough to declare that he could hold us in suspense about the adventures of a broomstick, with the aid of a yashmak and an ankle, may know the world; you had better not know him—that is my remark; and do not trust him.

He tells the story of the Old Buccaneer in fear of the public, for it was general property, but of course he finishes with a Nymney touch: 'So the Old Buccaneer is the doubloon she takes in exchange for a handful of silver pieces.' There is no such handful to exchange—not of the kind he sickeningly nudges at you. I will prove to you it was not Countess Fanny's naughtiness, though she was indeed very blamable. Women should walk in armour as if they were born to it; for these cold sneerers will never waste their darts on cuirasses. An independent brave young creature, exposing herself thoughtlessly in her reckless innocence, is the victim for them. They will bring all society down on her with one of their explosive sly words appearing so careless, the cowards. I say without hesitation, her conduct with regard to Kirby, the Old Buccaneer, as he was called, however indefensible in itself, warrants her at heart an innocent young woman, much to be pitied. Only to think of her, I could sometimes drop into a chair for a good cry. And of him too! and their daughter Carinthia Jane was the pair of them, as to that, and so was Chillon John, the son.

Those critics quoting Nymney should look at the portrait of her in the Long Saloon of Cresset Castle, where she stands in blue and white, completely dressed, near a table supporting a couple of holster pistols, and then let them ask themselves whether they would speak of her so if her little hand could move.

Well, and so the tale of her swim across the Shannon river and back drove the young Earl of Cresset straight over to Ireland to propose for her, he saying; that she was the girl to suit his book; not allowing her time to think of how much he might be the man to suit hers. The marriage was what is called a good one: both full of frolic, and he wealthy and rather handsome, and she quite lovely and spirited.

No wonder the whole town was very soon agog about the couple, until at the end of a year people began to talk of them separately, she going her way, and he his. She could not always be on the top of a coach, which was his throne of happiness.

Plenty of stories are current still of his fame as a four-in-hand coachman. They say he once drove an Emperor and a King, a Prince Chancellor and a pair of Field Marshals, and some ladies of the day, from the metropolis to Richmond Hill in fifty or sixty odd minutes, having the ground cleared all the way by bell and summons, and only a donkey-cart and man, and a deaf old woman, to pay for; and went, as you can imagine, at such a tearing gallop, that those Grand Highnesses had to hold on for their lives and lost their hats along the road; and a publican at Kew exhibits one above his bar to the present hour. And Countess Fanny was up among them, they say. She was equal to it. And some say, that was the occasion of her meeting the Old Buccaneer.

She met him at Richmond in Surrey we know for certain. It was on Richmond Hill, where the old King met his Lass. They say Countess Fanny was parading the hill to behold the splendid view, always admired so much by foreigners, with their Achs and Hechs! and surrounded by her crowned courtiers in frogged uniforms and moustachioed like sea-horses, a little before dinner time, when Kirby passed her, and the Emperor made a remark on him, for Kirby was a magnificent figure of a man, and used to be compared to a three-decker entering harbour after a victory. He stood six feet four, and was broad-shouldered and deep-chested to match, and walked like a king who has humbled his enemy. You have seen big dogs. And so Countess Fanny looked round. Kirby was doing the same. But he had turned right about, and appeared transfixed and like a royal beast angry, with his wound. If ever there was love at first sight, and a dreadful love, like a runaway mail-coach in a storm of wind and lightning at black midnight by the banks of a flooded river, which was formerly our comparison for terrible situations, it was when those two met.

And, what! you exclaim, Buccaneer Kirby full sixty-five, and Countess Fanny no more than three and twenty, a young beauty of the world of fashion, courted by the highest, and she in love with him! Go and gaze at one of our big ships coming out of an engagement home with all her flags flying and her crew manning the yards. That will give you an idea of a young woman's feelings for an old warrior never beaten down an inch by anything he had to endure; matching him, I dare say, in her woman's heart, with the Mighty Highnesses who had only smelt the outside edge of battle. She did rarely admire a valiant man. Old as Methuselah, he would have made her kneel to him. She was all heart for a real hero.

The story goes, that Countess Fanny sent her husband to Captain Kirby, at the emperor's request, to inquire his name; and on hearing it, she struck her hands on her bosom, telling his Majesty he saw there the bravest man in the king's dominions; which the emperor scarce crediting, and observing that the man must be, then, a superhuman being to be so distinguished in a nation of the brave, Countess Fanny related the well-known tale of Captain Kirby and the shipful of mutineers; and how when not a man of them stood by him, and he in the service of the first insurgent State of Spanish America, to save his ship from being taken over to the enemy,—he blew her up, fifteen miles from land: and so he got to shore swimming and floating alternately, and was called Old Sky-high by English sailors, any number of whom could always be had to sail under Buccaneer Kirby. He fought on shore as well; and once he came down from the tops of the Andes with a black beard turned white, and went into action with the title of Kirby's Ghost.

But his heart was on salt water; he was never so much at home as in a ship foundering or splitting into the clouds. We are told that he never forgave the Admiralty for striking him off the list of English naval captains: which is no doubt why in his old age he nursed a grudge against his country.

Ours, I am sure, was the loss; and many have thought so since. He was a mechanician, a master of stratagems; and would say, that brains will beat Grim Death if we have enough of them. He was a standing example of the lessons of his own MAXIMS FOR MEN, a very curious book, that fetches a rare price now wherever a copy is put up for auction. I shudder at them as if they were muzzles of firearms pointed at me; but they were not addressed to my sex; and still they give me an interest in the writer who would declare, that 'he had never failed in an undertaking without stripping bare to expose to himself where he had been wanting in Intention and Determination.'

There you may see a truly terrible man.

So the emperor being immensely taken with Kirby's method of preserving discipline on board ship, because (as we say to the madman, 'Your strait-waistcoat is my easy-chair') monarchs have a great love of discipline, he begged Countess Fanny's permission that he might invite Captain Kirby to his table; and Countess Fanny (she had the name from the ballad

'I am the star of Prince and Czar,
My light is shed on many,
But I wait here till my bold Buccaneer
Makes prize of Countess Fanny':—

for the popular imagination was extraordinarily roused by the elopement, and there were songs and ballads out of number), Countess Fanny despatched her husband to Captain Kirby again, meaning no harm, though the poor man is laughed at in the songs for going twice upon his mission.

None of the mighty people repented of having the Old Buccaneer—for that night, at all events. He sat in the midst of them, you may believe, like the lord of that table, with his great white beard and hair—not a lock of it shed—and his bronze lion-face, and a resolute but a merry eye that he had. He was no deep drinker of wine, but when he did drink, and the wine champagne, he drank to show his disdain of its powers; and the emperor wishing for a narrative of some of his exploits, particularly the blowing up of his ship, Kirby paid his Majesty the compliment of giving it him as baldly as an official report to the Admiralty. So disengaged and calm was he, with his bottles of champagne in him, where another would have been sparkling and laying on the colours, that he was then and there offered Admiral's rank in the Imperial navy; and the Old Buccaneer, like a courtier of our best days, bows to Countess Fanny, and asks her, if he is a free man to go: and, No, says she, we cannot spare you! And there was a pretty wrangle between Countess Fanny and the emperor, each pulling at the Old Buccaneer to have possession of him.

He was rarely out of her sight after their first meeting, and the ridiculous excuse she gave to her husband's family was, she feared he would be kidnapped and made a Cossack of! And young Lord Cressett, her husband, began to grumble concerning her intimacy with a man old enough to be her grandfather. As if the age were the injury! He seemed to think it so, and vowed he would shoot the old depredator dead, if he found him on the grounds of Cressett: 'like vermin,' he said, and it was considered that he had the right, and no jury would have convicted him. You know what those days were.

He had his opportunity one moonlight night, not far from the castle, and peppered Kirby with shot from a fowling-piece at, some say, five paces' distance, if not point-blank.

But Kirby had a maxim, Steady shakes them, and he acted on it to receive his enemy's fire; and the young lord's hand shook, and the Old Buccaneer stood out of the smoke not much injured, except in the coat-collar, with a pistol cocked in his hand, and he said:

'Many would take that for a declaration of war, but I know it 's only your lordship's diplomacy'; and then he let loose to his mad fun, astounding Lord Cressett and his gamekeeper, and vowed, as the young lord tried to relate subsequently, as well as he could recollect the words—here I have it in print:—'that he was a man pickled in saltpetre when an infant, like Achilles, and proof against powder and shot not marked with cross and key, and fetched up from the square magazine in the central depot of the infernal factory, third turning to the right off the grand arcade in Kingdom-come, where the night-porter has to wear wet petticoats, like a Highland chief, to make short work of the sparks flying about, otherwise this world and many another would not have to wait long for combustion.'

Kirby had the wildest way of talking when he was not issuing orders under fire, best understood by sailors. I give it you as it stands here printed. I do not profess to understand.

So Lord Cressett said: 'Diplomacy and infernal factories be hanged! Have your shot at me; it's only fair.' And Kirby discharged his pistol at the top twigs of an old oak tree, and called the young lord a Briton, and proposed to take him in hand and make a man of him, as nigh worthy of his wife as any one not an Alexander of Macedon could be.

So they became friendly, and the young lord confessed it was his family that had urged him to the attack; and Kirby abode at the castle, and all three were happy, in perfect honour, I am convinced: but such was not the opinion of the Cressetts and Levelliers. Down they trooped to Cressett Castle with a rush and a roar, crying on the disgrace of an old desperado like Kirby living there; Dukes, Marchionesses, Cabinet Ministers, leaders of fashion, and fire-eating colonels of the King's body-guard, one of whom Captain John Peter Kirby laid on his heels at ten paces on an April morning, when the duel was fought, as early as the blessed heavens had given them light to see to do it. Such days those were!

There was talk of shutting up the infatuated lady. If not incarcerated, she was rigidly watched. The earl her husband fell altogether to drinking and coaching, and other things. The ballad makes her say:

'My family my gaolers be,
My husband is a zany;
Naught see I clear save my bold Buccaneer
To rescue Countess Fanny!'

and it goes on:

'O little lass, at play on the grass,

Come earn a silver penny,
And you'll be dear to my bold Buccaneer
For news of his Countess Fanny.'

In spite of her bravery, that poor woman suffered!

We used to learn by heart the ballads and songs upon famous events in those old days when poetry was worshipped.

But Captain Kirby gave provocation enough to both families when he went among the taverns and clubs, and vowed before Providence over his big fist that they should rue their interference, and he would carry off the lady on a day he named; he named the hour as well, they say, and that was midnight of the month of June. The Levelliers and Cressetts foamed at the mouth in speaking of him, so enraged they were on account of his age and his passion for a young woman. As to blood, the Kirbys of Lincolnshire were quite equal to the Cressetts of Warwick. The Old Buccaneer seems to have had money too. But you can see what her people had to complain of: his insolent contempt of them was unexampled. And their tyranny had roused my lady's high spirit not a bit less; and she said right out: 'When he comes, I am ready and will go with him.'

There was boldness for you on both sides! All the town was laughing and betting on the event of the night in June: and the odds were in favour of Kirby; for though, Lord Cressett was quite the popular young English nobleman, being a capital whip and free of his coin, in those days men who had smelt powder were often prized above titles, and the feeling, out of society, was very strong for Kirby, even previous to the fight on the heath. And the age of the indomitable adventurer must have contributed to his popularity. He was the hero of every song.

"'What's age to me!" cries Kirby;
"Why, young and fresh let her be,
But it 's mighty better reasoned
For a man to be well seasoned,
And a man she has in me," cries Kirby.'

As to his exact age:

"'Write me down sixty-three," cries Kirby.'

I have always maintained that it was an understatement. We must remember, it was not Kirby speaking, but the song-writer. Kirby would not, in my opinion, have numbered years he was proud of below their due quantity. He was more, if he died at ninety-one; and Chillon Switzer John Kirby, born eleven months after the elopement, was, we know, twenty-three years old when the old man gave up the ghost and bequeathed him little besides a law-suit with the Austrian Government, and the care of Carinthia Jane, the second child of this extraordinary union; both children born in wedlock, as you will hear. Sixty-three, or sixty-seven, near upon seventy, when most men are reaping and stacking their sins with groans and weak knees, Kirby was a match for his juniors, which they discovered.

Captain John Peter Avason Kirby, son of a Lincolnshire squire of an ancient stock, was proud of his blood, and claimed descent from a chief of the Danish rovers.

"'What's rank to me!" cries Kirby;
"A titled lass let her be,
But unless my plans miscarry,
I'll show her when we marry;
As brave a pedigree," cries Kirby.'

That was the song-writer's answer to the charge that the countess had stooped to a degrading alliance.

John Peter was fourth of a family of seven children, all males, and hard at the bottle early in life: 'for want of proper occupation,' he says in his Memoirs, and applauds his brother Stanson, the clergyman, for being ahead of him in renouncing strong dunks, because he found that he 'cursed better upon water.' Water, however, helped Stanson Kirby to outlive his brothers and inherit the Lincolnshire property, and at the period of the great scandal in London he was palsied, and waited on by his grandson and heir Ralph Thorkill Kirby, the hero of an adventure celebrated in our Law courts and on the English stage; for he took possession of his coachman's wife, and was accused of compassing the death of the husband. He was not hanged for it, so we are bound to think him not guilty.

The stage-piece is called 'Saturday Night', and it had an astonishing run, but is only remembered now for the song of 'Saturday,' sung by the poor coachman and labourers at the village ale-house before he starts to capture his wife from the clutches of her seducer and meets his fate. Never was there a more popular song: you heard it everywhere. I recollect one verse:

'O Saturday money is slippery metal,
And Saturday ale it is tipsy stuff
At home the old woman is boiling her kettle,
She thinks we don't know when we've tippled enough.
We drink, and of never a man are we jealous,
And never a man against us will he speak
For who can be hard on a set of poor fellows
Who only see Saturday once a week!

You chorus the last two lines.

That was the very song the unfortunate coachman of Kirby Hall joined in singing before he went out to face his end for the woman he loved. He believed in her virtue to the very last.

'The ravished wife of my bosom,' he calls her all through the latter half of the play. It is a real tragedy. The songs of that day have lost their effect now, I suppose. They will ever remain pathetic to me; and to hear the poor coachman William Martin invoking the name of his dear stolen wife Elizabeth, jug in hand, so tearfully, while he joins the song of Saturday, was a most moving thing. You saw nothing but handkerchiefs out all over the theatre. What it is that has gone from our drama, I cannot tell: I am never affected now as I was then; and people in a low station of life could affect me then, without being flung at me, for I dislike an entire dish of them, I own. We were simpler in our habits and ways of thinking. Elizabeth Martin, according to report, was a woman to make better men than Ralph Thorkill act evilly— as to good looks, I mean. She was not entirely guiltless, I am afraid; though in the last scene, Mrs. Kempson, who played the part (as, alas, she could do to the very life!), so threw herself into the pathos of it that there were few to hold out against her, and we felt that Elizabeth had been misled. So much for morality in those days!

And now for the elopement.

CHAPTER II

MISTRESS GOSSIP TELLS OF THE ELOPEMENT OF THE COUNTESS OF CRESSETT WITH THE OLD BUCCANEER, AND OF CHARLES DUMP THE POSTILLION CONDUCTING THEM, AND OF A GREAT COUNTY FAMILY

The twenty-first of June was the day appointed by Captain Kirby to carry off Countess Fanny, and the time midnight: and ten minutes to the stroke of twelve, Countess Fanny, as if she scorned to conceal that she was in a conspiracy with her grey-haired lover, notwithstanding that she was watched and guarded, left the Marchioness of Arpington's ball-room and was escorted downstairs by her brother Lord Levellier, sworn to baffle Kirby. Present with him in the street and witness to the shutting of the carriage-door on Countess Fanny, were brother officers of his, General Abrane, Colonel Jack Potts, and Sir Upton Tomber.

The door fast shut, Countess Fanny kissed her hand to them and drew up the window, seeming merry, and as they had expected indignation and perhaps resistance, for she could be a spitfire in a temper and had no fear whatever of firearms, they were glad to have her safe on such good terms; and so General Abrane jumped up on the box beside the coachman, Jack Potts jumped up between the footmen, and Sir Upton Tomber and the one-armed lord, as soon as the carriage was disengaged from the ruck two deep, walked on each side of it in the road all the way to Lord Cressett's town house. No one thought of asking where that silly young man was—probably under some table.

Their numbers were swelled by quite a host going along, for heavy bets were on the affair, dozens having backed Kirby; and it must have appeared serious to them, with the lady in custody, and constables on the look-out, and Kirby and his men nowhere in sight. They expected an onslaught at some point of the procession, and it may be believed they wished it, if only that they might see something for their money. A beautiful bright moonlight night it happened to be. Arm in arm among them were Lord Pitscrew and Russett, Earl of Fleetwood, a great friend of Kirby's; for it was a device of the Old Buccaneer's that helped the earl to win the great Welsh heiress who made him, even before he took to hoarding and buying,—one of the wealthiest noblemen in England; but she was crazed by her marriage or the wild scenes leading to it; she never presented herself in society. She would sit on the top of Estlemont towers—as they formerly spelt it—all day and half the night in midwinter, often, looking for the mountains down in her native West country, covered with an old white flannel cloak, and on her head a tall hat of her Welsh women-folk; and she died of it, leaving a son in her likeness, of whom you will hear. Lord Fleetwood had lost none of his faith in Kirby, and went on booking bets giving him huge odds, thousands!

He accepted fifty to one when the carriage came to a stop at the steps of Lord Cressett's mansion; but he was anxious, and well he might be, seeing Countess Fanny alight and pass up between two lines of gentlemen all bowing low before her: not a sign of the Old Buccaneer anywhere to right or left! Heads were on the look out, and vows offered up for his appearance.

She was at the door and about to enter the house. Then it was; that with a shout of the name of some dreadful heathen god, Colonel Jack Potts roared out, 'She's half a foot short o' the mark!'

He was on the pavement, and it seems he measured her as she slipped by him, and one thing and another caused him to smell a cheat; and General Abrane, standing beside her near the door, cried: 'Where art flying now, Jack?' But Jack Potts grew more positive and bellowed, 'Peel her wig! we're done!'

And she did not speak a word, but stood huddled-up and hooded; and Lord Levellier caught her up by the arm as she was trying a dash into the hall, and Sir Upton Tomber plucked at her veil and raised it, and whistled:

'Phew!'—which struck the rabble below with awe of the cunning of the Old Buccaneer; and there was no need for them to hear General Abrane say: 'Right! Jack, we've a dead one in hand,' or Jack Potts reply:

'It's ten thousand pounds clean winged away from my pocket, like a string of wild geese!'

The excitement of the varletry in the square, they say, was fearful to hear. So the principal noblemen and gentlemen concerned thought it prudent to hurry the young woman into the house and bar the door; and there she was very soon stripped of veil and blonde false wig with long curls, the whole framing of her artificial resemblance to Countess Fanny, and she proved to be a good-looking foreign maid, a dark one, powdered, trembling very much, but not so frightened upon hearing that her penalty for the share she had taken in the horrid imposture practised upon them was to receive and return a salute from each of the gentlemen in rotation; which the hussy did with proper submission; and Jack Potts remarked, that 'it was an honest buss, but dear at ten thousand!'

When you have been the victim of a deceit, the explanation of the simplicity of the trick turns all the wonder upon yourself, you know, and the backers of the Old Buccaneer and the wagerers against him crowed and groaned in chorus at the maid's narrative of how the moment Countess Fanny had thrown up the window of her carriage, she sprang out to a carriage on the off side, containing Kirby, and how she, this little French jade, sprang in to take her place. One snap of the fingers and the transformation was accomplished. So for another kiss all round they let her go free, and she sat at the supper-table prepared for Countess Fanny and the party by order of Lord Levellier, and amused the gentlemen with stories of the ladies she had served, English and foreign. And that is how men are taught to think they know our sex and may despise it! I could preach them a lesson. Those men might as well not believe in the steadfastness of the very stars because one or two are reported lost out of the firmament, and now and then we behold a whole shower of fragments descending. The truth is, they have taken a stain from the life they lead, and are troubled puddles, incapable of clear reflection. To listen to the tattle of a chatting little slut, and condemn the whole sex upon her testimony, is a nice idea of justice. Many of the gentlemen present became notorious as woman-scorners, whether owing to Countess Fanny or other things. Lord Levellier was, and Lord Fleetwood, the wicked man! And certainly the hearing of naughty stories of us by the light of a grievous and vexatious instance of our misconduct must produce an impression. Countess Fanny's desperate passion for a man of the age of Kirby struck them as out of nature. They talked of it as if they could have pardoned her a younger lover.

All that Lord Cressett said, on the announcement of the flight of his wife, was: 'Ah! Fan! she never would run in my ribbons.'

He positively declined to persue. Lord Levellier would not attempt to follow her up without him, as it would have cost money, and he wanted all that he could spare for his telescopes and experiments. Who, then, was the gentleman who stopped the chariot, with his three mounted attendants, on the road to the sea, on the heath by the great Punch-Bowl?

That has been the question for now longer than half a century, in fact approaching seventy mortal years. No one has ever been able to say for certain.

It occurred at six o'clock on the summer morning. Countess Fanny must have known him, and not once did she open her mouth to breathe his name. Yet she had no objection to talk of the adventure and how Simon Fettle, Captain Kirby's old ship's steward in South America, seeing horsemen stationed on the ascent of the high road bordering the Bowl, which is miles round and deep, made the postillion cease jogging, and sang out to his master for orders, and Kirby sang back to him to look to his priming, and then the postillion was bidden proceed, and he did not like it, but he had to deal with pistols behind, where men feel weak, and he went bobbing on the saddle in dejection, as if upon his very heart he jogged; and soon the fray commenced. There was very little parleying between determined men.

Simon Fettle was a plain kindly creature without a thought of malice, who kept his master's accounts. He fired the first shot at the foremost man, as he related in after days, 'to reduce the odds.' Kirby said to

Countess Fanny, just to comfort her, never so much as imagining she would be afraid, 'The worst will be a bloody shirt for Simon to mangle,' for they had been arranging to live cheaply in a cottage on the Continent, and Simon Fettle to do the washing. She could not help laughing outright. But when the Old Buccaneer was down striding in the battle, she took a pistol and descended likewise; and she used it, too, and loaded again.

She had not to use it a second time. Kirby pulled the gentleman off his horse, wounded in the thigh, and while dragging him to Countess Fanny to crave her pardon, a shot intended for Kirby hit the poor gentleman in the breast, and Kirby stretched him at his length, and Simon and he disarmed the servant who had fired. One was insensible, one flying, and those two on the ground. All in broad daylight; but so lonely is that spot, nothing might have been heard of it, if at the end of the week the postillion who had been bribed and threatened with terrible threats to keep his tongue from wagging, had not begun to talk. So the scene of the encounter was examined, and on one spot, carefully earthed over, blood-marks were discovered in the green sand. People in the huts on the hill-top, a quarter of a mile distant, spoke of having heard sounds of firing while they were at breakfast, and a little boy named Tommy Wedger said he saw a dead body go by in an open coach that morning; all bloody and mournful. He had to appear before the magistrates, crying terribly, but did not know the nature of an oath, and was dismissed. Time came when the boy learned to swear, and he did, and that he had seen a beautiful lady firing and killing men like pigeons and partridges; but that was after Charles Dump, the postillion, had been telling the story.

Those who credited Charles Dump's veracity speculated on dozens of great noblemen—and gentlemen known to be dying in love with Countess Fanny. And this brings us to another family.

I do not say I know anything; I do but lay before you the evidence we have to fix suspicion upon a notorious character, perfectly capable of trying to thwart a man like Kirby, and with good reason to try, if she had bewitched him to a consuming passion, as we are told.

About eleven miles distant, as the crow flies and a bold huntsman will ride in that heath country, from the Punch-Bowl, right across the mounds and the broad water, lies the estate of the Fakenhams, who intermarried with the Coplestones of the iron mines, and were the wealthiest of the old county families until Curtis Fakenham entered upon his inheritance. Money with him was like the farm-wife's dish of grain she tosses in showers to her fowls. He was more than what you call a lady-killer, he was a woman-eater. His pride was in it as well as his taste, and when men are like that, indeed they are devourers!

Curtis was the elder brother of Commodore Baldwin Fakenham, whose offspring, like his own, were so strangely mixed up with Captain Kirby's children by Countess Fanny, as you will hear. And these two brothers were sons of Geoffrey Fakenham, celebrated for his devotion to the French Countess Jules d'Andreuze, or some such name, a courtly gentleman, who turned Papist on his death-bed in France, in Brittany somewhere, not to be separated from her in the next world, as he solemnly left word; wickedly, many think.

To show the oddness of things and how opposite to one another brothers may be, his elder, the uncle of Curtis, and Baldwin, was the renowned old Admiral Fakenham, better known along our sea-coasts and ports among sailors as 'Old Showery,' because of a remark he once made to his flag-captain, when cannon-balls were coming thick on them in a hard-fought action. 'Hot work, sir,' his captain said. 'Showery,' replied the admiral, as his cocked-hat was knocked off by the wind of a cannon-ball. He lost both legs before the war was over, and said merrily, 'Stumps for life' while they were carrying him below to the cockpit. In my girlhood the boys were always bringing home anecdotes of old Admiral Showery: not all of them true ones, perhaps, but they fitted him. He was a rough seaman, fond, as they say, of his glass and his girl, and utterly despising his brother Geoffrey for the airs he gave himself, and crawling on his knees to a female Parleyvoo; and when Geoffrey died, the admiral drank to his rest in the grave: 'There's to my brother Jeff,' he said, and flinging away the dregs of his glass: 'There 's to the Frog!' and flinging away the glass to shivers: 'There's to the Turncoat!'

He salted his language in a manner I cannot repeat; no epithet ever stood by itself. When I was young the boys relished these dreadful words because they seemed to smell of tar and battle-smoke, when every English boy was for being a sailor and daring the Black Gentleman below. In all truth, the bad words came from him; though an excellent scholar has assured me they should be taken for aspirates, and mean no harm; and so it may be, but heartily do I rejoice that aspirates, have been dropped by people of birth; for you might once hear titled ladies guilty of them in polite society, I do assure you.

We have greatly improved in that respect. They say the admiral's reputation as a British sailor of the old school made him, rather his name, a great favourite at Court; but to Court he could not be got to go, and if the tale be true, their Majesties paid him a visit on board his ship, in harbour one day, and sailors tell you that Old Showery gave his liege lord and lady a common dish of boiled beef with carrots and turnips, and a plain dumpling, for their dinner, with ale and port wine, the merit of which he swore to; and he became so elate, that after the cloth was removed, he danced them a hornpipe on his pair of wooden legs, whistling his tune, and holding his full tumbler of hot grog in his hand all the while, without so much as the spilling of a drop!—so earnest was he in everything he did. They say his limit was two bottles of port wine at a sitting, with his glass of hot grog to follow, and not a soul could induce him to go beyond that. In addition to being a great seaman, he was a very religious man and a stout churchman.

Well, now, the Curtis Fakenham of Captain Kirby's day had a good deal of his uncle as well as his father in him, the spirit of one and the outside, of the other; and, favoured or not, he had been distinguished among Countess Fanny's adorers: she certainly chose to be silent about the name of the assailant. And it has been attested on oath that two days and a night subsequent to the date furnished by Charles Dump, Curtis Fakenham was brought to his house, Hollis Grange, lame of a leg, with a shot in his breast, that he carried to the family vault; and his head gamekeeper, John Wiltshire, a resolute fellow, was missing from that hour. Some said they had a quarrel, and Curtis was wounded and John Wiltshire killed. Curtis was known to have been extremely attached to the man. Yet when Wiltshire was inquired for, he let fall a word of 'having more of Wiltshire than was agreeable to Hampshire'—his county. People asked what that meant. Yet, according to the tale, it was the surviving servant, by whom he, or whoever it may have been, was accidentally shot.

We are in a perfect tangle. On the other hand, it was never denied that Curtis and John Wiltshire were in London together at the time of Countess Fanny's flight: and Curtis Fakenham was one of the procession of armed gentleman conducting her in her carriage, as they supposed; and he was known to have started off, on the discovery of the cheat, with horrible imprecations against Frenchwomen. It became known, too; that horses of his were standing saddled in his innyard at midnight. And more, Charles Dump the postillion was taken secretly to set eyes on him as they wheeled him in his garden-walk, and he vowed it was the identical gentleman. But this coming by and by to the ear of Curtis, he had Charles Dump fetched over to confront him; and then the man made oath that he had never seen Mr. Curtis Fakenham anywhere but there, in his own house at Hollis! One does not really know what, to think of it.

This postillion made a small fortune. He was everywhere in request. People were never tired of asking him how he behaved while the fight was going on, and he always answered that he sat as close to his horse as he could, and did not dream of dismounting; for, he said, 'he was a figure on a horse, and naught when off it.' His repetition of the story, with some adornments, and that same remark, made him the popular man of the county; people said he might enter Parliament, and I think at one time it was possible. But a great success is full of temptations. After being hired at inns to fill them with his account of the battle, and tipped by travellers from London to show the spot, he set up for himself as innkeeper, and would have flourished, only he had contracted habits on his rounds, and he fell to contradicting himself, so that he came to be called Lying Charley; and the people of the country said it was 'he who drained the Punch-Bowl, for though he helped to put the capital into it, he took all the interest out of it.'

Yet we have the doctor of the village of Ipley, Dr. Cawthorne, a noted botanist, assuring us of the absolute credibility of Charles Dump, whom he attended in the poor creature's last illness, when Charles Dump confessed he had lived in mortal terror of Squire Curtis, and had got the trick of lying, through fear of telling the truth. Hence his ruin.

So he died delirious and contrite. Cawthorne, the great Turf man, inherited a portrait of him from his father the doctor. It was often the occasion of the story being told over again, and used to hang in the patients' reception room, next to an oil-painting of the Punch-Bowl, an admired landscape picture by a local artist, highly-toned and true to every particular of the scene, with the bright yellow road winding uphill, and the banks of brilliant purple heath, and a white thorn in bloom quite beautiful, and the green fir trees, and the big Bowl black as a cauldron,—indeed a perfect feast of harmonious contrasts in colours.

And now you know how it is that the names of Captain Kirby and Curtis Fakenham are alive to the present moment in the district.

We lived a happy domestic life in those old coaching days, when county affairs and county people were the topics of firesides, and the country enclosed us to make us feel snug in our own importance. My opinion is, that men and women grow to their dimensions only where such is the case. We had our alarms from the outside now and again, but we soon relapsed to dwell upon our private business and our pleasant little hopes and excitements; the courtships and the crosses and the scandals, the tea-parties and the dances, and how the morning looked after the stormy night had passed, and the coach coming down the hill with a box of news and perhaps a curious passenger to drop at the inn. I do believe we had a liking for the very highwaymen, if they had any reputation for civility. What I call human events, things concerning you and me, instead of the deafening catastrophes now afflicting and taking all conversation out of us, had their natural interest then. We studied the face of each morning as it came, and speculated upon the secret of the thing it might have in store for us or our heroes and heroines; we thought of them more than of ourselves. Long after the adventures of the Punch-Bowl, our county was anxious about Countess Fanny and the Old Buccaneer, wondering where they were and whether they were prospering, whether they were just as much in love as ever, and which of them would bury the other, and what the foreign people abroad thought of that strange pair.

CHAPTER III

CONTINUATION OF THE INTRODUCTORY MEANDERINGS OF DAME GOSSIP, TOGETHER WITH HER SUDDEN EXTINCTION

I have still time before me, according to the terms of my agreement with the person to whom I have, I fear foolishly, entrusted the letters and documents of a story surpassing ancient as well as modern in the wonderment it causes, that would make the Law courts bless their hearts, judges no less than the barristers, to have it running through them day by day, with every particular to wrangle over, and many to serve as a text for the pulpit. So to proceed.

It should be mentioned that the postillion Charles Dump is not represented, and I have no conception of the reason why not, sitting on horseback, in the portrait in the possession of the Cawthorne family. I have not seen it, I am bound to admit. We had offended Dr. Cawthorne, by once in an urgent case calling in another doctor, who, he would have it, was a quack, that ought to have killed us, and we ceased to visit; but a gentleman who was an established patient of Dr. Cawthorne's and had frequent opportunities of judging the portrait, in the course of a chronic malady, describes Charles Dump on his legs as a small man looking diminished from a very much longer one by shrinkage in thickish wrinkles from the shoulders to the shanks. His hat is enormous and very gay. He is rather of sad countenance. An elevation of his collar behind the ears, and pointed at the neck, gives you notions of his having dropped from some hook. He stands with his forefinger extended, like a disused semaphore-post, that seems tumbling and desponding on the hill by the highroad, in his attitude while telling the tale; if standing it may be called, where the whole figure appears imploring for a seat. That was his natural position, as one would suppose any artist must have thought, and a horse beneath him. But it has been suggested that the artist in question was no painter of animals. Then why did he not get a painter of animals to put in the horse? It is vain to ask, though it is notorious that artists combine without bickering to do these things; and one puts his name on the animal, the other on the human being or landscape.

My informant adds, that the prominent feature, telling a melancholy tale of its own, is of sanguine colour, and while plainly in the act of speaking, Charles Dump might be fancied about to drop off to sleep. He was impressed by the dreaminess of the face; and I must say I regard him as an interesting character. During my girlhood Napoleon Bonaparte alone would have been his rival for filling an inn along our roads. I have known our boys go to bed obediently and get up at night to run three miles to THE WHEATSHEAF, only to stand on the bench or traveller's-rest outside the window and look in at Charles Dump reciting, with just room enough in the crowd to point his finger, as his way was.

He left a child, Mary Dump, who grew up to become lady's maid to Livia Fakenham, daughter of Curtis, the beauty of Hampshire, equalled by no one save her cousin Henrietta Fakenham, the daughter of Commodore Baldwin; and they were two different kinds of beauties, not to be compared, and different were their fortunes; for this lady was likened to the sun going down on a cloudy noon, and that lady to the moon riding through a stormy night. Livia was the young widow of Lord Duffield when she accepted the Earl of Fleetwood, and was his third countess, and again a widow at eight-and-twenty, and stepmother to young Croesus, the Earl of Fleetwood of my story. Mary Dump testifies to her kindness of heart to her dependents. If we are to speak of goodness, I am afraid there are other witnesses.

I resent being warned that my time is short and that I have wasted much of it over 'the attractive Charles.' What I have done I have done with a purpose, and it must be a storyteller devoid of the rudiments of his art who can complain of my dwelling on Charles Dump, for the world to have a pause and pin its faith to him, which it would not do to a grander person—that is, as a peg. Wonderful events, however true they are, must be attached to something common and familiar, to make them credible.

Charles Dump, I say, is like a front-page picture to a history of those old quiet yet exciting days in England, and when once you have seized him the whole period is alive to you, as it was to me in the delicious dulness I loved, that made us thirsty to hear of adventures and able to enjoy to the utmost every thing occurring. The man is no more attractive to me than a lump of clay. How could he be? But supposing I took up the lump and told you that there where I found it, that lump of clay had been rolled over and flung off by the left wheel of the prophet's Chariot of Fire before it mounted aloft and disappeared in the heavens above!—you would examine it and cherish it and have the scene present with you, you may be sure; and magnificent descriptions would not be one-half so persuasive. And that is what we call, in my profession, Art, if you please.

So to continue: the Earl of Cressett fell from his coach-box in a fit, and died of it, a fortnight after the flight of his wife; and the people said she might as well have waited. Kirby and Countess Fanny were at Lucerne or Lausanne, or some such place, in Switzerland when the news reached them, and Kirby, without losing an hour, laid hold of an English clergyman of the Established Church and put him through the ceremony of celebrating his lawful union with the beautiful young creature he adored. And this he did, he said, for the world to guard his Fan in a wider circle than his two arms could compass, if not quite so well.

So the Old Buccaneer was ever after that her lawful husband, and as his wedded wife, not wedded to a fool, she was an example to her sex, like many another woman who has begun badly with a light-headed mate. It is hard enough for a man to be married to a fool, but a man is only half-cancelled by that burden, it has been said; whereas a woman finds herself on board a rudderless vessel, and often the desperate thing she does is to avoid perishing! Ten months, or eleven, some say, following the proclamation of the marriage-tie, a son was born to Countess Fanny, close by the castle of Chillon-on-the-lake, and he had the name of Chillon Switzer John Kirby given to him to celebrate the fact.

Two years later the girl was born, and for the reason of her first seeing the light in that Austrian province, she was christened Carinthia Jane. She was her old father's pet; but Countess Fanny gloried in the boy. She had fancied she would be a childless woman before he gave sign of coming; and they say she wrote a little volume of Meditations in Prospect of Approaching Motherhood, for the guidance of others in a similar situation.

I have never been able to procure the book or pamphlet, but I know she was the best of mothers, and of wives too. And she, with her old husband, growing like a rose out of a weather-beaten rock, proved she was that, among those handsome foreign officers poorly remarkable for their morals. Not once had the Old Buccaneer to teach them a lesson. Think of it and you will know that her feet did not stray—nor did her pretty eyes. Her heart was too full for the cravings of vanity. Innocent ladies who get their husbands into scrapes are innocent, perhaps; but knock you next door in their bosoms, where the soul resides, and ask for information of how innocence and uncleanness may go together. Kirby purchased a mine in Carinthia, on the borders of Styria, and worked it himself. His native land displeased him, so that he would not have been unwilling to see Chillon enter the Austrian service, which the young man was inclined for, subsequent to his return to his parents from one of the English public schools, notwithstanding his passionate love for Old England. But Lord Levellier explained the mystery in a letter to his half-forgiven sister, praising the boy for his defence of his mother's name at the school, where a big brutal fellow sneered at her, and Chillon challenged him to sword or pistol; and then he walked down to the boy's home in Staffordshire to force him to fight; and the father of the boy made him offer an apology. That was not much balm to Master Chillon's wound. He returned to his mother quite heavy, unlike a young man; and the unhappy lady, though she knew, him to be bitterly sensitive on the point of honour, and especially as to everything relating to her, saw herself compelled to tell him the history of her life, to save him, as she thought, from these chivalrous vindications of her good name. She may have even painted herself worse than she was, both to excuse her brother's miserliness to her son and the world's evil speaking of her. Wisely or not, she chose this course devotedly to protect him from the perils she foresaw in connection with the name of the once famous Countess Fanny in the British Isles. And thus are we stricken by the days of our youth. It is impossible to moralize conveniently when one is being hurried by a person at one's elbow.

So the young man heard his mother out and kissed her, and then he went secretly to Vienna and enlisted and served for a year as a private in the regiment of Hussars, called, my papers tell me, Liechtenstein, and what with his good conduct and the help of Kirby's friends, he would have obtained a commission from the emperor, when, at the right moment to keep a sprig of Kirby's growth for his country, Lord Levellier sent word that he was down for a cornetcy in a British regiment of dragoons. Chillon came home from a garrison town, and there was a consultation about his future career. Shall it be England? Shall it be Austria? Countess Fanny's voice was for England, and she carried the vote, knowing though she did that it signified separation, and it might be alienation—where her son would chance to hear things he could not refute. She believed that her son by such a man as Kirby would be of use to his country, and her voice, against herself, was for England.

It broke her heart. If she failed to receive the regular letter, she pined and was disconsolate. He has heard more of me! was in her mind. Her husband sat looking at her with his old large grey glassy eyes. You would have fancied him awaiting her death as the signal for his own release. But she, poor mother, behind her weeping lids beheld her son's filial love of her wounded and bleeding. When there was anything to be done for her, old Kirby was astir. When it was nothing, either in physic or assistance, he was like a great corner of rock. You may indeed imagine grief in the very rock that sees its flower fading to the withered shred. On the last night of her life this old man of past ninety carried her in his arms up a flight of stairs to her bed.

A week after her burial, Kirby was found a corpse in the mountain forest. His having called the death of his darling his lightning-stroke must have been the origin of the report that he died of lightning. He touched not a morsel of food from the hour of the dropping of the sod on her coffin of ebony wood. An old crust of their mahogany bread, supposed at first to be a specimen of quartz, was found in one of his coat pockets. He kissed his girl Carinthia before going out on his last journey from home, and spoke some wandering words. The mine had not been worked for a year. She thought she would find him at the mouth of the shaft, where he would sometimes be sitting and staring, already dead at heart with the death he saw coming to the beloved woman. They had to let her down with ropes, that she might satisfy herself he was not below. She and her great dog and a faithful man-servant discovered the body in the forest. Chillon arrived from England to see the common grave of both his parents.

And now good-bye to sorrow for a while. Keep your tears for the living. And first I am going to describe to you the young Earl of Fleetwood, son of the strange Welsh lady, the richest nobleman of his time, and how he persued and shunned the lady who had fascinated him, Henrietta, the daughter of Commodore Baldwin Fakenham; and how he met Carinthia Jane; and concerning that lovely Henrietta and Chillon Kirby-Levellier; and of the young poet of ordinary parentage, and the giant Captain Abrane, and Livia the widowed Countess of Fleetwood, Henrietta's cousin, daughter of Curtis Fakenham; and numbers of others; Lord Levellier, Lord Brailstone, Lord Simon Pitscrew, Chumley Potts, young Ambrose Mallard; and the English pugilist, such a man of honour though he drank; and the adventures of Madge, Carinthia Jane's maid. Just a few touches. And then the marriage dividing Great Britain into halves, taking sides.

After that, I trust you may go on, as I would carry you were we all twenty years younger, had I but sooner been in possession of these treasured papers. I promise you excitement enough, if justice is done to them. But I must and will describe the wedding. This young Earl of Fleetwood, you should know, was a very powder-magazine of ambition, and never would he break his word: which is right, if we are properly careful; and so he—

She ceases. According to the terms of the treaty, the venerable lady's time has passed. An extinguisher descends on her, giving her the likeness of one under condemnation of 'the Most Holy Inqusition, in the ranks of an 'auto da fe'; and singularly resembling that victim at the first sharp bite of the flames she will, be when she hears the version of her story.

CHAPTER IV

MORNING AND FAREWELL TO AN OLD HOME

Brother and sister were about to leave the mountainland for England. They had not gone to bed overnight, and from the windows of their deserted home, a little before dawn, they saw the dwindled moon, a late riser, break through droves of hunted cloud, directly topping their ancient guardian height, the triple peak and giant of the range, friendlier in his name than in aspect for the two young people clinging to the scene they were to quit. His name recalled old-days: the apparition of his head among the heavens drummed on their sense of banishment.

To the girl, this was a division of her life, and the dawn held the sword. She felt herself midswing across a gulf that was the grave of one half, without a light of promise for the other. Her passionate excess of attachment to her buried home robbed the future of any colours it might have worn to bid a young heart quicken. And England, though she was of British blood, was a foreign place to her, not alluring: her brother had twice come out of England reserved in speech; her mother's talk of England had been unhappy; her father had suffered ill-treatment there from a brutal institution termed the Admiralty, and had never regretted the not seeing England again. The thought that she was bound thitherward enfolded her like a frosty mist. But these bare walls, these loud floors, chill rooms, dull windows, and the vault-sounding of the ghostly house, everywhere the absence of the faces in the house told her she had no choice, she must go. The appearance of her old friend the towering mountain-height, up a blue night-sky, compelled her swift mind to see herself far away, yearning to him out of exile, an exile that had no local features; she would not imagine them to give a centre of warmth, her wilful grief preferred the blank. It resembled death in seeming some hollowness behind a shroud, which we shudder at.

The room was lighted by a stable-lantern on a kitchen-table. Their seat near the window was a rickety garden-bench rejected in the headlong sale of the furniture; and when she rose, unable to continue motionless while the hosts of illuminated cloud flew fast, she had to warn her brother to preserve his balance. He tacitly did so, aware of the necessity.

She walked up and down the long seven-windowed saloon, haunted by her footfall, trying to think, chafing at his quietness and acknowledging that he did well to be quiet. They had finished their packing of boxes and of wearing-apparel for the journey. There was nothing to think of, nothing further to talk of, nothing for her to do save to sit and look, and deaden her throbs by counting them. She soon returned to her seat beside her brother, with the marvel in her breast that the house she desired so much to love should be cold and repel her now it was a vacant shell. Her memories could not hang within it anywhere. She shut her eyes to be with the images of the dead, conceiving the method as her brother's happy secret, and imitated his posture, elbows propped on knees to support the chin. His quietness breathed of a deeper love than her own.

Meanwhile the high wind had sunk; the moon, after pushing her withered half to the zenith, was climbing the dusky edge, revealed fitfully; threads and wisps of thin vapour travelled along a falling gale, and branched from the dome of the sky in migratory broken lines, like wild birds shifting the order of flight, north and east, where the dawn sat in a web, but as yet had done no more than shoot up a glow along the central heavens, in amid the waves of deepened aloud: a mirror for night to see her dark self in her own hue. A shiver between the silent couple pricked their wits, and she said:

'Chillon, shall we run out and call the morning?'

It was an old game of theirs, encouraged by their hearty father, to be out in the early hour on a rise of ground near the house and 'call the morning.' Her brother was glad of the challenge, and upon one of the yawns following a sleepless night, replied with a return to boyishness: 'Yes, if you like. It's the last time we shall do her the service here. Let's go.'

They sprang up together and the bench fell behind them. Swinging the lantern he carried inconsiderately, the ring of it was left on his finger, and the end of candle rolled out of the crazy frame to the floor and was extinguished. Chillon had no match-box. He said to her:

'What do you think of the window?—we've done it before, Carin. Better than groping down stairs and passages blocked with lumber.'

'I'm ready,' she said, and caught at her skirts by instinct to prove her readiness on the spot.

A drop of a dozen feet or so from the French window to a flower—bed was not very difficult. Her father had taught her how to jump, besides the how of many other practical things. She leaped as lightly as her brother, never touching earth with her hands; and rising from the proper contraction of the legs in taking the descent, she quoted her father: 'Mean it when you're doing it.'

'For no enemy's shot is equal to a weak heart in the act,'

Chillon pursued the quotation, laying his hand on her shoulder for a sign of approval. She looked up at him.

They passed down the garden and a sloping meadow to a brook swollen by heavy rains; over the brook on a narrow plank, and up a steep and stony pathway, almost a watercourse, between rocks, to another meadow, level with the house, that led ascending through a firwood; and there the change to thicker darkness told them light was abroad, though whether of the clouded moon or of the first grey of the quiet revolution was uncertain. Metallic light of a subterranean realm, it might have been thought.

'You remember everything of father,' Carinthia said. 'We both do,' said Chillon.

She pressed her brother's arm. 'We will. We will never forget anything.'

Beyond the firwood light was visibly the dawn's. Half-way down the ravines it resembled the light cast off a torrent water. It lay on the grass like a sheet of unreflecting steel, and was a face without a smile above. Their childhood ran along the tracks to the forest by the light, which was neither dim nor cold, but grave; presenting tree and shrub and dwarf growth and grass austerely, not deepening or confusing them. They wound their way by borders of crag, seeing in a dell below the mouth of the idle mine begirt with weedy and shrub-hung rock, a dripping semi-circle. Farther up they came on the flat juniper and crossed a wet ground-thicket of whortleberry: their feet were in the moist moss among sprigs of heath; and a great fir-tree stretched his length, a peeled multitude of his dead fellows leaned and stood upright in the midst of scattered fire-stained members, and through their skeleton limbs the sheer precipice of slate-rock of the bulk across the chasm, nursery of hawk and eagle; wore a thin blue tinge, the sign of warmer light abroad.

'This way, my brother!' cried Carinthia, shuddering at a path he was about to follow.

Dawn in the mountain-land is a meeting of many friends. The pinnacle, the forest-head, the latschen-tufted mound, rock-bastion and defiant cliff and giant of the triple peak, were in view, clearly lined for a common recognition, but all were figures of solid gloom, unfeatured and bloomless. Another minute and they had flung off their mail, and changed to various, indented, intricate, succinct in ridge, scar and channel; and they had all a look of watchfulness that made them one company. The smell of rock-waters and roots of herb and moss grew keen; air became a wine that raised the breast high to breathe it; an uplifting coolness pervaded the heights. What wonder that the mountain-bred girl should let fly her voice. The natural carol woke an echo. She did not repeat it.

'And we will not forget our home, Chillon,' she said, touching him gently to comfort some saddened feeling.

The plumes of cloud now slowly entered into the lofty arch of dawn and melted from brown to purpleblack. The upper sky swam with violet; and in a moment each stray cloud-feather was edged with rose, and then suffused. It seemed that the heights fronted East to eye the interflooding of colours, and it was imaginable that all turned to the giant whose forehead first kindled to the sun: a greeting of god and king.

On the morning of a farewell we fluctuate sharply between the very distant and the close and homely: and even in memory the fluctuation occurs, the grander scene casting us back on the modestly nestling, and that, when it has refreshed us, conjuring imagination to embrace the splendour and wonder. But the wrench of an immediate division from what we love makes the things within us reach the dearest, we put out our hands for them, as violently-parted lovers do, though the soul in days to come would know a craving, and imagination flap a leaden wing, if we had not looked beyond them.

'Shall we go down?' said Carinthia, for she knew a little cascade near the house, showering on rock and fern, and longed to have it round her.

They descended, Chillon saying that they would soon have the mists rising, and must not delay to start on their journey.

The armies of the young sunrise in mountain-lands neighbouring the plains, vast shadows, were marching over woods and meads, black against the edge of golden; and great heights were cut with them, and bounding waters took the leap in a silvery radiance to gloom; the bright and dark-banded valleys were like night and morning taking hands down the sweep of their rivers. Immense was the range of vision scudding the peaks and over the illimitable Eastward plains flat to the very East and sources of the sun.

Carinthia said: 'When I marry I shall come here to live and die.'

Her brother glanced at her. He was fond of her, and personally he liked her face; but such a confident anticipation of marriage on the part of a portionless girl set him thinking of the character of her charms and the attraction they would present to the world of men. They were expressive enough; at times he had thought them marvellous in their clear cut of the animating mind.—No one could fancy her handsome; and just now her hair was in some disorder, a night without sleep had an effect on her complexion.

'It's not usually the wife who decides where to live,' said he.

Her ideas were anywhere but with the dream of a husband. 'Could we stay on another day?—'

'My dear girl! Another night on that crazy stool! 'Besides, Mariandl is bound to go to-day to her new place, and who's to cook for us? Do you propose fasting as well as watching?'

'Could I cook?' she asked him humbly.

'No, you couldn't; not for a starving regiment! Your accomplishments are of a different sort. No, it's better to get over the pain at once, if we can't escape it.

'That I think too,' said she, 'and we should have to buy provisions. Then, brother, instantly after breakfast. Only, let us walk it. I know the whole way, and it is not more than a two days' walk for you and me. Consent. Driving would be like going gladly. I could never bear to remember that I was driven away.

And walking will save money; we are not rich, you tell me, brother.'

'A few florins more or less!' he rejoined, rather frowning. 'You have good Styrian boots, I see. But I want to be over at the Baths there soon; not later than to-morrow.'

'But, brother, if they know we are coming they will wait for us. And we can be there to-morrow night or the next morning!'

He considered it. He wanted exercise and loved this mountain-land; his inclinations melted into hers; though he had reasons for hesitating. 'Well, we'll send on my portmanteau and your boxes in the cart; we'll walk it. You're a capital walker, you're a gallant comrade; I wouldn't wish for a better.' He wondered, as he spoke, whether any true-hearted gentleman besides himself would ever think the same of this lonely girl.

Her eyes looked a delighted 'No-really?' for the sweetest on earth to her was to be prized by her brother.

She hastened forward. 'We will go down and have our last meal at home,' she said in the dialect of the country. 'We have five eggs. No meat for you, dear, but enough bread and butter, some honey left, and plenty of coffee. I should like to have left old Mariandl more, but we are unable to do very much for poor people now. Milk, I cannot say. She is just the kind soul to be up and out to fetch us milk for an early first breakfast; but she may have overslept herself.'

Chillon smiled. 'You were right, Janet', about not going to bed last night; we might have missed the morning.'

'I hate sleep: I hate anything that robs me of my will,' she replied.

'You'd be glad of your doses of sleep if you had to work and study.'

'To fall down by the wayside tired out—yes, brother, a dead sleep is good. Then you are in the hands of God. Father used to say, four hours for a man, six for a woman.'

'And four and twenty for a lord,' added Chillon. 'I remember.'

'A lord of that Admiralty,' she appealed to his closer recollection. 'But I mean, brother, dreaming is what I detest so.'

'Don't be detesting, my dear; reserve your strength,' said he. 'I suppose dreams are of some use, now and then.'

'I shall never think them useful.'

'When we can't get what we want, my good Carin.'

'Then we should not waste ourselves in dreams.'

'They promise falsely sometimes. That's no reason why we should reject the consolation when we can't get what we want, my little sister.'

'I would not be denied.'

'There's the impossible.'

'Not for you, brother.'

Perhaps a half-minute after she had spoken, he said, 'pursuing a dialogue within himself aloud rather than revealing a secret: 'You don't know her position.'

Carinthia's heart stopped beating. Who was this person suddenly conjured up?

She fancied she might not have heard correctly; she feared to ask and yet she perceived a novel softness in him that would have answered. Pain of an unknown kind made her love of her brother conscious that if she asked she would suffer greater pain.

The house was in sight, a long white building with blinds down at some of the windows, and some wide open, some showing unclean glass: the three aspects and signs of a house's emptiness when they are seen together.

Carinthia remarked on their having met nobody. It had a serious meaning for them. Formerly they were proud of outstripping the busy population of the mine, coming down on them with wild wavings and shouts of sunrise. They felt the death again, a whole field laid low by one stroke, and wintriness in the season of glad life. A wind had blown and all had vanished.

The second green of the year shot lively sparkles off the meadows, from a fringe of coloured glovelets to a warm silver lake of dews. The firwood was already breathing rich and sweet in the sun. The half-moon fell rayless and paler than the fan of fleeces pushed up Westward, high overhead, themselves dispersing on the blue in downy feathers, like the mottled grey of an eagle's breast: the smaller of them bluish like traces of the beaked wood-pigeon.

She looked above, then below on the slim and straightgrown flocks of naked purple crocuses in bud and blow abounding over the meadow that rolled to the level of the house, and two of these she gathered.

CHAPTER V

A MOUNTAIN WALK IN MIST AND SUNSHINE

Chillon was right in his forecast of the mists. An over-moistened earth steaming to the sun obscured it before the two had finished breakfast, which was a finish to everything eatable in the ravaged dwelling, with the exception of a sly store for the midday meal, that old Mariandl had stuffed into Chillon's leather sack—the fruit of secret begging on their behalf about the neighbourhood. He found the sack heavy and bulky as he slung it over his shoulders; but she bade him make nothing of such a trifle till he had it inside him. 'And you that love tea so, my pretty one, so that you always laughed and sang after drinking a cup with your mother,' she said to Carinthia, 'you will find one pinch of it in your bag at the end of the left-foot slipper, to remember your home by when you are out in the world.'

She crossed the strap of the bag on her mistress's bosom, and was embraced by Carinthia and Chillon in turns, Carinthia telling her to dry her eyes, for that she would certainly come back and perhaps occupy the house one day or other. The old soul moaned of eyes that would not be awake to behold her; she begged a visit at her grave, though it was to be in a Catholic burial-place and the priests had used her dear master and mistress ill, not allowing them to lie in consecrated ground; affection made her a champion of religious tolerance and a little afraid of retribution. Carinthia soothed her, kissed her, gave the promise, and the parting was over.

She and Chillon had on the previous day accomplished a pilgrimage to the resting-place of their father and mother among humble Protestants, iron-smelters, in a valley out of the way of their present line of march to the glacier of the great snow-mountain marking the junction of three Alpine provinces of Austria. Josef, the cart-driver with the boxes, who was to pass the valley, vowed of his own accord to hang a fresh day's wreath on the rails. He would not hear of money for the purchase, and they humoured him. The family had been beloved. There was an offer of a home for Carinthia in the castle of Count Lebern, a friend of her parents, much taken with her, and she would have accepted it had not

Chillon overruled her choice, determined that, as she was English, she must come to England and live under the guardianship of her uncle, Lord Levellier, of whose character he did not speak.

The girl's cheeks were drawn thin and her lips shut as they departed; she was tearless. A phantom ring of mist accompanied her from her first footing outside the house. She did not look back. The house came swimming and plunging after her, like a spectral ship on big seas, and her father and mother lived and died in her breast; and now they were strong, consulting, chatting, laughing, caressing; now still and white, caught by a vapour that dived away with them either to right or left, but always with the same suddenness, leaving her to question herself whether she existed, for more of life seemed to be with their mystery than with her speculations. The phantom ring of mist enclosing for miles the invariable low-sweeping dark spruce-fir kept her thoughts on them as close as the shroud. She walked fast, but scarcely felt that she was moving. Near midday the haunted circle widened; rocks were loosely folded in it, and heads of trees, whose round intervolving roots grasped the yellow roadside soil; the mists shook like a curtain, and partly opened and displayed a tapestry-landscape, roughly worked, of woollen crag and castle and suggested glen, threaded waters, very prominent foreground, Autumn flowers on banks; a predominant atmospheric greyness. The sun threw a shaft, liquid instead of burning, as we see his beams beneath a wave; and then the mists narrowed again, boiled up the valleys and streams above the mountain, curled and flew, and were Python coils pierced by brighter arrows of the sun. A spot of blue signalled his victory above.

To look at it was to fancy they had been walking under water and had now risen to the surface. Carinthia's mind stepped out of the chamber of death. The different air and scene breathed into her a timid warmth toward the future, and between her naming of the lesser mountains on their side of the pass, she asked questions relating to England, and especially the ladies she was to see at the Baths beyond the glacier-pass. She had heard of a party of his friends awaiting him there, without much encouragement from him to ask particulars of them, and she had hitherto abstained, as she was rather shy of meeting her countrywomen. The ladies, Chillon said, were cousins; one was a young widow, the Countess of Fleetwood, and the other was Miss Fakenham, a younger lady.

Carinthia murmured in German: 'Poor soul!' Which one was she pitying? The widow, she said, in the tone implying, naturally.

Her brother assured her the widow was used to it, for this was her second widowhood.

'She marries again!' exclaimed the girl.

'You don't like that idea?' said he.

Carinthia betrayed a delicate shudder.

Her brother laughed to himself at her expressive present tense. 'And marries again!' he said. 'There will certainly be a third.'

'Husband?' said she, as at the incredible.

'Husband, let's hope,' he answered.

She dropped from her contemplation of the lady, and her look at her brother signified: It will not be you!

Chillon was engaged in spying for a place where he could spread out the contents of his bag. Sharp hunger beset them both at the mention of eating. A bank of sloping green shaded by a chestnut proposed the seat, and here he relieved the bag of a bottle of wine, slices of, meat, bread, hard eggs, and lettuce, a chipped cup to fling away after drinking the wine, and a supply of small butler-cakes known to be favourites with Carinthia. She reversed the order of the feast by commencing upon one of the cakes, to do honour to Mariandl's thoughtfulness. As at their breakfast, they shared the last morsel.

'But we would have made it enough for our dear old dog Pluto as well, if he had lived,' said Carinthia, sighing with her thankfulness and compassionate regrets, a mixture often inspiring a tender babbling melancholy. 'Dogs' eyes have such a sick look of love. He might have lived longer, though he was very old, only he could not survive the loss of father. I know the finding of the body broke his heart. He sprang forward, he stopped and threw up his head. It was human language to hear him, Chillon. He lay in the yard, trying to lift his eyes when I came to him, they were so heavy; and he had not strength to move his poor old tail more than once. He died with his head on my lap. He seemed to beg me, and I took him, and he breathed twice, and that was his end. Pluto! old dog! Well, for you or for me, brother, we could not have a better wish. As for me, death!... When we know we are to die! Only let my darling live! that is my prayer, and that we two may not be separated till I am taken to their grave. Father bought ground for four—his wife and himself and his two children. It does not oblige us to be buried there, but could we have any other desire?'

She stretched her hand to her brother. He kissed it spiritedly.

'Look ahead, my dear girl. Help me to finish this wine. There 's nothing like good hard walking to give common wine of the country a flavour—and out of broken crockery.'

'I think it so good,' Carinthia replied, after drinking from the cup. 'In England they, do not grow wine. Are the people there kind?'

'They're civilized people, of course.'

'Kind—warm to you, Chillon?'

'Some of them, when you know them. "Warm," is hardly the word. Winter's warm on skates. You must do a great deal for yourself. They don't boil over. By the way, don't expect much of your uncle.'

'Will he not love me?'

'He gives you a lodging in his house, and food enough, we'll hope. You won't see company or much of him.'

'I cannot exist without being loved. I do not care for company. He must love me a little.'

'He is one of the warm-hearted race—he's mother's brother; but where his heart is, I 've not discovered.

Bear with him just for the present, my dear, till I am able to support you.'

'I will,' she said.

The dreary vision of a home with an unloving uncle was not brightened by the alternative of her brother's having to support her. She spoke of money. 'Have we none, Chillon?'

'We have no debts,' he answered. 'We have a claim on the Government here for indemnification for property taken to build a fortress upon one of the passes into Italy. Father bought the land, thinking there would be a yield of ore thereabout; and they have seized it, rightly enough, but they dispute our claim for the valuation we put on it. A small sum they would consent to pay. It would be a very small sum, and I 'm father's son, I will have justice.'

'Yes!' Carthinia joined with him to show the same stout nature.

'We have nothing else except a bit to toss up for luck.'

'And how can I help being a burden on my brother?' she inquired, in distress.

'Marry, and be a blessing to a husband,' he said lightly.

They performed a sacrifice of the empty bottle and cracked cup on the site of their meal, as if it had been a ceremony demanded from travellers, and leaving them in fragments, proceeded on their journey refreshed.

Walking was now high enjoyment, notwithstanding the force of the sun, for they were a hardy couple, requiring no more than sufficient nourishment to combat the elements with an exulting blood. Besides they loved mountain air and scenery, and each step to the ridge of the pass they climbed was an advance in splendour. Peaks of ashen hue and pale dry red and pale sulphur pushed up, straight, forked, twisted, naked, striking their minds with an indeterminate ghostliness of Indian, so strange they were in shape and colouring. These sharp points were the first to greet them between the blue and green. A depression of the pass to the left gave sight of the points of black fir forest below, round the girths of the barren shafts. Mountain blocks appeared pushing up in front, and a mountain wall and woods on it, and mountains in the distance, and cliffs riven with falls of water that were silver skeins, down lower to meadows, villages and spires, and lower finally to the whole valley of the foaming river, field and river seeming in imagination rolled out from the hand of the heading mountain.

'But see this in winter, as I did with father, Chillon!' said Carinthia.

She said it upon love's instinct to halo the scene with something beyond present vision, and to sanctify it for her brother, so that this walk of theirs together should never be forgotten.

A smooth fold of cloud, moveless along one of the upper pastures, and still dense enough to be luminous in sunlight, was the last of the mist.

They watched it lying in the form of a fish, leviathan diminished, as they descended their path; and the head was lost, the tail spread peacockwise, and evaporated slowly in that likeness; and soft to a breath of air as gossamer down, the body became a ball, a cock, a little lizard, nothingness.

The bluest bright day of the year was shining. Chillon led the descent. With his trim and handsome figure before her, Carinthia remembered the current saying, that he should have been the girl and she the boy. That was because he resembled their mother in face. But the build of his limbs and shoulders was not feminine.

To her admiring eyes, he had a look superior to simple strength and grace; the look of a great sky-bird about to mount, a fountain-like energy of stature, delightful to her contemplation. And he had the mouth women put faith in for decision and fixedness. She did, most fully; and reflecting how entirely she did so, the thought assailed her: some one must be loving him!

She allowed it to surprise her, not choosing to revert to an uneasy sensation of the morning.

That some one, her process of reasoning informed her, was necessarily an English young lady. She reserved her questions till they should cease this hopping and heeling down the zigzag of the slippery path-track. When children they had been collectors of beetles and butterflies, and the flying by of a 'royal-mantle,' the purple butterfly grandly fringed, could still remind Carinthia of the event it was of old to spy and chase one. Chillon himself was not above the sentiment of their "very early days"; he stopped to ask if she had been that lustrous blue-wing, a rarer species, prized by youngsters, shoot through the chestnut trees: and they both paused for a moment, gazing into the fairyland of infancy, she seeing with her brother's eyes, this prince of the realm having escaped her. He owned he might have been mistaken, as the brilliant fellow flew swift and high between leaves, like an ordinary fritillary. Not the less did they get their glimpse of the wonders in the sunny eternity of a child's afternoon.

'An Auerhahn, Chillon!' she said, picturing the maturer day when she had scaled perilous heights with him at night to stalk the blackcock in the prime of the morning. She wished they could have had another such adventure to stamp the old home on his heart freshly, to the exclusion of beautiful English faces.

On the level of the valley, where they met the torrent-river, walking side by side with him, she ventured an inquiry: 'English girls are fair girls, are they not?'

'There are some dark also,' he replied.

'But the best-looking are fair?'

'Perhaps they are, with us.'

'Mother was fair.'

'She was.'

'I have only seen a few of them, once at Vies and at Venice, and those Baths we are going to; and at Meran, I think.'

'You considered them charming?'

'Not all.'

It was touching that she should be such a stranger to her countrywomen! He drew a portrait-case from his breast-pocket, pressing the spring, and handed it to her, saying: 'There is one.' He spoke indifferently, but as soon as she had seen the face inside it, with a look at him and a deep breath; she understood that he was an altered brother, and that they were three instead of two.

She handed it back to him, saying hushedly and only 'Yes.'

He did not ask an opinion upon the beauty she had seen. His pace increased, and she hastened her steps beside him. She had not much to learn when some minutes later she said; 'Shall I see her, Chillon?'

'She is one of the ladies we are to meet.'

'What a pity!' Carinthia stepped faster, enlightened as to his wish to get to the Baths without delay; and her heart softened in reflecting how readily he had yielded to her silly preference for going on foot.

Her cry of regret was equivocal; it produced no impression on him. They reached a village where her leader deemed it adviseable to drive for the remainder of the distance up the valley to the barrier snow-mountain. She assented instantly, she had no longer any active wishes of her own, save to make amends to her brother, who was and would ever be her brother: she could not be robbed of their relationship.

Something undefined in her feeling of possession she had been robbed of, she knew it by her spiritlessness; and she would fain have attributed it to the idle motion of the car, now and them stupidly jolting her on, after the valiant exercise of her limbs. They were in a land of waterfalls and busy mills, a narrowing vale where the runs of grass grew short and wild, and the glacier-river roared for the leap, more foam than water, and the savagery, naturally exciting to her, breathed of its lair among the rocks and ice-fields.

Her brother said: 'There he is.' She saw the whitecrowned king of the region, of whose near presence to her old home she had been accustomed to think proudly, end she looked at him without springing to him, and continued imaging her English home and her loveless uncle, merely admiring the scene, as if the fire of her soul had been extinguished.—'Marry, and be a blessing to a husband.' Chillon's words whispered of the means of escape from the den of her uncle.

But who would marry me! she thought. An unreproved sensation of melting pervaded her; she knew her capacity for gratitude, and conjuring it up in her 'heart, there came with it the noble knightly gentleman who would really stoop to take a plain girl by the hand, release her, and say: 'Be mine!' His vizor was down, of course. She had no power of imagining the lineaments of that prodigy. Or was he a dream? He came and went. Her mother, not unkindly, sadly, had counted her poor girl's chances of winning attention and a husband. Her father had doated on her face; but, as she argued, her father had been attracted by her mother, a beautiful woman, and this was a circumstance that reflected the greater hopelessness on her prospects. She bore a likeness to her father, little to her mother, though he fancied the reverse and gave her the mother's lips and hair. Thinking of herself, however, was destructive to the form of her mirror of knightliness: he wavered, he fled for good, as the rosy vapour born of our sensibility must do when we relapse to coldness, and the more completely when we try to command it. No, she thought, a plain girl should think of work, to earn her independence.

'Women are not permitted to follow armies, Chillon?' she said.

He laughed out. 'What 's in your head?'

The laugh abashed her; she murmured of women being good nurses for wounded soldiers, if they were good walkers to march with the army; and, as evidently it sounded witless to him, she added, to seem reasonable: 'You have not told me the Christian names of those ladies.'

He made queer eyes over the puzzle to connect the foregoing and the succeeding in her remarks, but answered straightforwardly: 'Livia is one, and Henrietta!'

Her ear seized on the stress of his voice. 'Henrietta!' She chose that name for the name of the person disturbing her; it fused best, she thought, with the new element she had been compelled to take into her system, to absorb it if she could.

'You're not scheming to have them serve as army hospital nurses, my dear?'

'No, Chillon.'

'You can't explain it, I suppose?'

'A sister could go too, when you go to war, Chillon.'

A sister could go, if it were permitted by the authorities, and be near her brother to nurse him in case of wounds; others would be unable to claim the privilege. That was her meaning, involved with the hazy project of earning an independence; but she could not explain it, and Chillon set her down for one of the inexplicable sex, which the simple adventurous girl had not previously seemed to be.

She was inwardly warned of having talked foolishly, and she held her tongue. Her humble and modest jealousy, scarce deserving the title, passed with a sigh or two. It was her first taste of life in the world.

A fit of heavy-mindedness ensued, that heightened the contrast her recent mood had bequeathed, between herself, ignorant as she was, and those ladies. Their names, Livia and Henrietta, soared above her and sang the music of the splendid spheres. Henrietta was closer to earth, for her features had been revealed; she was therefore the dearer, and the richer for him who loved her, being one of us, though an over-earthly one; and Carinthia gave her to Chillon, reserving for herself a handmaiden's place within the circle of their happiness.

This done, she sat straight in the car. It was toiling up the steep ascent of a glen to the mountain village, the last of her native province. Her proposal to walk was accepted, and the speeding of her blood, now that she had mastered a new element in it, soon restored her to her sisterly affinity with natural glories. The sunset was on yonder side of the snows. Here there was a feast of variously-tinted sunset shadows on snow, meadows, rock, river, serrated cliff. The peaked cap of the rushing rock-dotted sweeps of upward snow caught a scarlet illumination: one flank of the white in heaven was violetted wonderfully.

At nightfall, under a clear black sky, alive with wakeful fires round head and breast of the great Alp, Chillon and Carinthia strolled out of the village, and he told her some of his hopes. They referred to inventions of destructive weapons, which were primarily to place his country out of all danger from a world in arms; and also, it might be mentioned, to bring him fortune. 'For I must have money!' he said, sighing it out like a deliberate oath. He and his uncle were associated in the inventions. They had an improved rocket that would force military chiefs to change their tactics: they had a new powder, a rifle, a model musket—the latter based on his own plans; and a scheme for fortress artillery likely to turn the preponderance in favour of the defensive once again. 'And that will be really doing good,' said Chillon, 'for where it's with the offensive, there's everlasting bullying and plundering.'

Carinthia warmly agreed with him, but begged him be sure his uncle divided the profits equally. She discerned what his need of money signified.

Tenderness urged her to say: 'Henrietta! Chillon.'

'Well?' he answered quickly.

'Will she wait?'

'Can she, you should ask.'

'Is she brave?'

'Who can tell, till she has been tried?'

'Is she quite free?'

'She has not yet been captured.'

'Brother, is there no one else...?'

'There's a nobleman anxious to bestow his titles on her.'

'He is rich?'

'The first or second wealthiest in Great Britain, they say.'

'Is he young?'

'About the same age as mine.'

'Is he a handsome young man?'

'Handsomer than your brother, my girl.'

'No, no, no!' said she. 'And what if he is, and your Henrietta does not choose him? Now let me think what I long to think. I have her close to me.'

She rocked a roseate image on her heart and went to bed with it by starlight.

By starlight they sprang to their feet and departed the next morning, in the steps of a guide carrying, Chillon said, 'a better lantern than we left behind us at the smithy.'

'Father!' exclaimed Carinthia on her swift inward breath, for this one of the names he had used to give to her old home revived him to her thoughts and senses fervently.

CHAPTER VI

THE NATURAL PHILOSOPHER

Three parts down a swift decline of shattered slate, where travelling stones loosened from rows of scree hurl away at a bound after one roll over, there sat a youth dusty and torn, nursing a bruised leg, not in the easiest of postures, on a sharp tooth of rock, that might at any moment have broken from the slanting slab at the end of which it formed a stump, and added him a second time to the general crumble of the mountain. He had done a portion of the descent in excellent imitation of the detached fragments, and had parted company with his alpenstock and plaid; preserving his hat and his knapsack. He was alone, disabled, and cheerful; in doubt of the arrival of succour before he could trust his left leg to do him further service unaided; but it was morning still, the sun was hot, the air was cool; just the tempering opposition to render existence pleasant as a piece of vegetation, especially when there has been a question of your ceasing to exist; and the view was of a sustaining sublimity of desolateness: crag and snow overhead; a gloomy vale below; no life either of bird or herd; a voiceless region where there had once been roars at the bowling of a hill from a mountain to the deep, and the third flank of the mountain spoke of it in the silence.

He would have enjoyed the scene unremittingly, like the philosopher he pretended to be, in a disdain of civilization and the ambitions of men, had not a contest with earth been forced on him from time to time to keep the heel of his right foot, dug in shallow shale, fixed and supporting. As long as it held he was happy and maintained the attitude of a guitar-player, thrumming the calf of the useless leg to accompany tuneful thoughts, but the inevitable lapse and slide of the foot recurred, and the philosopher was exhibited as an infant learning to crawl. The seat, moreover, not having been fashioned for him or for any soft purpose, resisted his pressure and became a thing of violence, that required to be humiliatingly coaxed. His last resource to propitiate it was counselled by nature turned mathematician: tenacious extension solved the problem; he lay back at his length, and with his hat over his eyes consented to see nothing for the sake of comfort. Thus he was perfectly rational, though when others beheld him he appeared the insanest of mortals.

A girl's voice gave out the mountain carol ringingly above. His heart and all his fancies were in motion at the sound. He leaned on an elbow to listen; the slide threatened him, and he resumed his full stretch, determined to take her for a dream. He was of the class of youths who, in apprehension that their bright season may not be permanent, choose to fortify it by a systematic contempt of material realities unless they come in the fairest of shapes, and as he was quite sincere in this feeling and election of the right way to live, disappointment and sullenness overcame him on hearing men's shouts and steps; despite his helpless condition he refused to stir, for they had jarred on his dream. Perhaps his temper, unknown to himself, had been a little injured by his mishap, and he would not have been sorry to charge them with want of common humanity in passing him; or he did not think his plight so bad, else he would have bawled after them had they gone by: far the youths of his description are fools only upon system,— however earnestly they indulge the present self-punishing sentiment. The party did not pass; they stopped short, they consulted, and a feminine tongue more urgent than the others, and very musical, sweet to hear anywhere, put him in tune. She said, 'Brother! brother!' in German. Our philosopher flung off his hat.

'You see!' said the lady's brother.

'Ask him, Anton,' she said to their guide.

'And quick!' her brother added.

The guide scrambled along to him, and at a closer glance shouted: 'The Englishman!' wheeling his finger to indicate what had happened to the Tomnoddy islander.

His master called to know if there were broken bones, as if he could stop for nothing else.

The cripple was raised. The gentleman and lady made their way to him, and he tried his hardest to keep from tottering on the slope in her presence. No injury had been done to the leg; there was only a stiffness, and an idiotic doubling of the knee, as though at each step his leg pronounced a dogged negative to the act of walking. He said something equivalent to 'this donkey leg,' to divert her charitable eyes from a countenance dancing with ugly twitches. She was the Samaritan. A sufferer discerns his friend, though it be not the one who physically assists him: he is inclined by nature to put material aid at a lower mark than gentleness, and her brief words of encouragement, the tone of their delivery yet more, were medical to his blood, better help than her brother's iron arm, he really believed. Her brother and the guide held him on each side, and she led to pick out the safer footing for him; she looked round and pointed to some projection that would form a step; she drew attention to views here and there, to win excuses for his resting; she did not omit to soften her brother's visible impatience as well, and this was the art which affected her keenly sensible debtor most.

'I suppose I ought to have taken a guide,' he said.

'There's not a doubt of that,' said Chillon Kirby.

Carinthia halted, leaning on her staff: 'But I had the same wish. They told us at the inn of an Englishman who left last night to sleep on the mountain, and would go alone; and did I not say, brother, that must be true love of the mountains?'

'These freaks get us a bad name on the Continent,' her brother replied. He had no sympathy with nonsense, and naturally not with a youth who smelt of being a dreamy romancer and had caused the name of Englishman to be shouted in his ear in derision. And the fellow might delay his arrival at the Baths and sight of the lady of his love for hours!

They managed to get him hobbling and slipping to the first green tuft of the base, where long black tongues of slate-rubble pouring into the grass, like shore-waves that have spent their burden, seem about to draw back to bring the mountain down. Thence to the level pasture was but a few skips performed sliding.

'Well, now,' said Chillon, 'you can stand?'

'Pretty well, I think.' He tried his foot on the ground, and then stretched his length, saying that it only wanted rest. Anton pressed a hand at his ankle and made him wince, but the bones were sound, leg and hip not worse than badly bruised. He was advised by Anton to plant his foot in the first running water he came to, and he was considerate enough to say to Chillon:

'Now you can leave me; and let me thank you. Half an hour will set me right. My name is Woodseer, if ever we meet again.'

Chillon nodded a hurried good-bye, without a thought of giving his name in return. But Carinthia had thrown herself on the grass. Her brother asked her in dismay if she was tired. She murmured to him: 'I should like to hear more English.'

'My dear girl, you'll have enough of it in two or three weeks.'

'Should we leave a good deed half done, Chillon?'

'He shall have our guide.'

'He may not be rich.'

'I'll pay Anton to stick to him.'

'Brother, he has an objection to guides.'

Chillon cast hungry eyes on his watch: 'Five minutes, then.' He addressed Mr. Woodseer, who was reposing, indifferent to time, hard-by: 'Your objection to guides might have taught you a sharp lesson. It 's like declining to have a master in studying a science—trusting to instinct for your knowledge of a bargain. One might as well refuse an oar to row in a boat.'

'I 'd rather risk it,' the young man replied. 'These guides kick the soul out of scenery. I came for that and not for them.'

'You might easily have been a disagreeable part of the scene.'

'Why not here as well as elsewhere?'

'You don't care for your life?'

'I try not to care for it a fraction more than Destiny does.'

'Fatalism. I suppose you care for something?'

'Besides I've a slack purse, and shun guides and inns when I can. I care for open air, colour, flowers, weeds, birds, insects, mountains. There's a world behind the mask. I call this life; and the town's a boiling pot, intolerably stuffy. My one ambition is to be out of it. I thank heaven I have not another on earth. Yes, I care for my note-book, because it's of no use to a human being except me. I slept beside a spring last night, and I never shall like a bedroom so well. I think I have discovered the great secret: I may be wrong, of course.' And if so, he had his philosophy, the admission was meant to say.

Carinthia expected the revelation of a notable secret, but none came; or if it did it eluded her grasp:—he was praising contemplation, he was praising tobacco. He talked of the charm of poverty upon a settled income of a very small sum of money, the fruit of a compact he would execute with the town to agree to his perpetual exclusion from it, and to retain his identity, and not be the composite which every townsman was. He talked of Buddha. He said: 'Here the brook's the brook, the mountain's the mountain: they are as they always were.'

'You'd have men be the same,' Chillon remarked as to a nursling prattler, and he rejoined: 'They've lost more than they've gained; though, he admitted, 'there has been some gain, in a certain way.'

Fortunately for them, young men have not the habit of reflecting upon the indigestion of ideas they receive from members of their community, sometimes upon exchange. They compare a view of life with their own view, to condemn it summarily; and he was a curious object to Chillon as the perfect opposite of himself.

'I would advise you,' Chillon said, 'to get a pair of Styrian boots, if you intend to stay in the Alps. Those boots of yours are London make.'

'They 're my father's make,' said Mr. Woodseer.

Chillon drew out his watch. 'Come, Carinthia, we must be off.' He proposed his guide, and, as Anton was rejected, he pointed the route over the head of the valley, stated the distance to an inn that way, saluted and strode.

Mr. Woodseer, partly rising, presumed, in raising his hat and thanking Carinthia, to touch her fingers. She smiled on him, frankly extending her open hand, and pointing the route again, counselling him to rest at the inn, even saying: 'You have not yet your strength to come on with us?'

He thought he would stay some time longer: he had a disposition to smoke.

She tripped away to her brother and was watched through the whiffs of a pipe far up the valley, guiltless of any consciousness of producing an impression. But her mind was with the stranger sufficiently to cause her to say to Chillon, at the close of a dispute between him and Anton on the interesting subject of the growth of the horns of chamois: 'Have we been quite kind to that gentleman?'

Chillon looked over his shoulder. 'He's there still; he's fond of solitude. And, Carin, my dear, don't give your hand when you are meeting or parting with people it's not done.'

His uninstructed sister said: 'Did you not like him?'

She was answered with an 'Oh,' the tone of which balanced lightly on the neutral line. 'Some of the ideas he has are Lord Fleetwood's, I hear, and one can understand them in a man of enormous wealth, who doesn't know what to do with himself and is dead-sick of flattery; though it seems odd for an English nobleman to be raving about Nature. Perhaps it's because none else of them does.'

'Lord Fleetwood loves our mountains, Chillon?'

'But a fellow who probably has to make his way in the world!—and he despises ambition!'... Chillon dropped him. He was antipathetic to eccentrics, and his soldierly and social training opposed the profession of heterodox ideas: to have listened seriously to them coming from the mouth of an unambitious bootmaker's son involved him in the absurdity. He considered that there was no harm in the lad, rather a commendable sort of courage and some notion of manners; allowing for his ignorance of the convenable in putting out his hand to take a young lady's, with the plea of thanking her. He hoped she would be more on her guard.

Carinthia was sure she had the name of the nobleman wishing to bestow his title upon the beautiful Henrietta. Lord Fleetwood! That slender thread given her of the character of her brother's rival who loved the mountains was woven in her mind with her passing experience of the youth they had left behind them, until the two became one, a highly transfigured one, and the mountain scenery made him very threatening to her brother. A silky haired youth, brown-eyed, unconquerable in adversity, immensely rich, fond of solitude, curled, decorated, bejewelled by all the elves and gnomes of inmost solitude, must have marvellous attractions, she feared. She thought of him so much, that her humble spirit conceived the stricken soul of the woman as of necessity the pursuer; as shamelessly, though timidly, as she herself pursued in imagination the enchanted secret of the mountain-land. She hoped her brother would not supplicate, for it struck her that the lover who besieged the lady would forfeit her roaming and hunting fancy.

'I wonder what that gentleman is doing now,' she said to Chillon.

He grimaced slightly, for her sake; he would have liked to inform her, for the sake of educating her in the customs of the world she was going to enter, that the word 'gentleman' conveys in English a special signification.

Her expression of wonder whether they were to meet him again gave Chillon the opportunity of saying:

'It 's the unlikeliest thing possible—at all events in England.'

'But I think we shall,' said she.

'My dear, you meet people of your own class; you don't meet others.'

'But we may meet anybody, Chillon!'

'In the street. I suppose you would not stop to speak to him in the street.'

'It would be strange to see him in the street!' Carinthia said.

'Strange or not!'

.... Chillon thought he had said sufficient. She was under his protectorship, otherwise he would not have alluded to the observance of class distinctions. He felt them personally in this case because of their seeming to stretch grotesquely by the pretentious heterodoxy of the young fellow, whom, nevertheless, thinking him over now that he was mentioned, he approved for his manliness in bluntly telling his origin and status.

A chalet supplied them with fresh milk, and the inn of a village on a perch with the midday meal. Their appetites were princely and swept over the little inn like a conflagration. Only after clearing it did they remember the rearward pedestrian, whose probable wants Chillon was urged by Carthinia to speak of to their host. They pushed on, clambering up, scurrying down, tramping gaily, till by degrees the chambers of Carinthia's imagination closed their doors and would no longer intercommunicate. Her head refused to interest her, and left all activity to her legs and her eyes, and the latter became unobservant, except of foot-tracks, animal-like. She felt that she was a fine machine, and nothing else: and she was rapidly approaching those ladies!

'You will tell them how I walked with you,' she said.

'Your friends over yonder?' said he.

'So that they may not think me so ignorant, brother.' She stumbled on the helpless word in a hasty effort to cloak her vanity.

He laughed. Her desire to meet the critical English ladies with a towering reputation in one department of human enterprise was comprehensible, considering the natural apprehensiveness of the half-wild girl before such a meeting. As it often happens with the silly phrases of simple people, the wrong word, foolish although it was, went to the heart of the hearer and threw a more charitable light than ridicule on her. So that they may know I can do something they cannot do, was the interpretation. It showed her deep knowledge of her poorness in laying bare the fact.

Anxious to cheer her, he said: 'Come, come, you can dance. You dance well, mother has told me, and she was a judge. You ride, you swim, you have a voice for country songs, at all events. And you're a bit of a botanist too. You're good at English and German; you had a French governess for a couple of years. By the way, you understand the use of a walking-stick in self-defence: you could handle a sword on occasion.'

'Father trained me,' said Carthinia. 'I can fire a pistol, aiming.'

'With a good aim, too. Father told me you could. How fond he was of his girl! Well, bear in mind that father was proud of you, and hold up your head wherever you are.'

'I will,' she said.

He assured her he had a mind to have a bugle blown at the entrance of the Baths for a challenge to the bathers to match her in warlike accomplishments.

She bit her lips: she could not bear much rallying on the subject just then:

'Which is the hard one to please?' she asked.

'The one you will find the kinder of the two.'

'Henrietta?'

He nodded.

'Has she a father?'

'A gallant old admiral: Admiral Baldwin Fakenham.'

'I am glad of that!' Carinthia sighed out heartily. 'And he is with her? And likes you, Chillon?'

'On the whole, I think he does.'

'A brave officer!' Such a father would be sure to like him.

So the domestic prospect was hopeful.

At sunset they stood on the hills overlooking the basin of the Baths, all enfolded in swathes of pink and crimson up to the shining grey of a high heaven that had the fresh brightness of the morning.

'We are not tired in the slightest,' said Carinthia, trifling with the vision of a cushioned rest below. 'I could go on through the night quite comfortably.'

'Wait till you wake up in your little bed to-morrow,' Chillon replied stoutly, to drive a chill from his lover's heart, that had seized it at the bare suggestion of their going on.

CHAPTER VII

THE LADY'S LETTER

Is not the lover a prophet? He that fervently desires may well be one; his hurried nature is alive with warmth to break the possible blow: and if his fears were not needed they were shadows; and if fulfilled, was he not convinced of his misfortune by a dark anticipation that rarely erred? Descending the hills, he remembered several omens: the sun had sunk when he looked down on the villas and clustered houses, not an edge of the orb had been seen; the admiral's quarters in the broad-faced hotel had worn an appearance resembling the empty house of yesterday; the encounter with the fellow on the rocks had a bad whisper of impish tripping. And what moved Carinthia to speak of going on?

A letter was handed to Chillon in the hall of the admiral's hotel, where his baggage had already been delivered. The manager was deploring the circumstance that his rooms were full to the roof, when Chillon said:

'Well, we must wash and eat'; and Carinthia, from watching her brother's forehead during his perusal of the letter, declared her readiness for anything. He gave her the letter to read by herself while preparing to sit at table, unwilling to ask her for a further tax on her energies—but it was she who had spoken of going on! He thought of it as of a debt she had contracted and might be supposed to think payable to their misfortune.

She read off the first two sentences.

'We can have a carriage here, Chillon; order a carriage; I shall get as much sleep in a carriage as in a bed: I shall enjoy driving at night,' she said immediately, and strongly urged it and forced him to yield, the manager observing that a carriage could be had.

In the privacy of her room, admiring the clear flowing hand, she read the words, delicious in their strangeness to her, notwithstanding the heavy news, as though they were sung out of a night-sky:

'Most picturesque of Castles!
May none these marks efface,
For they appeal from Tyranny...'

'We start at noon to-day. Sailing orders have been issued, and I could only have resisted them in my own person by casting myself overboard. I go like the boat behind the vessel. You were expected yesterday, at latest this morning. I have seen boxes in the hall, with a name on them not foreign to me. Why does the master tarry? Sir, of your valliance you should have held to your good vow,—quoth the damozel, for now you see me sore perplexed and that you did not your devoir is my affliction. Where lingers chivalry, she should have proceeded, if not with my knight? I feast on your regrets. I would not have you less than miserable: and I fear the reason is, that I am not so very, very sure you will be so at all or very hugely, as I would command it of you for just time enough to see that change over your eyebrows I know so well.

'If you had seen a certain Henrietta yesterday you would have the picture of how you ought to look. The admiral was heard welcoming a new arrival—you can hear him. She ran down the stairs quicker than any cascade of this district, she would have made a bet with Livia that it could be no one else—her hand was out, before she was aware of the difference it was locked in Lord F.'s!

'Let the guilty absent suffer for causing such a betrayal of disappointment. I must be avenged! But if indeed you are unhappy and would like to chide the innocent, I am full of compassion for the poor gentleman inheriting my legitimate feelings of wrath, and beg merely that he will not pour them out on me with pen and paper, but from his lips and eyes.

'Time pressing, I chatter no more. The destination is Livia's beloved Baden. We rest a night in the city of Mozart, a night at Munich, a night at Stuttgart. Baden will detain my cousin full a week. She has Captain Abrane and Sir Meeson Corby in attendance—her long shadow and her short: both devoted to Lord F., to win her smile, and how she drives them! The captain has been paraded on the promenade, to the stupefaction of the foreigner. Princes, counts, generals, diplomats passed under him in awe. I am told that he is called St. Christopher.

'Why do we go thus hastily?—my friend, this letter has to be concealed. I know some one who sees in the dark.

'Think no harm of Livia. She is bent upon my worldly advantage, and that is plain even to the person rejecting it. How much more so must it be to papa, though he likes you, and when you are near him would perhaps, in a fit of unworldliness, be almost as reckless as the creature he calls madcap and would rather call countess. No! sooner with a Will-o'-the-wisp, my friend. Who could ever know where the man was when he himself never knows where he is. He is the wind that bloweth as it listeth— because it is without an aim or always with a new one. And am I the one to direct him? I need direction. My lord and sovereign must fix my mind. I am volatile, earthly, not to be trusted if I do not worship. He himself said to me that—he reads our characters. "Nothing but a proved hero will satisfy Henrietta," his words! And the hero must be shining like a beacon-fire kept in a blaze. Quite true; I own it. Is Chillon Kirby satisfied? He ought to be.

'But oh!—to be yoked is an insufferable thought, unless we name all the conditions. But to be yoked to a creature of impulses! Really I could only describe his erratic nature by commending you to the study of a dragon-fly. It would map you an idea of what he has been in the twenty-four hours since we had him here. They tell me a vain sort of person is the cause. Can she be the cause of his resolving to have a residence here, to buy up half the valley—erecting a royal palace—and marking out the site—raving about it in the wildest language, poetical if it had been a little reasonable—and then, after a night, suddenly, unaccountably, hating the place, and being under the necessity of flying from it in hot haste, tearing us all away, as if we were attached to a kite that will neither mount nor fall, but rushes about headlong. Has he heard, or suspected? or seen certain boxes bearing a name? Livia has no suspicion, though she thinks me wonderfully contented in so dull a place, where it has rained nine days in a fortnight. I ask myself whether my manner of greeting him betrayed my expectation of another. He has brains. It is the greatest of errors to suppose him at all like the common run of rich young noblemen. He seems to thirst for brilliant wits and original sayings. His ambition is to lead all England in everything! I readily acknowledge that he has generous ideas too; but try to hold him, deny him his liberty, and it would be seen how desperate and relentless he would be to get loose. Of this I am convinced: he would be either the most abject of lovers, or a woman (if it turned out not to be love) would find him the most unscrupulous of yoke-fellows. Yoke-fellow! She would not have her reason in consenting. A lamb and a furious bull! Papa and I have had a serious talk. He shuts his ears to my comparisons, but admits, that as I am the principal person concerned, etc. Rich and a nobleman is too tempting for an anxious father; and Livia's influence is paramount. She has not said a syllable in depreciation of you. That is to her credit. She also admits that I must yield freely if at all, and she grants me the use of similes; but her tactics are to contest them one by one, and the admirable pretender is not as shifty as the mariner's breeze, he is not like the wandering spark in burnt paper, of which you cannot say whether it is chasing or chased: it is I who am the shifty Pole to the steadiest of magnets. She is a princess in other things besides her superiority to Physics. There will be wild scenes at Baden.

'My Diary of to-day is all bestowed on you. What have I to write in it except the pair of commas under the last line of yesterday—"He has not come!" Oh! to be caring for a he.

'O that I were with your sister now, on one side of her idol, to correct her extravagant idolatry! I long for her. I had a number of nice little phrases to pet her with.

'You have said (I have it written) that men who are liked by men are the best friends for women. In which case, the earl should be worthy of our friendship; he is liked. Captain Abrane and Sir Meeson, in spite of the hard service he imposes on them with such comical haughtiness, incline to speak well of him, and Methuen Rivers—here for two days on his way to his embassy at Vienna—assured us he is the rarest of gentlemen on the point of honour of his word. They have stories of him, to confirm Livia's eulogies, showing him punctilious to chivalry. No man alive is like him in that, they say. He grieves me. All that you have to fear is my pity for one so sensitive. So speed, sir! It is not good for us to be much alone, and I am alone when you are absent.

'I hear military music!

'How grand that music makes the dullest world appear in a minute. There is a magic in it to bring you to me from the most dreadful of distances.—Chillon! it would kill me!—Writing here and you perhaps behind the hill, I can hardly bear it;—I am torn away, my hand will not any more. This music burst out to mock me! Adieu.

'I am yours.

'Your HENRIETTA.

'A kiss to the sister. It is owing to her.'

Carinthia kissed the letter on that last line. It seemed to her to end in a celestial shower.

She was oppressed by wonder of the writer who could run like the rill of the mountains in written speech; and her recollection of the contents perpetually hurried to the close, which was more in her way of writing, for there the brief sentences had a throb beneath them.

She did not speak of the letter to her brother when she returned it. A night in the carriage, against his shoulder, was her happy prospect, in the thought that she would be with her dearest all night, touching him asleep, and in the sweet sense of being near to the beloved of the fairest angel of her sex. They pursued their journey soon after Anton was dismissed with warm shakes of the hand and appointments for a possible year in the future.

The blast of the postillion's horn on the dark highway moved Chillon to say: 'This is what they call posting, my dear.'

She replied: 'Tell me, brother: I do not understand, "Let none these marks efface," at the commencement, after most "picturesque of Castles":—that is you.'

'They are quoted from the verses of a lord who was a poet, addressed to the castle on Lake Leman. She will read them to you.'

'Will she?'

The mention of the lord set Carinthia thinking of the lord whom that beautiful SHE pitied because she was forced to wound him and he was very sensitive. Wrapped in Henrietta, she slept through the joltings of the carriage, the grinding of the wheels, the blowing of the horn, the flashes of the late moonlight and the kindling of dawn.

CHAPTER VIII

OF THE ENCOUNTER OF TWO STRANGE YOUNG MEN AND THEIR CONSORTING: IN WHICH THE MALE READER IS REQUESTED TO BEAR IN MIND WHAT WILD CREATURE HE WAS IN HIS YOUTH, WHILE THE FEMALE SHOULD MARVEL CREDULOUSLY.

The young man who fancied he had robed himself in the plain homespun of a natural philosopher at the age of twenty-three journeyed limping leisurely in the mountain maid Carinthia's footsteps, thankful to the Fates for having seen her; and reproving the remainder of superstition within him, which would lay him open to smarts of evil fortune if he, encouraged a senseless gratitude for good; seeing that we are simply to take what happens to us. The little inn of the village on the perch furnished him a night's lodging and a laugh of satisfaction to hear of a young lady and gentleman, and their guide, who had devoured everything eatable half a day in advance of him, all save the bread and butter, and a few scraps of meat, apologetically spread for his repast by the maid of the inn: not enough for, a bantam cock, she said, promising eggs for breakfast. He vowed with an honest heart, that it was more than enough, and he was nourished by sympathy with the appetites of his precursors and the maid's description of their deeds. That name, Carinthia, went a good way to fill him.

Farther on he had plenty, but less contentment. He was compelled to acknowledge that he had expected to meet Carinthia again at the Baths. Her absence dealt a violent shock to the aerial structure he dwelt in; for though his ardour for the life of the solitudes was unfeigned, as was his calm overlooking of social distinctions, the self-indulgent dreamer became troubled with an alarming sentience, that for him to share the passions of the world of men was to risk the falling lower than most. Women are a cause of dreams, but they are dreaded enemies of his kind of dream, deadly enemies of the immaterial dreamers; and should one of them be taken on board a vessel of the vapourish texture young Woodseer sailed in above the clouds lightly while he was in it alone, questions of past, future, and present, the three weights upon humanity, bear it down, and she must go, or the vessel sinks. And cast out of it, what was he? The asking exposed him to the steadiest wind the civilized world is known to blow. From merely thinking upon one of the daughters of earth, he was made to feel his position in that world, though he refused to understand it, and assisted by two days of hard walking he reduced Carinthia to an abstract enthusiasm, no very serious burden. His note-book sustained it easily. He wrote her name in simple fondness of the name; a verse, and hints for more, and some sentences, which he thought profound. They were composed as he sat by the roadway, on the top of hills, and in a boat crossing a dark green lake deep under wooded mountain walls: things of priceless value.

It happened, that midway on the lake he perceived his boatman about to prime a pistol to murder the mild-eyed stillness, and he called to the man in his best German to desist. During the altercation, there passed a countryman of his in another of the punts, who said gravely: 'I thank you for that.' It was early morning, and they had the lake to themselves, each deeming the other an intruder; for the courtship of solitude wanes when we are haunted by a second person in pursuit of it; he is discolouring matter in our pure crystal cup. Such is the worship of the picturesque; and it would appear to say, that the spirit of man finds itself yet in the society of barbarians. The case admits of good pleading either way, even upon the issue whether the exclusive or the vulgar be the more barbarous. But in those days the solicitation of the picturesque had been revived by a poet of some impassioned rhetoric, and two devotees could hardly meet, as the two met here, and not be mutually obscurants.

They stepped ashore in turn on the same small shoot of land where a farm-house near a chapel in the shadow of cliffs did occasional service for an inn. Each had intended to pass a day and a night in this lonely dwelling-place by the lake, but a rival was less to be tolerated there than in love, and each awaited the other's departure, with an air that said, 'You are in my sunlight'; and going deeper, more sternly: 'Sir, you are an offence to Nature's pudency!'

Woodseer was the more placable of the two; he had taken possession of the bench outside, and he had his note-book and much profundity to haul up with it while fish were frying. His countryman had rushed inside to avoid him, and remained there pacing the chamber like a lion newly caged. Their boatmen were brotherly in the anticipation of provision and payment.

After eating his fish, Woodseer decided abruptly, that as he could not have the spot to himself, memorable as it would have been to intermarry with Nature in so sacred a welldepth of the mountains, he had better be walking and climbing. Another boat paddling up the lake had been spied: solitude was not merely shared with a rival, but violated by numbers. In the first case, we detest the man; in the second, we fly from an outraged scene. He wrote a line or so in his book, hurriedly paid his bill, and started, full of the matter he had briefly committed to his pages.

At noon, sitting beside the beck that runs from the lake, he was overtaken by the gentleman he had left behind, and accosted in the informal English style, with all the politeness possible to a nervously blunt manner: 'This book is yours,—I have no doubt it is yours; I am glad to be able to restore it; I should be glad to be the owner-writer of the contents, I mean. I have to beg your excuse; I found it lying open; I looked at the page, I looked through the whole; I am quite at your mercy.'

Woodseer jumped at the sight of his note-book, felt for the emptiness of his pocket, and replied: 'Thank you, thank you. It's of use to me, though to no one else.'

'You pardon me?'

'Certainly. I should have done it myself.'

'I cannot offer you my apologies as a stranger.' Lord Fleetwood was the name given.

Woodseer's plebeian was exchanged for it, and he stood up.

The young lord had fair, straight, thin features, with large restless eyes that lighted quickly, and a mouth that was winning in his present colloquial mood.

'You could have done the same? I should find it hard to forgive the man who pried into my secret thoughts,' he remarked.

'There they are. If one puts them to paper!...' Woodseer shrugged.

'Yes, yes. They never last long enough with me. So far I'm safe. One page led to another. You can meditate. I noticed some remarks on Religions. You think deeply.'

Woodseer was of that opinion, but modesty urged him to reply with a small flourish. 'Just a few heads of ideas. When the wind puffs down a sooty chimney the air is filled with little blacks that settle pretty much like the notes in this book of mine. There they wait for another puff, or my fingers to stamp them.'

'I could tell you were the owner of that book,' said Lord Fleetwood. He swept his forehead feverishly. 'What a power it is to relieve one's brain by writing! May I ask you, which one of the Universities...?'

The burden of this question had a ring of irony to one whom it taught to feel rather defiantly, that he carried the blazon of a reeking tramp. 'My University,' Woodseer replied, 'was a merchant's office in Bremen for some months. I learnt more Greek and Latin in Bremen than business. I was invalided home, and then tried a merchant's office in London. I put on my hat one day, and walked into the country. My College fellows were hawkers, tinkers, tramps and ploughmen, choughs and crows. A volume of our Poets and a History of Philosophy composed my library. I had scarce any money, so I learnt how to idle inexpensively—a good first lesson. We're at the bottom of the world when we take to the road; we see men as they were in the beginning—not so eager for harness till they get acquainted with hunger, as I did, and studied in myself the old animal having his head pushed into the collar to earn a feed of corn.'

Woodseer laughed, adding, that he had been of a serious mind in those days of the alternation of smooth indifference and sharp necessity, and he had plucked a flower from them.

His nature prompted him to speak of himself with simple candour, as he had done spontaneously to Chillon Kirby, yet he was now anxious to let his companion know at once the common stuff he was made of, together with the great stuff he contained. He grew conscious of an over-anxiety, and was uneasy, recollecting how he had just spoken about his naturalness, dimly if at all apprehending the cause of this disturbance within. What is a lord to a philosopher! But the world is around us as a cloak, if not a coat; in his ignorance he supposed it specially due to a lord seeking acquaintance with him, that he should expose his condition: doing the which appeared to subject him to parade his intellectual treasures and capacity for shaping sentences; and the effect upon Lord Fleetwood was an incentive to the display. Nevertheless he had a fretful desire to escape from the discomposing society of a lord; he fixed his knapsack and began to saunter.

The young lord was at his elbow. 'I can't part with you. Will you allow me?'

Woodseer was puzzled and had to say: 'If you wish it.'

'I do wish it: an hour's walk with you. One does not meet a man like you every day. I have to join a circle of mine in Baden, but there's no hurry; I could be disengaged for a week. And I have things to ask you, owing to my indiscretion—but you have excused it.'

Woodseer turned for a farewell gaze at the great Watzmann, and saluted him.

'Splendid,' said Lord Fleetwood; 'but don't clap names on the mountains.—I saw written in your book: "A text for Dada." You write: "A despotism would procure a perfect solitude, but kill the ghost." That was my thought at the place where we were at the lake. I had it. Tell me—though I could not have written it, and "ghost" is just the word, the exact word—tell me, are you of Welsh blood? "Dad" is good Welsh—pronounce it hard.'

Woodseer answered: 'My mother was a Glamorganshire woman. My father, I know, walked up from Wales, mending boots on his road for a livelihood. He is not a bad scholar, he knows Greek enough to like it. He is a Dissenting preacher. When I strike a truism, I 've a habit of scoring it to give him a peg or tuning-fork for one of his discourses. He's a man of talent; he taught himself, and he taught me more than I learnt at school. He is a thinker in his way. He loves Nature too. I rather envy him in some respects. He and I are hunters of Wisdom on different tracks; and he, as he says, "waits for me." He's patient!'

Ah, and I wanted to ask you,' Lord Fleetwood observed, bursting with it, 'I was puzzled by a name you write here and there near the end, and permit me to ask, it: Carinthia! It cannot be the country? You write after, the name: "A beautiful Gorgon—a haggard Venus." It seized me. I have had the face before my eyes ever since. You must mean a woman. I can't be deceived in allusions to a woman: they have heart in them. You met her somewhere about Carinthia, and gave her the name? You write—may I refer to the book?'

He received the book and flew through the leaves:

'Here—"A panting look": you write again: "A look of beaten flame: a look of one who has run and at last beholds!" But that is a living face: I see her! Here again: "From minute to minute she is the rock that loses the sun at night and reddens in the morning." You could not create an idea of a woman to move you like that. No one could, I am certain of it, certain; if so, you 're a wizard—I swear you are. But that's a face high over beauty. Just to know there is a woman like her, is an antidote. You compare her to a rock. Who would imagine a comparison of a woman to a rock! But rock is the very picture of beautiful Gorgon, haggard Venus. Tell me you met her, you saw her. I want only to hear she lives, she is in the world. Beautiful women compared to roses may whirl away with their handsome dragoons! A pang from them is a thing to be ashamed of. And there are men who trot about whining with it! But a Carinthia makes pain honourable. You have done what I thought impossible—fused a woman's face and grand scenery, to make them inseparable. She might be wicked for me. I should see a bright rim round hatred of her!—the rock you describe. I could endure horrors and not annihilate her! I should think her sacred.'

Woodseer turned about to have a look at the man who was even quicker than he at realizing a person from a hint of description, and almost insanely extravagant in the pitch of the things he uttered to a stranger. For himself, he was open with everybody, his philosophy not allowing that strangers existed on earth. But the presence of a lord brought the conventional world to his feelings, though at the same time the title seemed to sanction the exceptional abruptness and wildness of this lord. As for suspecting him to be mad, it would have been a common idea: no stretching of speech or overstepping of social rules could waken a suspicion so spiritless in Woodseer.

He said: 'I can tell you I met her and she lives. I could as soon swim in that torrent or leap the mountain as repeat what she spoke, or sketch a feature of her. She goes into the blood, she is a new idea of women. She has the face that would tempt a gypsy to evil tellings. I could think of it as a history written in a line: Carinthia, Saint and Martyr! As for comparisons, they are flowers thrown into the fire.'

'I have had that—I have thought that,' said Lord Fleetwood. 'Go on; talk of her, pray; without comparisons. I detest them. How did you meet her? What made you part? Where is she now? I have no wish to find her, but I want thoroughly to believe in her.'

Another than Woodseer would have perceived the young lord's malady. Here was one bitten by the serpent of love, and athirst for an image of the sex to serve for the cooling herb, as youth will be. Woodseer put it down to a curious imaginative fellowship with himself. He forgot the lord, and supposed he had found his own likeness, less gifted in speech. After talking of Carinthia more and more in the abstract, he fell upon his discovery of the Great Secret of life, against which his hearer struggled for a time, though that was cooling to him too; but ultimately there was no resistance, and so deep did they sink into the idea of pure contemplation, that the idea of woman seemed to have become a part of it. No stronger proof of their aethereal conversational earnestness could be offered. A locality was given to the Great Secret, and of course it was the place where the most powerful recent impression had been stamped on the mind of the discoverer: the shadowy valley rolling from the slate-rock. Woodseer was too artistic a dreamer to present the passing vision of Carinthia with any associates there. She passed: the solitude accepted her and lost her; and it was the richer for the one swift gleam: she brought no trouble, she left no regrets; she was the ghost of the rocky obscurity. But now remembering her mountain carol, he chanced to speak of her as a girl.

'She is a girl?' cried Lord Fleetwood, frowning over an utter revolution of sentiment at the thought of the beautiful Gorgon being a girl; for, rapid as he was to imagine, he had raised a solid fabric upon his conception of Carinthia the woman, necessarily the woman—logically. Who but the woman could look the Gorgon! He tried to explain it to be impossible for a girl to wear the look: and his notion evidently was, that it had come upon a beautiful face in some staring horror of a world that had bitten the tender woman. She touched him sympathetically through the pathos.

Woodseer flung out vociferously for the contrary. Who but a girl could look the beautiful Gorgon! What other could seem an emanation of the mountain solitude? A woman would instantly breathe the world on it to destroy it. Hers would be the dramatic and not the poetic face. It would shriek of man, wake the echoes with the tale of man, slaughter all. quietude. But a girl's face has no story of poisonous intrusion. She indeed may be cast in the terrors of Nature, and yet be sweet with Nature, beautiful because she is purely of Nature. Woodseer did his best to present his view irresistibly. Perhaps he was not clear; it was a piece of skiamachy, difficult to render clear to the defeated.

Lord Fleetwood had nothing to say but 'Gorgon! a girl a Gorgon!' and it struck Woodseer as intensely unreasonable, considering that he had seen the girl whom, in his effort to portray her, he had likened to a beautiful Gorgon. He recounted the scene of the meeting with her, pictured it in effective colours, but his companion gave no response, nor a nod. They ceased to converse, and when the young lord's hired carriage drew up on the road, Woodseer required persuasion to accompany him. They were both in their different stations young tyrants of the world, ready to fight the world and one another for not having their immediate view of it such as they wanted it. They agreed, however, not to sleep in the city. Beds were to be had near the top of a mountain on the other side of the Salza, their driver informed them, and vowing themselves to that particular height, in a mutual disgust of the city, they waxed friendlier, with a reserve.

Woodseer soon had experience that he was receiving exceptional treatment from Lord Fleetwood, whose manservant was on the steps of the hotel in Salzburg on the lookout for his master.

'Sir Meeson has been getting impatient, my lord,' said the man.

Sir Meeson Corby appeared; Lord Fleetwood cut him short: 'You 're in a hurry; go at once, don't wait for me; I join you in Baden.—Do me the favour to eat with me,' he turned to Woodseer. 'And here, Corby! tell the countess I have a friend to bear me company, and there is to be an extra bedroom secured at her hotel. That swinery of a place she insists on visiting is usually crammed. With you there,' he turned to Woodseer, 'I might find it agreeable.—You can take my man, Corby; I shall not want the fellow.'

'Positively, my dear Fleetwood, you know,' Sir Meeson expostulated, 'I am under orders; I don't see how—I really can't go on without you.'

'Please yourself. This gentleman is my friend, Mr. Woodseer.'

Sir Meeson Corby was a plump little beau of forty, at war with his fat and accounting his tight blue tail coat and brass buttons a victory. His tightness made his fatness elastic; he looked wound up for a dance, and could hardly hold on a leg; but the presentation of a creature in a battered hat and soiled garments, carrying a tattered knapsack half slung, lank and with disorderly locks, as the Earl of Fleetwood's friend—the friend of the wealthiest nobleman of Great Britain!—fixed him in a perked attitude of inquiry that exhausted interrogatives. Woodseer passed him, slouching a bow. The circular stare of Sir Meeson seemed unable to contract. He directed it on Lord Fleetwood, and was then reminded that he dealt with prickles.

'Where have you been?' he said, blinking to refresh his eyeballs. 'I missed you, I ran round and round the town after you.'

'I have been to the lake.'

'Queer fish there!' Sir Meeson dropped a glance on the capture.

Lord Fleetwood took Woodseer's arm. 'Do you eat with us?' he asked the baronet, who had stayed his eating for an hour and was famished; so they strode to the dining-room.

'Do you wash, sir, before eating?' Sir Meeson said to Woodseer, caressing his hands when they had seated themselves at table. 'Appliances are to be found in this hotel.'

'Soap?' said Lord Fleetwood.

'Soap—at least, in my chamber.'

'Fetch it, please.'

Sir Meeson, of course, could not hear that. He requested the waiter to show the gentleman to a room.

Lord Fleetwood ordered the waiter to bring a handbasin and towel. 'We're off directly and must eat at once,' he said.

'Soap—soap! my dear Fleetwood,' Sir Meeson knuckled on the table, to impress it that his appetite and his gorge demanded a thorough cleansing of those fingers, if they were to sit at one board.

'Let the waiter fetch it.'

'The soap is in my portmanteau.'

'You spoke of it as a necessity for this gentleman and me. Bring it.'

Woodseer had risen. Lord Fleetwood motioned him down. He kept an eye dead—as marble on Corby, who muttered: 'You can't mean that you ask me...?' But the alternative was forced on Sir Meeson by too strong a power of the implacable eye; there was thunder in it, a continuity of gaze forcefuller than repetitions of the word. He knew Lord Fleetwood. Men privileged to attend on him were dogs to the flinty young despot: they were sure to be called upon to expiate the faintest offence to him. He had hastily to consider, that he was banished beyond appeal, with the whole torture of banishment to an adorer of the Countess Livia, or else the mad behest must be obeyed. He protested, shrugged, sat fast, and sprang up, remarking, that he went with all the willingness imaginable. It could not have been the first occasion.

He was affecting the excessively obsequious when he came back bearing his metal soap-case. The performance was checked by another look solid as shot, and as quick. Woodseer, who would have done for Sir Meeson Corby or Lazarus what had been done for him, thought little of the service, but so intense a peremptoriness in the look of an eye made him uncomfortable in his own sense of independence. The humblest citizen of a free nation has that warning at some notable exhibition of tyranny in a neighbouring State: it acts like a concussion of the air.

Lord Fleetwood led an easy dialogue with him and Sir Meeson, on their different themes immediately, which was not less impressive to an observer. He listened to Sir Meeson's entreaties that he should start at once for Baden, and appeared to pity the poor gentleman, condemned by his office to hang about him in terror of his liege lady's displeasure. Presently, near the close of the meal, drawing a ring from his finger, he handed it to the baronet, and said, 'Give her that. She knows I shall follow that.' He added to himself:—I shall have ill-luck till I have it back! and he asked Woodseer whether he put faith in the virtue of talismans.

'I have never possessed one,' said Woodseer, with his natural frankness. 'It would have gone long before this for a night's lodging.'

Sir Meeson heard him, and instantly urged Lord Fleetwood not to think of dismissing his man Francis. 'I beg it, Fleetwood! I beg you to take the man. Her ladyship will receive me badly, ring or no ring, if she hears of your being left alone. I really can't present myself. I shall not go, not go. I say no.'

'Stay, then,' said Fleetwood.

He turned to Woodseer with an air of deference, and requested the privilege of glancing at his notebook again, and scanned it closely at one of the pages. 'I believe it true,' he cried; 'I had a half recollection of it—I have had some such thought, but never could put it in words. You have thought deeply.'

'That is only a surface thought, or common reflection,' said Woodseer.

Sir Meeson stared at them in turn. Judging by their talk and the effect produced on the earl, he took Woodseer for a sort of conjuror.

It was his duty to utter a warning.

He drew Fleetwood aside. A word was whispered, and they broke asunder with a snap. Francis was called. His master gave him his keys, and despatched him into the town to purchase a knapsack or bag for the outfit of a jolly beggar. The prospect delighted Lord Fleetwood. He sang notes from the deep chest, flaunting like an opera brigand, and contemplating his wretched satellite's indecision with brimming amusement.

'Remember, we fight for our money. I carry mine,' he said to Woodseer.

'Wouldn't it be expedient, Fleetwood...' Sir Meeson suggested a treasurer in the person of himself.

'Not a florin, Corby! I should find it all gambled away at Baden.'

'But I am not Abrane, I'm not Abrane! I never play, I have no mania, none. It would be prudent, Fleetwood.'

'The slightest bulging of a pocket would show on you, Corby; and they would be at you, they would fall on you and pluck you to have another fling. I 'd rather my money should go to a knight of the road than feed that dragon's jaw. A highwayman seems an honest fellow compared with your honourable corporation of fly-catchers. I could surrender to him with some satisfaction after a trial of the better man. I 've tried these tables, and couldn't stir a pulse. Have you?'

It had to be explained to Woodseer what was meant by trying the tables. 'Not I,' said he, in strong contempt of the queer allurement.

Lord Fleetwood studied him half a minute, as if measuring and discarding a suspicion of the young philosopher's possible weakness under temptation.

Sir Meeson Corby accompanied the oddly assorted couple through the town and a short way along the road to the mountain, for the sake of quieting his conscience upon the subject of his leaving them together. He could not have sat down a second time at a table with those hands. He said it:—he could not have done the thing. So the best he could do was to let them go. Like many of his class, he had a mind open to the effect of striking contrasts, and the spectacle of the wealthiest nobleman in Great Britain tramping the road, pack on back, with a young nobody for his comrade, a total stranger, who might be a cut-throat, and was avowedly next to a mendicant, charged him with quantities of interjectory matter, that he caught himself firing to the foreign people on the highway. Hundreds of thousands a year, and tramping it like a pedlar, with a beggar for his friend! He would have given something to have an English ear near him as he watched them rounding under the mountain they were about to climb.

CHAPTER IX

CONCERNING THE BLACK GODDESS FORTUNE AND THE WORSHIP OF HER, TOGETHER WITH AN INTRODUCTION OF SOME OF HER VOTARIES

In those early days of Fortune's pregnant alternations of colour between the Red and the Black, exhibited publicly, as it were a petroleum spring of the ebony-fiery lake below, Black-Forest Baden was the sprightliest' of the ante-chambers of Hades. Thither in the ripeness of the year trooped the devotees of the sable goddess to perform sacrifice; and annually among them the beautiful Livia, the Countess of Fleetwood; for nowhere else had she sensation of the perfect repose which is rocked to a slumber by gales.

She was not of the creatures who are excited by an atmosphere of excitement; she took it as the nymph of the stream her native wave, and swam on the flood with expansive languor, happy to have the master passions about her; one or two of which her dainty hand caressed, fearless of a sting; the lady petted them as her swans. It surprised her to a gentle contempt of men and women, that they should be ruffled either by love or play. A withholding from the scene will naturally arouse disturbing wishes; but to be present lulls; for then we live, we are in our element. And who could expect, what sane person can desire, perpetual good luck? Fortune, the goddess, and young Love, too, are divine in their mutability: and Fortune would resemble a humdrum housewife, Love a droning husband, if constancy were practised by them. Observe the staggering and plunging of the blindfold wretch seeking to be persuaded of their faithfulness.

She could make for herself a quiet centre in the heart of the whirlwind, but the whirlwind was required. The clustered lights at the corner of the vale under forest hills, the burst of music, the blazing windows of the saloons of the Furies, and the gamblers advancing and retreating, with their totally opposite views of consequences, and fashions of wearing or tearing the mask; and closer, the figures shifting up and down the promenade, known and unknown faces, and the histories half known, half woven, weaving fast, which flew their threads to provoke speculation; pleasantly embraced and diverted the cool-blooded lady surrounded by her courtiers, who could upon occasion supply the luminous clue or anecdote. She had an intuitive liveliness to detect interchanges of eyes, the shuttle of intrigue; the mild hypocrisy, the clever audacity, the suspicion confirmed, the complication threatening to become resonant and terrible; and the old crossing the young and the young outwitting the old, wiles of fair traitors and dark, knaves of all suits of the pack. A more intimate acquaintance with their lineaments inspired a regard for them, such as poets may feign the throned high moon to entertain for objects causing her rays to flash.

The simple fools, performing in character, were a neutral people, grotesques and arabesques wreathed about the margins of the scene. Venus or Fortune smote them to a relievo distinguishing one from another. Here, however, as elsewhere, the core of interest was with the serious population, the lovers and the players in earnest, who stood round the furnace and pitched themselves into it, not always under a miscalculation of their chances of emerging transfigured instead of serving for fuel. These, the tragical children of folly, were astute: they played with lightning, and they knew the conditions of the game; victories were to be had.

The ulterior conditions of the game, the price paid for a victory, they thought little of: for they were feverish worshippers of the phantasmal deity called the Present; a god reigning over the Past, appreciable only in the Future; whose whiff of actual being is composed of the embryo idea of the union of these two periods. Still he is occasionally a benevolent god to the appetites; which have but to be continuous to establish him in permanence; and as nothing in us more readily supposes perpetuity than the appetite rushing to destroy itself, the rational nature of the most universal worship on earth is perceived at once.

Now, the price paid for a victory is this: that having been favoured in a single instance by the spouse of the aforesaid eminent divinity—the Black Goddess of the golden fringes—men believe in her for ever after, behold her everywhere, they belong to her. Their faith as to sowing and reaping has gone; and so has their capacity to see the actual as it is: she has the power to attach them to her skirts the more by rewarding their impassioned devotion with cuffs and scorns. They have ceased to have a first notion upon anything without a second haunting it, which directs them to propitiate Fortune.

But I am reminded by the convulsions of Dame Gossip, that the wisdom of our ancestors makes it a mere hammering of commonplace to insist on such reflections. Many of them, indeed, took the union of the Black Goddess and the Rosy Present for the composition of the very Arch-Fiend. Some had a shot at the strange conjecture, figuring her as tired of men in the end and challengeing him below—equally tired of his easy conquests of men since the glorious old times of the duelling saints. By virtue of his one incorrigible weakness, which we know him to have as long as we have it ourselves: viz., the belief in her existence, she is to get the better of him.

Upon this point the experience of Captain Abrane has a value. Livia was a follower of the Red and Black and the rounding ball in the person of the giant captain, through whom she received her succession of sweetly teasing thrills and shocks, as one of the adventurous company they formed together. The place was known to him as the fair Philistine to another muscular hero; he had been shorn there before, and sent forth tottering, treating the friends he met as pillars to fall with him; and when the operation was done thoroughly, he pronounced himself refreshed by it, like a more sensible Samson, the cooler for his clipping. Then it was that he relapsed undistractedly upon processes of his mind and he often said he thought Fortune would beat the devil.

Her power is shown in the moving of her solicitors to think, instantly after they have made their cast, that the reverse of it was what they intended. It comes as though she had withdrawn the bandage from her forehead and dropped a leaden glance on them, like a great dame angry to have her signal misinterpreted. Well, then, distinguished by the goddess in such a manner, we have it proved to us how she wished to favour: for the reverse wins, and we who are pinched blame not her cruelty but our blind folly. This is true worship. Henceforth the pain of her nip is mingled with the dream of her kiss; between the positive and the imagined of her we remain confused until the purse is an empty body on a gallows, honour too, perhaps.

Captain Abrane was one of the Countess Livia's numerous courtiers on the border of the promenade under the lighted saloons. A colossus inactive, he had little to say among the chattering circle; for when seated, cards were wanted to animate him: and he looked entirely out of place and unfitted, like a great vessel's figure-head in a shipwright's yard.

She murmured: 'Not this evening?'

Abrane quoted promptly a line of nursery song 'How shall he cut it without e'er a knife?'

'Have we run it down so low?' said she, with no reproach in her tone.

The captain shrugged over his clean abyss, where nothing was.

Yesterday their bank presented matronly proportions. But an importuned goddess reduces the most voluminous to bare stitches within a few winks of an eye.

Livia turned to a French gentleman of her court, M. de St. Ombre, and pursued a conversation. He was a stately cavalier of the Gallicized Frankish outlines, ready, but grave in his bearing, grave in his delivery, trimly moustached, with a Guise beard.

His profound internal question relating to this un-English beauty of the British Isles:—had she no passion in her nature? was not convinced by her apparent insensibility to Fortune's whips.

Sir Meeson Corby inserted a word of Bull French out of place from time to time.

As it might be necessary to lean on the little man for weapons of war, supposing Lord Fleetwood delayed his arrival yet another day, Livia was indulgent. She assisted him to think that he spoke the foreign tongue.

Mention of Lord Fleetwood set Sir Meeson harping again on his alarms, in consideration of the vagabond object of the young lord had roamed away with.

'You forget that Russett has gypsy in him: Welsh! it's about the same,' said Livia. 'He can take excellent care of himself and his purse.'

'Countess, he is a good six days overdue.'

'He will be in time for the ball at the Schloss.'

Sir Meeson Corby produced an aspect of the word 'if,' so perkily, that the dejected Captain Abrane laughed outright and gave him double reason to fret for Lord Fleetwood's arrival, by saying: 'If he hangs off much longer, I shall have to come on you for another fifty.'

Our two pedestrians out of Salzburg were standing up in the night of cloud and pines above the glittering pool, having made their way along the path from the hill anciently dedicated to the god Mercury; and at the moment when Sir Meeson put forth his frilled wrists to say: 'If you had seen his hands—the creature Fleetwood trotted off alone with!—you'd be a bit anxious too'; the young lord called his comrade to gaze underneath them: 'There they are, hard at it, at their play!—it's the word used for the filthiest gutter scramble.'

They had come to know something of one another's humours; which are taken by young men for their characters; and should the humours please, they are friends, until further humours develop, trying these nascent conservatives hard to suit them to their moods as well as the accustomed. Lord Fleetwood had discovered in his companion, besides the spirit of independence and the powers of thought impressed on him by Woodseer's precocious flashes, a broad playfulness, that trenched on buffoonery; it astonished, amused, and relieved him, loosening the spell of reverence cast over him by one who could so wonderfully illumine his brain. Prone to admire and bend the knee where he admired, he chafed at subjection, unless he had the particular spell constantly renewed. A tone in him once or twice of late, different from the comrade's, had warned Woodseer to be guarded.

Susceptible, however, of the extreme contrast between the gamblers below and Nature's lover beside him, Fleetwood returned to his enthusiasm without thinking it a bondage.

'I shall never forget the walk we 've had. I have to thank you for the noblest of pleasures. You 've taught me—well, a thousand things; the things money can't buy. What mornings they were! And the dead-tired nights! Under the rock and up to see the snowy peak pink in a gap of thick mist. You were right: it made a crimsoning colour shine like a new idea. Up in those mountains one walks with the divinities, you said. It's perfectly true. I shall remember I did. I have a treasure for life! Now I understand where you get your ideas. The life we lead down there is hoggish. You have chosen the right. You're right, over and over again, when you say, the dirty sweaters are nearer the angels for cleanliness than my Lord and Lady Sybarite out of a bath, in chemical scents. A man who thinks, loathes their High Society. I went through Juvenal at college. But you—to be sure, you add example—make me feel the contempt of it more. I am everlastingly indebted to you. Yes, I won't forget: you preach against the despising of anything.

This was pleasant in Woodseer's ears, inasmuch as it established the young nobleman as the pupil of his philosophy for the conduct of life; and to fortify him, he replied:

'Set your mind on the beauty, and there'll be no room for comparisons. Most of them are unjust, precious few instructive. In this case, they spoil both pictures: and that scene down there rather hooks me; though I prefer the Dachstein in the wane of the afterglow. You called it Carinthia.'

'I did: the beautiful Gorgon, haggard Venus—if she is to be a girl!' Fleetwood rejoined. 'She looked burnt out—a spectre.'

'One of the admirably damned,' said Woodseer, and he murmured with enjoyment: 'Between the lights—that 's the beauty and the tragedy of Purgatory!'

His comrade fell in with the pictured idea: 'You hit it:—not what you called the "sublimely milky," and not squalid as you'll see the faces of the gambling women at the tables below. Oblige me—may I beg?—don't clap names on the mountains we've seen. It stamps guide-book on them, English tourist, horrors. We'll moralize over the crowds at the tables down there. On the whole, it's a fairish game: you know the odds against you, as you don't on the Turf or the Bourse. Have your fling; but don't get bitten. There's a virus. I'm not open to it. Others are.'

Hereupon Woodseer, wishing to have his individuality recognised in the universality it consented to, remarked on an exchequer that could not afford to lose, and a disposition free of the craving to win.

These were, no doubt, good reasons for abstaining, and they were grand morality. They were, at the same time, customary phrases of the unfleshed in folly. They struck Fleetwood with a curious reminder of the puking inexperienced, whom he had seen subsequently plunge suicidally. He had a sharp vision of the attractive forces of the game; and his elemental nature exulted in siding with the stronger against a pretender to the superhuman. For Woodseer had spoken a trifle loftily, as quite above temptation. To see a forewarned philosopher lured to try the swim on those tides, pulled along the current, and caught by the undertug of the lasher, would be fun.

'We'll drop down on them, find our hotel, and have a look at what they're doing,' he said, and stepped.

Woodseer would gladly have remained. The starlit black ridges about him and the dragon's mouth yawing underneath were an opposition of spiritual and mundane; innocent, noxious; exciting to the youthful philosopher. He had to follow, and so rapidly in the darkness that he stumbled and fell on an arm; a small matter.

Bed-chambers awaited them at the hotel, none of the party: and Fleetwood's man-servant was absent.

'Gambling, the rascal!' he said. Woodseer heard the first note of the place in that.

His leader was washed, neatly dressed, and knocking at his door very soon, impatient to be off, and he flung a promise of 'supper presently' to one whose modest purse had fallen into a debate with this lordly hostelry, counting that a supper and a night there would do for it. They hurried on to the line of promenaders, a river of cross-currents by the side of seated groups; and the willowy swish of silken dresses, feminine perfumery, cigar-smoke, chatter, laughter, told of pleasure reigning.

Fleetwood scanned the groups. He had seen enough in a moment and his face blackened. A darting waiter was called to him.

He said to Woodseer, savagely, as it sounded: 'You shall have something to joint your bones!' What cause of wrath he had was past a guess: a wolf at his vitals bit him, hardening his handsome features.

The waiter darted back, bearing a tray and tall glasses filled each with piled parti-coloured liqueurs, on the top of which an egg-yolk swam. Fleetwood gave example. Swallowing your egg, the fiery-velvet triune behind slips after it, in an easy milky way, like a princess's train on a state-march, and you are completely, transformed, very agreeably; you have become a merry demon. 'Well, yes, it's next to magic,' he replied to Woodseer's astonished snigger after the draught, and explained, that it was a famous Viennese four-of-the-morning panacea, the revellers' electrical restorer. 'Now you can hold on for an hour or two, and then we'll sup. At Rome?'

'Ay! Druids to-morrow!' cried the philosopher bewitched.

He found himself bowing to a most heavenly lady, composed of day and night in her colouring, but more of night, where the western edge has become a pale steel blade. Men were around her, forming a semi-circle. The world of men and women was mere timber and leafage to this flower of her sex, glory of her kind. How he behaved in her presence, he knew not; he was beyond self-criticism or conscious reflection; simply the engine of the commixed three liqueurs, with parlous fine thoughts, and a sense of steaming into the infinite.

To leave her was to have her as a moon in the heavens and to think of her creatively. A swarm of images rushed about her and away, took lustre and shade. She was a miracle of greyness, her eyes translucently grey, a dark-haired queen of the twilights; and his heart sprang into his brain to picture the novel beauty; language became a flushed Bacchanal in a ring of dancing similes. Lying beside a bank of silvery cinquefoil against a clear evening sky, where the planet Venus is a point of new and warmer light, one has the vision of her. Or something of Persephone rising to greet her mother, when our beam of day first melts through her as she kneels to gather an early bud of the year, would be near it. Or there is a lake in mid-forest, that curls part in shadow under the foot of morning: there we have her.

He strained to the earthly and the skyey likenesses of his marvel of human beauty because they bestowed her on him in passing. All the while, he was gazing on a green gaming-table.

The gold glittered, and it heaped or it vanished. Contemptuous of money, beyond the limited sum for his needs, he gazed; imagination was blunted in him to the hot drama of the business. Moreover his mind was engaged in insisting that the Evening Star is not to be called Venus, because of certain stories; and he was vowed to defend his lady from any allusion to them. This occupied him. By degrees, the visible asserted its authority; his look on the coin fell to speculating. Oddly, too, he was often right;—the money, staked on the other side, would have won. He considered it rather a plain calculation than a guess.

Philosophy withdrew him from his temporary interest in the tricks of a circling white marble ball. The chuck farthing of street urchins has quite as much dignity. He compared the creatures dabbling, over the board to summer flies on butcher's meat, periodically scared by a cloth. More in the abstract, they were snatching at a snapdragon bowl. It struck him, that the gamblers had thronged on an invitation to drink the round of seed-time and harvest in a gulp. Again they were desperate gleaners, hopping, skipping, bleeding, amid a whizz of scythe-blades, for small wisps of booty. Nor was it long before the presidency of an ancient hoary Goat-Satan might be perceived, with skew-eyes and pucker-mouth, nursing a hoof on a knee.

Our mediaeval Enemy sat symbolical in his deformities, as in old Italian and Dutch thick-line engravings of him. He rolled a ball for souls, excited like kittens, to catch it, and tumbling into the dozens of vacant pits. So it seemed to Woodseer, whose perceptions were discoloured by hereditary antagonism. Had he preserved his philosopher's eye, he would have known that the Hoofed One is too wily to show himself, owing to his ugliness. The Black Goddess and no other presides at her own game. She (it is good for us to know it) is the Power who challenges the individual, it is he who spreads the net for the mass. She liquefies the brain of man; he petrifies or ossifies the heart. From her comes craziness, from him perversity: a more provocative and, on the whole, more contagious disease. The gambler does not seek to lead his fellows into perdition; the snared of the Demon have pleasure in the act. Hence our naturally interested forecasts of the contests between them: for if he is beaten, as all must be at the close of an extended game with her, we have only to harden the brain against her allurements and we enter a clearer field.

Woodseer said to Fleetwood: 'That ball has a look of a nymph running round and round till she changes to one of the Fates.'

'We'll have a run with her,' said Fleetwood, keener for business than for metaphors—at the moment.

He received gold for a bank-note. Captain Abrane hurriedly begged a loan. Both of them threw. Neither of them threw on the six numbers Woodseer would have selected, and they lost. He stated that the number of 17 had won before. Abrane tried the transversal enclosing this favoured number. 'Of course!' he cried, with foul resignation and a hostile glare: the ball had seated itself and was grinning at him from the lowest of the stalls.

Fleetwood quitted the table-numbers to throw on Pair; he won, won again, pushed his luck and lost, dragging Abrane with him. The giant varied his tone of acquiescence in Fortune's whims: 'Of course! I 've only to fling! Luck hangs right enough till I put down my stake.'

'If the luck has gone three times, the chances....' Woodseer was rather inquiring than pronouncing.... Lord Fleetwood cut him short. 'The chances are equally the contrary!' and discomposed his argumentative mind.

As argument in such a place was impossible, he had a wild idea of example—'just to see'—; and though he smiled, his brain was liquefying. Upon a calculation of the chances, merely for the humour of it, he laid a silver piece on the first six, which had been neglected. They were now blest. He laid his winnings on the numbed 17. Who would have expected it? why, the player, surely! Woodseer comported himself like a veteran: he had proved that you can calculate the chances. Instead of turning in triumph to Lord Fleetwood, he laid gold pieces to hug the number 17, and ten in the centre. And it is the truth, he hoped then to lose and have done with it—after proving his case. The ball whirled, kicked, tried for seat in two, in three points, and entered 17. The usual temporary wonderment flew round the table; and this number was courted in dread, avoided with apprehension.

Abrane let fly a mighty breath: 'Virgin, by Jove!'

Success was a small matter to Gower Woodseer. He displayed his contempt of fortune by letting his heap of bank-notes lie on Impair, and he won. Abrane bade him say 'Maximum' in a furious whisper. He did so, as one at home with the word; and winning repeatedly, observed to Fleetwood: 'Now I can understand what historians mean, in telling us of heroes rushing into the fray and vainly seeking death. I always thought death was to be had, if you were in earnest.'

Fleetwood scrutinized the cast of his features and the touch of his fingers on the crispy paper.

'Come to another of these "green fields,"' he returned briefly. 'The game here is child's play.'

Urging Virgin Luck not to quit his initiatory table, the captain reluctantly went at their heels. Shortly before the tables were clad in mantles for the night, he reported to Livia one of the great cases of Virgin Luck; described it, from the silver piece to the big heap of notes, and drew on his envy of the fellow to sketch the indomitable coolness shown in following or in quitting a run. 'That fellow it is, Fleetwood's tag-rag; holds his head like a street-fiddler; Woodler or some name. But there's nothing to be done if we don't cultivate him. He must have pocketed a good three thousand and more. They had a quarrel about calculations of chances, and Fleet ran the V up his forehead at a piece of impudence. Fellow says some high-flying stuff; Fleet brightens like a Sunday chimney-sweep. If I believed in Black Arts, upon my word!'

'Russett is not usually managed with ease,' the lady said.

Her placid observation was directed on the pair then descending the steps.

'Be careful how you address, this gentleman,' she counselled Abrane. 'The name is not Woodier, I know. It must be the right name or none.'

Livia's fairest smile received them. She heard the captain accosting the child of luck as Mr. Woodier, and she made a rustle in rising to take Fleetwood's arm.

'We haven't dined, we have to sup,' said he.

'You are released at the end of the lamps. You redeem your ring, Russett, and I will restore it. I have to tell you, Henrietta is here to-morrow.'

'She might be in a better place.'

'The place where she is to be seen is not generally undervalued by men. It is not her fault that she is absent. The admiral was persuaded to go and attend those cavalry manoeuvres with the Grand Duke, to whom he had been civil when in command of the Mediterranean squadron. You know, the admiral believes he has military—I mean soldierly-genius; and the delusion may have given him wholesome exercise and helped him to forget his gout. So far, Henrietta will have been satisfied. She cannot have found much amusement among dusty troopers or at that court at Carlsruhe. Our French milliner there has helped in retarding her quite against her will. She has had to choose a balldress for the raw mountain girl they have with them, and get her fitted, and it's a task! Why take her to the ball? But the admiral's infatuated with this girl, and won't hear of her exclusion—because, he says, she understands a field of battle; and the Ducal party have taken to her. Ah, Russett, you should not have flown! No harm, only Henrietta does require a trifle of management. She writes, that she is sure of you for the night at the Schloss.'

'Why, ma'am?'

'You have given your word. "He never breaks his lightest word," she says.'

'It sounds like the beginning of respect.'

'The rarest thing men teach women to feel for them!'

'A respectable love match—eh? Good Lord! You'll be civil to my friend. You have struck him to the dust. You have your one poetical admirer in him.'

'I am honoured, Russett.'

'Cleared out, I suppose? Abrane is a funnel for pouring into that Bank. Have your fun as you like it! I shall get supplies to-morrow. By the way, you have that boy Cressett here. What are you doing with him?'

Livia spoke of watching over him and guarding him:

'He was at the table beside me, bursting to have a fling; and my friend Mr. Woodseer said, it was "Adonis come to spy the boar":—the picture!'

Prompt as bugle to the breath, Livia proposed to bet him fifty pounds that she would keep young Cressett from gambling a single louis. The pretty saying did not touch her.

Fleetwood moved and bowed. Sir Meeson Corby simulated a petrifaction of his frame at seeing the Countess of Fleetwood actually partly bent with her gracious acknowledgement of the tramp's gawky homage.

BOOK II

CHAPTER X

SMALL CAUSES

A clock sounded one of the later morning hours of the night as Gower Woodseer stood at his hotel door, having left Fleetwood with a band of revellers. The night was now clear. Stars were low over the ridge of pines, dropped to a league of our strange world to record the doings. Beneath this roof lay the starry She. He was elected to lie beneath it also: and he beheld his heavenly lady floating on the lull of soft white cloud among her sister spheres. After the way of imaginative young men, he had her features more accurately now she was hidden, and he idealized her more. He could escape for a time from his coil of similes and paint for himself the irids of her large, long, grey eyes darkly rimmed; purest water-grey, lucid within the ring, beneath an arch of lashes. He had them fast; but then he fell to contemplating their exceeding rareness; And the mystery of the divinely grey swung a kindled fancy to the flight with some queen-witch of woods, of whom a youth may dream under the spell of twilights, East or West, among forest branches.

She had these marvellous eyes and the glamour for men. She had not yet met a man with the poetical twist in the brain to prize her elementally. All admitted the glamour; none of her courtiers were able to name it, even the poetical head giving it a name did not think of the witch in her looks as a witch in her deeds, a modern daughter of the mediaeval. To her giant squire the eyes of the lady were queer: they were unlit glass lamps to her French suppliant; and to the others, they were attractively uncommon; the charm for them being in her fine outlines, her stature, carriage of her person, and unalterable composure; particularly her latent daring. She had the effect on the general mind of a lofty crag-castle with a history. There was a whiff of gunpowder exciting the atmosphere in the anecdotal part of the history known.

Woodseer sat for a certain time over his note-book. He closed it with a thrilling conceit of the right thing written down; such as entomologists feel when they have pinned the rare insect. But what is butterfly or beetle compared with the chiselled sentences carved out of air to constitute us part owner of the breathing image and spirit of an adored fair woman? We repeat them, and the act of repeating them makes her come close on ours, by virtue of the eagle thought in the stamped gold of the lines.

Then, though she is not ever to be absolutely ours (and it is an impoverishing desire that she should be), we have beaten out the golden sentence—the essential she and we in one. But is it so precious after all? A suspicious ring of an adjective drops us on a sickening descent.

The author dashed at his book, examined, approved, keenly enjoyed, and he murderously scratched the adjective. She stood better without it, as a bright planet star issuing from clouds, which are perhaps an adornment to our hackneyed moon. This done, he restored the book to his coat's breast-pocket, smiling or sneering at the rolls of bank-notes there, disdaining to count them. They stuffed an inner waistcoat pocket and his trousers also. They at any rate warranted that we can form a calculation of the chances, let Lord Fleetwood rave as he may please.

Woodseer had caught a glimpse of the elbow-point of his coat when flinging it back to the chair. There was distinctly abrasion. Philosophers laugh at such things. But they must be the very ancient pallium philosophers, ensconced in tubs, if they pretend to merriment over the spectacle of nether garments gapped at the spot where man is most vulnerable. He got loose from them and held them up to the candle, and the rays were admitted, neither winking nor peeping. Serviceable old clothes, no doubt. Time had not dealt them the final kick before they scored a good record.

They dragged him, nevertheless, to a sort of confession of some weakness, that he could not analyze for the swirl of emotional thoughts in the way; and they had him to the ground. An eagle of the poetic becomes a mere squat toad through one of these pretty material strokes. Where then is Philosophy? But who can be philosopher and the fervent admirer of a glorious lady? Ask again, who in that frowzy garb can presume to think of her or stand within fifty miles of her orbit?

A dreary two hours brought round daylight. Woodseer quitted his restless bed and entered the abjured habiliments, chivalrous enough to keep from denouncing them until he could cast the bad skin they now were to his uneasy sensations. He remembered having stumbled and fallen on the slope of the hill into this vale, and probably then the mischief had occurred though a brush would have, been sufficient, the slightest collision. Only, it was odd that the accident should have come to pass just previous to his introduction. How long antecedent was it? He belaboured his memory to reckon how long it was from the moment of the fall to the first sight of that lady.

His window looked down on the hotel stable-yard. A coach-house door was open. Odd or not—and it certainly looked like fate—that he should be bowing to his lady so shortly after the mishap expelling him, he had to leave the place. A groom in the yard was hailed, and cheerily informed him he could be driven to Carlsruhe as soon as the coachman had finished his breakfast. At Carlsruhe a decent refitting might be obtained, and he could return from exile that very day, thanks to the praiseworthy early hours of brave old Germany.

He had swallowed a cup of coffee with a roll of stale bread, in the best of moods, and entered his carriage; he was calling the order to start when a shout surprised his ear: 'The fiddler bolts!'

Captain Abrane's was the voice. About twenty paces behind, Abrane, Fleetwood, and one whom they called Chummy Potts, were wildly waving arms. Woodseer could hear the captain's lowered roar: 'Race you, Chummy, couple of louis, catch him first!' The two came pelting up to the carriage abreast.

They were belated revellers, and had been carelessly strolling under the pinky cloudlets bedward, after a prolonged carousal with the sons and daughters of hilarious nations, until the apparition of Virgin Luck on the wing shocked all prospect of a dead fight with the tables that day.

'Here, come, no, by Jove, you, Mr. Woodsir! won't do, not a bit! can't let you go,' cried Abrane, as he puffed. 'What! cut and run and leave us, post winnings—bankers—knock your luck on the head! What a fellow! Can't let you. Countess never forgive us. You promised—swore it—play for her. Struck all aheap to hear of your play! You've got the trick. Her purse for you in my pocket. Never a fellow played like you. Cool as a cook over a-gridiron! Comme un phare! St. Ombre says—that Frenchman. You astonished the Frenchman! And now cut and run? Can't allow it. Honour of the country at stake.'

'Hands off!' Woodseer bellowed, feeling himself a leaky vessel in dock, his infirmities in danger of exposure. 'If you pull!—what the deuce do you want? Stop!'

'Out you come,' said the giant, and laughed at the fun to his friends, who were entirely harmonious when not violently dissenting, as is the way with Night's rollickers before their beds have reconciled them to the day-beams.

Woodseer would have had to come and was coming; he happened to say: 'Don't knock my pipe out of my mouth,' and touched a chord in the giant.

'All—right; smoke your pipe,' was answered to his remonstrance.

During the amnesty, Fleetwood inquired: 'Where are you going?'

'Far a drive,—to be sure. Don't you see!'

'You'll return?'

'I intend to return.'

'He's beastly excited,' quoth Abrane.

Fleetwood silenced him, though indeed Woodseer appeared suspiciously restive.

'Step down and have a talk with me before you start. You're not to go yet.'

'I must. I'm in a hurry.'

'What 's the hurry?'

'I want to smoke and think.'

'Takes a carriage on the top of the morning to smoke and think! Hark at that!' Abrane sang out. 'Oh, come along quietly, you fellow, there's a good fellow! It concerns us all, every man Jack; we're all bound up in your fortunes. Fellow with luck like yours can't pretend to behave independently. Out of reason!'

'Do you give me your word you return?' said Fleetwood.

Woodseer replied: 'Very well, I do; there, I give my word. Hang it! now I know what they mean by "anything for a quiet life." Just a shake brings us down on that cane-bottomed chair!'

'You return to-day?'

'To-day, yes, yes.'

Fleetwood signified the captive's release; and Abrane immediately suggested:

'Pop old Chummy in beside the fellow to mount guard.'

Potts was hustled and precipitated into the carriage by the pair, with whom he partook this last glimmer of their night's humorous extravagances, for he was an easy creature. The carriage drove off.

'Keep him company!' they shouted.

'Escort him back!' said he, nodding.

He remarked to Woodseer: 'With your permission,' concerning the seat he took, and that 'a draught of morning air would do him good.' Then he laughed politely, exchanged wavy distant farewells with his comrades, touched a breast-pocket for his case of cigars, pulled forth one, obtained 'the loan of a light,' blew clouds and fell into the anticipated composure, quite understanding the case and his office.

Both agreed as to the fine morning it was. Woodseer briefly assented to his keeper's reiterated encomium on the morning, justified on oath. A fine morning, indeed. 'Damned if I think I ever saw so fine a morning!' Potts cried. He had no other subject of conversation with this hybrid: and being equally disposed for hot discourse or for sleep, the deprivation of the one and the other forced him to seek amusement in his famous reading of character; which was profound among the biped equine, jockeys, turfmen, sharpers, pugilists, demireps. He fronted Woodseer with square shoulders and wide knees, an elbow on one, a fist on the other, engaged in what he termed the 'prodding of his eel,' or 'nicking of his man,' a method of getting straight at the riddle of the fellow by the test of how long he could endure a flat mute stare and return look for look unblinking. The act of smoking fortifies and partly covers the insolence. But if by chance an equable, not too narrowly focussed, counterstare is met, our impertinent inquisitor may resemble the fisherman pulled into deep waters by his fish. Woodseer perused his man, he was not attempting to fathom him: he had besides other stuff in his head. Potts had naught, and the poor particle he was wriggled under detection.

'Tobacco before breakfast!' he said disgustedly tossing his cigar to the road. 'Your pipe holds on. Bad thing, I can tell you, that smoking on an empty stomach. No trainer'd allow it, not for a whole fee or double. Kills your wind. Let me ask you, my good sir, are you going to turn? We've sat a fairish stretch. I begin to want my bath and a shave, linen and coffee. Thirsty' as a dog.'

He heard with stupefaction, that he could alight on the spot, if he pleased, otherwise he would be driven into Carlsruhe. And now they had a lingual encounter, hot against cool; but the eyes of Chummy Potts having been beaten, his arguments and reproaches were not backed by the powerful looks which are an essential part of such eloquence as he commanded. They fled from his enemy's currishly, even while he was launching epithets. His pathetic position subjected him to beg that Woodseer would direct the driver to turn, for he had no knowledge of 'their German lingo.' And said he: 'You've nothing to laugh at, that I can see. I'm at your mercy, you brute; caught in a trap. I never walk;—and the sun fit to fry a mackerel along that road! I apologize for abusing you; I can't do more. You're an infernally clever player—there! And, upon my soul, I could drink ditchwater! But if you're going in for transactions at Carlsruhe, mark my words, your luck's gone. Laugh as much as you like.'

Woodseer happened to be smiling over the excellent reason for not turning back which inflicted the wofulness. He was not without sympathy for a thirsty wretch, and guessing, at the sight of an avenue of limes to the left of the road, that a wayside inn was below, he said: 'You can have coffee or beer in two minutes,' and told the driver where to pull up.

The sight of a grey-jacketed, green-collared sportsman, dog at heel, crossing the flat land to the hills of the forest, pricked him enviously, and caused him to ask what change had come upon him, that he should be hurrying to a town for a change of clothes. Just as Potts was about to jump out, a carriage, with a second behind it, left the inn door. He rubbed a hand on his unshaven chin, tried a glance at his shirt-front, and remarking: 'It won't be any one who knows me,' stood to let the carriages pass. In the first were a young lady and a gentleman: the lady brilliantly fair, an effect of auburn hair and complexion, despite the signs of a storm that had swept them and had not cleared from her eyelids. Apparently her maid, a damsel sitting straight up, occupied the carriage following; and this fresh-faced young person twice quickly and bluntly bent her head as she was driven by. Potts was unacquainted with the maid. But he knew the lady well, or well enough for her inattention to be the bigger puzzle. She gazed at the Black Forest hills in the steadiest manner, with eyes betraying more than they saw; which solved part of the puzzle, of course. Her reasons for declining to see him were exposed by the presence of the gentleman beside her. At the same time, in so highly bred a girl, a defenceless exposure was unaccountable. Half a nod and the shade of a smile would have been the proper course; and her going along on the road to the valley seemed to say it might easily have been taken; except that there had evidently been a bit of a scene.

Potts ranked Henrietta's beauty far above her cousin Livia's. He was therefore personally offended by her disregard of him, and her bit of a scene with the fellow carrying her off did him injury on behalf of his friend Fleetwood. He dismissed Woodseer curtly. Thirsting more to gossip than to drink, he took a moody draught of beer at the inn, and by the aid of a conveyance, hastily built of rotten planks to serve his needs, and drawn by a horse of the old wars,' as he reported on his arrival at Baden,—reached that home of the maltreated innocents twenty minutes before the countess and her party were to start for lunch up the Lichtenthal. Naturally, he was abused for letting his bird fly: but as he was shaven, refreshed, and in clean linen, he could pull his shirt-cuffs and take seat at his breakfast-table with equanimity while Abrane denounced him.

'I'll bet you the fellow's luck has gone,' said Potts. 'He 's no new hand and you don't think him so either, Fleet. I've looked into the fellow's eye and seen a leery old badger at the bottom of it. Talks vile stuff. However, 'perhaps I didn't drive out on that sweltering Carlsruhe road for nothing.'

He screwed a look at the earl, who sent Abrane to carry a message and heard the story Potts had to tell.

'Henrietta Fakenham! no mistake about her; driving out from a pothouse; man beside her, military man; might be a German. And, if you please, quite unacquainted with your humble servant, though we were as close as you to me. Something went wrong in that pothouse. Red eyes. There had been a scene, one could swear. Behind the lady another carriage, and her maid. Never saw the girl before, and sets to bowing and smirking at me, as if I was the-fellow of all others! Comical. I made sure they were bound for this place. They were on the Strasburg road. No sign of them?'

'You speak to me?' said Fleetwood.

Potts muttered. He had put his foot into it.

'You have a bad habit of speaking to yourself,' Fleetwood remarked, and left him. He suffered from the rustics he had to deal with among his class, and it was not needed that he should thunder at them to make his wrath felt.

Livia swam in, asking: 'What has come to Russett? He passed me in one of his black fits.'

The tale of the Carlsruhe road was repeated by Potts. She reproved him. 'How could you choose Russett for such a report as that! The admiral was on the road behind. Henrietta—you're sure it was she? German girls have much the same colouring. The gentleman with her must have been one of the Court equerries. They were driving to some chateau or battlefield the admiral wanted to inspect. Good-looking man? Military man?'

'Oh! the man! pretty fair, I dare say,' Potts rejoined. 'If it wasn't Henrietta Fakenham, I see with the back of my head. German girl! The maid was a German girl.'

'That may well be,' said Livia.

She conceived the news to be of sufficient importance for her to countermand the drive up the Lichtenthal, and take the Carlsruhe road instead; for Henrietta was weak, and Chillon Kirby an arch-plotter, and pleader too, one of the desperate lovers. He was outstaying his leave of absence already, she believed; he had to be in England. If he feared to lose Henrietta, he would not hesitate to carry her off. Livia knew him, and knew the power of his pleading with a firmer woman than Henrietta.

CHAPTER XI

THE PRISONER OF HIS WORD

Nothing to rouse alarm was discovered at Carlsruhe. Livia's fair cousin was there with the red-haired gaunt girl of the mountains; and it was frankly stated by Henrietta, that she had accompanied the girl a certain distance along the Strasburg road, for her to see the last of her brother Chillon on his way to England. Livia was not the woman to push inquiries. On that subject, she merely said, as soon as they were alone together:

'You seem to have had the lion's share of the parting.'

'Yes, we passed Mr. Chumley Potts,' was Henrietta's immediate answer; and her reference to him disarmed Livia.

They smiled at his name transiently, but in agreement: the tattler-spout of their set was, a fatal person to encounter, and each deemed the sudden apparition of him in the very early morning along the Carlsruhe road rather magical.

'You place particular confidence in Russett's fidelity to his word, Riette—as you have been hearing yourself called. You should be serious by this time. Russett won't bear much more. I counted on the night of the Ball for the grand effect. You will extinguish every woman there—and if he is absent?'

'I shall excuse him.'

'You are not in a position to be so charitable. You ought to know your position, and yourself too, a little better than you do. How could you endure poverty? Chillon Kirby stands in his uniform, and all's told. He can manoeuvre, we know. He got the admiral away to take him to those reviews cleverly. But is he thinking of your interests when he does it? He requires twenty years of active service to give you a roof to your head. I hate such allusions. But look for a moment at your character: you must have ordinary luxuries and pleasures, and if you were to find yourself grinding against common necessities—imagine it! Russett is quite manageable. He is, trust me! He is a gentleman; he has more ability than most young men: he can do anything he sets his mind to do. He has his great estates and fortune all in his own hands. We call him eccentric. He is only young, with a lot of power. Add, he's in love, and some one distracts him. Not love, do you say?—you look it. He worships. He has no chance given him to show himself at his best. Perhaps he is off again now. Will you bet me he is not?'

'I should incline to make the bet, if I betted,' said Henrietta. 'His pride is in his word, and supposing he's in love, it's with his pride, which never quits him.'

'There's firmness in a man who has pride of that kind. You must let me take you back to Baden. I hold to having you with me to-day. You must make an appearance there. The admiral will bring us his Miss Kirby to-morrow, if he is bound to remain here to-night. There's no harm in his bachelor dinners. I suspect his twinges of gout come of the prospect of affairs when he lands in England. Remember our bill with Madame Clemence. There won't be the ghost of a bank-note for me if Russett quits the field; we shall all be stranded.'

Henrietta inquired: 'Does it depend on my going with you to-day?'

'Consider, that he is now fancying a thousand things. We won't talk of the road to Paris.'

A shot of colour swept over Henrietta.

'I will speak to papa:—if he can let me go. He has taken to Miss Kirby.'

'Does she taste well?'

Henrietta debated. 'It's impossible to dislike her. Oh! she is wild! She knows absolutely nothing of the world. She can do everything we can't—or don't dare to try.—Men would like her. Papa's beginning to doat. He says she would have made a first-rate soldier. She fears blood as little as her morning cup of milk. One of the orderlies fell rather badly from a frightened horse close by our carriage. She was out in a moment and had his head on her lap, calling to papa to keep the carriage fast and block the way of the squadron, for the man's leg was hurt. I really thought we were lost. At these manoeuvres anything may happen, at any instant. Papa will follow the horse-artillery. You know his vanity to be a military quite as much as a naval commander like the Greeks and Romans, he says. We took the bruised man into our carriage and drove him to camp, Carinthia nursing him on the way.'

'Carinthia! She's well fitted with her name. What with her name and her hair and her build and her singular style of attire, one wonders at her coming into civilized parts. She 's utterly unlike Chillon.'

Henrietta reddened at the mention of one of her own thoughts in the contrasting of the pair.

They had their points of likeness, she said.

It did not concern Livia to hear what these were. Back to Baden, with means to procure the pleasant shocks of the galvanic battery there, was her thought; for she had a fear of the earl's having again departed in a huff at Henrietta's behaviour.

The admiral consented that his daughter should go, as soon as he heard that Miss Kirby was to stay. He had when a young man met her famous father; he vowed she was the Old Buccaneer young again in petticoats and had made prize of an English man-of-war by storm; all the profit, however, being his. This he proved with a courteous clasp of the girl and a show of the salute on her cheek, which he presumed to take at the night's farewell. 'She's my tonic,' he proclaimed heartily. She seemed to Livia somewhat unstrung and toneless. The separation from her brother in the morning might account for it. And a man of the admiral's age could be excused if he exalted the girl. Senility, like infancy, is fond of plain outlines for the laying on of its paints. The girl had rugged brows, a short nose, red hair; no young man would look at her twice. She was utterly unlike Chillon! Kissing her hand to Henrietta from the steps of the hotel, the girl's face improved.

Livia's little squire, Sir Meeson Corby, ejaculated as they were driving down the main street, 'Fleetwood's tramp! There he goes. Now see, Miss Fakenham, the kind of object Lord Fleetwood picks up and calls friend!—calls that object friend!.. But, what? He has been to a tailor and a barber!'

'Stop the coachman. Run, tell Mr. Woodseer I wish him to join us,' Livia said, and Sir Meeson had to thank his tramp for a second indignity. He protested, he simulated remonstrance,—he had to go, really feeling a sickness.

The singular-looking person, whose necessities or sense of the decencies had, unknown to himself and to the others, put them all in motion that day, swung round listening to the challenge to arms, as the puffy little man's delivery of the countess's message sounded. He was respectably clad, he thought, in the relief of his escape from the suit of clothes discarded, and he silently followed Sir Meeson's trot to the carriage. 'Should have mistaken you for a German to-day, sir,' the latter said, and trotted on.

'A stout one,' Woodseer replied, with his happy indifference to his exterior.

His dark lady's eyes were kindly overlooking, like the heavens. Her fair cousin, to whom he bowed, awakened him to a perception of the spectacle causing the slight, quick arrest of her look, in an astonishment not unlike the hiccup in speech, while her act of courtesy proceeded. At once he was conscious of the price he paid for respectability, and saw the Teuton skin on the slim Cambrian, baggy at shoulders, baggy at seat, pinched at the knees, short at the heels, showing outrageously every spot where he ought to have been bigger or smaller. How accept or how reject the invitation to drive in such company to Baden!

'You're decided enough, sir, in your play, they tell me,' the vindictive little baronet commented on his hesitation, and Woodseer sprang to the proffered vacant place. But he had to speak of his fly waiting for him at the steps of a certain hotel.

'Best hotel in the town!' Sir Beeson exclaimed pointedly to Henrietta, reading her constraint with this comical object before her. It was the admiral's hotel they stopped at.

'Be so good as to step down and tell the admiral he is to bring Madame Clemence in his carriage to-morrow; and on your way, you will dismiss Mr. Woodseer's fly,' Livia mildly addressed her squire. He stared: again he had to go, muttering: 'That nondescript's footman!' and his mischance in being checked and crossed and humiliated perpetually by a dirty-fisted vagabond impostor astounded him. He sent the flyman to the carriage for orders.

Admiral Fakenham and Carinthia descended. Sir Meeson heard her cry out: 'Is it you!' and up stood the pretentious lout in the German sack, affecting the graces of a born gentleman fresh from Paris,—bowing, smirking, excusing himself for something; and he jumped down to the young lady, he talked intimately with her, with a joker's air; he roused the admiral to an exchange of jokes, and the countess and Miss Fakenham more than smiled; evidently at his remarks, unobservant of the preposterous figure he cut. Sir Meeson Corby had intimations of the disintegration of his country if a patent tramp burlesquing in those clothes could be permitted to amuse English ladies of high station, quite at home with them. Among the signs of England's downfall, this was decidedly one. What to think of the admiral's favourite when, having his arm paternally on her shoulder, she gave the tramp her hand at parting, and then blushed! All that the ladies had to say about it was, that a spread of colour rather went to change the character of her face.

Carinthia had given Woodseer her hand and reddened under the recollection of Chillon's words to her as they mounted the rise of the narrow vale, after leaving the lame gentleman to his tobacco on the grass below the rocks. Her brother might have counselled her wisely and was to be obeyed. Only, the great pleasure in seeing the gentleman again inspired gratitude: he brought the scene to her; and it was alive, it chatted and it beckoned; it neighboured her home; she had passed it on her walk away from her home; the gentleman was her link to the mountain paths; he was just outside an association with her father and mother. At least, her thinking of them led to him, he to them. Now that she had lost Chillon, no one was near to do so much. Besides, Chillon loved Henrietta; he was her own. His heart was hers and his mind his country's. This gentleman loved the mountains; the sight of him breathed mountain air. To see him next day was her anticipation: for it would be at the skirts of hilly forest land, where pinetrees are a noble family, different from the dusty firs of the weariful plains, which had tired her eyes of late.

Baden was her first peep at the edges of the world since she had grown to be a young woman. She had but a faint idea of the significance of gambling. The brilliant lights, the band music, the sitting groups and company of promenaders were novelties; the Ball of the ensuing night at the Schloss would be a wonder, she acknowledged in response to Henrietta, who was trying to understand her; and she admired her ball-dress, she said, looking unintelligently when she heard that she would be guilty of slaying numbers of gentlemen before the night was over. Madame Clemence thought her chances in that respect as good as any other young lady's, if only she could be got to feel interested. But at a word of the pine forest, and saying she intended to climb the hills early with the light in the morning, a pointed eagerness flushed Carinthia, the cold engraving became a picture of colour.

She was out with the earliest light. Yesterday's parting between Chillon and Henrietta had taught her to know some little about love; and if her voice had been heeded by Chillon's beloved, it would not have been a parting. Her only success was to bring a flood of tears from Henrietta. The tears at least assured her that her brother's beautiful girl had no love for the other one,—the young nobleman of the great wealth, who was to be at the Ball, and had 'gone flying,' Admiral Fakenham shrugged to say; for Lord Fleetwood was nowhere seen.

The much talk of him on the promenade overnight fetched his name to her thoughts; he scarcely touched a mind that her father filled when she was once again breathing early morning air among the stems of climbing pines, broken alleys of the low-sweeping spruce branches and the bare straight shafts carrying their heads high in the march upward. Her old father was arch-priest of such forest land, always recoverable to her there. The suggestion of mountains was enough to make her mind play, and her old father and she were aware of one another without conversing in speech. He pointed at things to observe; he shared her satisfied hunger for the solitudes of the dumb and growing and wild sweet-smelling. He would not let a sorrowful thought backward or an apprehensive idea forward disturb the scene. A half-uprooted pine-tree stem propped mid-fall by standing comrades, and the downy drop to ground and muted scurry up the bark of long-brush squirrels, cocktail on the wary watch, were noticed by him as well as by her; even the rotting timber drift, bark and cones on the yellow pine needles, and the tortuous dwarf chestnut pushing level out, with a strain of the head up, from a crevice of mossed rock, among ivy and ferns; he saw what his girl saw. Power of heart was her conjuring magician.

She climbed to the rock-slabs above. This was too easily done. The poor bit of effort excited her frame to desire a spice of danger, her walk was towering in the physical contempt of a mountain girl for petty lowland obstructions. And it was just then, by the chance of things—by the direction of events, as Dame Gossip believes it to be—while colour, expression, and her proud stature marked her from her sex, that a gentleman, who was no other than Lord Fleetwood, passed Carinthia, coming out of the deeper pine forest.

Some distance on, round a bend of the path, she was tempted to adventure by a projected forked head of a sturdy blunted and twisted little rock-fostered forest tree pushing horizontally for growth about thirty feet above the lower ground. She looked on it, and took a step down to the stem soon after.

Fleetwood had turned and followed, merely for the final curious peep at an unexpected vision; he had noticed the singular shoot of thick timber from the rock, and the form of the goose-neck it rose to, the sprout of branches off the bill in the shape of a crest. And now a shameful spasm of terror seized him at sight of a girl doing what he would have dreaded to attempt. She footed coolly, well-balanced, upright. She seated herself.

And there let her be. She was a German girl, apparently. She had an air of breeding, something more than breeding. German families of the nobles give out, here and there, as the Great War showed examples of, intrepid young women, who have the sharp lines of character to render them independent of the graces. But, if a young woman out alone in the woods was hardly to be counted among the well-born, she held rank above them. Her face and bearing might really be taken to symbolize the forest life. She was as individual a representative as the Tragic and Comic masks, and should be got to stand between them for sign of the naturally straight-growing untrained, a noble daughter of the woods.

Not comparable to Henrietta in feminine beauty, she was on an upper plateau, where questions as to beauty are answered by other than the shallow aspect of a girl. But would Henrietta eclipse her if they were side by side? Fleetwood recalled the strange girl's face. There was in it a savage poignancy in serenity unexampled among women—or modern women. One might imagine an apotheosis of a militant young princess of Goths or Vandals, the glow of blessedness awakening her martial ardours through the languor of the grave:—Woodseer would comprehend and hit on the exact image to portray her in a moment, Fleetwood thought, and longed for that fellow.

He walked hurriedly back to the stunted rock tree. The damsel had vanished. He glanced below. She had not fallen. He longed to tell Woodseer he had seen a sort of Carinthia sister, cousin, one of the family. A single glimpse of her had raised him out of his grovelling perturbations, cooled and strengthened him, more than diverting the course of the poison Henrietta infused, and to which it disgraced him to be so subject. He took love unmanfully; the passion struck at his weakness; in wrath at the humiliation, if only to revenge himself for that, he could be fiendish; he knew it, and loathed the desired fair creature who caused and exposed to him these cracks in his nature, whence there came a brimstone stench of the infernal pits. And he was made for better. Of this he was right well assured. Superior to station and to wealth, to all mundane advantages, he was the puppet of a florid puppet girl; and he had slept at the small inn of a village hard by, because it was intolerable to him to see the face that had been tearful over her lover's departure, and hear her praises of the man she trusted to keep his word, however grievously she wounded him.

He was the prisoner of his word;—rather like the donkeys known as married men: rather more honourable than most of them. He had to be present at the ball at the Schloss and behold his loathed Henrietta, suffer torture of chains to the rack, by reason of his having promised the bitter coquette he would be there. So hellish did the misery seem to him, that he was relieved by the prospect of lying a whole day long in loneliness with the sunshine of the woods, occasionally conjuring up the antidote face of the wood-sprite before he was to undergo it. But, as he was not by nature a dreamer, only dreamed of the luxury of being one, he soon looked back with loathing on a notion of relief to come from the state of ruminating animal, and jumped up and shook off another of men's delusions—that they can, if they have the heart to suffer pain, deaden it with any semi-poetical devices, similar to those which Rufus Abrane's 'fiddler fellow' practised and was able to carry out because he had no blood. The spite of a present entire opposition to Woodseer's professed views made him exult in the thought, that the mouther of sentences was likely to be at work stultifying them and himself in the halls there below during the day. An imp of mischief offered consolatory sport in those halls of the Black Goddess; already he regarded his recent subservience to the conceited and tripped peripatetic philosopher as among the ignominies he had cast away on his road to a general contempt; which is the position of a supreme elevation for particularly sensitive young men.

Pleasure in the scenery had gone, and the wood-sprite was a flitted vapour; he longed to be below there, observing Abrane and Potts and the philosopher confounded, and the legible placidity of Countess Livia. Nevertheless, he hung aloft, feeding where he could, impatient of the solitudes, till night, when, according to his guess, the ladies were at their robing.

Half the fun was over: but the tale of it, narrated in turn by Abrane and his Chummy Potts on the promenade, was a very good half. The fiddler had played for the countess and handed her back her empty purse, with a bow and a pretty speech. Nothing had been seen of him since. He had lost all his own money besides. 'As of course he would,' said Potts. 'A fellow calculating the chances catches at a knife in the air.'

'Every franc-piece he had!' cried Abrane. 'And how could the jackass expect to keep his luck! Flings off his old suit and comes back here with a rig of German bags—you never saw such a figure!—Shoreditch Jew's holiday!—why, of course, the luck wouldn't stand that.'

They confessed ruefully to having backed him a certain distance, notwithstanding. 'He took it so coolly, just as if paying for goods across a counter.'

'And he had something to bear, Braney, when you fell on him,' said Potts, and murmured aside: 'He can be smartish. Hears me call Braney Rufus, and says he, like a fellow-chin on his fiddle—"Captain Mountain, Rufus Mus'. Not bad, for a counter."'

Fleetwood glanced round: he could have wrung Woodseer's hand. He saw young Cressett instead, and hailed him: 'Here you are, my gallant! You shall flash your maiden sword tonight. When I was under your age by a long count, I dealt sanctimoniousness a flick o' the cheek, and you shall, and let 'em know you're a man. Come and have your first boar-hunt along with me. Petticoats be hanged.'

The boy showed some recollection of the lectures of his queen, but he had not the vocables for resistance to an imperative senior at work upon sneaking inclinations. 'Promised Lady F.'—do you hear him?' Fleetwood called to the couple behind; and as gamblers must needs be parasites, manly were the things they spoke to invigorate the youthful plunger and second the whim of their paymaster.

At half-past eleven, the prisoner of his word entered under the Schloss partico, having vowed to himself on the way, that he would satisfy the formulas to gain release by a deferential bow to the great personages, and straightway slip out into the heavenly starlight, thence down among the jolly Parisian and Viennese Bacchanals.

CHAPTER XII

HENRIETTA'S LETTER TREATING OF THE GREAT EVENT

By the first light of an autumn morning, Henrietta sat at her travelling-desk, to shoot a spark into the breast of her lover with the story of the great event of the night. For there had been one, one of our biggest, beyond all tongues and trumpets and possible anticipations. Wonder at it hammered on incredulity as she wrote it for fact, and in writing had vision of her lover's eyes over the page.

'Monsieur Du Lac!

'Grey Dawn. 'You are greeted. This, if you have been tardy on the journey home, will follow close on the heels of the prowest, I believe truest, of knights, and bear perhaps to his quick mind some help to the solution he dropped a hint of seeking.

'The Ball in every way a success. Grand Duke and Duchess perfect in courtesy, not a sign of the German morgue. Livia splendid. Compared to Day and Night. But the Night eclipses the Day. A summer sea of dancing. Who, think you, eclipsed those two?

'I tell you the very truth when I say your Carinthia did. If you had seen her,—the "poor dear girl" you sigh to speak of,—with the doleful outlook on her fortunes: "portionless, unattractive!" Chillon, she was magical!

You cannot ever have seen her irradiated with happiness. Her pleasure in the happiness of all around her was part of the charm. One should be a poet to describe her. It would task an artist to paint the rose-crystal she became when threading her way through the groups to be presented. This is not meant to say that she looked beautiful. It was the something above beauty—more unique and impressive—like the Alpine snow-cloak towering up from the flowery slopes you know so well and I a little.

'You choose to think, is it Riette who noticed my simple sister so closely before...? for I suppose you to be reading this letter a second time and reflecting as you read. In the first place, acquaintance with her has revealed that she is not the simple person—only in her manner. Under the beams of subsequent events, it is true I see her more picturesquely. But I noticed also just a suspicion of the "grenadier" stride when she was on the march to make her curtsey. But Livia had no cause for chills and quivers. She was not the very strange bird requiring explanatory excuses; she dances excellently, and after the first dance, I noticed she minced her steps in the walk with her partner. She catches the tone readily. If not the image of her mother, she has inherited her mother's bent for the graces; she needs but a small amount of practice.

'Take my assurance of that; and you know who has critical eyes. Your anxiety may rest; she is equal to any station.

'As expected by me, my Lord Tyrant appeared, though late, near midnight. I saw him bowing to the Ducal party. Papa had led your "simple sister" there. Next I saw the Tyrant and Carinthia conversing. Soon they were dancing together, talking interestedly, like cheerful comrades. Whatever his faults, he has the merit of being a man of his word. He said he would come, he did not wish to come, and he came.

'His word binds him—I hope not fatally; irrevocably, it certainly does. There is charm of character in that. His autocrat airs can be forgiven to a man who so profoundly respects his word.

'It occurred during their third dance. Your Riette was not in the quadrille. O but she was a snubbed young woman last night! I refrain—the examples are too minute for quotation.

'A little later and he had vanished. Carinthia Kirby may already be written Countess of Fleetwood! His hand was offered and hers demanded in plain terms. Her brother would not be so astounded if he had seen the brilliant creature she was—is, I could say; for when she left me here, to go to her bed, she still wore the "afterglow." She tripped over to me in the ball-room to tell me. I might doubt, she had no doubt whatever. I fancied he had subjected her to some degree of trifling. He was in a mood. His moods are known to me. But no, he was precise; her report of him strikes the ear as credible, in spite of the marvel it insists on our swallowing.

"'Lord Fleetwood had asked me to marry him." Neither assurance nor bashfulness; newspaper print; aid an undoubting air of contentment.

'Imagine me hearing it.

'"To be his wife?"

'"He said wife."

'"And you replied?"

'"I—said I would."

'"Tell me all?"

'"He said we were plighted."

'Now, "wife" is one of the words he abhors; and he loathes the hearing of a girl as "engaged." However, "plighted" carried a likeness.

'I pressed her: "My dear Carinthia, you thought him in earnest?"

'"He was."

'"How do you judge?"

'"By his look when he spoke."

'"Not by his words?"

'"I repeat them to you."

'She has repeated them to me here in my bedroom. There is no variation. She remembers every syllable. He went so far as to urge her to say whether she would as willingly utter consent if they were in a church and a clergyman at the altar-rails.

'That was like him.

'She made answer: "Wherever it may be, I am bound, if I say yes."

'She then adds: "He told me he joined hands with me."

'"Did he repeat the word 'wife'?"

'"He said it twice."

'I transcribe verbatim scrupulously. There cannot be an error, Chillon. It seems to show, that he has embraced the serious meaning of the word—or seriously embraced the meaning, reads' better. I have seen his lips form "wife."

'But why wonder so staringly? They both love the mountains. Both are wildish. She was looking superb. And he had seen her do a daring thing on the rocks on the heights in the early morning, when she was out by herself, unaware of a spectator, he not knowing who she was;—the Fates had arranged it so. That was why he took to her so rapidly. So he told her. She likes being admired. The preparation for the meeting does really seem "under direction." She likes him too, I do think. Between her repetitions of his compliments, she praised his tone of voice, his features. She is ready to have the fullest faith in the sincerity of his offer; speaks without any impatience for the fulfilment. If it should happen, what a change in the fortunes of a girl—of more than one, possibly.

'Now I must rest "eyelids fall." It will be with a heart galloping. No rest for me till this letter flies. Good morning is my good night to you, in a world that has turned over.'

Henrietta resumes:

'Livia will not hear of it, calls up all her pretty languor to put it aside. It is the same to-day as last night. "Why mention Russett's nonsense to me?" Carinthia is as quietly circumstantial as at first. She and the Tyrant talked of her native home. Very desirous to see it! means to build a mansion there! "He said it must be the most romantic place on earth."

'I suppose I slept. I woke with my last line to you on my lips, and the great news thundering. He named Esslemont and his favourite—always uninhabited—Cader Argau. She speaks them correctly. She has an unfailing memory. The point is, that it is a memory.

'Do not forget also—Livia is affected by her distaste—that he is a gentleman. He plays with his nobility. With his reputation of gentleman, he has never been known to play. You will understand the slightly hypocritical air—it is not of sufficient importance for it to be alluded to in papa's presence—I put on with her.

'Yes, I danced nearly all the dances. One, a princeling in scarlet uniform, appearing fresh from under earth; Prussian: a weighty young Graf in green, between sage and bottle, who seemed to have run off a tree in the forest, and was trimmed with silver like dew-drops: one in your Austrian white, dragon de Boheme, if I caught his French rightly. Others as well, a list. They have the accomplishment. They are drilled in it young, as girls are, and so few Englishmen—even English officers. How it may be for campaigning, you can pronounce; but for dancing, the pantalon collant is the perfect uniform. Your critical Henrietta had not to complain of her partners, in the absence of the one.

'I shall be haunted by visions of Chillon's amazement until I hear or we meet. I serve for Carinthia's mouthpiece, she cannot write it, she says. It would be related in two copybook lines, if at all.

'The amazement over London! The jewel hand of the kingdom gone in a flash, to "a raw mountain girl," as will be said. I can hear Lady Endor, Lady Eldritch, Lady Cowry. The reasonable woman should be Lady Arpington. I have heard her speak of your mother, seen by her when she was in frocks.

'Enter the "plighted." Poor Livia! to be made a dowager of by any but a damsel of the family. She may well ridicule "that nonsense of Russett's last night"! Carinthia kisses, embraces, her brother. I am to say: "What Henrietta tells you is true, Chillon." She is contented though she has not seen him again and has not the look of expecting to see him. She still wears the kind of afterglow.

'Chillon's Viennese waltz was played by the band: played a second time, special request, conveyed to the leader by Prince Ferdinand. True, most true, she longs to be home across the water. But be it admitted, that to any one loving colour, music, chivalry, the Island of Drab is an exile. Imagine, then, the strange magnetism drawing her there! Could warmer proof be given?

'Adieu. Livia's "arch-plotter" will weigh the letter he reads to the smallest fraction of a fraction before he moves a step.

'I could leave it and come to it again and add and add. I foresee in Livia's mind a dread of the aforesaid "arch," and an interdict. So the letter must be closed, sealed and into the box, with the hand I still call mine, though I should doubt my right if it were contested fervently. I am singing the waltz.

'Adieu,
'Ever and beyond it,
'Your obedient Queen,
'HENRIETTA.

'P.S.-My Lord Tyrant has departed—as on other occasions. The prisoner of his word is sure to take his airing before he presents himself to redeem it. His valet is left to pay bills, fortunately for Livia. She entrusted her purse yesterday to a man picked up on the road by my lord, that he might play for her. Captain Abrane assured her he had a star, and Mr. Potts thought him a rush compere, an adept of those dreadful gambling tables. Why will she continue to play! The purse was returned to her, without so much as a piece of silver in it; the man has flown. Sir M. Corby says, he is a man whose hands betray him—or did to Sir M.; expects to see him one day on the wrong side of the criminal bar. He struck me as not being worse than absurd. He was, in any case, an unfit companion, and our C. would help to rescue the Eccentric from such complicating associates. I see worlds of good she may do. Happily, he is no slave of the vice of gambling; so she would not suffer that anxiety. I wish it could be subjoined, that he has no malicious pleasure in misleading others. Livia is inconsolable over her pet, young Lord Cressett, whom he yesterday induced to "try his luck"—with the result. We leave, if bills are paid, in two days. Captain Abrane and Mr. Potts left this afternoon; just enough to carry them home. Papa and your blissful sister out driving. Riette within her four walls and signing herself,

'THE PRISONER OF CHILLON.'

CHAPTER XIII

AN IRRUPTION. OF MISTRESS GOSSIP IN BREACH OF THE CONVENTION

'It is a dark land,' Carinthia said, on seeing our Island's lowered clouds in swift motion, without a break of their folds, above the sheer white cliffs. —She said it, we know. That poor child Carinthia Jane, when first she beheld Old England's shores, tossing in the packet-boat on a wild Channel sea, did say it and think it, for it is in the family that she did; and no wonder that she should, the day being showery from the bed of the sun, after a frosty three days, at the close of autumn. We used to have an eye of our own for English weather before printed Meteorological Observations and Forecasts undertook to supplant the shepherd and the poacher, and the pilot with his worn brown leather telescope tucked beneath his arm. All three would have told you, that the end of a three days' frost in the late season of the year and the early, is likely to draw the warm winds from the Atlantic over Cornish Land's End and Lizard.

Quite by chance of things, Carinthia Jane looked on the land of her father and mother for the first time under those conditions. There can be no harm in quoting her remark. Only—I have to say it—experience causes apprehension, that we are again to be delayed by descriptions, and an exposition of feelings; taken for granted,—of course, in a serious narrative; which it really seems these moderns think designed for a frequent arrest of the actors in the story and a searching of the internal state of this one or that one of them: who is laid out stark naked and probed and expounded, like as in the celebrated picture by a great painter—and we, thirsting for events as we are, are to stop to enjoy a lecture on Anatomy. And all the while the windows of the lecture-room are rattling, if not the whole fabric shaking, with exterior occurrences or impatience for them to come to pass. Every explanation is sure to be offered by the course events may take; so do, in mercy, I say, let us bide for them.

She thought our Island all the darker because Henrietta had induced her to talk on the boat of her mountain home and her last morning there for the walk away with Chillon John. Soon it was to appear supernaturally bright, a very magician's cave for brilliancy.

Now, this had happened—and comment on it to yourselves, remembering always, that Chillon John was a lover, and a lover has his excuses, though they will not obviate the penalties he may incur; and dreadful they were. After reading Henrietta's letter to him, he rode out of his Canterbury quarters across the country to the borders of Sussex, where his uncle Lord Levellier lived, on the ridge of ironstone, near the wild land of a forest, Croridge the name of the place. Now, Chillon John knew his uncle was miserly, and dreaded the prospect of having to support a niece in the wretched establishment at Lekkatts, or, as it was popularly called, Leancats; you can understand why. But he managed to assure himself he must in duty consult with the senior and chief member of his family on a subject of such importance as the proposal of marriage to his lordship's niece.

The consultation was short: 'You will leave it to me,' his uncle said: and we hear of business affairs between them, involving payment of moneys due to the young man; and how, whenever he touched on them, his uncle immediately fell back on the honour of the family and Carinthia Jane's reputation, her good name to be vindicated, and especially that there must be no delays, together with as close a reckoning as he could make of the value of Lord Fleetwood's estates in Kent and in Staffordshire and South Wales, and his house property in London.

'He will have means to support her,' said the old lord, shrugging as if at his own incapacity for that burden.

The two then went to the workshops beside a large pond, where there was an island bordered with birch trees and workmen's cottages near the main building; and that was an arsenal containing every kind of sword and lance and musket, rifle and fowling-piece and pistol, and more gunpowder than was, I believe, allowed by law. For they were engaged in inventing a new powder for howitzer shells, of tremendous explosive power.

Nothing further did either of them say, concerning the marriage. Nor did Carinthia Jane hear any mention of Lord Fleetwood from her brother on the landing-place at Dover. She was taken to Admiral Baldwin Fakenham's house in Hampshire; and there she remained, the delight of his life, during two months, patiently expecting and rebuking the unmaidenliness of her expectations, as honest young women in her position used to do. So did they sometimes wait for years; they have waited until they withered into their graves, like the vapours of a brief winter's day: a moving picture of a sex restrained by modesty in those purer times from the taking of one step forward unless inquired for.

Two months she waited in our 'dark land.' January arrived, and her brother. Henrietta communicated the news:

'My Janey, you are asked by Lord Fleetwood whether it is your wish that he should marry you.'

Now, usually a well-born young woman's answer, if a willing one, is an example of weak translation. Here it was the heart's native tongue, without any roundabout, simple but direct.

'Oh, I will, I am ready, tell him.'

Remember, she was not speaking publicly.

Henrietta knew the man enough to be glad he did not hear. She herself would have felt a little shock on his behalf: only, that answer suited the scheme of the pair of lovers.

How far those two were innocent in not delivering the whole of Lord Fleetwood's message to Carinthia Jane through Lord Levellier, we are unable to learn. We may suspect the miserly nobleman of curtailing it for his purposes; and such is my idea. But the answer would have been the same, I am sure.

In consequence and straight away, Chillon John betakes him to Admiral Baldwin and informs him of Lord Fleetwood's proposal on the night at Baden, and renewal of it through the mouth of Lord Levellier, not communicating, however (he may really not have known), the story of how it had been wrung from the earl by a surprise movement on the part of the one-armed old lord, who burst out on him in the street from the ambush of a Club-window, where he had been stationed every day for a fortnight, indefatigably to watch for the passing of the earl, as there seemed no other way to find him. They say, indeed, there was a scene, judging by the result, and it would have been an excellent scene for the stage; though the two noblemen were to all appearance politely exchanging their remarks. But the audience hearing what passes, appreciates the courteous restraint of an attitude so contrasting with their tempers. Behind the ostentation of civility, their words were daggers.

For it chanced, that the young earl, after a period of refuge at his Welsh castle, supposing, as he well might, that his latest mad freak of the proposal of his hand and title to the strange girl in a quadrille at a foreign castle had been forgotten by her, and the risks of annoyance on the subject had quite blown over, returned to town, happy in having done the penance for his impulsiveness, and got clean again— that is to say, struck off his fetters and escaped from importunities—the very morning of the day when Lord Levellier sprang upon him! It shows the old campaigner's shrewdness in guessing where his prey would come, and not putting him on his guard by a call at his house. Out of the window he looked for all the hours of light during an entire fortnight. 'In the service of my sister's child,' he said. 'To save him from the cost of maintaining her,' say his enemies. At any rate he did it.

He was likely to have done the worse which I suspect.

Now, the imparting of the wonderful news to Admiral Baldwin Fakenham was, we read, the whiff of a tropical squall to lay him on his beam ends. He could not but doubt; and his talk was like the sails of a big ship rattling to the first puff of wind. He had to believe; and then, we read, he was for hours like a vessel rolling in the trough of the sea. Of course he was a disappointed father. Naturally his glance at the loss to Henrietta of the greatest prize of the matrimonial market of all Europe and America was vexing and saddening. Then he woke up to think of the fortunes of his 'other girl,' as he named her, and cried: 'Crinny catches him!'

He cried it in glee and rubbed his hands.

So thereupon, standing before him, Chillon John, from whom he had the news, bent to him slightly, as his elegant manner was, and lengthened the admiral's chaps with another proposal; easy, deliberate, precise, quite the respectful bandit, if you please, determined on having his daughter by all means, only much preferring the legal, formal, and friendly. Upon that, in the moment of indecision, Henrietta enters, followed by Admiral Baldwin's heroine, his Crinny, whom he embraced and kissed, congratulated and kissed again. One sees the contrivance to soften him.

So it was done, down in that Hampshire household on the heights near the downs, whence you might behold, off a terra firma resembling a roll of billows, England's big battle-ships in line fronting the island; when they were a spectacle of beauty as well as power: which now they are no more, but will have to be, if they are both to float and to fight. For I have, had quoted to me by a great admirer of the Old Buccaneer, one of the dark sayings in his MAXIMS FOR MEN, where Captain John Peter Kirby commends his fellow-men to dissatisfaction with themselves if they have not put an end to their enemy handsomely.. And he advises the copying of Nature in this; whose elements have always, he says, a pretty, besides a thorough, style of doing it, when they get the better of us; and the one by reason of the other. He instances the horse, the yacht, and chiefly the sword, for proof, that the handsomest is the most effective. And he prints large: 'UGLY IS ONLY HALF WAY TO A THING.' To an invention, I suppose he intends to say. But looking on our huge foundering sea-monsters and the disappearance of the unwieldy in Nature, and the countenances of criminals, who are, he bids us observe, always in the long run beaten, I seem to see a meaning our country might meditate on.

So, as I said, it was done; for Admiral Baldwin could refuse his Crinny nothing; as little as he would deny anything to himself, the heartiest of kindly hosts, fathers, friends. Carinthia Jane's grand good fortune covered that pit, the question of money, somehow, and was, we may conceive, a champagne wine in their reasoning faculties. The admiral was in debt, Henrietta had no heritage, Chillon John was the heir of a miserly uncle owing him sums and evading every application for them, yet they behaved as people who had the cup of golden wishes. Perhaps it was because Henrietta and her lover were so handsome a match as to make it seem to them and others they must marry; and as to character, her father could trust her to the man of her choice more readily than to the wealthy young nobleman; of whose discreetness he had not the highest opinion. He reconciled this view with his warm feeling for the Countess of Fleetwood to be, by saying: 'Crinny will tame him!' His faith was in her dauntless bold spirit, not thinking of the animal she was to tame.

Countess Livia, after receiving Henrietta's letter of information, descended on them and thought them each and all a crazed set. Love, as a motive of action for a woman, she considered the female's lunacy and suicide. Men are born subject to it, happily, and thus the balance between the lordly half of creation and the frail is rectified. We women dress, and smile, sigh, if you like, to excite the malady. But if we are the fools to share it, we lose our chance; instead of the queens, we are the slaves, and instead of a life of pleasure, we pass from fever to fever at a tyrant's caprice: he does rightly in despising us. Ay, and many a worthy woman thinks the same. Educated in dependency as they are, they come to the idea of love to snatch at it for their weapon of the man's weakness. For which my lord calls them heartless, and poets are angry with them, rightly or wrongly.

It must, I fear, be admitted for a truth, that sorrow is the portion of young women who give the full measure of love to the engagement, marrying for love. At least, Countess Livia could declare subsequently she had foretold it and warned her cousin. Not another reflection do you hear from me, if I must pay forfeit of my privilege to hurry you on past descriptions of places and anatomy of character and impertinent talk about philosophy in a story. When we are startled and offended by the insinuated tracing of principal incidents to a thread-bare spot in the nether garments of a man of no significance, I lose patience.

Henrietta's case was a secondary affair. What with her passion—it was nothing less—and her lover's cunning arts, and her father's consent given, and in truth the look of the two together, the dissuasion of them from union was as likely to keep them apart as an exhortation addressed to magnet and needle. Countess Livia attacked Carinthia Jane and the admiral backing her. But the admiral, having given his consent to his daughter's marriage, in consequence of the earl's pledged word to 'his other girl,' had become a zealot for this marriage and there was only not a grand altercation on the subject because Livia shunned annoyances. Alone with Carinthia Jane, as she reported to Henrietta, she spoke to a block, that shook a head and wore a thin smile and nursed its own idea of the better knowledge of Edward Russett, Earl of Fleetwood, gained in the run of a silly quadrille at a ball:

What is a young man's word to his partner in a quadrille?

Livia put the question, she put it twice rather sternly, and the girl came out with: 'Oh, he meant it!'

The nature, the pride, the shifty and furious moods of Lord Fleetwood were painted frightful to her.

She had conceived her own image of him.

Whether to set her down as an enamoured idiot or a creature not a whit less artful than her brother, was Countess Livia's debate. Her inclination was to misdoubt the daughter of the Old Buccaneer: she might be simple, at her age, and she certainly was ignorant; but she clung to her prize. Still the promise was extracted from her, that she would not worry the earl to fulfil the word she supposed him to mean in its full meaning.

The promise was unreluctantly yielded. No, she would not write. Admiral Fakenham, too, engaged to leave the matter to a man of honour.

Meanwhile, Chillon John had taken a journey to Lekkatts; following which, his uncle went to London. Lord Fleetwood heard that Miss Kirby kept him bound. He was again the fated prisoner of his word.

And following that, not so very long, there was the announcement of the marriage of Chillon John Kirby Levellier, Lieutenant in the King's Own Hussars, and Henrietta, daughter of Admiral Baldwin Fakenham. A county newspaper paragraph was quoted for its eulogy of the Beauty of Hampshire—not too strong, those acquainted with her thought. Interest at Court obtained an advancement for the bridegroom: he was gazetted Captain during his honeymoon, and his prospects under his uncle's name were considered fair, though certain people said at the time, it was likely to be all he would get while old Lord Levellier of Leancats remained in the flesh.

Now, as it is good for those to tell who intend preserving their taste for romance and hate anatomical lectures, we never can come to the exact motives of any extraordinary piece of conduct on the part of man or woman. Girls are to read; and the study of a boy starts from the monkey. But no literary surgeon or chemist shall explain positively the cause of the behaviour of men and women in their relations together; and speaking to rescue my story, I say we must with due submission accept the facts. We are not a bit the worse for wondering at them. So it happened that Lord Fleetwood's reply to Lord Levellier's hammer—hammer by post and messenger at his door, one may call it, on the subject of the celebration of the marriage of the young Croesus and Carinthia Jane, in which there was demand for the fixing of a date forthwith, was despatched on the day when London had tidings of Henrietta Pakenham's wedding.

The letter, lost for many years, turned up in the hands of a Kentish auctioneer, selling it on behalf of a farm-serving man, who had it from Lord Levellier's cook and housemaid, among the things she brought him as her wifely portion after her master's death, and this she had not found saleable in her husband's village at her price, but she had got the habit of sticking to the scraps, being proud of hearing it said that she had skinned Leancats to some profit: and her expectation proved correct after her own demise, for her husband putting it up at the auction; our relative on the mother's side, Dr. Glossop, interested in the documents and particulars of the story as he was, had it knocked down to him, in contest with an agent of a London gentleman, going as high as two pounds ten shillings, for the sum of two pounds and fifteen shillings. Count the amount that makes for each word of a letter a marvel of brevity, considering the purport! But Dr. Glossop was right in saying he had it cheap. The value of that letter may now be multiplied by ten: nor for that sum would he part with it.

Thus it ran, I need not refer to it in Bundle No. 3:

'MY LORD: I drive to your church-door on the fourteenth of the month at ten A.M., to keep my appointment with Miss C. J. Kirby, if I do not blunder the initials.
'Your lordship's obedient servant,
'FLEETWOOD.'

That letter will ever be a treasured family possession with us.

That letter was dated from Lord Fleetwood's Kentish mansion, Esslemont, the tenth of the month. He must have quitted London for Esslemont, for change of scene, for air, the moment after the news of Henrietta's marriage. Carinthia Jane received the summons without transmission of the letter from her uncle on the morning of the twelfth. It was a peremptory summons.

Unfortunately, Admiral Fakenham, a real knight and chevalier of those past times, would not let her mount the downs to have her farewell view of the big ships unaccompanied by him; and partly and largely in pure chivalry, no doubt; but her young idea of England's grandeur, as shown in her great vessels of war, thrilled him, too, and restored his youthful enthusiasm for his noble profession or made it effervesce. However it was, he rode beside her and rejoiced to hear the young girl's talk of her father as a captain of one of England's thunderers, and of the cruelty of that Admiralty to him: at which Admiral Baldwin laughed, but had not the heart to disagree with her, for he could belabour the Admiralty in season, cause or no cause. Altogether he much enjoyed the ride, notwithstanding intimations of the approach of 'his visitor,' as he called his attacks of gout.

Riding home, however, the couple passed through a heavy rainfall, and the next day, when he was to drive with the bride to Lekkatts, gout, the fiercest he had ever known, chained him fast to his bed. Such are the petty accidents affecting circumstances. They are the instruments of Destiny.

There he lay, protesting that the ceremony could not possibly be for the fourteenth, because Countess Livia had, he now remembered, written of her engagement to meet Russett on the night of that day at a ball at Mrs. Cowper Quillett's place, Canleys, lying south of the Surrey hills: a house famed for its gatherings of beautiful women; whither Lord Fleetwood would be sure to engage to go, the admiral now said; and it racked him like gout in his mind, and perhaps troubled his conscience about handing the girl to such a young man. But he was lying on his back, the posture for memory to play the fiend with us, as we read in the BOOK of MAXIMS of the Old Buccaneer. Admiral Baldwin wished heartily to be present at his Crinny's wedding 'to see her launched,' if wedding it was to be, and he vowed the date of the fourteenth, in Lord Levellier's announcement of it, must be an error and might be a month in advance, and ought to be. But it was sheer talking and raving for a solace to his disappointment or his anxiety. He had to let Carinthia Jane depart under the charge of his housekeeper, Mrs. Carthew, a staid excellent lady, poorly gifted with observation.

Her report of the performance of the ceremony at Croridge village church, a half mile from Lekkatts, was highly reassuring to the anxious old admiral still lying on his back with memory and gout at their fiend's play, and livid forecasts hovering. He had recollected that there had been no allusion in Lord Levellier's message to settlements or any lawyer's preliminaries, and he raged at himself for having to own it would have been the first of questions on behalf of his daughter.

'All passed off correctly,' Mrs. Carthew said. 'The responses of the bride and bridegroom were particularly articulate.'

She was reserved upon the question of the hospitality of Lekkatts. The place had entertained her during her necessitated residence there, and honour forbade her to smile concordantly at the rosy admiral's mention of Leancats. She took occasion, however, to praise the Earl of Fleetwood's eminently provident considerateness for his bride, inasmuch as he had packed a hamper in his vehicle, which was a four-in-hand, driven by himself.

Admiral Baldwin inquired: 'Bride inside?'

He was informed: 'The Countess of Fleetwood sat on the box on the left of my lord.'

She had made no moan about the absence of bridesmaids.

'She appeared too profoundly happy to meditate an instant upon deficiencies.'

'How did the bridegroom behave?'

'Lord Fleetwood was very methodical. He is not, or was not, voluntarily a talker.'

'Blue coat, brass buttons, hot-house flower? old style or new?'

'His lordship wore a rather low beaver and a buttoned white overcoat, not out of harmony with the bride's plain travelling-dress.'

'Ah! he's a good whip, men say. Keeps first-rate stables, hacks, and bloods. Esslemont hard by will be the place for their honeymoon, I guess. And he's a lucky dog, if he knows his luck.'

So said Admiral Baldwin. He was proceeding to say more, for he had a prodigious opinion of the young countess and the benefit of her marriage to the British race. As it concerned a healthy constitution and motherhood, Mrs. Carthew coughed and retired. Nor do I reprove either of them. The speculation and the decorum are equally commendable. Masculine ideas are one thing; but let feminine ever be feminine, or our civilization perishes.

At Croridge village church, then, one of the smallest churches in the kingdom, the ceremony was performed and duly witnessed, names written in the vestry book, the clergyman's fee, the clerk, and the pew-woman, paid by the bridegroom. And thus we see how a pair of lovers, blind with the one object of lovers in view; and a miserly uncle, all on edge to save himself the expense of supporting his niece; and an idolatrous old admiral, on his back with gout; conduced in turn and together to the marriage gradually exciting the world's wonder, till it eclipsed the story of the Old Buccaneer and Countess Fanny, which it caused to be discussed afresh.

Mrs. Carthew remembered Carinthia Jane's last maiden remark and her first bridal utterance. On the way, walking to the church of Croridge from Lekkatts, the girl said: 'Going on my feet, I feel I continue the mountain walk with my brother when we left our home.' And after leaving the church, about to mount the coach, she turned to Mrs. Carthew, saying, as she embraced her:

'A happy bride's kiss should bring some good fortune.' And looking down from her place on the top of the coach:

'Adieu, dear Mrs. Carthew. A day of glory it is to-day.' She must actually have had it in her sight as a day of glory: and it was a day of the clouds off our rainy quarter, similar in every way to the day of her stepping on English soil and saying: 'It is a dark land.' For the heart is truly declared to be our colourist. A day having the gale in its breast, sweeping the whole country and bending the trees for the twigs to hiss like spray of the billows around our island, was a day of golden splendour to the young bride of the Earl of Fleetwood, though he scarcely addressed one syllable to her, and they sat side by side all but dumb, he like a coachman driving an unknown lady fare, on a morning after a night when his wife's tongue may have soured him for the sex.

CHAPTER XIV

A PENDANT OF THE FOREGOING

Mention has been omitted or forgotten by the worthy Dame, in her vagrant fowl's treatment of a story she cannot incubate, will not relinquish, and may ultimately addle, that the bridegroom, after walking with a disengaged arm from the little village church at Croridge to his coach and four at the cross of the roads to Lekkatts and the lowland, abruptly, and as one pursuing a deferential line of conduct he had prescribed to himself, asked his bride, what seat she would prefer.

He shouted: 'Ives!'

A person inside the coach appeared to be effectually roused.

The glass of the window dropped. The head of a man emerged. It was the head of one of the bargefaced men of the British Isles, broad, and battered flattish, with sentinel eyes.

In an instant the heavy-headed but not ill-looking fellow was nimble and jumped from the coach.

'Napping, my lord,' he said.

Heavy though the look of him might be, his feet were light; they flipped a bar of a hornpipe at a touch of the ground. Perhaps they were allowed to go with their instinct for the dance, that his master should have a sample of his wakefulness. He quenched a smirk and stood to take orders; clad in a flat blue cap, a brown overcoat, and knee-breeches, as the temporary bustle of his legs had revealed.

Fleet-wood heard the young lady say: 'I would choose, if you please, to sit beside you.'

He gave a nod of enforced assent, glancing at the vacated box.

The man inquired: 'A knee and a back for the lady to mount up, my lord?'

'In!' was the smart command to him; and he popped in with the agility of his popping out.

Then Carinthia made reverence to the grey lean figure of her uncle and kissed Mrs. Carthew. She needed no help to mount the coach. Fleetwood's arm was rigidly extended, and he did not visibly wince when this foreign girl sprang to the first hand-grip on the coach and said: 'No, my husband, I can do it'; unaided,' was implied.

Her stride from the axle of the wheel to the step higher would have been a graceful spectacle on Alpine crags.

Fleetwood swallowed that, too, though it conjured up a mocking recollection of the Baden woods, and an astonished wild donkey preparing himself for his harness. A sour relish of the irony in his present position sharpened him to devilish enjoyment of it, as the finest form of loathing: on the principle that if we find ourselves consigned to the nether halls, we do well to dance drunkenly. He had cried for Romance—here it was!

He raised his hat to Mrs. Carthew and to Lord Levellier. Previous to the ceremony, the two noblemen had interchanged the short speech of mannered duellists punctiliously courteous in the opening act. Their civility was maintained at the termination of the deadly work. The old lord's bosom thanked the young one for not requiring entertainment and a repast; the young lord's thanked the old one for a strict military demeanour at an execution and the abstaining from any nonsensical talk over the affair.

A couple of liveried grooms at the horses' heads ran and sprang to the hinder seats as soon as their master had taken the reins. He sounded the whip caressingly: off those pretty trotters went.

Mrs. Carthew watched them, waving to the bride. She was on the present occasion less than usually an acute or a reflective observer, owing to her admiration of lordly state and masculine commandership; and her thought was: 'She has indeed made a brilliant marriage!'

The lady thought it, notwithstanding an eccentricity in the wedding ceremony, such as could not but be noticeable. But very wealthy noblemen were commonly, perhaps necessarily, eccentric, for thus they proved themselves egregious, which the world expected them to be.

Lord Levellier sounded loud eulogies of the illustrious driver's team. His meditation, as he subsequently stated to Chillon, was upon his vanquished antagonist's dexterity, in so conducting matters, that he had to be taken at once, with naught of the customary preface and apology for taking to himself the young lady, of which a handsome settlement, is the memorial.

We have to suppose, that the curious occupant of the coach inside aroused no curiosity in the pair of absorbed observers.

Speculations regarding the chances of a fall of rain followed the coach until it sank and the backs of the two liveried grooms closed the chapter of the wedding, introductory to the honeymoon at Esslemont, seven miles distant by road, to the right of Lekkatts. It was out of sight that the coach turned to the left, Northwestward.

CHAPTER XV

OPENING STAGE OF THE HONEYMOON

A famous maxim in the book of the Old Buccaneer, treating of PRECAUTION, as 'The brave man's clean conscience,' with sound counsel to the adventurous, has it:—

'Then you sail away into the tornado, happy as a sealed bottle of ripe wine.'

It should mean, that brave men entering the jaws of hurricanes are found to have cheerful hearts in them when they know they have done their best. But, touching the picture of happiness, conceive the bounteous Bacchic spirit in the devoutness of a Sophocles, and you find comparison neighbour closely between the sealed wine-flask and the bride, who is being driven by her husband to the nest of the unknown on her marriage morn.

Seated beside him, with bosom at heave and shut mouth, in a strange land, travelling cloud-like, rushing like the shower-cloud to the vale, this Carinthia, suddenly wedded, passionately grateful for humbleness exalted, virginly sensible of treasures of love to give, resembled the inanimate and most inspiring, was mindless and inexpressive, past memory, beyond the hopes, a thing of the thrilled blood and skylark air, since she laid her hand in this young man's. His not speaking to her was accepted. Her blood rather than recollection revived their exchanges during the dance at Baden, for assurance that their likings were one, their aims rapturously one; that he was she, she he, the two hearts making one soul.

Could she give as much as he? It was hardly asked. If we feel we can give our breath of life, the strength of the feeling fully answers. It bubbles perpetually from the depth like a well-spring in tumult. Two hearts that make one soul do not separately count their gifts.

For the rest, her hunger to admire disposed her to an absorbing sentience of his acts; the trifles, gestures, manner of this and that; which were seized as they flew, and swiftly assimilated to stamp his personality. Driving was the piece of skill she could not do. Her husband's mastery of the reins endowed him with the beauty of those harmonious trotters he guided and kept to their pace; and the humming rush of the pace, the smooth torrent of the brown heath-knolls and reddish pits and hedge-lines and grass-flats and copses pouring the counter-way of her advance, belonged to his wizardry. The bearing of her onward was her abandonment to him. Delicious as mountain air, the wind sang; it had a song of many voices. Quite as much as on the mountains, there was the keen, the blissful, nerve-knotting catch of the presence of danger in the steep descents, taken as if swallowed, without swerve or check. She was in her husband's hands. At times, at the pitch of a rapid shelving, that was like a fall, her heart went down; and at the next throb exalted before it rose, not reasoning why;—her confidence was in him; she was his comrade whatever chanced. Up over the mountain-peaks she had known edged moments, little heeded in their passage, when life is poised as a crystal pitcher on the head, in peril of a step. Then she had been dependent on herself. Now she had the joy of trusting to her husband.

His hard leftward eye had view of her askant, if he cared to see how she bore the trial; and so relentlessly did he take the slopes, that the man inside pushed out an inquiring pate, the two grooms tightened arms across their chests. Her face was calmly set, wakeful, but unwrinkled: the creature did not count among timid girls—or among civilized. She had got what she wanted from her madman—mad in his impulses, mad in his reading of honour. She was the sister of Henrietta's husband. Henrietta bore the name she had quitted. Could madness go beyond the marrying of the creature? He chafed at her containment, at her courage, her silence, her withholding the brazen or the fawnish look-up, either of which he would have hated.

He, however, was dragged to look down. Neither Gorgon nor Venus, nor a mingling of them, she had the chasm of the face, recalling the face of his bondage, seen first that night at Baden. It recalled and it was not the face; it was the skull of the face, or the flesh of the spirit. Occasionally she looked, for a twinkle or two, the creature or vision she had been, as if to mock by reminding him. She was the abhorred delusion, who captured him by his nerves, ensnared his word—the doing of a foul witch. How had it leapt from his mouth? She must have worked for it. The word spoken she must have known it he was bound, or the detested Henrietta would have said: Not even true to his word!

To see her now, this girl, insisting to share his name, for a slip of his tongue, despite the warning sent her through her uncle, had that face much as a leaden winter landscape pretends to be the country radiant in colour. She belonged to the order of the variable animals—a woman indeed!—womanish enough in that. There are men who love women—the idea of woman. Woman is their shepherdess of sheep. He loved freedom, loathed the subjection of a partnership; could undergo it only in adoration of an ineffable splendour. He had stepped to the altar fancying she might keep to her part of the contract by appearing the miracle that subdued him. Seen by light of day, this bitter object beside him was a witch without her spells; that is, the skeleton of the seductive, ghastliest among horrors and ironies. Let her have the credit of doing her work thoroughly before the exposure. She had done it. She might have helped—such was the stipulation of his mad freak in consenting to the bondage—yes, she might have helped to soften the sting of his wound. She was beside him bearing his name, for the perpetual pouring of an acid on the wound that vile Henrietta—poisoned honey of a girl!—had dealt.

He glanced down at his possession:—heaven and the yawning pit were the contrast! Poisoned honey is after all honey while you eat it. Here there was nothing but a rocky bowl of emptiness. And who was she? She was the sister of Henrietta's husband. He was expected to embrace the sister of Henrietta's husband. Those two were on their bridal tour.

This creature was also the daughter of an ancient impostor and desperado called the Old Buccaneer; a distinguished member of the family of the Lincolnshire Kirbys, boasting a present representative grimly acquitted, men said, on a trial for murder. An eminent alliance! Society considered the Earl of Fleetwood wildish, though he could manage his affairs. He and his lawyers had them under strict control. How of himself? The prize of the English marriage market had taken to his bosom for his winsome bride the daughter of the Old Buccaneer. He was to mix his blood with the blood of the Lincolnshire Kirbys, lying pallid under the hesitating acquittal of a divided jury.

How had he come to this pass, which swung him round to think almost regretfully of the scorned multitude of fair besiegers in the market, some of whom had their unpoetic charms?

He was renowned and unrivalled as the man of stainless honour: the one living man of his word. He had never broken it—never would. There was his distinction among the herd. In that, a man is princely above princes. The nobility of Edward Russett, Earl of Fleetwood, surpassed the nobility of common nobles. But, by all that is holy, he pays for his distinction.

The creature beside him is a franked issue of her old pirate of a father in one respect—nothing frightens her. There she sits; not a screw of her brows or her lips; and the coach rocked, they were sharp on a spill midway of the last descent. It rocks again. She thinks it scarce worth while to look up to reassure him. She is looking over the country.

'Have you been used to driving?' he said.

She replied: 'No, it is new to me on a coach.'

Carinthia felt at once how wild the wish or half expectation that he would resume the glowing communion of the night which had plighted them.

She did not this time say 'my husband,' still it flicked a whip at his ears.

She had made it more offensive, by so richly toning the official title just won from him as to ring it on the nerves; one had to block it or be invaded. An anticipation that it would certainly recur haunted every opening of her mouth.

Now that it did not, he felt the gap, relieved, and yet pricked to imagine a mimicry of her tones, for the odd foreignness of the word and the sound. She had a voice of her own besides her courage. At the altar, her responses had their music. No wonder: the day was hers. 'My husband' was a manner of saying 'my fish.'

He, spoke very civilly. 'Oblige me by telling me what name you are accustomed to answer to.'

She seemed unaware of an Arctic husband, and replied: 'My father called me Carin—short for Carinthia. My mother called me Janey; my second name is Jane. My brother Chillon says both. Henrietta calls me Janey.'

The creature appeared dead flesh to goads. But the name of her sister-in-law on her lips returned the stroke neatly. She spared him one whip, to cut him with another.

'You have not informed me which of these names you prefer.'

'Oh, my husband, it is as you shall please.'

Fleetwood smartened the trot of his team, and there was a to-do with the rakish leaders.

Fairies of a malignant humour in former days used to punish the unhappiest of the naughty men who were not favourites, by suddenly planting a hump on their backs. Off the bedevilled wretches pranced, and they kicked, they snorted, whinnied, rolled, galloped, outflying the wind, but not the dismal rider. Marriage is our incubus now. No explanation is offered of why we are afflicted; we have simply offended, or some one absent has offended, and we are handy. The spiteful hag of power ties a wife to us; perhaps for the reason, that we behaved in the spirit of a better time by being chivalrously honourable. Wives are just as inexplicable curses, just as ineradicable and astonishing as humps imposed on shapely backs.

Fleetwood lashed his horses until Carinthia's low cry of entreaty rose to surprise. That stung him.

'Leave the coachman to his devices: we have an appointment and must keep it,' he said.

'They go so willingly.'

'Good beasts, in their way.'

'I do not like the whip.'

'I have the same objection.'

They were on the level of the vale, going along a road between farms and mansions, meadows and gardenplots and park-palings. A strong warm wind drove the pack of clouds over the tree-tops and charged at the branches. English scenery, animating air; a rouse to the blood and the mind. Carinthia did not ask for hues. She had come to love of the dark land with the warm lifting wind, the big trees and the hedges, and the stately houses, and people requiring to be studied, who mean well and are warm somewhere below, as chimneypots are, though they are so stiff.

English people dislike endearments, she had found. It might be that her husband disliked any show of fondness. He would have to be studied very much. He was not like others, as Henrietta had warned her. From thinking of him fervidly, she was already past the marvel of the thought that she called him husband. At the same time, a curious intimation, gathered she knew not whence, of the word 'husband' on a young wife's lips as being a foreign sound in England, advised her to withhold it. His behaviour was instructing her.

'Are you weather-wise?—able to tell when the clouds will hold off or pelt,' he said, to be very civil to a neighbour.

She collected her understanding, apparently; treating a conversational run of the tongue as a question to be pondered; and the horses paid for it. Ordinarily he was gentle with his beasts. He lashed at her in his heart for perverting the humanest of men.

'Father was,' she replied.

'Oh! I have heard of him.'

Her face lightened. 'Father had a great name in England.'

'The Old Buccaneer, I think.'

'I do not know. He was a seaman of the navy, like Admiral Fakenham is. Weather at sea, weather on the mountains, he could foretell it always. He wrote a book; I have a copy you will read. It is a book of Maxims. He often speaks of the weather. English weather and women, he says. But not my mother. My mother he stood aside by herself—pas capricieuse du tout! Because she would be out in the weather and brave the weather. She rode, she swam, best of any woman. If she could have known you, what pleasure for me! Mother learnt to read mountain weather from father. I did it too. But sometimes on the high fields' upper snows it is very surprising. Father has been caught. Here the cloud is down near the earth and the strong wind keeps the rain from falling. How long the wind will blow I cannot guess. But you love the mountains. We spoke... And mountains' adventures we both love. I will talk French if you like, for, I think, German you do not speak. I may speak English better than French; but I am afraid of my English with you.'

'Dear me!' quoth Fleetwood, and he murmured politely and cursorily, attentive to his coachman business. She had a voice that clove the noise of the wheels, and she had a desire to talk—that was evident. Talk of her father set her prattling. It became clear also to his not dishonest, his impressionable mind, that her baby English might be natural. Or she was mildly playing on it, to give herself an air.

He had no remembrance of such baby English at Baden. There, however, she was in a state of enthusiasm—the sort of illuminated transparency they show at the end of fireworks. Mention of her old scapegrace of a father lit her up again. The girl there and the girl here were no doubt the same. It could not be said that she had duped him; he had done it for himself—acted on by a particular agency. This creature had not the capacity to dupe. He had armed a bluntwitted young woman with his idiocy, and she had dealt the stroke; different in scarce a degree by nature from other young women of prey.

But her look at times, and now and then her voice, gave sign that she counted on befooling him as well, to reconcile him to his bondage. The calculation was excessive. No woman had done it yet. Idiocy plunged him the step which reawakened understanding; and to keep his whole mind alert on guard against any sort of satisfaction with his bargain, he frankly referred to the cause. Not female arts, but nature's impulses, it was his passion for the wondrous in the look of a woman's face, the new morning of the idea of women in the look, and the peep into imaginary novel character, did the trick of enslaving him. Call it idiocy. Such it was. Once acknowledged, it is not likely to recur. An implacable reason sits in its place, with a keen blade for efforts to carry the imposture further afield or make it agreeable. Yet, after giving his word to Lord Levellier, he had prodded himself to think the burden of this wild young woman might be absurdly tolerable and a laugh at the world.

A solicitude for the animal was marked by his inquiry 'You are not hungry yet?'

'Oh no, not yet,' said she, oddly enlivened.

They had a hamper and were independent of stoppages for provision, he informed her. What more delightful? cried her look, seeing the first mid-day's rest and meal with Chillon on the walk over the mountain from their empty home.

She could get up enthusiasm for a stocked hamper! And when told of some business that drew him to a meadow they were nearing, she said she would be glad to help, if she could. 'I learn quickly, I know.'

His head acquiesced. The daughter of the Old Buccaneer might learn the business quickly, perhaps; a singularly cutting smile was on his tight lips, in memory of a desire he had as a boy to join hands with an Amazonian damsel and be out over the world for adventures, comrade and bride as one. Here the creature sat. Life is the burlesque of young dreams; or they precipitate us on the roar and grin of a recognized beast world.

The devil possessing him gnawed so furiously that a partial mitigation of the pain was afforded by sight of waving hats on a hill-rise of the road. He flourished his whip. The hats continued at wind-mill work. It signified brisk news to him, and prospect of glee to propitiate any number of devils.

'You will want a maid to attend on you,' he said.

She replied: 'I am not used to attendance on me. Henrietta's maid would help. I did not want her. I had no maid at home. I can do for myself. Father and mother liked me to be very independent.'

He supposed he would have to hear her spelling her words out next.

The hill-top was gained; twenty paces of pretty trotting brought up the coach beside an inn porch, in the style of the finish dear to whips, and even imperative upon them, if they love their art. Two gentlemen stood in the road, and a young woman at the inn door; a dark-haired girl of an anxious countenance. Her puckers vanished at some signal from inside the coach.

'All right, Madge; nothing to fear,' Fleetwood called to her, and she curtseyed.

He alighted, saying to her, before he spoke to his friends: 'I've brought him safe; had him under my eye the last four and twenty hours. He'll do the trick to-day. You don't bet?'

'Oh! my lord, no.'

'Help the lady down. Out with you, Ines!'

The light-legged barge-faced man touched ground capering. He was greeted 'Kit' by the pair of gentlemen, who shook hands with him, after he had faintly simulated the challenge to a jig with Madge. She flounced from him, holding her arms up to the lady. Landlord, landlady, and hostler besought the lady to stay for the fixing of a ladder. Carinthia stepped, leaped, and entered the inn, Fleetwood remarking:

'We are very independent, Chummy Potts.'

'Cordy bally, by Jove!' Potts cried. But the moment after this disengaged ejaculation, he was taken with a bewilderment. 'At the Opera?' he questioned of his perplexity.

'No, sir, not at the Opera,' Fleetwood rejoined. 'The lady's last public appearance was at the altar.'

'Sort of a suspicion of having seen her somewhere. Left her husband behind, has she?'

'You see: she has gone in.'

The scoring of a proposition of Euclid on the forehead of Potts amused him and the other gentleman, who was hailed 'Mallard!' and cared nothing for problems involving the female of man when such work was to the fore as the pugilistic encounter of the Earl of Fleetwood's chosen Kit Ines, with Lord Brailstone's unbeaten and well-backed Ben Todds.

Ines had done pretty things from the age of seventeen to his twenty-third year. Remarkably clever things they were, to be called great in the annals of the Ring. The point, however, was, that the pockets of his backers had seriously felt his latest fight. He received a dog's licking at the hands of Lummy Phelps, his inferior in skill, fighting two to one of the odds; and all because of his fatal addiction to the breaking of his trainer's imposed fast in liquids on, the night before the battle. Right through his training, up to that hour, the rascal was devout; the majority's money rattled all on the snug safe side. And how did he get at the bottle? His trainers never could say. But what made him turn himself into a headlong ass, when he had only to wait a night to sit among friends and worshippers drinking off his tumbler upon tumbler with the honours? It was past his wits to explain. Endurance of his privation had snapped in him; or else, which is more likely, this Genius of the Ring was tempted by his genius on the summit of his perfected powers to believe the battle his own, and celebrate it, as became a victor despising the drubbed antagonist.

In any case, he drank, and a minor man gave him the dog's licking.. 'Went into it puffy, came out of it bunged,' the chronicle resounding over England ran. Old England read of an 'eyeless carcase' heroically stepping up to time for three rounds of mashing punishment. If he had won the day after all, the country would have been electrified. It sympathized on the side of his backers too much to do more than nod a short approval of his fortitude. To sink with flag flying is next to sinking the enemy. There was talk of a girl present at the fight, and of how she received the eyeless, almost faceless, carcase of her sweetheart Kit, and carried him away in a little donkey-cart, comfortably cushioned to meet disaster. This petty incident drew the attention of the Earl of Fleetwood, then beginning to be known as the diamond of uncounted facets, patron of the pick of all departments of manly activity in England.

The devotion of the girl Madge to her sweetheart was really a fine story. Fleetwood touched on it to Mr. Mallard, speaking of it like the gentleman he could be, while Chumley Potts wagged impatient acquiescence in a romantic episode of the Ring, that kept the talk from the hotter theme.

'Money's Bank of England to-day, you think?' he interposed, and had his answer after Mallard had said:

'The girl 's rather good-looking, too.'

'You may double your bets, Chummy. I had the fellow to his tea at my dinner-table yesterday evening; locked him in his bedroom, and had him up and out for a morning spin at six. His trainer, Flipper's on the field, drove from Esslemont at nine, confident as trumps.'

'Deuce of a good-looking girl,' Potts could now afford to say; and he sang out: 'Feel fit, lucky dog?'

'Concert pitch!' was the declaration of Kit Ives.

'How about Lord Brailstone's man?'

'Female partner in a quadrille, sir.'

'Ah!' Potts doated on his limbs with a butcher's eye for prize joints.

'Cock-sure has crowed low by sunset,' Mallard observed.

Fleetwood offered him to take his bets.

'You're heavy on it with Brailstone?' said Mallard.

'Three thousand.'

'I'd back you for your luck blindfold.'

A ruffle of sourness shot over the features of the earl, and was noticed by both eager betters, who exchanged a glance.

Potts inspected his watch, and said half aloud: 'Liver, ten to one! That never meant bad luck—except bad to act on. We slept here last night, you know. It 's a mile and a quarter from the Royal Sovereign to the field of glory. Pretty well time to start. Brailstone has a drive of a couple of miles. Coaches from London down by this time. Abrane's dead on Ben Todds, any odds. Poor old Braney! "Steady man, Todds." Backs him because he's a "respectable citizen,"—don't drink. A prize-fighter total abstainer has no spurts. Old Draney's branded for the losing side. You might bet against Draney blindfold, Mallard. How long shall you take to polish him off, Kit Ines?'

The opponent of Ben Todds calculated.

'Well, sir, steady Benny ought to be satisfied with his dose in, say, about forty minutes. Maybe he won't own to it before an hour and ten. He's got a proud English stomach.'

'Shall we be late?' Potts asked.

'Jump in,' Fleetwood said to his man. 'We may be five minutes after time, Chummy. I had a longer drive, and had to get married on the way, and—ah, here they are!'

'Lady coming?'

'I fancy she sticks to the coach; I don't know her tastes. Madge must see her through it, that's positive.'

Potts deferred his astonishment at the things he was hearing and seeing, which were only Fleetwood's riddles. The fight and the bets rang every other matter out of his head. He beheld the lady, who had come down from the coach like a columbine, mount it like Bean-stalk Jack. Madge was not half so clever, and required a hand at her elbow.

After, giving hurried directions to Rundles, the landlord of the Royal Sovereign, Fleetwood took the reins, and all three gentlemen touched hats to the curtseying figure of Mrs. Rundles.

'You have heard, I dare say—it's an English scene,' he spoke, partly turning his face, to Carinthia; 'particularly select to-day. Their Majesties might look on, as the Caesars did in Rome. Pity we can't persuade them. They ought to set the fashion. Here we have the English people at their grandest, in prime condition, if they were not drunk overnight; and dogged, perfectly awake, magnanimous, all for fair play; fine fellows, upon my word. A little blood, of course.'

But the daughter of the Old Buccaneer would have inherited a tenderness for the sight of blood. She should make a natural Lady Patroness of England's National Sports. We might turn her to that purpose; wander over England with a tail of shouting riff-raft; have exhibitions, join in them, display our accomplishments; issue challenges to fence, shoot, walk, run, box, in time: the creature has muscle. It's one way of crowning a freak; we follow the direction, since the deed done can't be undone; and a precious poetical life, too! You may get as royally intoxicated on swipes as on choice wine; win a name for yourself as the husband of such a wife; a name in sporting journals and shilling biographies: quite a revival of the Peerage they have begun to rail at!

'I would not wish to leave you,' said Carinthia.

'You have chosen,' said Fleetwood.

CHAPTER XVI

IN WHICH THE BRIDE FROM FOREIGN PARTS IS GIVEN A TASTE OF OLD ENGLAND

Cheers at an open gate of a field saluted the familiar scarlet of the Earl of Fleetwood's coach in Kentish land. They were chorister cheers, the spontaneous ringing out of English country hearts in homage to the nobleman who brightened the heaviness of life on English land with a spectacle of the noble art distinguishing their fathers. He drove along over muffling turf; ploughboys and blue butcher-boys, and smocked old men, with an approach to a hundred-weight on their heels, at the trot to right and left; all hoping for an occasional sight of the jewel called Kitty, that he carried inside. Kitty was there.

Kitty's eyes are shut. Think of that: cradled innocence and angels' dreams and the whole of the hymn just before ding-dong-bang on noses and jaws! That means confidence? Looks like it. But Kitty's not asleep you try him. He's only quiet because he has got to undergo great exertion. Last fight he was knocked out of time, because he went into it honest drunk, they tell. And the earl took him up, to give him a chance of recovering his good name, and that's Christian. But the earl, he knows a man as well as a horse. He's one to follow. Go to a fayte down at Esslemont, you won't forget your day. See there, he's brought a lady on the top o' the coach. That seems for to signify he don't expect it's going to be much of a bloody business. But there's no accounting. Anyhow, Broadfield 'll have a name in the papers for Sunday reading. In comes t' other lord's coach. They've timed it together closes they have.

They were pronounced to be both the right sort of noblemen for the country. Lord Brailstone's blue coach rattled through an eastern gate to the corner of the thirty-acre meadow, where Lord Fleetwood had drawn up, a toss from the ring. The meeting of the blue and scarlet coaches drew forth Old England's thunders; and when the costly treasures contained in them popped out heads, the moment was delirious. Kit Ines came after his head on a bound. Ben Todds was ostentatiously deliberate: his party said he was no dancing-master. He stepped out, grave as a barge emerging from a lock, though alive to the hurrahs of supporters and punctilious in returning the formal portion of his rival's too roguish nod. Their look was sharp into the eyes, just an instant.

Brailstone and Fleetwood jumped to the grass and met, talking and laughing, precise upon points of business, otherwise cordial: plenipotentiaries of great powers, whom they have set in motion and bind to the ceremonial opening steps, according to the rules of civilized warfare. They had a short colloquy with newspaper reporters;—an absolutely fair, square, upright fight of Britons was to be chronicled. Captain Abrane, a tower in the crowd, registered bets whenever he could. Curricles, gigs, carts, pony-traps, boys on ponies, a swarm on legs, flowed to the central point and huddled there.

Was either champion born in Kent? An audacious boy proclaimed Kit Ines a man of Kent. Why, of course he was! and that was why the Earl of Fleetwood backed our cocky Kitty, and means to land him on the top of his profession. Ben Todds was shuffled aside; as one of their Londoners, destitute of county savour.

All very well, but have a spy at Benny Todds. Who looks the square man? And hear what that big gentleman of the other lord's party says. A gentleman of his height and weight has a right to his opinion. He 's dead against Kit Ines: it's fists, not feet, he says, 'll do it to-day; stamina, he says. Benny has got the stamina.

Todds' possession of the stamina, and the grand voice of Captain Abrane, and the Father Christmas, roast-beef-of-Old England face of the umpire declared to be on the side of Lord Brailstone's colour blue, darkened the star of Kit Ines till a characteristic piece of behaviour was espied. He dashed his cap into the ring and followed it, with the lightest of vaults across the ropes. There he was, the first in the ring: and that stands for promise of first blow, first blood, first flat knock-down, and last to cry for quarter. His pair of seconds were soon after him. Fleetwood mounted his box.

'Is it to fight?' said Carinthia.

'To see which is the master.'

'They fight to see?'

'Generally until one or the other can't see. You are not obliged to see it; you can be driven away if you wish.'

'I will be here, if you are here.'

'You choose it.'

Fleetwood leaned over to Chumley Potts on the turf. 'Abrane's ruining himself.'

Potts frankly hoped that his friend might be doing so. 'Todds is jolly well backed. He's in prime condition. He's the favourite of the knowing ones.'

'You wouldn't have the odds, if he weren't.'

'No; but the odds are like ten per cent.: they conjure the gale, and be hanged,' said Potts; he swore at his betting mania, which destroyed the pleasure of the show he loved.

All in the ring were shaking hands. Shots of a desire to question and comment sped through Carinthia's veins and hurt her. She had gathered that she spoke foolishly to her husband's ear, so she kept her mouth shut, though the unanswered of her inquisitive ignorance in the strange land pricked painfully at her bosom. She heard the girl behind her say: 'Our colours!' when the colour scarlet unwound with Lord Brailstone's blue was tied to the stake: and her husband nodded; he smiled; he liked to hear the girl.

Potts climbed up, crying: 'Toilets complete! Now for paws out, and then at it, my hearties!'

Choice of corners under the leaden low cloud counted for little. A signal was given; a man outside the ring eyed a watch, raised a hand; the two umpires were on foot in their places; the pair of opposing seconds hurried out cheery or bolt-business words to their men; and the champions advanced to the scratch. Todds first, by the courtesy of Ines, whose decorous control of his legs at a weighty moment was rightly read by his party.

Their hands grasped firmly: thereupon becoming fists of a hostile couple in position. And simply to learn which of us two is the better man! Or in other words, with four simple fists to compass a patent fact and stand it on the historic pedestal, with a little red writing underneath: you never can patent a fact without it. But mark the differences of this kind of contention from all other—especially the Parliamentary: this is positive, it has a beginning and an end; and it is good-humoured from beginning to end; trial of skill, trial of stamina; Nature and Art; Old English; which made us what we are; and no rancours, no vows of vengeance; the beaten man of the two bowing to the bit of history he has helped to make.

Kittites had need to be confident in the skill of their lither lad. His facer looked granite. Fronting that mass, Kit you might—not to lash about for comparisons—call a bundle of bamboo. Ay, but well knitted, springy, alive every inch of him; crafty, too, as you will soon bear witness. He knows he has got his task, and he's the man to do it.

There was wary sparring, and mirrors watched them.

'Bigger fellow: but have no fear,' the earl said over his shoulder to Madge.

She said in return: 'Oh, I don't know, I'm praying.'

Kit was now on his toes, all himself, like one who has found the key. He feinted. Quick as lightning, he landed a bolt on Ben's jib, just at the toll-bar of the bridge, between the eyes, and was off, out of reach, elastic; Ben's counter fell short by a couple of inches. Cheers for first blow.

The earl clucked to Madge. Her gaze at the ring was a sullen intensity.

Will you believe it?—Ben received a second spanking cracker on the spectacles-seat: neat indeed; and, poor payment for the compliment, he managed to dig a drive at the ribs. As much of that game as may suit you, sturdy Ben! But hear the shout, and behold!

First blood to Kit Ines! That tell-tale nose of old Ben's has mounted the Earl of Fleetwood's colours, and all his party are looking Brailstone-blue.

'So far!' said Fleetwood. His grooms took an indication: the hamper was unfastened; sandwiches were handed. Carinthia held one; she tried to nibble, in obedience to her husband's example. Madge refused a bite of food.

Hearing Carinthia say to her: 'I hope he will not be beaten, I hope, I hope,' she made answer: 'You are very good, Miss'; and the young lady flushed.

Gentlemen below were talking up to the earl. A Kentish squire of an estate neighbouring Esslemont introduced a Welsh squire he had driven to see the fun, by the name of Mr. Owain Wythan, a neighbour of the earl's down in Wales. Refreshments were offered. Carinthia submissively sipped the sparkling wine, which stings the lips when they are indisposed to it. The voice of the girl Madge rang on the tightened chords of her breast. Madge had said she was praying: and to pray was all that could be done by two women. Her husband could laugh loudly with Mr. Potts and the other gentlemen and the strangers. He was quite sure the man he supported would win; he might have means of knowing. Carinthia clung to his bare words, for the sake of the girl.

A roaring peal went up from the circle of combat. Kit had it this time. Attacking Ben's peepers, he was bent on defending his own, and he caught a bodyblow that sent him hopping back to his pair of seconds, five clear hops to the rear, like a smashed surge-wave off the rock. He was respectful for the remainder of the round. But hammering at the system he had formed, in the very next round he dropped from a tremendous repetition of the blow, and lay flat as a turbot. The bets against him had simultaneously a see-saw rise.

'Bellows, he appears to have none,' was the comment of Chumley Potts.

'Now for training, Chummy!' said Lord Fleetwood.

'Chummy!' signifying a crow over Potts, rang out of the hollows of Captain Abrane on Lord Brailstone's coach.

Carinthia put a hand behind her to Madge. It was grasped, in gratitude for sympathy or in feminine politeness. The girl murmured: 'I've seen worse.' She was not speaking to ears.

Lord Fleetwood sat watch in hand. 'Up,' he said; and, as if hearing him, Kit rose from the ministering second's knee. He walked stiffly, squared after the fashion of a man taught caution. Ben made play. They rounded the ring, giving and taking. Ben rushed, and had an emollient; spouted again and was corked; again, and received a neat red-waxen stopper. He would not be denied at Kit's door, found him at home and hugged him. Kit got himself to grass, after a spell of heavy fibbing, Ben's game.

It did him no great harm; it might be taken for an enlivener; he was dead on his favourite spot the ensuing round, played postman on it. So cleverly, easily, dancingly did he perform the double knock and the retreat, that Chumley Potts was moved to forget his wagers and exclaim: 'Racket-ball, by Jove!'

'If he doesn't let the fellow fib the wind out of him,' Mallard addressed his own crab eyeballs.

Lord Fleetwood heard and said coolly: 'Tightstrung. I kept him fasting since he earned his breakfast. You don't wind an empty rascal fit for action. A sword through the lungs won't kill when there's no air in them.'

That was printed in the 'Few Words before the Encounter', in the Book Of MAXIMS FOR MEN. Carinthia, hearing everything her husband uttered, burned to remind him of the similarity between his opinions and her father's.

She was learning, that for some reason, allusions to her father were not acceptable. She squeezed the hand of Madge, and felt a pressure, like a scream, telling her the girl's heart was with the fight beneath them. She thought it natural for her. She wished she could continue looking as intently. She looked because her husband looked. The dark hills and clouds curtaining the run of the stretch of fields relieved her sight.

The clouds went their way; the hills were solid, but like a blue smoke; the scene here made them very distant and strange. Those two men were still hitting, not hating one another; only to gratify a number of unintelligible people and win a success. But the earth and sky seemed to say, What is the glory? They were insensible to it, as they are not—they are never insensible to noble grounds of strife. They bless the spot, they light lamps on it; they put it into books of history, make it holy, if the cause was a noble one or a good one.

Or supposing both those men loved the girl, who loved one of them! Then would Carinthia be less reluctantly interested in their blows.

Her infant logic stumbled on for a reason while she repressed the torture the scene was becoming, as though a reason could be found by her submissive observation of it. And she was right in believing that a reason for the scene must or should exist. Only, like other bewildered instinctive believers, she could not summon the great universe or a life's experience to unfold it. Her one consolation was in squeezing the hand of the girl from time to time.

Not stealthily done, it was not objected to by the husband whose eye was on all. But the persistence in doing it sank her from the benignity of her station to the girl's level: it was conduct much too raw, and grated on the deed of the man who had given her his name.

Madge pleased him better. She had the right to be excited, and she was very little demonstrative. She had—well, in justice, the couple of them had, only she had it more—the tone of the women who can be screwed to witness a spill of blood, peculiarly catching to hear;—a tone of every string in them snapped except the silver string. Catching to hear? It is worth a stretching of them on the rack to hear that low buzz-hum of their inner breast... By heaven! we have them at their best when they sing that note.

His watch was near an hour of the contest, and Brailstone's man had scored first knock-down blow, a particularly clean floorer. Thinking of that, he was cheered by hearing Chummy Potts, whose opinions he despised, cry out to Abrane:—

'Yeast to him!' For the face of Todds was visibly swelling to the ripest of plums from Kit's deliveries.

Down he went. He had the sturdy legs which are no legs to a clean blow. Odds were offered against him.

'Oh! pretty play with your right, Kit!' exclaimed Mallard, as Kit fetched his man an ugly stroke on the round of the waist behind, and the crowd sent up the name of the great organs affected: a sickener of a stroke, if dealt soundly. It meant more than 4 showed. Kit was now for taking liberties. Light as ever on his pins, he now and then varied his attentions to the yeasty part, delivering a wakener in unexpected quarters: masterly as the skilled cook's carving of a joint with hungry guests for admirers.

'Eh, Madge?' the earl said.

She kept her sight fixed, replying: 'Yes, I think...' Carinthia joined with her: 'I must believe it that he will: but will the other man, poor man, submit? I entreat him to put away his pride. It is his—oh, poor man!'

Ben was having it hot and fast on a torso physiognomy.

The voices of these alien women thrilled the fray and were a Bardic harp to Lord Fleetwood.

He dropped a pleasant word on the heads in the curricle.

Mr. Owain Wythan looked up. 'Worthy of Theocritus. It's the Boxing Twin and the Bembrycian giant. The style of each. To the letter!'

'Kit is assiduously fastening Ben's blinkers,' Potts remarked.

He explained to the incomprehensible lady he fancied he had somewhere seen, that the battle might be known as near the finish by the behaviour on board Lord Brailstone's coach.

'It's like Foreign Affairs and the Stock Exchange,' he said to the more intelligent males. 'If I want to know exactly how the country stands, I turn to the Money Article in the papers. That's a barometrical certainty. No use inquiring abroad. Look at old Rufus Abrane. I see the state of the fight on the old fellow's mug. He hasn't a bet left in him!'

'Captain Mountain—Rufus Mus!' cried Lord Fleetwood, and laughed at the penetrative portrait Woodseer's epigram sketched; he had a desire for the presence of the singular vagabond.

The Rufus Mus in the Captain Mountain exposed his view of the encounter, by growing stiller, apparently growing smaller, without a squeak, like the entrapped; and profoundly contemplative, after the style of the absolutely detached, who foresee the fatal crash, and are calculating, far ahead of events, the means for meeting their personal losses.

The close of the battle was on the visage of Rufus Abrane fifteen minutes before that Elgin marble under red paint in the ring sat on the knee of a succouring seconder, mopped, rubbed, dram-primed, puppy-peeping, inconsolably comforted, preparatory to the resumption of the great-coat he had so hopefully cast from his shoulders. Not downcast by any means. Like an old Roman, the man of the sheer hulk with purple eyemounds found his legs to do the manful thing, show that there was no bad blood, stand equal to all forms. Ben Todds, if ever man in Old England, looked the picture you might label 'Bellyful,' it was remarked. Kit Ines had an appearance of springy readiness to lead off again. So they faced on the opening step of their march into English History.

Vanquisher and vanquished shook hands, engaged in a parting rally of good-humoured banter; the beaten man said his handsome word; the best man capped it with a compliment to him. They drink of different cups to-day. Both will drink of one cup in the day to come. But the day went too clearly to crown the light and the tight and the right man of the two, for moralizing to wag its tail at the end. Oldsters and youngsters agreed to that. Science had done it: happy the backers of Science! Not one of them alluded to the philosophical 'hundred years hence.' For when England, thanks to a spirited pair of our young noblemen, has exhibited one of her characteristic performances consummately, Philosophy is bidden fly; she is a foreign bird.

CHAPTER XVII

RECORDS A SHADOW CONTEST CLOSE ON THE FOREGOING

Kit Ines cocked an eye at Madge, in the midst of the congratulations and the paeans pumping his arms. As he had been little mauled, he could present a face to her, expecting a wreath of smiles for the victor.

What are we to think of the contrarious young woman who, when he lay beaten, drove him off the field and was all tenderness and devotion? She bobbed her head, hardly more than a trifle pleased, one might say. Just like females. They're riddles, not worth spelling. Then, drunk I'll get to-night, my pretty dear! the man muttered, soured by her inopportune staidness, as an opponent's bruisings could never have rendered him.

She smiled a lively beam in answer to the earl; 'Oh yes I 'm glad. It's your doing, my lord.' Him it was that she thanked, and for the moment prized most. The female riddle is hard to read, because it is compounded of sensations, and they rouse and appeal to the similar cockatrices in us, which either hiss back or coil upon themselves. She admired Kit Ines for his valour: she hated that ruinous and besotting drink. It flung skeletons of a married couple on the wall of the future. Nevertheless her love had been all maternal to him when he lay chastised and disgraced on account of his vice. Pity had done it. Pity not being stirred, her admiration of the hero declared victorious, whose fortunes in uncertainty had stopped the beating of her heart, was eclipsed by gratitude toward his preserver, and a sentiment eclipsed becomes temporarily coldish, against our wish and our efforts, in a way to astonish; making her think that she cannot hold two sentiments at a time; when it is but the fact that she is unable to keep the two equally warm.

Carinthia said to her: 'He is brave.'

'Oh yes, he's brave,' Madge assented.

Lord Brailstone, flourishing his whip, cried out: 'At Canleys to-night?'

The earl nodded: 'I shall be there.'

'You, too, Chummy?' came from Abrane.

'To see you dance,' Potts rejoined, and mumbled

'But will he dance! Old Braney's down on his luck; he's a specimen of a fellow emptier and not lighter. And won't be till supper-time. But, I say, Fleet, how the deuce?—funny sort of proceeding!—You haven't introduced me.'

'The lady bears my name, Mr. Chumley Potts.'

With a bow to the lady's profile and a mention of a glimpse at Baden, Potts ejaculated: 'It happened this morning?'

'You allude to the marriage. It happened this morning.'

'How do I get to Canleys?'

'I drive you. Another team from the Esslemont stables is waiting at the Royal.'

'You stay at Canleys?'

'No.'

'No? Oh! Funny, upon my word. Though I don't know why not—except that people...'

'Count your winnings, Chummy.'

Fleetwood remarked to his bride: 'Our friend has the habit of soliloquizing in company. I forgot to tell you of an appointment of mine at a place called Canleys, about twenty miles or more from here. I gave my word, so I keep it. The landlady at the inn, Mrs. Rundles, motherly kind of woman; she will be attentive. They don't cook badly, for an English inn, I have heard. Madge here will act as your lady's-maid for the time. You will find her serviceable; she's a bruiser's lass and something above it. Ines informed me, Madge, you were going to friends of yours at the Wells. You will stay at the Royal and wait on this lady, who bears my name. You understand?—A girl I can trust for courage, if the article is in request,' he resumed to his bride; and talked generally of the inn and the management of it, and its favoured position outside the village and contiguous to the river, upon which it subsisted.

Carinthia had heard. She was more than ever the stunned young woman she had been since her mounting of the coach, between the village church and Lekkatts.

She said not a word. Why should she? her object was won. Give her that, and a woman's tongue will consent to rest. The dreaded weapon rest, also when she is kept spinning by the whip. She gives out a pleasant hum, too. Her complexion must be pronounced dull in repose. A bride on her travels with an aspect of wet chalk, rather helps to scare mankind from marriage: which may be good or bad; but she reflects a sicklier hue on the captured Chessman calling her his own. Let her shine in privacy.

Fleetwood drew up at the Royal Sovereign, whereof the reigning monarch, in blue uniform on the signboard, curtseyed to his equally windy subjects; and a small congregation of the aged, and some cripples and infants, greeted the patron of Old England's manfullest display, cheering at news of the fight, brought them by many little runners.

'Your box has been conveyed to your room,' he said to his bride.

She bowed. This time she descended the coach by the aid of the ladder.

Ines, victorious in battle, had scant notice from his love. 'Yes, I 'm glad,' and she passed him to follow her newly constituted mistress. His pride was dashed, all the foam of the first draw on the top of him blown off, as he figuratively explained the cause of his gloom to the earl. 'I drink and I gets a licking—that girl nurses and cossets me. I don't drink and I whops my man—she shows me her back. Ain't it encouragement, my lord?'

'You ought to know them by this time, you dolt,' returned his patron, and complimented him on his bearing in the fight. 'You shall have your two hundred, and something will be added. Hold handy here till I mount. I start in ten minutes.'

Whether to speak a polite adieu to the bride, whose absurd position she had brought on her own head, was debated for half a minute. He considered that the wet chalk-quarry of a beauty had at all events the merit of not being a creature to make scenes. He went up to the sitting-room. If she was not there, he would leave his excuses.

She was there, and seated; neither crying, nor smiling, nor pointedly serious in any way, not conventionally at her ease either. And so clearly was he impressed by her transparency in simplicity of expression, that he took without a spurn at it the picture of a woman half drained of her blood, veiling the wound. And a young woman, a stranger to suffering: perhaps—as the creatures do looking for the usual flummery tenderness, what they call happiness; wondering at the absence of it and the shifty ghost of a husband she has got by floundering into the bog known as Marriage. She would have it, and here she was!

He entered the situation and was possessed by the shivering delicacy of it. Surface emotions were not seen on her. She might be a creature with a soul. Here and there the thing has been found in women. It is priceless when found, and she could not be acting. One might swear the creature had no power to act.

She spoke without offence, the simplest of words, affected no solicitudes, put on no gilt smiles, wore no reproaches: spoke to him as if so it happened—he had necessarily a journey to perform. One could see all the while big drops falling from the wound within. One could hear it in her voice. Imagine a crack of the string at the bow's deep stress. Or imagine the bow paralyzed at the moment of the deepest sounding. And yet the voice did not waver. She had now the richness of tone carrying on a music through silence.

Well, then, at least, he had not been the utterly duped fool he thought himself since the consent was pledged to wed her.

More, she had beauty—of its kind. Or splendour or grandeur, was the term for it. But it bore no name. None of her qualities—if they were qualities—had a name. She stood with a dignity that the word did not express. She endured meekly, when there was no meekness. Pain breathed out of her, and not a sign of pain was visible. She had, under his present observation of her, beauty, with the lines of her face breaking in revolt from beauty—or requiring a superterrestrial illumination to show the harmony. He, as he now saw, had erred grossly in supposing her insensitive, and therefore slow of a woman's understanding. She drew the breath of pain through the lips: red lips and well cut. Her brown eyes were tearless, not alluring or beseeching or repelling; they did but look, much like the skies opening high aloof on a wreck of storm. Her reddish hair-chestnut, if you will—let fall a skein over one of the rugged brows, and softened the ruggedness by making it wilder, as if a great bird were winging across a shoulder of the mountain ridges. Conceived of the mountains, built in their image, the face partook alternately of mountain terror or splendour; wholly, he remembered, of the splendour when her blood ran warm. No longer the chalk-quarry face,—its paleness now was that of night Alps beneath a moon chasing the shadows.

She might be casting her spells again.

'You remember I told you,' he said, 'I have given my word—I don't break it—to be at a Ball. Your uncle was urgent to have the ceremony over. These clashes occur. The people here—I have spoken of that: people of good repute for attention to guests. I am uncertain of the time... we have all to learn to wait. So then, good-bye till we meet.'

He was experiencing a novel nip of torment, of just the degree which takes a partial appeasement from the inflicting of it, and calls up a loathed compassion. She might have been in his arms for a step, though she would not have been the better loved.

He was allowed his escape, bearing with him enough of husband to execrate another enslaving pledge of his word, that begat a frenzy to wreak some caresses on the creature's intolerably haunting image. Of course, he could not return to her. How would she receive him? There was no salt in the thought of it; she was too submissive.

However, there would be fun with Chummy Potts on the drive to Canleys; fun with Rufus Abrane at Mrs. Cowper Quillett's; and with the Countess Livia, smothered, struggling, fighting for life with the title of Dowager. A desire for unbridled fun had hold of any amount of it, to excess in any direction. And though this cloud as a dry tongue after much wine craves water, glimpses of his tramp's walk with a fellow tramp on a different road, enjoying strangely healthy vagabond sensations and vast ideas; brought the vagrant philosopher refreshfully to his mind: chiefly for the reason that while in Woodseer's company he had hardly suffered a stroke of pain from the thought of Henrietta. She was now a married woman, he was a married man by the register. Stronger proof of the maddest of worlds could not be furnished.

Sane in so mad a world, a man is your flabby citizen among outlaws, good for plucking. Fun, at any cost, is the one object worth a shot in such a world. And the fun is not to stop. If it does, we are likely to be got hold of, and lugged away to the altar—the terminus. That foul disaster has happened, through our having temporarily yielded to a fit of the dumps and treated a mad world's lunatic issue with some seriousness. But fun shall be had with the aid of His Highness below. The madder the world, the madder the fun. And the mixing in it of another element, which it has to beguile us—romance—is not at all bad cookery. Poetic romance is delusion—a tale of a Corsair; a poet's brain, a bottle of gin, and a theatrical wardrobe. Comic romance is about us everywhere, alive for the tapping.

A daughter of the Old Buccaneer should participate in it by right of birth: she would expect it in order to feel herself perfectly at home. Then, be sure, she finds an English tongue and prattles away as merrily as she does when her old scapegrace of a father is the theme. Son-in-law to him! But the path of wisdom runs in the line of facts, and to have wild fun and romance on this pantomime path, instead of kicking to break away from it, we follow things conceived by the genius of the situation, for the delectation of the fair Countess of Fleetwood and the earl, her delighted husband, quite in the spirit of the Old Buccaneer, father of the bride.

Carinthia sat beside the fire, seeing nothing in the room or on the road. Up in her bedchamber, the girl Madge was at her window. She saw Lord Fleetwood standing alone, laughing, it seemed, at some thought; he threw up his head. Was it a newly married man leaving his bride and laughing? The bride was a dear lady, fit for better than to be driven to look on at a prize-fight—a terrible scene to a lady. She was left solitary: and this her wedding day? The earl had said it, he had said she bore his name, spoke of coming from the altar, and the lady had blushed to hear herself called Miss. The pressure of her hand was warm with Madge: her situation roused the fervid latent sisterhood in the breast of women.

Before he mounted the coach, Lord Fleetwood talked to Kit Ives. He pointed at an upper window, seemed to be issuing directions. Kit nodded; he understood it, whatever it was. You might have said, a pair of burglars. The girl ran downstairs to bid her lover good-bye and show him she really rejoiced in his victory. Kit came to her saying: 'Given my word of honour I won't make a beast of myself to-night. Got to watch over you and your lady.'

Lord Fleetwood started his fresh team, casting no glance at the windows of the room where his bride was. He and the gentlemen on the coach were laughing.

His leaving of his young bride to herself this day was classed among the murky flashes which distinguished the deeds of noblemen. But his laughter on leaving her stamped it a cruelty; of the kind that plain mortals, who can be monsters, commit. Madge conceived a pretext for going into the presence of her mistress, whose attitude was the same as when she first sat in the chair. The lady smiled and said: 'He is not hurt much?' She thought for them about her.

The girl's, heart of sympathy thumped, and her hero became a very minute object. He had spoken previously of the making or not making a beast of himself; without inflicting a picture of the beast. His words took shape now, and in consequence a little self-pity began to move. It stirred to swell the great wave of pity for the lady, that was in her bosom. 'Oh, he!' she said, and extinguished the thought of him; and at once her under-lip was shivering, her eyes filled and poured.

Carinthia rose anxiously. The girl dropped at her feet. 'You have been so good to me to-day, my lady! so good to me to-day! I can't help it—I don't often just for this moment; I've been excited. Oh, he's well, he will do; he's nothing. You say "poor child!" But I'm not; it's only. excitement. I do long to serve you the best I can.'

She stood up in obedience and had the arms of her young mistress pressing her. Tears also were streaming from Carinthia's eyes. Heartily she thanked the girl for the excuse to cry.

They were two women. On the road to Canleys, the coach conveying men spouted with the lusty anecdote, relieved of the interdict of a tyrannical sex.

CHAPTER XVIII

DOWN WHITECHAPEL WAY

Contention begets contention in a land of the pirate races. Gigs were at high rival speed along the road from the battle-field to London. They were the electrical wires of the time for an expectant population bursting to have report of so thundering an event as the encounter of two champion light weights, nursed and backed by a pair of gallant young noblemen, pick of the whole row of coronets above. London panted gaping and the gigs flew with the meat to fill it.

Chumley Potts offered Ambrose Mallard fair odds that the neat little trap of the chief sporting journal, which had a reputation to maintain, would be over one or other of the bridges crossing the Thames first. Mallard had been struck by the neat little trap of an impudent new and lower-priced journal, which had a reputation to gain. He took the proffered odds, on the cry as of a cracker splitting. Enormous difficulties in regard to the testimony and the verifications were discussed; they were overcome. Potts was ready for any amount of trouble; Mallard the same. There was clearly a race. There would consequently be a record. Visits to the offices of those papers, perhaps half a day at the south end of London or on Westminster bridge, examining witnesses, corner shopmen, watermen, and the like, would or should satisfactorily establish the disputed point.

Fleetwood had his fun; insomuch that he laughed himself into a sentiment of humaneness toward the couple of donkeys and forgot his contempt of them. Their gamblings and their bets increased his number of dependents; and imbeciles were preferable to dolts or the dry gilt figures of the circle he had to move in. Matter for some astonishment had been furnished to the latter this day; and would cause an icy Signor stare and rather an angry Signora flutter. A characteristic of that upper circle, as he knew it, is, that the good are dull, the vicious very bad. They had nothing to please him but manners. Elsewhere this land is a land of no manners. Take it and make the most of it, then, for its quality of brute honesty: which is found to flourish best in the British prize-ring.

His irony landed him there. It struck the country a ringing blow. But it struck an almost effacing one at the life of the young nobleman of boundless wealth, whose highest renown was the being a patron of prizefighters. Husband of the daughter of the Old Buccaneer as well! perchance as a result. That philosopher tramp named her 'beautiful Gorgon.' She has no beauty; and as for Gorgon, the creature has a look of timid softness in waiting behind her rocky eyes. A barbaric damsel beginning to nibble at civilization, is nearer the mark; and ought she to be discouraged?

Fleetwood's wrath with his position warned him against the dupery of any such alcove thoughts. For his wrath revenged him, and he feared the being stripped of it, lest a certain fund of his own softness, that he knew of; though few did, should pull him to the creature's feet. She belonged to him indeed; so he might put her to the trial of whether she had a heart and personal charm, without the ceremony of wooing—which, in his case, tempted to the feeling desperately earnest and becoming enslaved. He speculated upon her eyelids and lips, and her voice, when melting, as women do in their different ways; here and there with an execrable—perhaps pardonable—art; one or two divinely. The vision drew him to a headlong plunge and swim of the amorous mind, occupying a minute, filling an era. He corrected the feebleness, and at the same time threw a practical coachman's glance on peculiarities of the road, requiring some knowledge of it if traversed backward at a whipping pace on a moonless night. The drive from Canleys to the Royal Sovereign could be done by good pacers in an hour and a half, little more— with Ives and the stables ready, and some astonishment in a certain unseen chamber. Fleetwood chuckled at a vision of romantic devilry—perfectly legitimate too. Something, more to inflict than enjoy, was due to him.

He did, not phrase it, that a talk with the fellow Woodseer of his mountains and his forests, and nature, philosophy, poetry, would have been particularly healthy for him, almost as good as the good counsel be needed and solicited none to give him. It swept among his ruminations while he pricked Potts and Mallard to supply his craving for satanical fare.

Gower Woodseer; the mention of whom is a dejection to the venerable source of our story, was then in the act of emerging from the Eastward into the Southward of the line of Canterbury's pilgrims when they set forth to worship, on his homeward course, after a walk of two days out of Dover. He descended London's borough, having exactly twopence halfpenny for refreshment; following a term of prudent starvation, at the end of the walk. It is not a district seductive to the wayfarer's appetite; as, for example, one may find the Jew's fry of fish in oil, inspiriting the Shoreditch region, to be. Nourishment is afforded, according to the laws of England's genius in the arts of refection, at uninviting shops, to the necessitated stomach. A penn'orth of crumb of bread, assisted on its laborious passage by a penn'orth of the rinsings of beer, left the natural philosopher a ha'penny for dessert at the stall of an applewoman, where he withstood an inclination toward the juicy fruit and chose nuts. They extend a meal, as a grimace broadens the countenance, illusorily; but they help to cheat an emptiness in time, where it is nearly as offensive to our sensations as within us; and that prolonged occupation of the jaws goes a length to persuade us we are filling. All the better when the substance is indigestible. Tramps of the philosophical order, who are the practically sagacious, prefer tough grain for the teeth. Woodseer's munching of his nuts awakened to fond imagination the picture of his father's dinner, seen one day and little envied: a small slice of cold boiled mutton-flesh in a crescent of white fat, with a lump of dry bread beside the plate.

Thus he returned to the only home he had, not disheartened, and bearing scenes that outvied London's print-shops for polychrome splendour, an exultation to recall. His condition, moreover, threw his father's life and work into colour: the lean Whitechapel house of the minister among the poor; the joy in the saving of souls, if he could persuade himself that such good labour advanced: and at the fall of light, the pastime task of bootmaking—a desireable occupation for a thinker. Thought flies best when the hands are easily busy. Cobblers have excursive minds. Their occasional rap at the pegs diversifies the stitchings and is often happily timed to settle an internal argument. Seek in a village for information concerning the village or the state of mankind, you will be less disappointed at the cobbler's than elsewhere, it has been said.

As Gower had anticipated, with lively feelings of pleasure, Mr. Woodseer was at the wonted corner of his back room, on the stool between two tallow candleflames, leather scented strongly, when the wanderer stood before him, in the image of a ball that has done with circling about a stable point.

'Back?' the minister sang out at once, and his wrinkles gleamed:

Their hands grasped.

'Hungry, sir, rather.'

'To be sure, you are. One can read it on your boots. Mrs. Jones will spread you a table. How many miles to-day? Show the soles. They tell a tale of wear.'

They had worn to resemble the thin-edged layers of still upper cloud round the peep of coming sky.

'About forty odd to-day, sir. They've done their hundreds of miles and have now come to dock. I 'll ask Mrs. Jones to bring me a plate here.'

Gower went to the housekeeper in the kitchen. His father's front door was unfastened by day; she had not set eyes on him yet, and Mr. Woodseer murmured:

'Now she's got the boy. There 's clasping and kissing. He's all wild Wales to her.'

The plate of meat was brought by Mary Jones with Gower beside her, and a sniffle of her happiness audible. She would not, although invited to stay and burning to hear Gower, wait in the room where father and son had to talk together after a separation, long to love's counting. She was a Welshwoman of the pure blood, therefore delicately mannered by nature.

'Yes, dear lad, tobacco helps you on to the marrow of your story, and I too will blow the cloud,' said Mr. Woodseer, when the plate was pushed aside and the pipe appeared.

So Gower's recital of his wanderings began, more puffs than speech at the commencement. He was alternately picturesque and sententious until he reached Baden; there he became involved, from thinking of a revelation of beauty in woman.

Mr. Woodseer rapped the leather on his block.

'A place where they have started public gambling, I am told.'

'We must look into all the corners of the world to know it, sir, and the world has to be riddled or it riddles us.'

'Ah. Did you ever tell a lie, Gower Woodseer?'

'I played.'

'You played. The Lord be thanked you have kept your straight tongue! The Lord can always enter a heart of truth. Sin cannot dwell with it. But you played for gain, and that was a licenced thieving; and that was a backsliding; and there will have to be a climbing up. And what that means, your hold on truth will learn. Touch sin and you accommodate yourself to its vileness. Ay, you love nature. Nature is not anchorage for vessels like men. If you loved the Book you would float in harbour. You played. I do trust you lost.'

'You have your wish, sir.'

'To have won their money, Gower! Rather starve.'

'I did.'

'Your reason for playing, poor lad?'

'The reason eludes reason.'

'Not in you.'

'Sight of the tables; an itch to try them—one's self as well; a notion that the losers were playing wrong. In fine, a bit of a whirl of a medley of atoms; I can't explain it further.'

'Ah. The tippler's fumes in his head! Spotty business, Gower Woodseer. "Lead us not into temptation" is worldly wisdom in addition to heavenly.'

After listening to an extended homily, with a general assent and tobacco's phlegm, Gower replied to his father's 'You starved manfully?' nodding: 'From Baden to Nancy. An Alsatian cottager at times helped me along, milk and bread.'

'Wholesome for body and for soul.'

'Entering Nancy I subscribed to the dictum of our first fathers, which dogs would deliver, if they could speak: that there is no driver like stomach: and I went head on to the College, saw the Principal: plea of urgency. No engagement possible, to teach either French or English. But he was inquisitive touching the urgency. That was my chance. The French are humane when they are not suspicious of you. They are generous, if you put a light to their minds. As I was dealing with a scholarly one, I made use of such ornamental literary skill as I possessed, to prove urgency. He supplied me with bread, fruit, and wine. In the end he procured me pupils. I lodged over a baker's shop. I had food walks, and learnt something of forestry there—a taking study. When I had saved enough to tramp it home, I said my adieux to that good friend and tramped away, entering London with about the same amount in small coin as when I entered Nancy. A manner of exactly hitting the mark, that some would not find so satisfactory as it is to me.'

The minister sighed. 'There comes in the "philosophy," I suppose. When will you understand, that this "philosophy" is only the passive of a religious faith? It seems to suit you gentlemen of the road while you are young. Work among the Whitechapel poor. It would be a way for discovering the shallows of your "philosophy" earlier.'

Gower asked him: 'Going badly here, sir?'

'Murders, robberies, misusage of women, and misconduct of women!—Drink, in short: about the same amount. Drink is their death's river, rolling them on helpless as corpses, on to—may they find mercy! I and a few stand—it's in the tide we stand here, to stop them, pluck them out, make life a bit sweet to them before the poor bodies go beneath. But come! all's not dark, we have our gleams. I speak distressed by one of our girls: a good girl, I believe; and the wilfullest that ever had command of her legs. A well-favoured girl! You'll laugh, she has given her heart to a prize-fighter. Well, you can say, she might have chosen worse. He drinks, she hates it; she loves the man and hates his vice. He swears amendment, is hiccupping at night; fights a match on the morrow, and gets beaten out of formation. No matter: whenever, wherever, that man goes to his fight, that girl follows to nurse him after it. He's her hero. Women will have one, and it's their lottery. You read of such things; here we have it alive and walking. I am led to think they 're an honest couple. They come of established families. Her mother was out of Caermarthen; died under my ministration, saintly, forgiving the drunkard. You may remember the greengrocer, Tobias Winch? He passed away in shrieks for one drop. I had to pitch my voice to the top notes to get hearing for the hymn. He was a reverent man, with the craving by fits. That should have been a lesson to Madge.'

'A little girl at the greengrocer's hard by? She sold me apples; rather pretty,' said Gower.

'A fine grown girl now—Madge Winch; a comely wench she is. It breaks her sister Sarah's heart. They both manage the little shop; they make it prosper in a small way; enough, and what need they more? Then Christopher Ines has on one of his matches. Madge drives her cart out, if it 's near town. She's off down into Kent to-day by coach, Sarah tells me. A great nobleman patronizes Christopher; a Lord Fleetwood, a lord of wealth. And he must be thoughtful for these people: he sent Sarah word that Christopher should not touch drink. You may remember a butcher Ines in the street next to us. Christopher was a wild lad, always at "best man" with every boy he met: went to sea—ran away. He returned a pugilist. The girl will be nursing him now. I have spoken to her of him; and I trust to her; but I mourn her attachment to the man who drinks.'

'The lord's name?' said Gower.

'Lord Fleetwood, Sarah named him. And so it pleases him to spend his money!'

'He has other tastes. I know something of him, sir. He promises to be a patron of Literature as well. His mother was a South Wales woman.'

'Could he be persuaded to publish a grand edition of the Triads?' Mr. Woodseer said at once.

'No man more likely '

'If you see him, suggest it.'

'Very little chance of my meeting him again. But those Triads! They're in our blood. They spring to tie knots in the head. They push me to condense my thoughts to a tight ball. They were good for primitive times: but they—or the trick of the mind engendered by them—trip my steps along the lines of composition. I produce pellets instead of flowing sheets. It'll come right. At present I 'm so bent to pick and perfect, polish my phrase, that I lose my survey. As a consequence, my vocabulary falters.'

'Ah,' Mr. Woodseer breathed and smote. 'This Literature is to be your profession for the means of living?'

'Nothing else. And I'm so low down in the market way of it, that I could not count on twenty pounds per annum. Fifty would give me standing, an independent fifty.'

'To whom are you crying, Gower?'

'Not to gamble, you may be sure.'

'You have a home.'

'Good work of the head wants an easy conscience. I've too much of you in me for a comfortable pensioner.'

'Or is it not, that you have been living the gentleman out there, with just a holiday title to it?'

Gower was hit by his father's thrust. 'I shall feel myself a pieman's chuckpenny as long as I'm unproductive, now I 've come back and have to own to a home,' he said.

Tea brought in by Mrs. Mary Jones rather brightened him until he considered that the enlivenment was due to a purchase by money, of which he was incapable, and he rejected it, like an honourable man. Simultaneously, the state of depression threw critic shades on a prized sentence or two among his recent confections. It was rejected for the best of reasons and the most discomforting: because it racked our English; signifying, that he had not yet learnt the right use of his weapons.

He was in this wrestle, under a placid demeanour, for several days, hearing the shouts of Whitechapel Kit's victory, and hearing of Sarah Winch's anxiety on account of her sister Madge; unaffected by sounds of joy or grief, in his effort to produce a supple English, with Baden's Madonna for sole illumination of his darkness. To her, to the illimitable gold-mist of perspective and the innumerable images the thought of her painted for him, he owed the lift which withdrew him from contemplation of himself in a very disturbing stagnant pool of the wastes; wherein often will strenuous youth, grown faint, behold a face beneath a scroll inscribed Impostor. All whose aim was high have spied into that pool, and have seen the face. His glorious lady would not let it haunt him.

The spell she cast had likewise power to raise him clean out of a neighbourhood hinting Erebus to the young man with thirst for air, solitudes, and colour. Scarce imaginable as she was, she reigned here, in the idea of her, more fixedly than where she had been visible; as it were, by right of her being celestially removed from the dismal place. He was at the same time not insensible to his father's contented ministrations among these homes of squalor; they pricked the curiosity, which was in the youthful philosopher a form of admiration. For his father, like all Welshmen, loved the mountains. Yet here he lived, exhorting, ministering, aiding, supported up to high good cheer by some, it seemed, superhuman backbone of uprightness;—his religious faith? Well, if so, the thing might be studied. But things of the frozen senses, lean and hueless things, were as repellent to Gower's imagination as his father's dishes to an epicure. What he envied was, the worthy old man's heart of feeling for others: his feeling at present for the girl Sarah Winch and her sister Madge, who had not been heard of since she started for the fight. Mr. Woodseer had written to her relatives at the Wells, receiving no consolatory answer.

He was relieved at last; and still a little perplexed. Madge had returned, he informed Gower. She was well, she was well in health; he had her assurances that she was not excited about herself.

'She has brought a lady with her, a great lady to lodge with her. She has brought the Countess of Fleetwood to lodge with her.'

Gower heard those words from his father; and his father repeated them. To the prostrate worshipper of the Countess of Fleetwood, they were a blow on the head; madness had set in here, was his first recovering thought, or else a miracle had come to pass. Or was it a sham Countess of Fleetwood imposing upon the girl? His father was to go and see the great lady, at the greengrocer's shop; at her request, according to Madge. Conjectures shot their perishing tracks across a darkness that deepened and made shipwreck of philosophy. Was it the very Countess of Fleetwood penitent for her dalliance with the gambling passion, in feminine need of pastor's aid, having had report from Madge of this good shepherd? His father expressed a certain surprise; his countenance was mild. He considered it a merely strange occurrence.

Perhaps, in a crisis, a minister of religion is better armed than a philosopher. Gower would not own that, but he acknowledged the evidences, and owned to envy; especially when he accompanied his father to the greengrocer's shop, and Mr. Woodseer undisturbedly said:

'Here is the place.' The small stuffed shop appeared to grow portentously cavernous and waveringly illumined.

CHAPTER XIX

THE GIRL MADGE

Customers were at the counter of the shop, and these rational figures, together with the piles of cabbages, the sacks of potatoes, the pale small oranges here and there, the dominant smell of red herrings, denied the lurking of an angelical presence behind them.

Sarah Winch and a boy served at the counter. Sarah led the Mr. Woodseers into a corner knocked off the shop and called a room. Below the top bars of a wizened grate was a chilly fire. London's light came piecemeal through a smut-streaked window. If the wonderful was to occur, this was the place to heighten it.

'My son may be an intruder,' Mr. Woodseer said. 'He is acquainted with a Lord Fleetwood...'

'Madge will know, sir,' replied Sarah, and she sent up a shrill cry for Madge from the foot of the stairs.

The girl ran down swiftly. She entered listening to Sarah, looking at Gower; to whom, after a bob and pained smile where reverence was owing, she said, 'Can you tell me, sir, please, where we can find Lord Fleetwood now?'

Gower was unable to tell. Madge turned to Mr. Woodseer, saying soon after: 'Oh, she won't mind; she'll be glad, if he knows Lord Fleetwood. I'll fetch her.'

The moments were of the palpitating order for Gower, although his common sense lectured the wildest of hearts for expecting such a possibility as the presence of his lofty lady here.

And, of course, common sense proved to be right: the lady was quite another. But she struck on a sleeping day of his travels. Her face was not one to be forgotten, and to judge by her tremble of a smile, she remembered him instantly.

They were soon conversing, each helping to paint the scene of the place where they had met.

'Lord Fleetwood has married me,' she said.

Gower bent his head; all stood silent.

'May I?' said Madge to her. 'It is Lord Fleetwood's wedded wife, sir. He drove her from her uncle's, on her wedding day, the day of a prize-fight, where I was; he told me to wait on his lady at an inn there, as I 've done and will. He drove away that evening, and he hasn't'—the girl's black eyebrows worked: 'I've not seen him since. He's a great nobleman, yes. He left his lady at the inn, expenses paid. He left her with no money. She stayed on till her heart was breaking. She has come to London to find him. She had to walk part of the way. She has only a change of linen we brought in a parcel. She's a stranger to England: she knows nobody in London. She had no place to come to but this poor hole of ours she 's so good as let welcome her. We can't do better, and it 's no use to be ashamed. She 's not a lady to scorn poor people.'

The girl's voice hummed through Gower.

He said: 'Lord Fleetwood may not be in London,' and chafed at himself for such a quaver.

'It's his house we want, sir, he has not been at his house in Kent. We want his London house.'

'My dear lady,' said Mr. Woodseer; 'it might be as well to communicate the state of things to your family without delay. My son will call at any address you name; or if it is a country address, I can write the items, with my assurances of your safety under my charge, in my house, which I beg you to make your home. My housekeeper is known to Sarah and Madge for an excellent Christian woman.'

Carinthia replied: 'You are kind to me, sir. I am grateful. I have an uncle; I would not disturb my uncle; he is inventing guns and he wishes peace. It is my husband I have come to find. He did not leave me in anger.'

She coloured. With a dimple of tenderness at one cheek, looking from Sarah to Madge, she said: 'I would not leave my friends; they are sisters to me.' Sarah, at these words, caught up her apron. Madge did no more than breathe deep and fast.

An unoccupied cold parlour in Mr. Woodseer's house that would be heated for a guest, urged him to repeat his invitation, but he took the check from Gower, who suggested the doubt of Mary Jones being so good an attendant upon Lady Fleetwood as Madge. 'And Madge has to help in the shop at times.'

Madge nodded, looked into the eyes of her mistress, which sanctioned her saying: 'She will like it best here, she is my lady and I understand her best. My lady gives no trouble: she is hardy, she's not like other ladies. I and Sarah sleep together in the room next. I can hear anything she wants. She takes us as if she was used to it.'

Sarah had to go to serve a customer. Madge made pretence of pricking her ears and followed into the shop.

'Your first visit to London is in ugly weather, Lady Fleetwood,' said Gower.

'It is my first,' she answered.

How the marriage came about, how the separation, could not be asked and was not related.

'Our district is not all London, my dear lady,' said Mr. Woodseer. 'Good hearts are here, as elsewhere, and as many, if one looks behind the dirt. I have found it since I laboured amongst them, now twenty years. Unwashed human nature, though it is natural to us to wash, is the most human, we find.'

Gower questioned the naturalness of human nature's desire to wash; and they wrangled good-humouredly, Carinthia's eyes dwelling on them each in turn; until Mr. Woodseer, pursuing the theme started by him to interest her, spoke of consolations derived from his labours here, in exchange for the loss of his mountains. Her face lightened.

'You love the mountains?'

'I am a son of the mountains.'

'Ah, I love them! Father called me a daughter of the mountains. I was born in the mountains. I was leaving my mountains on the day, I think it yesterday, when I met this gentleman who is your son.'

'A glorious day it was!' Gower exclaimed.

'It was a day of great glory for me,' said Carinthia. 'Your foot did not pain you for long?'

'The length of two pipes. You were with your brother.'

'With my brother. My brother has married a most beautiful lady. He is now travelling his happy time—my Chillon!'

There came a radiance on her under-eyelids. There was no weeping.

Struck by the contrast between the two simultaneous honeymoons, and a vision of the high-spirited mountain girl, seen in this place a young bride seeking her husband, Gower Woodseer could have performed that unphilosophical part. He had to shake himself. She seemed really a soaring bird brought down by the fowler.

Lord Fleetwood's manner of abandoning her was the mystery.

Gower stood waiting for her initiative, when the minister interposed: 'There are books, books of our titled people-the Peers, books of the Peerage. They would supply the address. My son will discover where to examine them. He will find the address. Most of the great noblemen have a London house.'

'My husband has a house in London,' Carinthia said.

'I know him, to some degree,' said Gower.

She remarked: 'I have heard that you do.'

Her lips were shut, as to any hint at his treatment of her.

Gower went into the shop to speak with Madge. The girl was talking in the business tone to customers; she finished her commission hurriedly and joined him on the pavement by the doorstep. Her voice was like the change for the swing of a door from street to temple.

'You've seen how brave she is, sir. She has things to bear. Never cries, never frets. Her marriage day—leastways... I can't, no girl can tell. A great nobleman, yes. She waited, believing in him; she does. She hasn't spoken to me of what she's had to bear. I don't know; I guess; I'm sure I'm right—and him a man! Girls learn to know men, call them gentlemen or sweeps. She thinks she has only to meet him to persuade him she 's fit to be loved by him. She thinks of love. Would he—our tongues are tied except among ourselves to a sister. Leaves her by herself, with only me, after—it knocks me dumb! Many a man commits a murder wouldn't do that. She could force him to—no, it isn't a house she wants, she wants him. He's her husband, Mr. Woodseer. You will do what you can to help; I judge by your father. I and Sarah 'll slave for her to be as comfortable—as we—can make her; we can't give her what she 's used to. I shall count the hours.'

'You sold me apples when your head was just above the counter,' said Gower.

'Did I?—you won't lose time, sir?' she rejoined. 'Her box is down at the beastly inn in Kent. Kind people, I dare say; their bill was paid any extent, they said. And he might do as he liked in it—enter it like a thief, if it pleased him, and off like one, and they no wiser. She walked to his big house Esslemont for news of him. And I'm not a snivelling wench either; but she speaks of him a way to make a girl drink her tears, if they ain't to be let fall.'

'But you had a victory down there,' Gower hinted congratulations.

'Ah,' said she.

'Christopher Ines is all right now?'

'I've as good as lost my good name for Kit Ines, Mr. Woodseer.'

'Not with my dad, Madge.'

'The minister reads us at the heart. Shall we hear the street of his house in London before night?'

'I may be late.'

'I'll be up, any hour, for a rap at the shutters. I want to take her to the house early next morning. She won't mind the distance. She lies in bed, her eyes shut or open, never sleeping, hears any mouse. It shouldn't go on, if we can do a thing to help.'

'I'm off,' said Gower, unwontedly vexed at his empty pocket, that could not offer the means for conveyance to a couple of young women.

The dark-browed girl sent her straight eyes at him. They pushed him to hasten. On second thoughts, he stopped and hailed her; he was moved to confirm an impression of this girl's features.

His mind was directed to the business burning behind them, honestly enough, as soon as he had them in sight again.

'I ought to have the address of some of her people, in case,' he said.

'She won't go to her uncle, I 'm sure of that,' said Madge. 'He 's a lord and can't be worried. It 's her husband to find first.'

'If he's to be found!—he's a lord, too. Has she no other relatives or friends?'

'She loves her brother. He's an officer. He's away on honeymoon. There 's an admiral down Hampshire way, a place I've been near and seen. I'd not have you go to any of them, sir, without trying all we can do to find Lord Fleetwood. It's Admiral Fakenham she speaks of; she's fond of him. She's not minded to bother any of her friends about herself.'

'I shall see you to-night,' said Gower, and set his face Westward, remembering that his father had named Caermarthen as her mother's birthplace.

Just in that tone of hers do Welshwomen talk of their country; of its history, when at home, of its mountains, when exiled: and in a language like hers, bare of superlatives to signify an ardour conveyed by the fire of the breath. Her quick devotion to a lady exciting enthusiasm through admiring pity for the grace of a much-tried quiet sweetness, was explained; apart from other reasons, feminine or hidden, which might exist. Only a Welsh girl would be so quick and all in it, with a voice intimating a heated cauldron under her mouth. None but a Welsh-blooded girl, risking her good name to follow and nurse the man she considered a hero, would carry her head to look virgin eyes as she did. One could swear to them, Gower thought. Contact with her spirited him out of his mooniness.

He had the Cymric and Celtic respect of character; which puts aside the person's environments to face the soul. He was also an impressionable fellow among his fellows, a philosopher only at his leisure, in his courted solitudes. Getting away some strides from this girl of the drilling voice,—the shudder-voice, he phrased it,—the lady for whom she pleaded came clearer into his view and gradually absorbed him; though it was an emulation with the girl Madge, of which he was a trifle conscious, that drove him to do his work of service in the directest manner. He then fancied the girl had caught something of the tone of her lady: the savage intensity or sincerity; and he brooded on Carinthia's position, the mixture of the astounding and the woful in her misadventure. One could almost laugh at our human fate, to think of a drop off the radiant mountain heights upon a Whitechapel greengrocer's shop, gathering the title of countess midway.

But nothing of the ludicrous touched her; no, and if we bring reason to scan our laugh at pure humanity, it is we who are in the place of the ridiculous, for doing what reason disavows. Had he not named her, Carinthia, Saint and Martyr, from a first perusal of her face? And Lord Fleetwood had read and repeated it. Lord Fleetwood had become the instrument to martyrize her? That might be; there was a hoard of bad stuff in his composition besides the precious: and this was a nobleman owning enormous wealth, who could vitiate himself by disposing of a multitude of men and women to serve his will, a shifty will. Wealth creates the magician, and may breed the fiend within him. In the hands of a young man, wealth is an invitation to devilry. Gower's idea of the story of Carinthia inclined to charge Lord Fleetwood with every possible false dealing. He then quashed the charge, and decided to wait for information.

At the second of the aristocratic Clubs of London's West, into which he stepped like an easy member, the hall-porter did not examine his clothing from German hat to boots, and gave him Lord Fleetwood's town address. He could tell Madge at night by the door of the shuttered shop, that Lord Fleetwood had gone down to Wales.

'It means her having to wait,' she said. 'The minister has been to the coach-office, to order up her box from that inn. He did it in his name; they can't refuse; no money's owing. She must have a change. Sally has fifteen pounds locked up in case of need.'

Sally's capacity and economy fetched the penniless philosopher a slap.

'You've taken to this lady,' he said.

'She held my hand, while Kit Ines was at his work; and I was new to her, and a prize-fighter's lass, they call me:—upon the top of that nobleman's coach, where he made me sit, behind her, to see the fight; and she his wedded lady that morning. A queer groom. He may keep Kit Ines from drink, he's one of you men, and rides over anything in his way. I can't speak about it; I could swear it before a judge, from what I know. Those Rundles at that inn don't hear anything it suits him to do. All the people down in those parts are slaves to him. And I thought he was a real St. George before,—yes, ready I was to kiss the ground his feet crossed. If you could, it's Chinningfold near where Admiral Fakenham lives, down Hampshire way. Her friends ought to hear what's happened to her. They'll find her in a queer place. She might go to the minister's. I believe she's happier with us girls.'

Gower pledged his word to start for Chinningfold early as the light next day. He liked the girl the better, in an amicable fashion, now that his nerves had got free of the transient spell of her kettle tone—the hardly varied one note of a heart boiling with sisterly devotion to a misused stranger of her sex;—and, after the way of his race, imagination sprang up in him, at the heels of the quieted senses, releasing him from the personal and physical to grasp the general situation and place the protagonist foremost.

He thought of Carinthia, with full vision of her. Some wrong had been done, or some violation of the right, to guess from the girl Madge's molten words in avoidance of the very words. It implied—though it might be but one of Love's shrewder discords—such suspected traitorous dealing of a man with their sister woman as makes the world of women all woman toward her. They can be that, and their being so illuminates their hidden sentiments in relation to the mastering male, whom they uphold.

But our uninformed philosopher was merely picking up scraps of sheddings outside the dark wood of the mystery they were to him, and playing imagination upon them. This primary element of his nature soon enthroned his chosen lady above their tangled obscurities. Beneath her tranquil beams, with the rapture of the knowledge that her name on earth was Livia, he threaded East London's thoroughfares,— on a morning when day and night were made one by fog, to journey down to Chinningfold, by coach, in the service of the younger Countess of Fleetwood, whose right to the title he did not doubt, though it directed surprise movements at his understanding from time to time.

BOOK III

CHAPTER XX

STUDIES IN FOG, GOUT, AN OLD SEAMAN, A LOVELY SERPENT, AND THE MORAL EFFECTS THAT MAY COME OF A BORROWED SHIRT

Money of his father's enabled Gower to take the coach; and studies in fog, from the specked brown to the woolly white, and the dripping torn, were proposed to the traveller, whose preference of Nature's face did not arrest his observation of her domino and petticoats; across which blank sheets he curiously read backward, that he journeyed by the aid of his father's hard-earned, ungrudged piece of gold. Without it, he would have been useless in this case of need. The philosopher could starve with equanimity, and be the stronger. But one had, it seemed here clearly, to put on harness and trudge along a line, if the unhappy were to have one's help. Gradual experiences of his business among his fellows were teaching an exercised mind to learn in regions where minds unexercised were doctorial giants beside it.

The study of gout was offered at Chinningfold. Admiral Fakenham's butler refused at first to take a name to his master. Gower persisted, stating the business of his mission; and in spite of the very suspicious glib good English spoken by a man wearing such a hat and suit, the butler was induced to consult Mrs. Carthew.

She sprang up alarmed. After having seen the young lady happily married and off with her lordly young husband, the arrival of a messenger from the bride gave a stir the wrong way to her flowing recollections; the scenes and incidents she had smothered under her love of the comfortable stood forth appallingly. The messenger, the butler said, was no gentleman. She inspected Gower and heard him speak. An anomaly had come to the house; for he had the language of a gentleman, the appearance of a nondescript; he looked indifferent, he spoke sympathetically; and he was frank as soon as the butler was out of hearing. In return for the compliment, she invited him to her sitting-room. The story of the young countess, whom she had seen driven away by her husband from the church in a coach and four, as being now destitute, praying to see her friends, in the Whitechapel of London—the noted haunt of thieves and outcasts, bankrupts and the abandoned; set her asking for the first time, who was the man with dreadful countenance inside the coach? A previously disregarded horror of a man. She went trembling to the admiral, though his health was delicate, his temper excitable. It was, she considered, an occasion for braving the doctor's interdict.

Gower was presently summoned to the chamber where Admiral Fakenham reclined on cushions in an edifice of an arm-chair. He told a plain tale. Its effect was to straighten the admiral's back, and enlarge in grey glass a pair of sea-blue eyes. And, 'What's that? Whitechapel?' the admiral exclaimed,—at high pitch, far above his understanding. The particulars were repeated, whereupon the sick-room shook with,

'Greengrocer?' He stunned himself with another of the monstrous points in his pet girl's honeymoon: 'A prizefight?'

To refresh a saving incredulity, he took a closer view of the messenger. Gower's habiliments were those of the 'queer fish,' the admiral saw. But the meeting at Carlsruhe was recalled to him, and there was a worthy effort to remember it. 'Prize-fight!—Greengrocer! Whitechapel!' he rang the changes rather more moderately; till, swelling and purpling, he cried: 'Where's the husband?'

That was the emissary's question likewise.

'If I could have found him, sir, I should not have troubled you.'

'Disappeared? Plays the man of his word, then plays the madman! Prize-fight the first day of her honeymoon? Good Lord! Leaves her at the inn?'

'She was left.'

'When was she left?'

'As soon as the fight was over—as far as I understand.'

The admiral showered briny masculine comments on that bridegroom.

'Her brother's travelling somewhere in the Pyrenees—married my daughter. She has an uncle, a hermit.' He became pale. 'I must do it. The rascal insults us all. Flings her off the day he married her! It 's a slap in the face to all of us. You are acquainted with the lady, sir. Would you call her a red-haired girl?'

'Red-gold of the ballads; chestnut-brown, with threads of fire.'

'She has the eyes for a man to swear by. I feel the loss of her, I can tell you. She was wine and no penalty to me. Is she much broken under it?—if I 'm to credit... I suppose I must. It floors me.'

Admiral Baldwin's frosty stare returned on him. Gower caught an image of it, as comparable, without much straining, to an Arctic region smitten by the beams.

'Nothing breaks her courage,' he said.

'To be sure, my poor dear! Who could have guessed when she left my house she was on her way to a prizefight and a greengrocer's in Whitechapel. But the dog's not mad, though his bite 's bad; he 's an eccentric mongrel. He wants the whip; ought to have had it regularly from his first breeching. He shall whistle for her when he repents; and he will, mark me. This gout here will be having a snap at the vitals if I don't start to-night. Oblige me, half a minute.'

The admiral stretched his hand for an arm to give support, stood, and dropped into the chair, signifying a fit of giddiness in the word 'Head.'

Before the stupor had passed, Mrs. Carthew entered, anxious lest the admittance of a messenger of evil to her invalid should have been an error of judgement. The butler had argued it with her. She belonged to the list of persons appointed to cut life's thread when it strains, their general kindness being so liable to misdirection.

Gower left the room and went into the garden. He had never seen a death; and the admiral's peculiar pallor intimated events proper to days of cold mist and a dripping stillness. How we go, was the question among his problems:—if we are to go! his youthful frame insistingly added.

The fog down a wet laurel-walk contracted his mind with the chilling of his blood, and he felt that he would have to see the thing if he was to believe in it. Of course he believed, but life throbbed rebelliously, and a picture of a desk near a lively fire-grate, books and pen and paper, and a piece of writing to be approved of by the Hesper of ladies, held ground with a pathetic heroism against the inevitable. He got his wits to the front by walking faster; and then thought of the young countess and the friend she might be about to lose. She could number her friends on her fingers. Admiral Fakenham's exclamations of the name of the place where she now was, conveyed an inky idea of the fall she had undergone. Counting her absent brother, with himself, his father, and the two Whitechapel girls, it certainly was an unexampled fall, to say of her, that they and those two girls had become by the twist of circumstances the most serviceable of her friends.

Her husband was the unriddled riddle we have in the wealthy young lord,—burning to possess, and making, tatters of all he grasped, the moment it was his own. Glints of the devilish had shot from him at the gamingtables,—fine haunts for the study of our lower man. He could be magnificent in generosity; he had little humaneness. He coveted beauty in women hungrily, and seemed to be born hostile to them; or so Gower judged by the light of the later evidence on unconsidered antecedent observations of him. Why marry her to cast her off instantly? The crude philosopher asked it as helplessly as the admiral. And, further, what did the girl Madge mean by the drop of her voice to a hum of enforced endurance under injury, like the furnace behind an iron door? Older men might have understood, as he was aware; he might have guessed, only he had the habit of scattering meditation upon the game of hawk and fowl.

Dame Gossip boils. Her one idea of animation is to have her dramatis persona in violent motion, always the biggest foremost; and, indeed, that is the way to make them credible, for the wind they raise and the succession of collisions. The fault of the method is, that they do not instruct; so the breath is out of them before they are put aside; for the uninstructive are the humanly deficient: they remain with us like the tolerated old aristocracy, which may not govern, and is but socially seductive. The deuteragonist or secondary person can at times tell us more of them than circumstances at furious heat will help them to reveal; and the Dame will have him only as an index-post. Hence her endless ejaculations over the mystery of Life, the inscrutability of character,—in a plain world, in the midst of such readable people! To preserve Romance (we exchange a sky for a ceiling if we let it go), we must be inside the heads of our people as well as the hearts, more than shaking the kaleidoscope of hurried spectacles, in days of a growing activity of the head.

Gower Woodseer could not know that he was drawn on to fortune and the sight of his Hesper by Admiral Fakenham's order that the visitor was to stay at his house until he should be able to quit his bed, and journey with him to London, doctor or no doctor. The doctor would not hear of it. The admiral threatened it every night for the morning, every morning for the night; and Gower had to submit to postponements balefully affecting his linen. Remonstrance was not to be thought of; for at a mere show of reluctance the courtly admiral flushed, frowned, and beat the bed where he lay, a gouty volcano. Gower's one shirt was passing through the various complexions, and had approached the Nubian on its way to negro. His natural candour checked the downward course. He mentioned to Mrs. Carthew, with incidental gravity, on a morning at breakfast, that this article of his attire 'was beginning to resemble London snow.' She was amused; she promised him a change more resembling country snow. 'It will save me from buttoning so high up,' he said, as he thanked her. She then remembered the daily increase of stiffness in his figure: and a reflection upon his patient waiting, and simpleness, and lexicographer speech to expose his minor needs, touched her unused sense of humour on the side where it is tender in women, from being motherly.

In consequence, she spoke of him with a pleading warmth to the Countess Livia, who had come down to see the admiral 'concerning an absurd but annoying rumour running over London.' Gower was out for a walk. He knew of the affair, Mrs. Carthew said, for an introduction to her excuses of his clothing.

'But I know the man,' said Livia. 'Lord Fleetwood picked him up somewhere, and brought him to us. Clever: Why, is he here?'

'He is here, sent to the admiral, as I understand, my lady.'

'Sent by whom?'

Having but a weak vocabulary to defend a delicate position, Mrs. Carthew stuttered into evasions, after the way of ill-armed persons; and naming herself a stranger to the circumstances, she feebly suggested that the admiral ought not to be disturbed before the doctor's next visit; Mr. Woodseer had been allowed to sit by his bed yesterday only for ten minutes, to divert him with his talk. She protected in this wretched manner the poor gentleman she sacrificed and emitted such a smell of secresy, that Livia wrote three words on her card, for it to be taken to Admiral Baldwin at once. Mrs. Carthew supplicated faintly; she was unheeded.

The Countess of Fleetwood mounted the stairs—to descend them with the knowledge of her being the Dowager Countess of Fleetwood! Henrietta had spoken of the Countess of Fleetwood's hatred of the title of Dowager. But when Lady Fleetwood had the fact from the admiral, would she forbear to excite him? If she repudiated it, she would provoke him to fire 'one of his broadsides,'—as they said in the family, to assert its and that might exhaust him; and there was peril in that. And who was guilty? Mrs. Carthew confessed her guilt, asking how it could have been avoided. She made appeal to Gower on his return, transfixing him.

Not only is he no philosopher who has an idol, he has to learn that he cannot think rationally; his due sense of weight and measure is lost, the choice of his thoughts as well. He was in the house with his devoutly, simply worshipped, pearl of women, and his whole mind fell to work without ado upon the extravagant height of the admiral's shirt-collar cutting his ears. The very beating of his heart was perplexed to know whether it was for rapture or annoyance. As a result he was but histrionically master of himself when the Countess Livia or the nimbus of the lady appeared in the room.

She received his bow; she directed Mrs. Carthew to have the doctor summoned immediately. The remorseful woman flew.

'Admiral Fakenham is very ill, Mr. Woodseer, he has had distracting news. Oh, no, the messenger is not blamed. You are Lord Fleetwood's friend and will not allow him to be prejudged. He will be in town shortly. I know him well, you know him; and could you hear him accused of cruelty—and to a woman? He is the soul of chivalry. So, in his way, is the admiral. If he were only more patient! Let us wait for Lord

Fleetwood's version. I am certain it will satisfy me. The admiral wishes you to step up to him. Be very quiet; you will be; consent to everything. I was unaware of his condition: the things I heard were incredible. I hope the doctor will not delay. Now go. Beg to retire soon.'

Livia spoke under her breath; she had fears.

Admiral Baldwin lay in his bed, submitting to a nurse-woman-sign of extreme exhaustion. He plucked strength from the sight of Gower and bundled the woman out of the room, muttering: 'Kill myself? Not half so quick as they'd do it. I can't rest for that Whitechapel of yours. Please fetch pen and paper: it's a letter.'

The letter began, 'Dear Lady Arpington.'

The dictation of it came in starts. Atone moment it seemed as if life's ending shook the curtains on our stage and were about to lift. An old friend in the reader of the letter would need no excuse for its jerky brevity. It said that his pet girl, Miss Kirby, was married to the Earl of Fleetwood in the first week of last month, and was now to be found at a shop No. 45 Longways, Whitechapel; that the writer was ill, unable to stir; that he would be in London within eight-and-forty hours at furthest. He begged Lady Arpington to send down to the place and have the young countess fetched to her, and keep her until he came.

Admiral Baldwin sat up to sign the letter.

'Yes, and write "miracles happen when the devil's abroad"—done it!' he said, sinking back. 'Now seal, you'll find wax—the ring at my watch-chain.'

He sighed, as it were the sound of his very last; he lay like a sleeper twitched by a dream. There had been a scene with Livia. The dictating of the letter took his remainder of strength out of him.

Gower called in the nurse, and went downstairs. He wanted the address of Lady Arpington's town house.

'You have a letter for her?' said Livia, and held her hand for it in a way not to be withstood.

'There's no superscription,' he remarked.

'I will see to that, Mr. Woodseer.'

'I fancy I am bound, Lady Fleetwood.'

'By no means.' She touched his arm. 'You are Lord Fleetwood's friend.'

A slight convulsion of the frame struck the admiral's shirt-collar at his ears; it virtually prostrated him under foot of a lady so benign in overlooking the spectacle he presented. Still, he considered; he had wits alive enough, just to perceive a duty.

'The letter was entrusted to me, Lady Fleetwood.'

'You are afraid to entrust it to the post?'

'I was thinking of delivering it myself in town.'

'You will entrust it to me.'

'Anything on earth of my own.'

'The treasure would be valued. This you confide to my care.'

'It is important.'

'No.'

'Indeed it is.'

'Say that it is, then. It is quite safe with me. It may be important that it should not be delivered. Are you not Lord Fleetwood's friend? Lady Arpington is not so very, very prominent in the list with you and me. Besides, I don't think she has come to town yet. She generally sees out the end of the hunting season. Leave the letter to me: it shall go. You, with your keen observation missing nothing, have seen that my uncle has not his whole judgement at present. There are two sides to a case. Lord Fleetwood's friend will know that it would be unfair to offer him up to his enemies while he is absent. Things going favourably here, I drive back to town to-morrow, and I hope you will accept a seat in my carriage.'

He delivered his courtliest; he was riding on cloud.

They talked of Baden. His honourable surrender of her defeated purse was a subject for gentle humour with her, venturesome compliment with him. He spoke well; and though his hands were clean of Sir Meeson Corby's reproach of them, the caricature of presentable men blushed absurdly and seemed uneasy in his monstrous collar. The touching of him again would not be required to set him pacing to her steps. His hang of the head testified to the unerring stamp of a likeness Captain Abrane could affix with a stroke: he looked the fiddler over his bow, playing wonderfully to conceal the crack of a string. The merit of being one of her army of admirers was accorded to him. The letter to Lady Arpington was retained.

Gower deferred the further mention of the letter until a visit to the admiral's chamber should furnish an excuse; and he had to wait for it. Admiral Baldwin's condition was becoming ominous. He sent messages downstairs by the doctor, forbidding his guest's departure until they two could make the journey together next day. The tortured and blissful young man, stripped of his borrowed philosopher's cloak, hung conscience-ridden in this delicious bower, which was perceptibly an antechamber of the vaults, offering him the study he thirsted for, shrank from, and mixed with his cup of amorous worship.

CHAPTER XXI

IN WHICH WE HAVE FURTHER GLIMPSES OF THE WONDROUS MECHANISM OF OUR YOUNGER MAN

The report of Admiral Baldwin Fakenham as having died in the arms of a stranger visiting the house, hit nearer the mark than usual. He yielded his last breath as Gower Woodseer was lowering him to his pillow, shortly after a husky whisper of the letter to Lady Arpington; and that was one of Gower's crucial trials. It condemned him, for the pacifying of a dying man, to the murmur and shuffle, which was a lie; and the lie burnt him, contributed to the brand on his race. He and his father upheld a solitary bare staff, where the Cambrian flag had flown, before their people had been trampled in mire, to do as the worms. His loathing of any shadow of the lie was a protest on behalf of Welsh blood against an English charge, besides the passion for spiritual cleanliness: without which was no comprehension, therefore no enjoyment, of Nature possible to him. For Nature is the Truth.

He begged the countess to let him have the letter; he held to the petition, with supplications; he spoke of his pledged word, his honour; and her countenance did not deny to such an object as she beheld the right to a sense of honour. 'We all have the sentiment, I hope, Mr. Woodseer,' she said, stupefying the worshipper, who did not see it manifested. There was a look of gentle intimacy, expressive of common grounds between them, accompanying the dead words. Mistress of the letter, and the letter safe under lock, the admiral dead, she had not to bestow a touch of her hand on his coatsleeve in declining to return it. A face languidly and benevolently querulous was bent on him, when he, so clever a man, resumed his very silly petition.

She was moon out of cloud at a change of the theme. Gower journeyed to London without the letter, intoxicated, and conscious of poison; enamoured of it, and straining for health. He had to reflect at the journey's end, that he had picked up nothing on the road, neither a thing observed nor a thing imagined; he was a troubled pool instead of a flowing river.

The best help to health for him was a day in his father's house. We are perpetually at our comparisons of ourselves with others; and they are mostly profitless; but the man carrying his religious light, to light the darkest ways of his fellows, and keeping good cheer, as though the heart of him ran a mountain water through the grimy region, plucked at Gower with an envy to resemble him in practice. His philosophy, too, reproached him for being outshone. Apart from his philosophy, he stood confessed a bankrupt; and it had dwindled to near extinction. Adoration of a woman takes the breath out of philosophy. And if one had only to say sheer donkey, he consenting to be driven by her! One has to say worse in this case; for the words are, liar and traitor.

Carinthia's attitude toward his father conduced to his emulous respect for the old man, below whom, and indeed below the roadway of ordinary principles hedged with dull texts, he had strangely fallen. The sight of her lashed him. She made it her business or it was her pleasure to go the rounds beside Mr. Woodseer visiting his poor people. She spoke of the scenes she witnessed, and threw no stress on the wretchedness, having only the wish to assist in ministering. Probably the great wretchedness bubbling over the place blunted her feeling of loss at the word of Admiral Baldwin's end; her bosom sprang up: 'He was next to father,' was all she said; and she soon reverted to this and that house of the lodgings of poverty. She had descended on the world. There was of course a world outside Whitechapel, but Whitechapel was hot about her; the nests of misery, the sharp note of want in the air, tricks of an urchin who had amused her.

As to the place itself, she had no judgement to pronounce, except that: 'They have no mornings here'; and the childish remark set her quivering on her heights, like one seen through a tear, in Gower's memory. Scarce anything of her hungry impatience to meet her husband was visible: she had come to London to meet him; she hoped to meet him soon: before her brother's return, she could have added.

She mentioned the goodness of Sarah Winch in not allowing that she was a burden to support. Money and its uses had impressed her; the quantity possessed by some, the utter need of it for the first of human purposes by others. Her speech was not of so halting or foreign an English. She grew rapidly wherever she was planted.

Speculation on the conduct of her husband, empty as it might be, was necessitated in Gower. He pursued it, and listened to his father similarly at work: 'A young lady fit for any station, the kindest of souls, a born charitable human creature, void of pride, near in all she—does and thinks to the Shaping Hand, why should her husband forsake her on the day of their nuptials.

She is most gracious; the simplicity of an infant. Can you imagine the doing of an injury by a man to a woman like her?'

Then it was that Gower screwed himself to say:

'Yes, I can imagine it, I'm doing it myself. I shall be doing it till I've written a letter and paid a visit.'

He took a meditative stride or two in the room, thinking without revulsion of the Countess Livia under a similitude of the bell of the plant henbane, and that his father had immunity from temptation because of the insensibility to beauty. Out of which he passed to the writing of the letter to Lord Fleetwood, informing his lordship that he intended immediately to deliver a message to the Marchioness of Arpington from Admiral Baldwin Fakenham, in relation to the Countess of Fleetwood. A duty was easily done by Gower when he had surmounted the task of conceiving his resolution to do it; and this task, involving an offence to the Lady Livia and intrusion of his name on a nobleman's recollection, ranked next in severity to the chopping off of his fingers by a man suspecting them of the bite of rabies.

An interview with Lady Arpington was granted him the following day.

She was a florid, aquiline, loud-voiced lady, evidently having no seat for her wonderments, after his account of the origin of his acquaintance with the admiral had quieted her suspicions. The world had only to stand beside her, and it would hear what she had heard. She rushed to the conclusion that Lord Fleetwood had married a person of no family.

'Really, really, that young man's freaks appear designed for the express purpose of heightening our amazement!' she exclaimed. 'He won't easily get beyond a wife in the east of London, at a shop; but there's no knowing. Any wish of Admiral Baldwin Fakenham's I hold sacred. At least I can see for myself. You can't tell me more of the facts? If Lord Fleetwood's in town, I will call him here at once. I will drive down to this address you give me. She is a civil person?'

'Her breeding is perfect,' said Gower.

'Perfect breeding, you say?' Lady Arpington was reduced to a murmur. She considered the speaker: his outlandish garb, his unprotesting self-possession. He spoke good English by habit, her ear told her. She was of an eminence to judge of a man impartially, even to the sufferance of an opinion from him, on a subject that lesser ladies would have denied to his clothing. Outwardly simple, naturally frank, though a tangle of the complexities inwardly, he was a touchstone for true aristocracy, as the humblest who bear the main elements of it must be. Certain humorous turns in his conversation won him an amicable smile when he bowed to leave: they were the needed finish of a favourable impression.

One day later the earl arrived in town, read Gower Woodseer's brief words, and received the consequently expected summons, couched in a great lady's plain imperative. She was connected with his family on the paternal side.

He went obediently; not unwillingly, let the deputed historian of the Marriage, turning over documents, here say. He went to Lady Arpington disposed for marital humaneness and jog-trot harmony, by condescension; equivalent to a submitting to the drone of an incessant psalm at the drum of the ear. He was, in fact, rather more than inclined that way. When very young, at the age of thirteen, a mood of religious fervour had spiritualized the dulness of Protestant pew and pulpit for him. Another fit of it, in the Roman Catholic direction, had proposed, during his latest dilemma, to relieve him of the burden of his pledged word. He had plunged for a short space into the rapturous contemplation of a monastic life—'the clean soul for the macerated flesh,' as that fellow Woodseer said once: and such as his friend, the Roman Catholic Lord Feltre, moodily talked of getting in his intervals. He had gone down to a young and novel trial establishment of English penitents in the forest of a Midland county, and had watched and envied, and seen the escape from a lifelong bondage to the 'beautiful Gorgon,' under cover of a white flannel frock. The world pulled hard, and he gave his body into chains of a woman, to redeem his word.

But there was a plea on behalf of this woman. The life she offered might have psalmic iteration; the dead monotony of it in prospect did, nevertheless, exorcise a devil. Carinthia promised, it might seem to chase and keep the black beast out of him permanently, as she could, he now conceived: for since the day of the marriage with her, the devil inhabiting him had at least been easier, 'up in a corner.'

He held an individual memory of his bride, rose-veiled, secret to them both, that made them one, by subduing him. For it was a charm; an actual feminine, an unanticipated personal, charm; past reach of tongue to name, wordless in thought. There, among the folds of the incense vapours of our heart's holy of holies, it hung; and it was rare, it was distinctive of her, and alluring, if one consented to melt to it, and accepted for compensation the exorcising of a devil.

Oh, but no mere devil by title!—a very devil. It was alert and frisky, flushing, filling the thin cold idea of Henrietta at a thought; and in the thought it made Carinthia's intimate charm appear as no better than a thing to enrich a beggar, while he knew that kings could never command the charm. Not love, only the bathing in Henrietta's incomparable beauty and the desire to be, desire to have been, the casket of it, broke the world to tempest and lightnings at a view of Henrietta the married woman—married to the brother of the woman calling him husband:—'It is my husband.' The young tyrant of wealth could have avowed that he did not love Henrietta; but not the less was he in the swing of a whirlwind at the hint of her loving the man she had married. Did she? It might be tried.

She? That Henrietta is one of the creatures who love pleasure, love flattery, love their beauty: they cannot love a man. Or the love is a ship that will not sail a sea.

Now, if the fact were declared and attested, if her shallowness were seen proved, one might get free of the devil she plants in the breast. Absolutely to despise her would be release, and it would allow of his tasting Carinthia's charm, reluctantly acknowledged; not 'money of the country' beside that golden Henrietta's.

Yet who can say?—women are such deceptions. Often their fairest, apparently sweetest, when brought to the keenest of the tests, are graceless; or worse, artificially consonant; in either instance barren of the poetic. Thousands of the confidently expectant among men have been unbewitched; a lamentable process; and the grimly reticent and the loudly discursive are equally eloquent of the pretty general disillusion. How they loathe and tear the mask of the sham attraction that snatched them to the hag yoke, and fell away to show its grisly horrors within the round of the month, if not the second enumeration of twelve by the clock! Fleetwood had heard certain candid seniors talk, delivering their minds in superior appreciation of unpretentious boor wenches, nature's products, not esteemed by him. Well, of a truth, she—'Red Hair and Rugged Brows,' as the fellow Woodseer had called her, in alternation with 'Mountain Face to Sun'—she at the unveiling was gentle, surpassingly; graceful in the furnace of the trial. She wore through the critic ordeal his burning sensitiveness to grace and delicacy cast about a woman, and was rather better than not withered by it.

On the borders between maidenly and wifely, she, a thing of flesh like other daughters of earth, had impressed her sceptical lord, inclining to contempt of her and detestation of his bargain, as a flitting hue, ethereal, a transfiguration of earthliness in the core of the earthly furnace. And how?—but that it must have been the naked shining forth of her character, startled to show itself:—'It is my husband':—it must have been love.

The love that they versify, and strum on guitars, and go crazy over, and end by roaring at as the delusion; this common bloom of the ripeness of a season; this would never have utterly captured a sceptic, to vanquish him in his mastery, snare him in her surrender. It must have been the veritable passion: a flame kept alive by vestal ministrants in the yewwood of the forest of Old Romance; planted only in the breasts of very favourite maidens. Love had eyes, love had a voice that night,-love was the explicable magic lifting terrestrial to seraphic. Though, true, she had not Henrietta's golden smoothness of beauty. Henrietta, illumined with such a love, would outdo all legends, all dreams of the tale of love. Would she? For credulous men she would be golden coin of the currency. She would not have a particular wild flavour: charm as of the running doe that has taken a dart and rolls an eye to burst the hunter's heart with pity.

Fleetwood went his way to Lady Arpington almost complacently, having fought and laid his wilder self. He might be likened to the doctor's patient entering the chemist's shop, with a prescription for a drug of healing virtue, upon which the palate is as little consulted as a robustious lollypop boy in the household of ceremonial parents, who have rung for the troop of their orderly domestics to sit in a row and hearken the intonation of good words.

CHAPTER XXII

A RIGHT-MINDED GREAT LADY

The bow, the welcome, and the introductory remarks passed rapidly as the pull at two sides of a curtain opening on a scene that stiffens courtliness to hard attention.

After the names of Admiral Baldwin and 'the Mr. Woodseer,' the name of Whitechapel was mentioned by Lady Arpington. It might have been the name of any other place.

'Ah, so far, then, I have to instruct you,' she said, observing the young earl. 'I drove down there yesterday. I saw the lady calling herself Countess of Fleetwood. By right? She was a Miss Kirby.'

'She has the right,' Fleetwood said, standing well up out of a discharge of musketry.

'Marriage not contested. You knew of her being in that place?—I can't describe it.'

'Your ladyship will pardon me?'

London's frontier of barbarism was named for him again, and in a tone to penetrate.

He refrained from putting the question of how she had come there.

As iron as he looked, he said: 'She stays there by choice.'

The great lady tapped her foot on the floor.

'You are not acquainted with the district.'

'One of my men comes out of it.'

'The coming out of it!... However, I understand her story, that she travelled from a village inn, where she had been left-without resources. She waited weeks; I forget how many. She has a description of maid in attendance on her. She came to London to find her husband. You were at the mines, we heard. Her one desire is to meet her husband. But, goodness! Fleetwood, why do you frown? You acknowledge the marriage, she has the name of the church; she was married out of that old Lord Levellier's house. You drove her—I won't repeat the flighty business. You left her, and she did her best to follow you. Will the young men of our time not learn that life is no longer a game when they have a woman for partner in the match!

You don't complain of her flavour of a foreign manner? She can't be so very... Admiral Baldwin's daughter has married her brother; and he is a military officer. She has germs of breeding, wants only a little rub of the world to smooth her. Speak to the point:—do you meet her here? Do you refuse?'

'At present? I do.'

'Something has to be done.'

'She was bound to stay where I left her.'

'You are bound to provide for her becomingly.'

'Provision shall be made, of course.'

'The story will... unless—and quickly, too.'

I know, I know!'

Fleetwood had the clang of all the bells of London chiming Whitechapel at him in his head, and he betrayed the irritated tyrant ready to decree fire and sword, for the defence or solace of his tender sensibilities.

The black flash flew.

'It 's a thing to mend as well as one can,' Lady Arpington said. 'I am not inquisitive: you had your reasons or chose to act without any. Get her away from that place. She won't come to me unless it 's to meet her husband. Ah, well, temper does not solve your problem; husband you are, if you married her. We'll leave the husband undiscussed: with this reserve, that it seems to me men are now beginning to play the misunderstood.'

'I hope they know themselves better,' said Fleetwood; and he begged for the name and number of the house in the Whitechapel street, where she who was discernibly his enemy, and the deadliest of enemies, had now her dwelling.

Her immediate rush to that place, the fixing of herself there for an assault on him, was a move worthy the daughter of the rascal Old Buccaneer; it compelled to urgent measures. He, as he felt horribly in pencilling her address, acted under compulsion; and a woman prodded the goad. Her mask of ingenuousness was flung away for a look of craft, which could be power; and with her changed aspect his tolerance changed to hatred.

'A shop,' Lady Arpington explained for his better direction: 'potatoes, vegetable stuff. Honest people, I am to believe. She is indifferent to her food, she says. She works, helping one of their ministers—one of their denominations: heaven knows what they call themselves! Anything to escape from the Church! She's likely to become a Methodist. With Lord Feltre proselytizing for his Papist creed, Lord Pitscrew a declared Mohammedan, we shall have a pretty English aristocracy in time. Well, she may claim to belong to it now. She would not be persuaded against visitations to pestiferous hovels. What else is there to do in such a place? She goes about catching diseases to avoid bilious melancholy in the dark back room of a small greengrocer's shop in Whitechapel. There—you have the word for the Countess of Fleetwood's present address.'

It drenched him with ridicule.

'I am indebted to your ladyship for the information,' he said, and maintained his rigidity.

The great lady stiffened.

'I am obliged to ask you whether you intend to act on it at once. The admiral has gone; I am in some sort deputed as a guardian to her, and I warn you—very well, very well. In your own interests, it will be. If she is left there another two or three days, the name of the place will stick to her.'

'She has baptized herself with it already, I imagine,' said Fleetwood. 'She will have Esslemont to live in.'

'There will be more than one to speak as to that. You should know her.'

'I do not know her.'

'You married her.'

'The circumstances are admitted.'

'If I may hazard a guess, she is unlikely to come to terms without a previous interview. She is bent on meeting you.'

'I am to be subjected to further annoyance, or she will take the name of the place she at present inhabits, and bombard me with it. Those are the terms.'

'She has a brother living, I remind you.'

'State the deduction, if you please, my lady.'

'She is not of 'a totally inferior family.'

'She had a father famous over England as the Old Buccaneer, and is a diligent reader of his book of MAXIMS FOR MEN.'

'Dear me! Then Kirby—Captain Kirby! I remember. That's her origin, is it?' the great lady cried, illumined. 'My mother used to talk of the Cressett scandal. Old Lady Arpington, too. At any rate, it ended in their union—the formalities were properly respected, as soon as they could be.'

'I am unaware.'

'I detest such a tone of speaking. Speaking as you do now—married to the daughter? You are not yourself, Lord Fleetwood.'

'Quite, ma'am, let me assure you. Otherwise the Kirby-Cressetts would be dictating to me from the muzzle of one of the old rapscallion's Maxims. They will learn that I am myself.'

'You don't improve as you proceed. I tell you this, you'll not have me for a friend. You have your troops of satellites; but take it as equal to a prophecy, you won't have London with you; and you'll hear of Lord Fleetwood and his Whitechapel Countess till your ears ache.'

The preluding box on them reddened him.

'She will have the offer of Esslemont.'

'Undertake to persuade her in person.'

'I have spoken on that head.'

'Well, I may be mistaken,—I fancied it before I knew of the pair she springs from: you won't get her consent to anything without your consenting to meet her. Surely it's the manlier way. It might be settled for to-morrow, here, in this room. She prays to meet you.'

With an indicated gesture of 'Save me from it,' Fleetwood bowed.

He left no friend thinking over the riddle of his conduct. She was a loud-voiced lady, given to strike out phrases. The 'Whitechapel Countess' of the wealthiest nobleman of his day was heard by her on London's wagging tongue. She considered also that he ought at least have propitiated her; he was in the position requiring of him to do something of the kind, and he had shown instead the dogged pride which calls for a whip. Fool as he must have been to go and commit himself to marriage with a girl of whom he knew nothing or little, the assumption of pride belonged to the order of impudent disguises intolerable to behold and not, in a modern manner, castigate.

Notwithstanding a dislike of the Dowager Countess of Fleetwood, Lady Arpington paid Livia an afternoon visit; and added thereby to the stock of her knowledge and the grounds of her disapprobation.

Down in Whitechapel, it was known to the Winch girls and the Woodseers that Captain Kirby and his wife had spent the bitterest of hours in vainly striving to break their immoveable sister's will to remain there.

At the tea-time of simple people, who make it a meal, Gower's appetite for the home-made bread of Mary Jones was checked by the bearer of a short note from Lord Fleetwood. The half-dozen lines were cordial, breathing of their walk in the Austrian highlands, and naming a renowned city hotel for dinner that day, the hour seven, the reply yes or no by messenger.

'But we are man to man, so there's no "No" between us two,' the note said, reviving a scene of rosy crag and pine forest, where there had been philosophical fun over the appropriate sexes of those our most important fighting-ultimately, we will hope, to be united-syllables, and the when for men, the when for women, to select the one of them as their weapon.

Under the circumstances, Gower thought such a piece of writing to him magnanimous.

'It may be the solution,' his father remarked.

Both had the desire; and Gower's reply was the yes, our brave male word, supposed to be not so compromising to men in the employment of it as a form of acquiescence rather than insistent pressure.

CHAPTER XXIII

IN DAME GOSSIP'S VEIN

Right soon the London pot began to bubble. There was a marriage.

'There are marriages by the thousand every day of the year that is not consecrated to prayer for the forgiveness of our sins,' the Old Buccaneer, writing it with simple intent, says, by way of preface to a series of Maxims for men who contemplate acceptance of the yoke.

This was a marriage high as the firmament over common occurrences, black as Erebus to confound; it involved the wreck of expectations, disastrous eclipse of a sovereign luminary in the splendour of his rise, Phaethon's descent to the Shades through a smoking and a crackling world. Asserted here, verified there, the rumour gathered volume, and from a serpent of vapour resolved to sturdy concrete before it was tangible. Contradiction retired into corners, only to be swept out of them. For this marriage, abominable to hear of, was of so wonderful a sort, that the story filled the mind, and the discrediting of the story threatened the great world's cranium with a vacuity yet more monstrously abominable.

For he, the planet Croesus of his time, recently, scarce later than last night, a glorious object of the mid-heavens above the market, has been enveloped, caught, gobbled up by one of the nameless little witches riding after dusk the way of the wind on broomsticks-by one of them! She caught him like a fly in the hand off a pane of glass, gobbled him with the customary facility of a pecking pullet.

But was the planet Croesus of his time a young man to be so caught, so gobbled?

There is the mystery of it. On his coming of age, that young man gave sign of his having a city head. He put his guardians deliberately aside, had his lawyers and bailiffs and stewards thoroughly under control: managed a particularly difficult step-mother; escaped the snares of her lovely cousin; and drove his team of sycophants exactly the road he chose to go and no other. He had a will.

The world accounted him wildish?

Always from his own offset, to his own ends. Never for another's dictation or beguilement. Never for a woman. He was born with a suspicion of the sex. Poetry decorated women, he said, to lime and drag men in the foulest ruts of prose.

We are to believe he has been effectively captured?

It is positively a marriage; he admits it.

Where celebrated?

There we are at hoodman-blind for the moment. Three counties claim the church; two ends of London.

She is not a person of society, lineage?

Nor of beauty. She is a witch; ordinarily petticoated and not squeaking like a shrew-mouse in her flights, but not a whit less a moon-shade witch. The kind is famous. Fairy tales and terrible romances tell of her; she is just as much at home in life, and springs usually from the mire to enthral our knightliest. Is it a popular hero? She has him, sooner or later. A planet Croesus? He falls to her.

That is, if his people fail to attach him in legal bonds to a damsel of a corresponding birth on the day when he is breeched.

Small is her need to be young—especially if it is the man who is very young. She is the created among women armed with the deadly instinct for the motive force in men, and shameless to attract it. Self-respecting women treat men as their tamed housemates. She blows the horn of the wild old forest, irresistible to the animal. O the droop of the eyelids, the curve of a lip, the rustle of silks, the much heart, the neat ankle; and the sparkling agreement, the reserve—the motherly feminine petition that she may retain her own small petted babe of an opinion, legitimate or not, by permission of superior authority!—proof at once of her intelligence and her appreciativeness. Her infinitesimal spells are seen; yet, despite experience, the magnetism in their repulsive display is barely apprehended by sedate observers until the astounding capture is proclaimed. It is visible enough then:—and O men! O morals! If she can but trick the smallest bit in stooping, she has the pick of men.

Our present sample shows her to be young: she is young and a foreigner. Mr. Chumley Potts vouches for it. Speaks foreign English. He thinks her more ninny than knave: she is the tool of a wily plotter, picked up off the highway road by Lord Fleetwood as soon as he had her in his eye. Sir Meeson Corby wrings his frilled hands to depict the horror of the hands of that tramp the young lord had her from. They afflict him malariously still. The man, he says, the man as well was an infatuation, because he talks like a Dictionary Cheap Jack, and may have had an education and dropped into vagrancy, owing to indiscretions. Lord Fleetwood ran about in Germany repeating his remarks. But the man is really an accomplished violinist, we hear. She dances the tambourine business. A sister of the man, perhaps, if we must be charitable. They are, some say, a couple of Hungarian gypsies Lord F. found at a show and brought over to England, and soon had it on his conscience that he ought to marry her, like the Quixote of honour that he is; which is equal to saying crazy, as there is no doubt his mother was.

The marriage is no longer disputable; poor Lady Fleetwood, whatever her faults as a step-mother, does no longer deny the celebration of a marriage; though she might reasonably discredit any such story if he, on the evening of the date of the wedding day, was at a Ball, seen by her at the supper-table; though it is admitted he left the Ball-room at night. But the next day he certainly was in his place among the Peers and voted against the Government, and then went down to his estates in Wales, being an excellent holder of the reins, whether on the coach box or over the cash box.

More and more wonderful, we hear that he drove his bride straight from the church to the field of a prizefight, arranged for her special delectation. She doats on seeing blood-shed and drinking champagne. Young Mr. Mallard is our authority; and he says, she enjoyed it, and cheered the victor for being her husband's man. And after the shocking exhibition, good-bye; the Countess of Fleetwood was left sole occupant of a wayside inn, and may have learnt in her solitude that she would have been wise to feign disgust; for men to the smallest degree cultivated are unable to pardon a want of delicacy in a woman who has chosen them, as they are taught to think by their having chosen her.

So talked, so twittered, piped and croaked the London world over the early rumours of the marriage, this Amazing Marriage; which it got to be called, from the number of items flocking to swell the wonder.

Ravens ravening by night, poised peregrines by day, provision-merchants for the dispensing of dainty scraps to tickle the ears, to arm the tongues, to explode reputations, those great ladies, the Ladies Endor, Eldritch, and Cowry, fateful three of their period, avenged and scourged both innocence and naughtiness; innocence, on the whole, the least, when their withering suspicion of it had hunted the unhappy thing to the bank of Ophelia's ditch. Mallard and Chumley Potts, Captain Abrane, Sir Meeson Corby, Lord Brailstone, were plucked at and rattled, put to the blush, by a pursuit of inquiries conducted with beaks. High-nosed dames will surpass eminent judges in their temerity on the border-line where Ahem sounds the warning note to curtained decency. The courtly M. de St. Ombre had to stand confused. He, however, gave another version of Captain Abrane's 'fiddler,' and precipitated the great ladies into the reflection, that French gentlemen, since the execrable French Revolution, have lost their proper sense of the distinctions of Class. Homme d'esprit, applied to a roving adventurer, a scarce other than vagabond, was either an undiscriminating epithet or else a further example of the French deficiency in humour.

Dexterous contriver, he undoubtedly is. Lady Cowry has it from Sir Meeson Corby, who had it from the poor dowager, that Lord Fleetwood has installed the man in his house and sits at the opposite end of his table; fished him up from Whitechapel, where the countess is left serving oranges at a small fruit-shop. With her own eyes, Lady Arpington saw her there; and she can't be got to leave the place unless her husband drives his coach down to fetch her. That he declines to do; so she remains the Whitechapel Countess, all on her hind heels against the offer of a shilling of her husband's money, if she 's not to bring him to his knees; and goes about at night with a low Methodist singing hymns along those dreadful streets, while Lord Fleetwood gives gorgeous entertainments. One signal from the man he has hired, and he stops drinking—he will stop speaking as soon as the man's mouth is open. He is under a complete fascination, attributable, some say, to passes of the hands, which the man won't wash lest he should weaken their influence.

For it cannot be simply his violin playing. They say he was a pupil of a master of the dark art in Germany, and can practise on us to make us think his commonest utterances extraordinarily acute and precious. Lord Fleetwood runs round quoting him to everybody, quite ridiculously. But the man's influence is sufficient to induce his patron to drive down and fetch the Whitechapel Countess home in state, as she insists—if the man wishes it. Depend upon it he is the key of the mystery.

Totally the contrary, Lady Arpington declares! the man is a learned man, formerly a Professor of English Literature in a German University, and no connection of the Whitechapel Countess whatever, a chance acquaintance at the most. He operates on Lord Fleetwood with doses of German philosophy; otherwise, a harmless creature; and has consented to wash and dress. It is my lord who has had the chief influence. And the Countess Livia now backs him in maintaining that there is nowhere a more honest young man to be found. She may have her reasons.

As for the Whitechapel Countess... the whole story of the Old Buccaneer and Countess Fanny was retold, and it formed a terrific halo, presage of rains and hurricane tempest, over the girl the young earl had incomprehensibly espoused to discard. Those two had a son and a daughter born aboard:—in wedlock, we trust. The girl may be as wild a one as the mother. She has a will as determined as her husband's. She is offered Esslemont, the earl's Kentish mansion, for a residence, and she will none of it until she has him down in the east of London on his knees to entreat her. The injury was deep on one side or the other. It may be almost surely prophesied that the two will never come together. Will either of them deal the stroke for freedom? And which is the likelier?

Meanwhile Lord Fleetwood and his Whitechapel Countess composed the laugh of London. Straightway Invention, the violent propagator, sprang from his shades at a call of the great world's appetite for more, and, rushing upon stationary Fact, supplied the required. Marvel upon marvel was recounted. The mixed origin of the singular issue could not be examined, where all was increasingly funny.

Always the shout for more produced it. She and her band of Whitechapel boys were about in ambush to waylay the earl wherever he went. She stood knocking at his door through a whole night. He dared not lug her before a magistrate for fear of exposure. Once, riding in the park with a troop of friends he had a young woman pointed out to him, and her finger was levelled, and she cried: 'There is the English nobleman who marries a girl and leaves her to go selling cabbages!'

He left town for the Island, and beheld his yacht sailing the Solent:—my lady the countess was on board! A pair of Tyrolese minstrels in the square kindled his enthusiasm at one of his dinners; he sent them a sovereign; their humble, hearty thanks were returned to him in the name of Die Grafin von Fleetwood.

The Ladies Endor, Eldritch, and Cowry sifted their best. They let pass incredible stories: among others, that she had sent cards to the nobility and gentry of the West End of London, offering to deliver sacks of potatoes by newly-established donkey-cart at the doors of their residences, at so much per sack, bills quarterly; with the postscript, Vive L'aristocratie! Their informant had seen a card, and the stamp of the Fleetwood dragoncrest was on it.

He has enemies, was variously said of the persecuted nobleman. But it was nothing worse than the parasite that he had. This was the parasite's gentle treason. He found it an easy road to humour; it pricked the slug fancy in him to stir and curl; gave him occasion to bundle and bustle his patron kindly. Abrane, Potts, Mallard, and Sir Meeson Corby were personages during the town's excitement, besought for having something to say. Petrels of the sea of tattle, they were buoyed by the hubbub they created, and felt the tipsy happiness of being certain to rouse the laugh wherever they alighted. Sir Meeson Corby, important to himself in an eminent degree, enjoyed the novel sense of his importance with his fellows. They crowded round the bore who had scattered them.

He traced the miserable catastrophe in the earl's fortunes to the cunning of the rascal now sponging on Fleetwood and trying to dress like a gentleman: a convicted tramp, elevated by the caprice of the young nobleman he was plotting to ruin. Sir Meeson quoted Captain Abrane's latest effort to hit the dirty object's name, by calling him 'Fleetwood's Mr. Woodlouse.' And was the rascal a sorcerer? Sir Meeson spoke of him in the hearing of the Countess Livia, and she, previously echoing his disgust, corrected him sharply, and said: 'I begin to be of Russett's opinion, that his fault is his honesty.' The rascal had won or partly won the empress of her sex! This Lady Livia, haughtiest and most fastidious of our younger great dames, had become the indulgent critic of the tramp's borrowed plumes! Nay, she would not listen to a depreciatory word on him from her cousin Henrietta Kirby-Levellier.

Perhaps, after all, of all places for an encounter between the Earl of Fleetwood and the countess, those vulgar Gardens across the water, long since abandoned by the Fashion, were the most suitable. Thither one fair June night, for the sake of showing the dowager countess and her beautiful cousin, the French nobleman, Sir Meeson Corby, and others, what were the pleasures of the London lower orders, my lord had the whim to conduct them,—merely a parade of observation once round;—the ladies veiled, the gentlemen with sticks, and two servants following, one of whom, dressed in quiet black, like the peacefullest of parsons, was my lord's pugilist, Christopher Ives.

Now, here we come to history: though you will remember what History is.

The party walked round the Gardens unmolested nor have we grounds for supposing they assumed airs of state in the style of a previous generation. Only, as it happened, a gentleman of the party was a wag; no less than the famous, well-seasoned John Rose Mackrell, bent on amusing Mrs. Kirby-Levellier, to hear her lovely laughter; and his wit and his anecdotes, both inexhaustible, proved, as he said, 'that a dried fish is no stale fish, and a smoky flavour to an old chimney story will often render it more piquant to the taste than one jumping fresh off the incident.' His exact meaning in 'smoky flavour' we are not to know; but whether that M. de St. Ombre should witness the effect of English humour upon them, or that the ladies could permit themselves to laugh, their voices accompanied the gentlemen in silvery volleys. There had been 'Mackrell' at Fleetwood's dinner-table; which was then a way of saying that dry throats made no count of the quantity of champagne imbibed, owing to the fits Rose Mackrell caused. However, there was loud laughter as they strolled, and it was noticed; and Fleetwood crying out, 'Mackrell! Mackrell!' in delighted repudiation of the wag's last sally, the cry of 'Hooray, Mackrell!' was caught up by the crowd. They were not the primary offenders, for loud laughter in an isolated party is bad breeding; but they had not the plea of a copious dinner.

So this affair began; inoffensively at the start, for my lord was good-humoured about it.

Kit Ines, of the mercurial legs, must now give impromptu display of his dancing. He seized a partner, in the manner of a Roman the Sabine, sure of pleasing his patron; and the maid, passing from surprise to merriment, entered the quadrille perforce, all giggles, not without emulation, for she likewise had the passion for the dance. Whereby it befell that the pair footed in a way to gather observant spectators; and if it had not been that the man from whom the maid was willy-nilly snatched, conceived resentment, things might have passed comfortably; for Kit's quips and cuts and high capers, and the Sunday gravity of the barge face while the legs were at their impish trickery, double motion to the music, won the crowd to cheer. They conjectured him to be a British sailor. But the destituted man said, sailor or no sailor,—bos'en be hanged! he should pay for his whistle.

Honourably at the close of the quadrille, Kit brought her back; none the worse for it, he boldly affirmed, and he thanked the man for the short loan of her.—The man had an itch to strike. Choosing rather to be struck first, he vented nasty remarks. My lord spoke to Kit and moved on. At the moment of the step, Rose Mackrell uttered something, a waggery of some sort, heard to be forgotten, but of such instantaneous effect, that the prompt and immoderate laugh succeeding it might reasonably be taken for a fling of scorn at himself, by an injured man. They were a party; he therefore proceeded to make one, appealing to English sentiment and right feeling. The blameless and repentant maid plucked at his coat to keep him from dogging the heels of the gentlemen. Fun was promised; consequently the crowd waxed.

'My lord,' had been let fall by Kit Ines. Conjoined to 'Mackrell,' it rang finely, and a trumpeting of 'Lord Mackrell' resounded. Lord Mackrell was asked for 'more capers and not so much sauce.' Various fish took part in his title of nobility. The wag Mackrell continuing to be discreetly silent, and Kit Ines acting as a pacific rearguard, the crowd fell in love with their display of English humour, disposed to the surly satisfaction of a big street dog that has been appeased by a smaller one's total cessation of growls.

All might have gone well but for the sudden appearance of two figures of young women on the scene. They fronted the advance of the procession. They wanted to have a word with Lord Mackrell. Not a bit of it—he won't listen, turns away; and one of the pair slips round him. It's regular imploring: 'my lord! my lord!'

O you naughty Surrey melodram villain of a Lord Mackrell! Listen to the young woman, you Mackrell, or you'll get Billingsgate! Here's Mr. Jig-and-Reel behind here, says she's done him! By Gosh! What's up now?

One of the young ladies of the party ahead had rushed up to the young woman dodging to stand in Lord Mackrell's way. The crowd pressed to see. Kit Ines and his mate shouldered them off. They performed an envelopment of the gentlemen and ladies, including the two young women. Kit left his mate and ran to the young woman hitherto the quieter of the two. He rattled at her. But she had a tongue of her own and rattled it at him. What did she say?

Merely to hear, for no other reason,' a peace-loving crowd of clerks and tradesmen, workmen and their girls, young aspirants to the professions, night-larks of different classes, both sexes, there in that place for simple entertainment, animated simply by the spirit of English humour, contracted, so closing upon the Mackrell party as to seem threatening to the most orderly and apprehensive member of it, who was the baronet, Sir Meeson Corby.

He was a man for the constables in town emergencies, and he shouted. 'Cock Robin crowing' provoked a jolly round of barking chaff. The noise in a dense ring drew Fleetwood's temper. He gave the word to Kit Ines, and immediately two men dropped; a dozen staggered unhit. The fists worked right and left; such a clearing of ground was never seen for sickle or scythe. And it was taken respectfully; for Science proclaimed her venerable self in the style and the perfect sufficiency of the strokes. A bruiser delivered them. No shame to back away before a bruiser. There was rather an admiring envy of the party claiming the nimble champion on their side, until the very moderate lot of the Mackrells went stepping forward along the strewn path with sticks pointed.

If they had walked it like gentlemen, they would have been allowed to get through. An aggressive minority, and with Cock Robin squealing for constables in the midst, is that insolent upstart thing which howls to have a lesson. The sticks were fallen on; bump came the mass. Kit Ines had to fight his way back to his mate, and the couple scoured a clearish ring, but the gentlemen were at short thrusts, affable in tone, to cheer the spirits of the ladies:—'All right, my friend, you're a trifle mistaken, it 's my stick, not yours.' Therewith the wrestle for the stick.

The one stick not pointed was wrenched from the grasp of Sir Meeson Corby; and by a woman, the young woman who had accosted my lord; not a common young woman either, as she appeared when beseeching him. Her stature rose to battle heights: she made play with Sir Meeson Corby's ebony stick, using it in one hand as a dwarf quarterstaff to flail the sconces, then to dash the point at faces; and she being a woman, a girl, perhaps a lady, her cool warrior method of cleaving way, without so much as tightening her lips, was found notable; and to this degree (vouched for by Rose Mackrell, who heard it), that a fellow, rubbing his head, cried: 'Damn it all, she's clever, though!' She took her station beside Lord Fleetwood.

He had been as cool as she, or almost. Now he was maddened; she defended him, she warded and thrust for him, only for him, to save him a touch; unasked, undesired, detested for the box on his ears of to-morrow's public mockery, as she would be, overwhelming him with ridicule. Have you seen the kick and tug at the straps of the mettled pony in stables that betrays the mishandling of him by his groom? Something so did Fleetwood plunge and dart to be free of her, and his desperate soul cried out on her sticking to him like a plaster!

Welcome were the constables. His guineas winked at their chief, as fair women convey their meanings, with no motion of eyelids; and the officers of the law knew the voice habituated to command, and answered two words of his: 'Right, my lord,' smelling my lord in the unerring manner of those days. My lord's party were escorted to the gates, not a little jeered; though they by no means had the worst of the tussle. But the puffing indignation of Sir Meesan Corby over his battered hat and torn frill and buttons plucked from his coat, and his threat of the magistrates, excited the crowd to derisive yells.

My lord spoke something to his man, handing his purse.

The ladies were spared the hearing of bad language. They, according to the joint testimony of M. de St. Ombre and Mr. Rose Mackrell, comported themselves throughout as became the daughters of a warrior race. Both gentlemen were emphatic to praise the unknown Britomart who had done such gallant service with Sir Meeson's ebony wand. He was beginning to fuss vociferously about the loss of the stick—a family stick, goldheaded, the family crest on it, priceless to the family—when Mrs. Kirby-Levellier handed it to him inside the coach.

'But where is she?' M. de St. Ombre said, and took the hint of Livia's touch on his arm in the dark.

At the silence following the question, Mr. Rose Mackrell murmured, 'Ah!'

He and the French gentleman understood that there might have been a manifestation of the notorious Whitechapel Countess.

They were two; and a slower-witted third was travelling to his ideas on the subject. Three men, witnesses of a remarkable incident in connection with a boiling topic of current scandal,—glaringly illustrative of it, moreover,—were unlikely to keep close tongues, even if they had been sworn to secrecy. Fleetwood knew it, and he scorned to solicit them; an exaction of their idle vows would be merely the humiliation of himself. So he tossed his dignity to recklessness, as the ultraconvivial give the last wink of reason to the wine-cup. Persecuted as he was, nothing remained for him but the nether-sublime of a statuesque desperation.

That was his feeling; and his way of cloaking it under light sallies at Sir Meeson and easy chat with Henrietta made it visible to her, from its being the contrary of what the world might expect a proud young nobleman to exhibit. She pitied him: she had done him some wrong. She read into him, too, as none else could. Seeing the solitary tortures behind the pleasant social mask, she was drawn to partake of them; and the mask seemed pathetic. She longed to speak a word in sympathy or relieve her bosom of tears. Carinthia had sunk herself, was unpardonable, hardly mentionable. Any of the tales told of her might be credited after this! The incorrigible cause of humiliation for everybody connected with her pictured, at a word of her name, the crowd pressing and the London world acting audience. Livia spoke the name when they had reached their house and were alone. Henrietta responded with the imperceptible shrug which is more eloquent than a cry to tell of the most monstrous of loads. My lord, it was thought by the ladies, had directed his man to convey her safely to her chosen home, whence she might be expected very soon to be issuing and striking the gong of London again.

CHAPTER XXIV

A KIDNAPPING AND NO GREAT HARM

Ladies who have the pride of delicate breeding are not more than rather violently hurled back on the fortress it is, when one or other of the gross mishaps of circumstance may subject them to a shock: and this happening in the presence of gentlemen, they are sustained by the within and the without to keep a smooth countenance, however severe their affliction. Men of heroic nerve decline similarly to let explosions shake them, though earth be shaken. Dragged into the monstrous grotesque of the scene at the Gardens, Livia and Henrietta went through the ordeal, masking any signs that they were stripped for a flagellation. Only, the fair cousins were unable to perceive a comic element in the scene: and if the world was for laughing, as their instant apprehension foresaw it, the world was an ignoble beast. They did not discuss Carinthia's latest craziness at night, hardly alluded to it while they were in the interjectory state.

Henrietta was Livia's guest, her husband having hurried away to Vienna: 'To get money! money!' her angry bluntness explained his absence, and dealt its blow at the sudden astounding poverty into which they had fallen. She was compelled to practise an excessive, an incredible economy:—'think of the smallest trifles!' so that her Chillon travelled unaccompanied, they were separated. Her iterations upon money were the vile constraint of an awakened interest and wonderment at its powers. She, the romantic Riette, banner of chivalry, reader of poetry, struck a line between poor and rich in her talk of people, and classed herself with the fallen and pinched; she harped on her slender means, on the enforced calculations preceding purchases, on the living in lodgings; and that miserly Lord Levellier's indebtedness to Chillon—large sums! and Chillon's praiseworthy resolve to pay the creditors of her father's estate; and of how he travelled like a common man, in consequence of the money he had given Janey—weakly, for her obstinacy was past endurance; but her brother would not leave her penniless, and penniless she had been for weeks, because of her stubborn resistance to the earl—quite unreasonably, whether right or wrong—in the foul retreat she had chosen; apparently with a notion that the horror of it was her vantage ground against him: and though a single sign of submission would place the richest purse in England at her disposal. 'She refuses Esslemont! She insists on his meeting her! No child could be so witless. Let him be the one chiefly or entirely to blame, she might show a little tact—for her brother's sake! She loves her brother? No: deaf to him, to me, to every consideration except her blind will.'

Here was the skeleton of the love match, earlier than Livia had expected.

It refreshed a phlegmatic lady's disposition for prophecy. Lovers abruptly tossed between wind and wave may still be lovers, she knew: but they are, or the weaker of the two is, hard upon any third person who tugs at them for subsistence or existence. The condition, if they are much beaten about, prepares true lovers, through their mutual tenderness, to be bitterly misanthropical.

Livia supposed the novel economic pinches to be the cause of Henrietta's unwonted harsh judgement of her sister-in-law's misconduct, or the crude expression of it. She could not guess that Carinthia's unhappiness in marriage was a spectre over the married happiness of the pair fretted by the conscience which told them they had come together by doing much to bring it to pass. Henrietta could see herself less the culprit when she blamed Carinthia in another's hearing.

After some repose, the cousins treated their horrible misadventure as a piece of history. Livia was cool; she had not a husband involved in it, as Henrietta had; and London's hoarse laugh surely coming on them, spared her the dread Henrietta suffered, that Chillon would hear; the most sensitive of men on any matter touching his family.

'And now a sister added to the list! Will there be names, Livia?'

'The newspapers!' Livia's shoulders rose.

'We ought to have sworn the gentlemen to silence.'

'M. de St. Ombre is a tomb until he writes his Memoirs. I hold Sir Meeson under lock. But a spiced incident, a notorious couple,—an anecdotal witness to the scene,—could you expect Mr. Rose Mackrell to contain it? The sacredest of oaths, my dear!'

That relentless force impelling an anecdotist to slaughter families for the amusement of dinner-tables, was brought home to Henrietta by her prospect of being a victim; and Livia reminding her of the excessive laughter at Rose Mackrell's anecdotes overnight, she bemoaned her having consented to go to those Gardens in mourning.

'How could Janey possibly have heard of the project to go?

'You went to please Russett, he to please you, and that wild-cat to please herself,' said Livia. 'She haunts his door, I suppose, and follows him, like a running footman. Every step she takes widens the breach. He keeps his temper, yes, keeps his temper as he keeps his word, and one morning it breaks loose, and all that's done has to be undone. It will bemust. That extravaganza, as she is called, is fatal, dogs him with burlesque—of all men!'

'Why not consent to meet her once, Chillon asks.'

'You are asking Russett to yield an inch on demand, and to a woman.'

'My husband would yield to a woman what he would refuse to all the men in Europe and America,' said Henrietta; and she enjoyed her thrill of allegiance to her chivalrous lord and courtier.

'No very extraordinary specimen of a newly married man, who has won the Beauty of England and America for his wife-at some cost to some people,' Livia rejoined.

There came a moisture on the eyelashes of the emotional young woman, from a touch of compassion for the wealthy man who had wished to call her wife, and was condemned by her rejection of him to call another woman wife, to be wifeless in wedding her, despite his wealth.

She thinks he loves her; it is pitiable, but she thinks it—after the treatment she has had. She begs to see him once.'

'And subdue him with a fit of weeping,' Livia was moved to say by sight of the tear she hated. 'It would harden Russett—on other eyes, too! Salt-water drops are like the forced agony scenes in a play: they bring down the curtain, they don't win the critics. I heard her "my husband" and saw his face.'

'You didn't hear a whimper with it,' Henrietta said. 'She's a mountain girl, not your city madam on the boards. Chillon and I had her by each hand, implored her to leave that impossible Whitechapel, and she trembled, not a drop was shed by her. I can almost fancy privation and squalor have no terrors for Janey. She sings to the people down there, nurses them. She might be occupying Esslemont—our dream of an English home! She is the destruction of the idea of romantic in connection with the name of marriage. I talk like a simpleton. Janey upsets us all. My lord was only—a little queer before he knew her: His Mr. Woodseer may be encouraging her. You tell me the creature has a salary from him equal to your jointure.'

'Be civil to the man while it lasts,' Livia said, attentive to a degradation of tone—in her cousin, formerly of supreme self-containment.

The beautiful young woman was reminded of her holiday in town. She brightened, and the little that it was, and the meanness of the satisfaction, darkened her. Envy of the lucky adventurer Mr. Woodseer, on her husband's behalf, grew horridly conscious for being reproved. So she plucked resolution to enjoy her holiday and forget the contrasts of life-palaces running profusion, lodgings hammered by duns; the pinch of poverty distracting every simple look inside or out. There was no end to it; for her husband's chivalrous honour forced him to undertake the payment of her father's heavy debts. He was right and admirable, it could not be contested; but the prospect for them was a grinding gloom, an unrelieved drag, as of a coach at night on an interminable uphill flinty road.

These were her sensations, and she found it diverting to be admired; admired by many while she knew herself to be absorbed in the possession of her by one. It bestowed the before and after of her marriage. She felt she was really, had rapidly become, the young woman of the world, armed with a husband, to take the flatteries of men for the needed diversion they brought. None moved her; none could come near to touching the happy insensibility of a wife who adored her husband, wrote to him daily, thought of him by the minute. Her former worshippers were numerous at Livia's receptions; Lord Fleetwood, Lord Brailstone, and the rest. Odd to reflect on—they were the insubstantial but coveted wealth of the woman fallen upon poverty, ignoble poverty! She could not discard her wealth. She wrote amusingly of them, and fully, vivacious descriptions, to Chillon; hardly so much writing to him as entering her heart's barred citadel, where he resided at his ease, heard everything that befell about her. If she dwelt on Lord Fleetwood's kindness in providing entertainments, her object was to mollify Chillon's anger in some degree. She was doing her utmost to gratify him, 'for the purpose of paving a way to plead Janey's case.' She was almost persuading herself she was enjoying the remarks of his friend, confidant, secretary, or what not, Livia's worshipper, Mr. Woodseer, 'who does as he wills with my lord; directs his charities, his pleasures, his opinions, all because he is believed to have wonderful ideas and be wonderfully honest.' Henrietta wrote: 'Situation unchanged. Janey still At that place'; and before the letter was posted, she and Livia had heard from Gower Woodseer of the reported disappearance of the Countess of Fleetwood and her maid. Gower's father had walked up from Whitechapel, bearing news of it to the earl, she said.

'And the earl is much disturbed?' was Livia's inquiry.

'He has driven down with my father,' Gower said carelessly, ambiguously in the sound.

Troubled enough to desire the show of a corresponding trouble, Henrietta read at their faces.

'May it not be—down there—a real danger?'

The drama, he could inform her, was only too naked down there for disappearances to be common.

'Will it be published that she is missing?'

'She has her maid with her, a stout-hearted girl. Both have courage. I don't think we need take measures just yet.'

'Not before it is public property?'

Henrietta could have bitten her tongue for laying her open to the censure implied in his muteness. Janey perverted her.

Women were an illegible manuscript, and ladies a closed book of the binding, to this raw philosopher, or he would not so coldly have judged the young wife, anxious on her husband's account, that they might escape another scorching. He carried away his impression.

Livia listened to a remark on his want of manners.

'Russett puts it to the credit of his honesty,' she said. 'Honesty is everything with us at present. The man has made his honesty an excellent speculation. He puts a piece on zero and the bank hands him a sackful. We may think we have won him to serve us, up comes his honesty. That's how we have Lady Arpington mixed in it—too long a tale. But be guided by me; condescend a little.'

'My dear! my whole mind is upon that unhappy girl. It would break Chillon's heart.'

Livia pished. 'There are letters we read before we crack the seal. She is out of that ditch, and it suits Russett that she should be. He's not often so patient. A woman foot to foot against his will—I see him throwing high stakes. Tyrants are brutal; and really she provokes him enough. You needn't be alarmed about the treatment she 'll meet. He won't let her beat him, be sure.'

Neither Livia nor Gower wondered at the clearing of the mystery, before it went to swell the scandal. A young nobleman of ready power, quick temper, few scruples, and a taxed forbearance, was not likely to stand thwarted and goaded-and by a woman. Lord Fleetwood acted his part, inscrutable as the blank of a locked door. He could not conceal that he was behind the door.

CHAPTER XXV

THE PHILOSOPHER MAN OF ACTION

Gower's bedroom window looked over the shrubs of the square, and as his form of revolt from a city life was to be up and out with the sparrows in the early flutter of morning, for a stretch of the legs where grass was green and trees were not enclosed, he rarely saw a figure below when he stood dressing. Now there appeared a petticoated one stationary against the rails, with her face lifted. She fronted the house, and while he speculated abstractedly, recognition rushed on him. He was down and across the roadway at leaps.

'It's Madge here!'

The girl panted for her voice.

'Mr. Woodseer, I'm glad; I thought I should have to wait hours. She's safe.'

'Where?'

'Will you come, sir?'

'Step ahead.'

Madge set forth to north of the square.

He judged of the well-favoured girl that she could steer her way through cities: mouth and brows were a warning to challenger pirate craft of a vessel carrying guns; and the red lips kept their firm line when they yielded to the pressure for speech.

'It's a distance. She's quite safe, no harm; she's a prisoner; she's well fed; she's not ill treated.'

'You're out?'

'That's as it happens. I'm lucky in seeing you early. He don't mean to hurt her; he won't be beaten. All she asks is ten minutes with him. If he would!—he won't. She didn't mean to do him offence t' other night in that place—you've heard. Kit Ines told me he was on duty there—going. She couldn't help speaking when she had eyes on her husband. She kisses the ground of his footsoles, you may say, let him be ever so unkind. She and I were crossing to the corner of Roper Street a rainy night, on way to Mile End, away down to one of your father's families, Mother Davis and her sick daughter and the little ones, and close under the public-house Goat and Beard we were seized on and hustled into a covered carriage that was there, and they drove sharp. She 's not one to scream. We weren't frightened. We both made the same guess. They drove us to the house she 's locked in, and me, too, up till three o'clock this morning.'

'You've seen nobody, Madge?'

'He 's fixed she 's to leave London, Mr. Woodseer. I've seen Kit Ines. And she 's to have one of the big houses to her use. I guessed Kit Ines was his broom. He defends it because he has his money to make— and be a dirty broom for a fortune! But any woman's sure of decent handling with Kit Ines—not to speak of lady. He and a mate guard the house. An old woman cooks.'

'He guards the house, and he gave you a pass?'

'Not he. His pride's his obedience to his "paytron"—he calls his master, and won't hear that name abused. We are on the first floor; all the lower doors are locked day and night. New Street, not much neighbours; she wouldn't cry out of the window. She 's to be let free if she'll leave London.'

'You jumped it!'

'If I'd broke a leg, Mr. Kit Ines would have had to go to his drams. It wasn't very high; and a flower-bed underneath. My mistress wanted to be the one. She has to be careful. She taught me how to jump down not to hurt. She makes you feel you can do anything. I had a bother to get her to let me and be quiet herself. She's not one to put it upon others, you'll learn. When I was down I felt like a stick in the ground and sat till I had my feet, she at the window waiting; and I started for you. She kissed her hand. I was to come to you, and then your father, you nowhere seen. I wasn't spoken to. I know empty London.'

'Kit Ines was left sleeping in the house?'

'Snoring, I dare say: He don't drink on duty.'

'He must be kept on duty.'

'Drink or that kind of duty, it's a poor choice.'

'You'll take him in charge, Madge.'

'I've got a mistress to look after.'

'You've warmed to her.'

'That's not new; Mr. Woodseer. I do trust you, and you his friend. But you are the minister's son, and any man not a great nobleman must have some heart for her. You'll learn. He kills her so because she's fond of him—loves him, however he strikes. No, not like a dog, as men say of us. She'd die for him this night, need were. Live with her, you won't find many men match her for brave; and she's good. My Sally calls her a Bible saint. I could tell you stories of her goodness, short the time though she's been down our way. And better there for her than at that inn he left her at to pine and watch the Royal Sovereign come swing come smirk in sailor blue and star to meet the rain—would make anybody disrespect Royalty or else go mad! He's a great nobleman, he can't buy what she's ready to give; and if he thinks he breaks her will now, it's because she thinks she's obeying a higher than him, or no lord alive and Kit Ines to back him 'd hold her. Women want a priest to speak to men certain times. I wish I dared; we have to bite our tongues. He's master now, but, as I believe God's above, if he plays her false, he's the one to be brought to shame. I talk.'

'Talk on, Madge,' said Gower, to whom the girl's short-syllabled run of the lips was a mountain rill compared with London park waters.

'You won't let him hurry her off where she'll eat her heart for never seeing him again? She prays to be near him, if she's not to see him.'

'She speaks in that way?'

'I get it by bits. I'm with her so, it's as good as if I was inside her. She can't obey when it goes the wrong way of her heart to him.'

'Love and wisdom won't pull together, and they part company for good at the church door,' said Gower. 'This matrimony's a bad business.'

Madge hummed a moan of assent. 'And my poor Sally 'll have to marry. I can't leave my mistress while she wants me, and Sally can't be alone. It seems we take a step and harm's done, though it's the right step we take.'

'It seems to me you've engaged yourself to follow Sally's lead, Madge.'

'Girls' minds turn corners, Mr. Woodseer.'

He passed the remark. What it was that girls' minds occasionally or habitually did, or whether they had minds to turn, or whether they took their whims for minds, were untroubled questions with a young man studying abstract and adoring surface nature too exclusively to be aware of the manifestation of her spirit in the flesh, as it is not revealed so much by men. However, she had a voice and a face that led him to be thoughtful over her devotedness to her mistress, after nearly losing her character for the prize-fighter, and he had to thank her for invigorating him. His disposition was to muse and fall slack, helpless to a friend. Here walked a creature exactly the contrary. He listened to the steps of the dissimilar pair on the detonating pavement, and eyed a church clock shining to the sun.

She was sure of the direction: 'Out Camden way, where the murder was.'

They walked at a brisk pace, conversing or not.

'Tired? You must be,' he said.

'Not when I'm hot to do a thing.'

'There's the word of the thoroughbred!'

'You don't tire, sir,' said she. 'Sally and I see you stalking out for the open country in the still of the morning. She thinks you look pale for want of food, and ought to have some one put a biscuit into your pocket overnight.'

'Who'd have guessed I was under motherly observation!'

'You shouldn't go so long empty, if you listen to trainers.'

'Capital doctors, no doubt. But I get a fine appetite.'

'You may grind the edge too sharp.'

He was about to be astonished, and reflected that she had grounds for her sagacity. His next thought plunged him into contempt for Kit Ines, on account of the fellow's lapses to sottishness. But there would be no contempt of Kit Ines in a tussle with him. Nor could one funk the tussle and play cur, if Kit's engaged young woman were looking on. We get to our courage or the show of it by queer screws.

Contemplative over these matters, the philosopher transformed to man of action heard Madge say she read directions in London by churches, and presently exclaiming disdainfully, and yet relieved, 'Spooner Villas,' she turned down a row of small detached houses facing a brickfield, that had just contributed to the erection of them, and threatened the big city with further defacements.

Madge pointed to the marks of her jump, deep in flower-bed earth under an open window.

Gower measured the height with sensational shanks.

She smote at the door. Carinthia nodded from her window. Close upon that, Kit Ines came bounding to the parlour window; he spied and stared. Gower was known to him as the earl's paymaster; so he went to the passage and flung the door open, blocking the way.

'Any commands, your honour?'

'You bring the countess to my lord immediately,' said Gower.

Kit swallowed his mouthful of surprise in a second look at Madge and the ploughed garden-bed beneath the chamber window.

'Are the orders written, sir?'

'To me?—for me to deliver to you?—for you to do my lord's bidding? Where's your head?'

Kit's finger-nails travelled up to it. Madge pushed past him. She and her mistress, and Kit's mate, and the old woman receiving the word for a cup of tea, were soon in the passage. Kit's mate had a ready obedience for his pay, nothing else,—no counsel at all, not a suggestion to a head knocked to a pudding by Madge's jump and my lord's paymaster here upon the scene.

'My lady was to go down Wales way, sir.'

'That may be ordered after.'

'I'm to take my lady to my lord?' and, 'Does it mean my lady wants a fly?' Kit asked, and harked back on whether Madge had seen my lord.

'At five in the morning?—don't sham donkey with me,' said Gower.

The business looked inclined to be leaky, but which the way for proving himself other than a donkey puzzled Kit: so much so, that a shove made him partly grateful. Madge's clever countermove had stunned his judgement. He was besides acting subordinate to his patron's paymaster; and by the luck of it, no voice of woman interposed. The countess and her maid stood by like a disinterested couple. Why be suspicious, if he was to keep the countess, in sight? She was a nice lady, and he preferred her good opinion. She was brave, and he did her homage. It might be, my lord had got himself round to the idea of thanking her for saving his nob that night, and his way was to send and have her up, to tell her he forgave her, after the style of lords. Gower pricked into him by saying aside: 'Mad, I suppose, in case of a noise?' And he could not answer quite manfully, lost his eyes and coloured. Neighbours might have required an explanation of shrieks, he confessed. Men have sometimes to do nasty work for their patrons.

They were afoot, walking at Carinthia's pace before half-past seven. She would not hear of any conveyance. She was cheerful, and, as it was pitiful to see, enjoyed her walk. Hearing of her brother's departure for the Austrian capital, she sparkled. Her snatches of speech were short flights out of the meditation possessing her. Gower noticed her easier English, that came home to the perpetual student he was. She made use of some of his father's words, and had assimilated them mentally besides appropriating them: the verbalizing of 'purpose,' then peculiar to his father, for example. She said, in reply to a hint from him: 'If my lord will allow me an interview, I purpose to be obedient.' No one could imagine of her that she spoke broken-spiritedly. Her obedience was to a higher than a mortal lord: and Gower was touched to the quick through the use of the word.

Contrasting her with Countess Livia and her cousin, the earl might think her inferior on the one small, square compartment called by them the world; but she carried the promise of growth, a character in expansion, and she had at least natural grace, a deerlike step. Although her picturesqueness did not swarm on him with images illuminating night, subduing day, like the Countess Livia's, it was marked, it could tower and intermittently eclipse; and it was of the uplifting and healing kind by comparison, not a delicious balefulness.

The bigger houses, larger shops, austere streets of private residences, were observed by the recent inhabitant of Whitechapel.

'My lord lives in a square,' she said.

'We shall soon be there now,' he encouraged her, doubtful though the issue appeared.

'It is a summer morning for the Ortler, the Gross-Glockner, the Venediger,—all our Alps, Mr. Woodseer.'

'If we could fly!'

'We love them.'

'Why, then we beat a wing—yes.'

'For I have them when I want them to sight. It is the feet are so desirous. I feel them so this morning, after prisonership. I could not have been driven to my lord.'

'I know the feeling,' said Gower; 'any movement of us not our own impulse, hurries the body and deadens the mind. And by the way, my dear lady, I spoke of the earl's commands to this man behind us walking with your Madge. My father would accuse me of Jesuitry. Ines mentioned commands, and I took advantage of it.'

'I feared,' said Carinthia. 'I go for my chance.'

Gower had a thought of the smaller creature, greater by position, to whom she was going for her chance. He alluded to his experience of the earl's kindness in relation to himself, from a belief in his 'honesty'; dotted outlines of her husband's complex character, or unmixed and violently opposing elements.

She remarked: 'I will try and learn.'

The name of the street of beautiful shops woke a happy smile on her mouth. 'Father talked of it; my mother, too. He has it written down in his Book of Maxims. When I was a girl, I dreamed of one day walking up Bond Street.'

They stepped from the pavement and crossed the roadway for a side-street leading to the square. With the swift variation of her aspect at times, her tone changed.

'We are near. My lord will not be troubled by me. He has only to meet me. There has been misunderstanding. I have vexed him; I could not help it. I will go where he pleases after I have heard him give orders. He thinks me a frightful woman. I am peaceful.'

Gower muttered her word 'misunderstanding.' They were at the earl's house door. One tap at it, and the two applicants for admission would probably be shot as far away from Lord Fleetwood as when they were on the Styrian heights last autumn. He delivered the tap, amused by the idea. It was like a summons to a genie of doubtful service.

My lord was out riding in the park.

Only the footman appeared at that early hour, and his countenance was blank whitewash as he stood rigid against the wall for the lady to pass. Madge followed into the morning room; Ines remained in the hall, where he could have the opening speech with his patron, and where he soon had communication with the butler.

This official entered presently to Gower, presenting a loaded forehead. A note addressed to Mrs. Kirby-Levellier at the Countess Livia's house hard by was handed to him for instant despatch. He signified a deferential wish to speak.

'You can speak in the presence of the Countess of Fleetwood, Mr. Waytes,' Gower said.

Waytes checked a bend of his shoulders. He had not a word, and he turned to send the note. He was compelled to think that he saw a well-grown young woman in the Whitechapel Countess.

Gower's note reached Henrietta on her descent to the breakfast-table. She was, alone, and thrown into a torture of perplexity: for she wanted advice as to the advice to be given to Janey, and Livia was an utterly unprofitable person to consult in the case. She thought of Lady Arpington, not many doors distant. Drinking one hasty cup of tea, she sent for her bonnet, and hastened away to the great lady, whom she found rising from breakfast with the marquis.

Lady Arpington read Gower's note. She unburdened herself: 'Oh! So it 's no longer a bachelor's household!'

Henrietta heaved the biggest of sighs. 'I fear the poor dear may have made matters worse.'

To which Lady Arpington said: 'Worse or better, my child!' and shrugged; for the present situation strained to snapping.

She proposed to go forthwith, and give what support she could to the Countess of Fleetwood.

They descended the steps of the house to the garden and the Green Park's gravel walk up to Piccadilly. There they had view of Lord Fleetwood on horseback leisurely turning out of the main way's tide. They saw him alight at the mews. As they entered the square, he was met some doors from the south corner by his good or evil genius, whose influence with him came next after the marriage in the amazement it caused, and was perhaps to be explained by it; for the wealthiest of young noblemen bestowing his name on an unknown girl, would be the one to make an absurd adventurer his intimate. Lord Fleetwood bent a listening head while Mr. Gower Woodseer, apparently a good genius for the moment, spoke at his ear.

How do we understand laughter at such a communication as he must be hearing from the man? Signs of a sharp laugh indicated either his cruel levity or that his presumptuous favourite trifled—and the man's talk could be droll, Lady Arpington knew: it had, she recollected angrily, diverted her, and softened her to tolerate the intruder into regions from which her class and her periods excluded the lowly born, except at the dinner-tables of stale politics and tattered scandal. Nevertheless, Lord Fleetwood mounted the steps to his house door, still listening. His 'Asmodeus,' on the tongue of the world, might be doing the part of Mentor really. The house door stood open.

Fleetwood said something to Gower; he swung round, beheld the ladies and advanced to them, saluting. 'My dear Lady Arpington! quite so, you arrive opportunely. When the enemy occupies the citadel, it's proper to surrender. Say, I beg, she can have the house, if she prefers it. I will fall back on Esslemont. Arrangements for her convenience will be made. I thank you, by anticipation.'

His bow included Henrietta loosely. Lady Arpington had exclaimed: 'Enemy, Fleetwood?' and Gower, in his ignorance of the smoothness of aristocratic manners, expected a remonstrance; but Fleetwood was allowed to go on, with his air of steely geniality and a decision, that his friend imagined he could have broken down like an old partition board under the kick of a sarcasm sharpening an appeal.

'Lord Fleetwood was on the point of going in,' he assured the great lady.

'Lord Fleetwood may regret his change of mind,' said she. 'The Countess of Fleetwood will have my advice to keep her footing in this house.'

She and Henrietta sat alone with Carinthia for an hour. Coming forth, Lady Arpington ejaculated to herself: 'Villany somewhere!—You will do well, Henrietta, to take up your quarters with her a day or two. She can hold her position a month. Longer is past possibility.'

A shudder of the repulsion from men crept over the younger lady. But she was a warrior's daughter, and observed: 'My husband, her brother, will be back before the month ends.'

'No need for hostilities to lighten our darkness,' Lady Arpington rejoined. 'You know her? trust her?'

'One cannot doubt her face. She is my husband's sister. Yes, I do trust her. I nail my flag to her cause.'

The flag was crimson, as it appeared on her cheeks; and that intimated a further tale, though not of so dramatic an import as the cognizant short survey of Carinthia had been.

These young women, with the new complications obtruded by them, irritated a benevolent great governing lady, who had married off her daughters and embraced her grandchildren, comfortably finishing that chapter; and beheld now the apparition of the sex's ancient tripping foe, when circumstances in themselves were quite enough to contend against on their behalf. It seemed to say, that nature's most burdened weaker must always be beaten. Despite Henrietta's advocacy and Carinthia's clear face, it raised a spectral form of a suspicion, the more effective by reason of the much required justification it fetched from the shades to plead apologies for Lord Fleetwood's erratic, if not mad, and in any case ugly, conduct. What otherwise could be his excuse? Such was his need of one, that the wife he crushed had to be proposed for sacrifice, in the mind of a lady tending strongly to side with her and condemn her husband.

Lady Arpington had counselled Carinthia to stay where she was, the Fates having brought her there. Henrietta was too generous to hesitate in her choice between her husband's sister and the earl. She removed from Livia's house to Lord Fleetwood's. My lord was at Esslemont two days; then established his quarters at Scrope's hotel, five minutes' walk from the wedded lady to whom the right to bear his title was granted, an interview with him refused. Such a squaring for the battle of spouses had never— or not in mighty London—been seen since that old fight began.

CHAPTER XXVI

AFTER SOME FENCING THE DAME PASSES OUR GUARD

Dame Gossip at this present pass bursts to give us a review of the social world siding for the earl or for his countess; and her parrot cry of 'John Rose Mackrell!' with her head's loose shake over the smack of her lap, to convey the contemporaneous tipsy relish of the rich good things he said on the subject of the contest, indicates the kind of intervention it would be.

To save the story from having its vein tied, we may accept the reminder, that he was the countess's voluble advocate at a period when her friends were shy to speak of her. After relating the Vauxhall Gardens episode in burlesque Homeric during the freshness of the scandal, Rose Mackrell's enthusiasm for the heroine of his humour set in. He tracked her to her parentage, which was new breath blown into the sunken tradition of some Old Buccaneer and his Countess Fanny: and, a turn of great good luck helping him to a copy of the book of the MAXIMS FOR MEN, he would quote certain of the racier ones, passages of Captain John Peter Kirby's personal adveres in various lands and waters illustrating the text, to prove that the old warrior acted by the rule of his recommendations. They had the repulsive attraction proper to rusty lumber swords and truncehons that have tasted brains. They wove no mild sort of halo for the head of a shillelagh-flourishing Whitechapel Countess descended from the writer and doer.

People were willing to believe in her jump of thirty feet or more off a suburban house-top to escape durance, and her midnight storming of her lord's town house, and ousting of him to go find his quarters at Scrope's hotel. He, too, had his band of pugilists, as it was known; and he might have heightened a rageing scandal. The nobleman forbore. A woman's blow gracefully taken adds a score of inches to our stature, floor us as it may; we win the world's after thoughts. Rose Mackrell sketched the earl;—always alert, smart, quick to meet a combination and protect a dignity never obtruded, and in spite of himself the laugh of the town. His humour flickered wildly round the ridiculous position of a prominent young nobleman, whose bearing and character were foreign to a position of ridicule.

Nevertheless, the earl's figure continuing to be classic sculpture, it allied him with the aristocracy of martyrs, that burn and do not wince. He propitiated none, and as he could not but suffer shrewdly, he gained esteem enough to shine through the woman's pitiless drenching of him. During his term at Scrope's hotel, the carousals there were quite old-century and matter of discourse. He had proved his return to sound sense in the dismissal of 'the fiddler,' notoriously the woman's lieutenant, or more; and nightly the revelry closed at the great gaming tables of St. James's Street, while Whitechapel held the coroneted square, well on her way to the Law courts, as Abrane and Potts reported; and positively so, 'clear case.' That was the coming development and finale of the Marriage. London waited for it.

A rich man's easy smile over losses at play, merely taught his emulous troop to feel themselves poor devils in the pocket. But Fleetwood's contempt of Sleep was a marvel, superhuman, and accused them of an inferior vigour, hard for young men to admit by the example. He never went to bed. Issuing from Fortune's hall-doors in the bright, lively, summer morning, he mounted horse and was away to the hills. Or he took the arm of a Roman Catholic nobleman, Lord Feltre, and walked with him from the green tables and the establishment's renowned dry still Sillery to a Papist chapel. As it was not known that he had given his word to abjure his religion, the pious gamblers did no worse than spread an alarm and quiet it, by the citation of his character for having a try at everything.

Henrietta despatched at this period the following letter to Chillon:

'I am with Livia to-morrow. Janey starts for Wales to-morrow morning, a voluntary exile. She pleaded to go back to that place where you had to leave her, promising she would not come Westward; but was persuaded. Lady Arpington approves. The situation was getting too terribly strained. We met and passed my lord in the park.

'He was walking his horse-elegant cavalier that he is: would not look on his wife. A woman pulled by her collar should be passive; if she pulls her way, she is treated as a dog. I see nothing else in the intention of poor Janey's last offence to him. There is an opposite counsel, and he can be eloquent, and he will be heard on her side. How could she manage the most wayward when she has not an idea of ordinary men! But, my husband, they have our tie between them; it may move him. It subdues her—and nothing else would have done that. If she had been in England a year before the marriage, she would, I think, have understood better how to guide her steps and her tongue for his good pleasure. She learns daily, very quickly: observes, assimilates; she reads and has her comments—would have shot far ahead of your Riette, with my advantages.

'Your uncle—but he will bear any charge on his conscience as long as he can get the burden off his shoulders. Do not fret, my own! Reperuse the above—you will see we have grounds for hope.

'He should have looked down on her! No tears from her eyes, but her eyes were tears. She does not rank among beautiful women. She has her moments for outshining them—the loveliest of spectres! She caught at my heart. I cannot forget her face looking up for him to look down. A great painter would have reproduced it, a great poet have rendered the impression. Nothing short of the greatest. That is odd to say of one so simple as she. But when accidents call up her reserves, you see mountain heights where mists were—she is actually glorified. Her friend—I do believe a friend—the Mr. Woodseer you are to remember meeting somewhere—a sprained ankle—has a dozen similes ready for what she is when pain or happiness vivify her. Or, it may be, tender charity. She says, that if she feels for suffering people, it is because she is the child of Chillon's mother. In like manner Chillon is the son of Janey's father.

'Mr. Woodseer came every other evening. Our only enlivenment. Livia followed her policy, in refusing to call. We lived luxuriously; no money, not enough for a box at the opera, though we yearned—you can imagine. Chapters of philosophy read out and expounded instead. Janey likes them. He sets lessons to her queer maid—reading, writing, pronunciation of English. An inferior language to Welsh, for poetical purposes, we are informed. So Janey—determining to apply herself to Welsh, and a chameleon Riette dreading that she will be taking a contrary view of the honest souls—as she feels them to be—when again under Livia's shadow.

'The message from Janey to Scrope's hotel was despatched half-an-hour after we had driven in from the park; fruit of a brown meditation. I wrote it—third person—a single sentence. Arrangements are made for her to travel comfortably. It is funny—the shops for her purchases of clothes, necessaries, etc., are specified; she may order to any extent. Not a shilling of money for her poor purse. What can be the secret of that? He does nothing without an object. To me, uniformly civil, no irony, few compliments. Livia writes, that I am commended for keeping Janey company. What can be the secret of a man scrupulously just with one hand, and at the same time cruel with the other? Mr. Woodseer says, his wealth:—"More money than is required for their needs, men go into harness to Plutus,"—if that is clever.

'I have written my husband—as Janey ceases to call her own; and it was pretty and touching to hear her "my husband."—Oh! a dull letter. But he is my husband though he keeps absent—to be longed for—he is my husband still, my husband always. Chillon is Henrietta's husband, the world cries out, and when she is flattered she does the like, for then it is not too presumptuous that she should name Henrietta Chillon's wife. In my ears, husband has the sweeter sound. It brings an angel from overhead. Will it bring him one-half hour sooner? My love! My dear! If it did, I should be lisping "husband, husband, husband" from cock-crow to owl's cry. Livia thinks the word foolish, if not detestable. She and I have our different opinions. She is for luxury. I choose poverty and my husband. Poverty has its beauty, if my husband is the sun of it. Elle radote. She would not have written so dull a letter to her husband if she had been at the opera last night, or listened to a distant street-band. No more—the next line would be bleeding. He should have her blood too, if that were her husband's—it would never be; but if it were for his good in the smallest way. Chillon's wish is to give his blood for them he loves. Never did woman try more to write worthily to her absent lord and fall so miserably into the state of dripping babe from bath on nurse's knee. Cover me, my lord; and love, my cause for—no, my excuse, my refuge from myself. We are one? Oh! we are one!—and we have been separated eight and twenty days.

'HENRIETTA KIRBY-LEVELLIER.'

That was a letter for the husband and lover to receive in a foreign land and be warmed.

The tidings of Carinthia washed him clean of the grimy district where his waxen sister had developed her stubborn insensibility;—resembling craziness, every perversion of the refinement demanded by young Englishmen of their ladies; and it pacified him with the belief that she was now at rest, the disturbed history of their father and mother at rest as well; his conscience in relation to the marriage likewise at rest. Chillon had a wife. Her writing of the welcome to poverty stirred his knowledge of his wife's nature. Carinthia might bear it and harden to flint; Henrietta was a butterfly for the golden rays. His thoughts, all his energies, were bent on the making of money to supply her need for the pleasure she flew in—a butterfly's grub without it. Accurately so did the husband and lover read his wife—adoring her the more.

Her letter's embracing close was costly to them. It hurried him to the compromise of a debateable business, and he fell into the Austrian Government's terms for the payment of the inheritance from his father; calculating that—his sister's share deducted-money would be in hand to pay pressing debts and enable Henrietta to live unworried by cares until he should have squeezed debts, long due and increasing, out of the miserly old lord, his uncle. A prospect of supplies for twelve months, counting the hack and carriage Henrietta had always been used to, seemed about as far as it was required to look by the husband hastening homeward to his wife's call. Her letter was a call in the night. Besides, there were his yet untried Inventions. The new gunpowder testing at Croridge promised to provide Henrietta with many of the luxuries she could have had, and had abandoned for his sake. The new blasting powder and a destructive shell might build her the palace she deserved. His uncle was, no doubt, his partner. If, however, the profits were divided, sufficient wealth was assured. But his uncle remained a dubious image. The husband and lover could enfold no positive prospect to suit his wife's tastes beyond the twelve months.

We have Dame Gossip upon us. —One minute let mention be of the excitement over Protestant England when that rumour disseminated, telling of her wealthiest nobleman's visit to a monastery, up in the peaks and snows; and of his dwelling among the monks, and assisting in all their services day and night, hymning and chanting, uttering not one word for one whole week: his Papistical friend, Lord Feltre, with him, of course, after Jesuit arts had allured him to that place of torrents and lightnings and canticles and demon echoes, all as though expressly contrived for the horrifying of sinners into penitence and confession and the monkish cowl up to life's end, not to speak of the abjuration of worldly possessions and donation of them into the keeping of the shaven brothers; when either they would have settled a band of them here in our very midst, or they would have impoverished—is not too strong a word—the country by taking the money's worth of the mines, estates, mansions, freehold streets and squares of our metropolis out of it without scruple; rejoicing so to bleed the Protestant faith. Underrate it now— then it was a truly justifiable anxiety: insomuch that you heard people of station, eminent titled persons, asking, like the commonest low Radicals, whether it was prudent legislation to permit of the inheritance of such vast wealth by a young man, little more than a boy, and noted for freaks. And some declared it could not be allowed for foreign monks to have a claim to inherit English property. There was a general consent, that if the Earl of Fleetwood went to the extreme of making over his property to those monks, he should be pronounced insane and incapable. Ultimately the world was a little pacified by hearing that a portion of it was entailed, Esslemont and the Welsh mines.

So it might be; but what if he had no child! The marriage amazing everybody scarcely promised fruit, it was thought. Countess Livia, much besought for her opinion, scouted the possibility. And Carinthia Jane was proclaimed by John Rose Mackrell (to his dying day the poor gentleman tried vainly to get the second syllable of his name accentuated) a young woman who would outlive twice over the husband she had. He said of his name, it was destined to pass him down a dead fish in the nose of posterity, and would affect his best jokes; which something has done, or the present generation has lost the sense of genuine humour.

Thanks to him, the talk of the Whitechapel Countess again sprang up, merrily as ever; and after her having become, as he said, 'a desiccated celebrity,' she outdid cabinet ministers and naughty wives for a living morsel in the world's mouth. She was denounced by the patriotic party as the cause of the earl's dalliance with Rome.

The earl, you are to know, was then coasting along the Mediterranean, on board his beautiful schooner yacht, with his Lord Feltre, bound to make an inspection of Syrian monasteries, and forget, if he could, the face of all faces, another's possession by the law.

Those two lords, shut up together in a yacht, were advised by their situation to be bosom friends, and they quarrelled violently, and were reconciled, and they quarrelled again; they were explosive chemicals; until the touch of dry land relieved them of what they really fancied the spell of the Fiend. For their argumentative topic during confinement was Woman, when it was not Theology; and even off a yacht, those are subjects to kindle the utmost hatred of dissension, if men are not perfectly concordant. They agreed upon land to banish any talk of Women or Theology, where it would have been comparatively innocent; so they both desiring to be doing the thing they had sworn they would not do, the thoughts of both were fastened on one or the other interdicted subject. They hardly spoke; they perceived in their longing minds, that the imagined spell of, the Fiend was indeed the bile of the sea, secreted thickly for want of exercise, and they both regretted the days and nights of their angry controversies; unfit pilgrims of the Holy Land, they owned.

To such effect, Lord Fleetwood wrote to Gower Woodseer, as though there had been no breach between them, from Jerusalem, expressing the wish to hear his cool wood-notes of the philosophy of Life, fresh drawn from Nature's breast; and urgent for an answer, to be addressed to his hotel at Southampton, that he might be greeted on his return home first by his 'friend Gower.'

He wrote in the month of January. His arrival at Southampton was on the thirteenth day of March; and there he opened a letter some weeks old, the bearer of news which ought by rights to make husbands proudly happy.

CHAPTER XXVII

WE DESCEND INTO A STEAMER'S ENGINE-ROOM

Fleetwood had dropped his friend Lord Feltre at Ancona; his good fortune was to be alone when the clang of bells rang through his head in the reading of Gower's lines. Other letters were opened: from the Countess Livia, from Lady Arpington, from Captain Kirby-Levellier. There was one from his lawyers, informing him of their receipt of a communication dated South Wales, December 11th, and signed Owain Wythan; to the effect, that the birth of a son to the Earl of Fleetwood was registered on the day of the date, with a copy of the document forwarded.

Livia scornfully stated the tattling world's 'latest.' The captain was as brief, in ordinary words, whose quick run to the stop could be taken for a challenge of the eye. It stamped the adversary's frown on Fleetwood reading. Lady Arpington was more politic; she wrote of 'a healthy boy,' and 'the healthy mother giving him breast,' this being 'the way for the rearing of strong men.' She condescended to the particulars, that she might touch him.

The earl had not been so reared: his mother was not the healthy mother. One of his multitudinous, shifty, but ineradicable ambitions was to exhibit an excellingly vigorous, tireless constitution. He remembered the needed refreshment of the sea-breezes aboard his yacht during the week following the sleep-discarded nights at Scrope's and the green tables. For a week he hung to the smell of brine, in rapturous amity with Feltre, until they yellowed, differed, wrangled, hated.

A powerful leaven was put into him by the tidings out of Wales. Gower, good fellow, had gone down to see the young mother three weeks after the birth of her child. She was already renewing her bloom. She had produced the boy in the world's early manner, lightly, without any of the tragic modern hovering over death to give the life. Gower compared it to a 'flush of the vernal orchard after a day's drink of sunlight.' That was well: that was how it should be. One loathes the idea of tortured women.

The good fellow was perhaps absurdly poetical. Still we must have poetry to hallow this and other forms of energy: or say, if you like, the right view of them impels to poetry. Otherwise we are in the breeding yards, among the litters and the farrows. It is a question of looking down or looking up. If we are poor creatures—as we are if we do but feast and gamble and beget—we shall run for a time with the dogs and come to the finish of swine. Better say, life is holy! Why, then have we to thank her who teaches it.

He gazed at the string of visions of the woman naming him husband, making him a father: the imagined Carinthia—beautiful Gorgon, haggard Venus; the Carinthia of the precipice tree-shoot; Carinthia of the ducal dancing-hall; and she at the altar rails; she on the coach box; she alternately softest of brides, doughtiest of Amazons. A mate for the caress, an electrical heroine, fronted him.

Yes, and she was Lord Fleetwood's wife, cracking sconces,—a demoiselle Moll Flanders,—the world's Whitechapel Countess out for an airing, infernally earnest about it, madly ludicrous; the schemer to catch his word, the petticoated Shylock to bind him to the letter of it; now persecuting, haunting him, now immoveable for obstinacy; malignant to stay down in those vile slums and direct tons of sooty waters on his head from its mains in the sight of London, causing the least histrionic of men to behave as an actor. He beheld her a skull with a lamp behind the eyeholes.

But this woman was the woman who made him a father; she was the mother of the heir of the House; and the boy she clasped and suckled as her boy was his boy. They met inseparably in that new life.

Truly, there could not be a woman of flesh so near to a likeness with the beatific image of Feltre's worshipped Madonna!

The thought sparkled and darkened in Fleetwood's mind, as a star passing into cloud. For an uproarious world claimed the woman, jeered at all allied with her; at her husband most, of course:—the punctilious noodle! the golden jackass, tethered and goaded! He had choice among the pick of women: the daughter of the Old Buccaneer was preferred by the wiseacre Coelebs. She tricked him cunningly and struck a tremendous return blow in producing her male infant.

By the way, was she actually born in wedlock? Lord Levellier's assurances regarding her origin were, by the calculation, a miser's shuffles to clinch his bargain. Assuming the representative of holy motherhood to be a woman of illegitimate birth, the history of the House to which the spotted woman gave an heir would suffer a jolt when touching on her. And altogether the history fumed rank vapours. Imagine her boy in his father's name a young collegian! No commonly sensitive lad could bear the gibes of the fellows raking at antecedents: Fleetwood would be the name to start roars. Smarting for his name, the earl chafed at the boy's mother. Her production of a man-child was the further and grosser offence.

The world sat on him. His confession to some degree of weakness, even to folly, stung his pride of individuality so that he had to soothe the pain by tearing himself from a thought of his folly's partner, shutting himself up and away from her. Then there was a cessation of annoyance, flatteringly agreeable: which can come to us only of our having done the right thing, young men will think. He felt at once warmly with the world, enjoyed the world's kind shelter, and in return for its eulogy of his unprecedented attachment to the pledge of his word, admitted an understanding of its laughter at the burlesque edition of a noble lady in the person of the Whitechapel Countess. The world sat on him heavily.

He recurred to Gower Woodseer's letter.

The pictures and images in it were not the principal matter,—the impression had been deep. A plain transcription of the young mother's acts and words did more to portray her: the reader could supply reflections.

Would her boy's father be very pleased to see him? she had asked.

And she spoke of a fear that the father would try to take her boy from her.

'Never that—you have my word!' Fleetwood said; and he nodded consentingly over her next remark—

'Not while I live, till he must go to school!'

The stubborn wife would be the last of women to sit and weep as a rifled mother.

A child of the Countess Carinthia (he phrased it) would not be deficient in will, nor would the youngster lack bravery.

For his part, comparison rushing at him and searching him, he owned that he leaned on pride. To think that he did, became a theme for pride. The mother had the primitive virtues, the father the developed: he was the richer mine. And besides, he was he, the unriddled, complex, individual he; she was the plain barbarian survival, good for giving her offspring bone, muscle, stout heart.

Shape the hypothesis of a fairer woman the mother of the heir to the earldom.

Henrietta was analyzed in a glimpse. Courage, animal healthfulness, she, too, might—her husband not obstructing—transmit; and good looks, eyes of the sapphire AEgean. And therewith such pliability as the Mother of Love requires of her servants.

Could that woman resist seductions?

Fleetwood's wrath with her for refusing him and inducing him in spite to pledge his word elsewhere, haphazard, pricked a curiosity to know whether the woman could be—and easily! easily! he wagered—led to make her conduct warrant for his contempt of her. Led,—that is, misled, you might say, if you were pleading for a doll. But it was necessary to bait the pleasures for the woman, in order to have full view of the precious fine fate one has escaped. Also to get well rid of a sort of hectic in the blood, which the woman's beauty has cast on that reflecting tide: a fever-sign, where the fever has become quite emotionless and is merely desirous for the stain of it to be washed out. As this is not the desire to possess or even to taste, contempt will do it. When we know that the weaver of the fascinations is purchasable, we toss her to the market where men buy; and we walk released from vile subjection to one of the female heap: subjection no longer, doubtless, and yet a stain of the past flush, often colouring our reveries, creating active phantasms of a passion absolutely extinct, if it ever was the veritable passion.

The plot—formless plot—to get release by the sacrifice or at least a crucial temptation of the woman, that should wash his blood clean of her image, had a shade of the devilish, he acknowledged; and the apology offered no improvement of its aspect. She might come out of the trial triumphant. And benefit for himself, even a small privilege, even the pressure of her hand, he not only shrank from the thought of winning,-he loathed the thought. He was too delicate over the idea of the married woman whom he fancied he loved in her maidenhood. Others might press her hand, lead her the dance: he simply wanted his release. She had set him on fire; he conceived a method for trampling the remaining sparks and erasing stain and scars; that was all. Henrietta rejected her wealthy suitor: she might some day hence be seen crawling abjectly to wealth, glad of a drink from the cup it holds, intoxicated with the draught. An injured pride could animate his wealth to crave solace of such a spectacle.

Devilish, if you like. He had expiated the wickedness in Cistercian seclusion. His wife now drove him to sin again.

She had given him a son. That fluted of home and honourable life. She had her charm, known to him alone.

But how, supposing she did not rub him to bristle with fresh irritations, how go to his wife while Henrietta held her throne? Consideration was due to her until she stumbled. Enough if she wavered. Almost enough is she stood firm as a statue in the winds, and proved that the first page of her was a false introduction. The surprising apparition of a beautiful woman with character; a lightly-thrilled, pleasure-loving woman devoted to her husband or protected by her rightful self-esteem, would loosen him creditably. It had to be witnessed, for faith in it. He reverenced our legendary good women, and he bowed to noble deeds; and he ascribed the former to poetical creativeness, the latter operated as a scourging to his flesh to yield its demoniacal inmates. Nothing of the kind was doing at present.

Or stay: a studious re-perusal of Gower Woodseer's letter enriched a little incident. Fleetwood gave his wife her name of Carinthia when he had read deliberately and caught the scene.

Mrs. Wythan down in Wales related it to Gower. Carinthia and Madge, trudging over the treeless hills, came on a birchen clump round a deep hollow or gullypit; precipitous, the earl knew, he had peeped over the edge in his infant days. There at the bottom, in a foot or so of water, they espied a lamb; and they rescued the poor beastie by going down to it, one or both. It must have been the mountain-footed one. A man would hesitate, spying below. Fleetwood wondered how she had managed to climb up, and carrying the lamb! Down pitches Madge Winch to help—they did it between them. We who stand aloof admire stupidly. To defend himself from admiring, he condemned the two women for the risk they ran to save a probably broken-legged little beast: and he escaped the melting mood by forcing a sneer at the sort of stuff out of which popular ballads are woven. Carinthia was accused of letting her adventurous impulses and sentimental female compassion swamp thought of a mother's duties. If both those women had broken their legs the child might have cried itself into fits for the mother, there she would have remained.

Gower wrote in a language transparent of the act, addressed to a reader whose memory was to be impregnated. His reader would have flown away from the simple occurrence on arabesques and modulated tones; and then envisaging them critically, would have tossed his poor little story to the winds, as a small thing magnified: with an object, being the next thought about it. He knew his Fleetwood so far.

His letter concluded: 'I am in a small Surrey village over a baker's shop, rent eight shillings per week, a dame's infant school opposite my window, miles of firwood, heath, and bracken openings, for the winged or the nested fancies. Love Nature, she makes you a lord of her boundless, off any ten square feet of common earth. I go through my illusions and come always back on that good truth. It says, beware of the world's passion for flavours and spices. Much tasted, they turn and bite the biter. My exemplars are the lately breeched youngsters with two pence in their pockets for the gingerbread-nut booth on a fair day. I learn more from one of them than you can from the whole cavalcade of your attendant Ixionides.'

Mounting the box of his coach for the drive to London, Fleetwood had the new name for the parasitic and sham vital troop at his ears.

'My Ixionides!' he repeated, and did not scorn them so much as he rejoiced to be enlightened by the title. He craved the presence of the magician who dropped illumination with a single word; wholesomer to think of than the whole body of those Ixionides—not bad fellows, here and there, he reflected, tolerantly, half laughing at some of their clownish fun. Gower Woodseer and he had not quarrelled? No, they had merely parted at one of the crossways. The plebeian could teach that son of the, genuflexions, Lord Feltre, a lesson in manners. Woodseer was the better comrade and director of routes. Into the forest, up on the heights; and free, not locked; and not parroting day and night, but quick for all that the world has learnt and can tell, though two-thirds of it be composed of Ixionides: that way lies wisdom, and his index was cut that way.

Arrived in town, he ran over the headings of his letters, in no degree anxious for a communication from Wales. There was none. Why none?

She might as well have scrawled her announcement of an event pleasing to her, and, by the calculation, important to him, if not particularly interesting. The mother's wifeish lines would, perhaps, have been tested in a furnace. He smarted at the blank of any, of even two or three formal words. She sulked? 'I am not a fallen lamb!' he said. Evidently one had to be a shivering beast in trouble, to excite her to move a hand.

Through so slight a fissure as this piece of discontent cracked in him, the crowd of his grievances with the woman rushed pell-mell, deluging young shoots of sweeter feelings. She sulked! If that woman could not get the command, he was to know her incapable of submission. After besmutting the name she had filched from him, she let him understand that there was no intention to repent. Possibly she meant war. In which case a man must fly, or stand assailed by the most intolerable of vulgar farces;—to be compared to a pelting of one on the stage.

The time came for him to knock at doors and face his public.

CHAPTER XXVIII

BY CONCESSIONS TO MISTRESS GOSSIP A FURTHER INTRUSION IS AVERTED

Livia welcomed him, with commiserating inquiry behind her languid eyelids. 'You have all the latest?' it said.

He struck on the burning matter.

'You wish to know the part you have to play, ma'am.' 'Tell me, Russett.'

'You will contradict nothing.'

Her eyebrows asked, 'It means?'

'You have authority from me to admit the facts.'

'They are facts?' she remarked.

'Women love teasing round certain facts, apparently; like the Law courts over their pet cases.'

'But, Russett, will you listen?'

'Has the luck been civil of late?'

'I think of something else at present. No, it has not.'

'Abrane?'

'Pray, attend to me. No, not Abrane.'

'I believe you've all been cleared out in my absence. St. Ombre?'

Her complexion varied. 'Mr. Ambrose Mallard has once or twice... But let me beg you—the town is rageing with it. My dear Russett, a bold front now; there 's the chance of your release in view.'

'A rascal in view! Name the sum.'

'I must reckon. My head is—can you intend to submit?'

'So it's Brosey Mallard now. You choose your deputy queerly. He's as bad as Abrane, with steam to it. Chummy Potts would have done better.'

'He wins one night; loses every pound-note he has the next; and comes vaunting—the "dry still Sillery" of the establishment,—a perpetual chorus to his losses!'

'His consolation to you for yours. That is the gentleman. Chummy doesn't change. Say, why not St. Ombre? He's cool.'

'There are reasons.'

'Let them rest. And I have my reasons. Do the same for them.'

'Yours concern the honour of the family.'

'Deeply: respect them.'

'Your relatives have to be thought of, though they are few and not too pleasant.'

'If I had thought much of them, what would our relations be? They object to dicing, and I to leading strings.'

She turned to a brighter subject, of no visible connection with the preceding.

'Henrietta comes in May.'

'The month of her colours.'

'Her money troubles are terrible.'

'Both of you appear unlucky in your partners,—if winning was the object. She shall have all the distractions we can offer.'

'Your visit to the Chartreuse alarmed her.'

'She has rejoiced her husband.'

'A girl. She feared the Jesuit in your friend.'

'Feltre and she are about equally affected by music. They shall meet.'

'Russett, this once: I do entreat you to take counsel with your good sense, and remember that you stand where you are by going against my advice. It is a perfect storm over London. The world has not to be informed of your generosity; but a chivalry that invites the most horrible of sneers at a man! And what can I say? I have said it was impossible.'

'Add the postscript: you find it was perfectly possible.'

'I have to learn more than I care to hear.'

'Your knowledge is not in request: you will speak in my name.'

'Will you consult your lawyers, Russett, before you commit yourself?'

'I am on my way to Lady Arpington.'

'You cannot be thinking how serious it is.'

'I rather value the opinion of a hard-headed woman of the world.'

'Why not listen to me?'

'You have your points, ma'am.'

'She's a torch.'

'She serves my purpose.'

Livia shrugged sadly. 'I suppose it serves your purpose to be unintelligible to me.'

He rendered himself intelligible immediately by saying, 'Before I go—a thousand?'

'Oh, my dear Russett!' she sighed.

'State the amount.'

She seemed to be casting unwieldly figures and he helped her with, 'Mr. Isaacs?'

'Not less than three, I fear.'

'Has he been pressing?'

'You are always good to us, Russett.'

'You are always considerate for the honour of the family, ma'am. Order for the money with you here to-morrow. And I thank you for your advice. Do me the favour to follow mine.

'Commands should be the word.'

'Phrase it as you please.'

'You know I hate responsibility.'

'The chorus in classical dramas had generally that sentiment, but the singing was the sweeter for it.'

'Whom do you not win when you condescend to the mood, you dear boy?'

He restrained a bitter reply, touching the kind of persons he had won: a girl from the mountains, a philosophical tramp of the roads, troops of the bought.

Livia spelt at the problem he was. She put away the task of reading it. He departed to see Lady Arpington, and thereby rivet his chains.

As Livia had said, she was a torch. Lady Endor, Lady Eldritch, Lady Cowry, kindled at her. Again there were flights of the burning brands over London. The very odd marriage; the no-marriage; the two-ends-of-the-town marriage; and the maiden marriage a fruitful marriage; the monstrous marriage of the countess productive in banishment, and the unreadable earl accepting paternity; this Amazing Marriage was again the riddle in the cracker for tattlers and gapers. It rattled upon the world's native wantonness, the world's acquired decorum: society's irrepressible original and its powerfully resisting second nature. All the rogues of the fine sphere ran about with it, male and female; and there was the narrative that suggestively skipped, and that which trod the minuet measure, dropping a curtsey to ravenous curiosity; the apology surrendering its defensible cause in supplications to benevolence; and the benevolence damnatory in a too eloquent urgency; followed by the devout objection to a breath of the subject, so blackening it as to call forth the profanely circumstantial exposition. Smirks, blushes, dead silences, and in the lower regions roars, hung round it.

But the lady, though absent, did not figure poorly at all. Granting Whitechapel and the shillelagh affair, certain whispers of her good looks, contested only to be the more violently asserted; and therewith Rose Mackrell's tale of her being a 'young woman of birth,' having a 'romantic story to tell of herself and her parentage,' made her latest performance the champagne event of it hitherto. Men sparkled when they had it on their lips.

How, then, London asked, would the Earl of Fleetwood move his pieces in reply to his countess's particularly clever indication of the check threatening mate?

His move had no relation to the game, it was thought at first. The world could not suppose that he moved a simple pawn on his marriage board. He purchased a shop in Piccadilly for the sale of fruit and flowers.

Lady Arpington was entreated to deal at the shop, Countess Livia had her orders; his friends, his parasites and satellites, were to deal there. Intensely earnest as usual, he besought great ladies to let him have the overflow of their hothouses; and they classing it as another of the mystifications of a purse crazy for repleteness, inquired: 'But is it you we are to deal with?' And he quite seriously said: 'With me, yes, at present.' Something was behind the curtain, of course. His gravity had the effect of the ultra-comical in concealing it.

The shop was opened. We have the assurance of Rose Mackrell, that he entered and examined the piles and pans of fruit, and the bouquets cunningly arranged by a hand smelling French. The shop was roomy, splendid windows lighted the yellow, the golden, the green and parti-coloured stores. Four doors off, a chemist's motley in bellied glasses crashed on the sight. Passengers along the pavement had presented to them such a contrast as might be shown if we could imagine the Lethean ferry-boatload brought sharp against Pomona's lapful. In addition to the plucked flowers and fruits of the shop, Rose Mackrell more attentively examined the samples doing service at the counters. They were three, under supervision of a watchful-eyed fourth. Dame Gossip is for quoting his wit. But the conclusion he reached, after quitting the shop and pacing his dozen steps, is important; for it sent a wind over the town to set the springs of tattle going as wildly as when the herald's trumpet blew the announcement for the world to hear out of Wales.

He had observed, that the young woman supervising was deficient in the ease of an established superior; her brows were troubled; she was, therefore, a lieutenant elevated from a lower grade; and, to his thinking, conducted the business during the temporary retirement of the mistress of the shop.

And the mistress of the shop?

The question hardly needs be put.

Rose Mackrell or his humour answered it in unfaltering terms.

London heard, with the variety of feelings which are indistinguishable under a flooding amazement, that the beautiful new fruit and flower shop had been purchased and stocked by the fabulously wealthy young Earl of Fleetwood, to give his Whitechapel Countess a taste for business, an occupation, and an honourable means of livelihood.

There was, Dame Gossip thumps to say, a general belief in this report. Crowds were on the pavement, peering through the shop-windows. Carriages driving by stopped to look. My lord himself had been visible, displaying his array of provisions to friends. Nor was credulity damped appreciably when over the shop, in gold letters, appeared the name of Sarah Winch. It might be the countess's maiden name, if she really was a married countess.

But, in truth, the better informed of the town, having begun to think its Croesus capable of any eccentricity, chose to believe. They were at the pitch of excitement which demands and will swallow a succession of wilder extravagances. To accelerate the delirium of the fun, nothing was too much, because any absurdity was anticipated. And the earl's readiness to be complimented on the shop's particular merits, his gratified air at an allusion to it, whirled the fun faster. He seemed entirely unconscious that each step he now took wakened peals.

For such is the fate of a man who has come to be dogged by the humourist for the provision he furnishes; and, as it happens, he is the more laughable if not in himself a laughable object. The earl's handsome figure, fine style, and contrasting sobriety heightened the burlesque of his call to admiration of a shop where Whitechapel would sit in state-according to the fiction so closely under the lee of fact that they were not strictly divisible. Moreover, Sarah Winch, whom Chumley Potts drew into conversation, said, he vowed, she came up West from Whitechapel. She said it a little nervously, but without blushing. Always on the side of the joke, he could ask: 'Who can doubt?' Indeed, scepticism poisoned the sport.

The Old Buccaneer has written: Friends may laugh; I am not roused. My enemy's laugh is a bugle blown in the night.

Our enemy's laugh at us rouses to wariness, he would say. He can barely mean, that a condition of drowsihead is other than providently warned by laughter of friends. An old warrior's tough fibre would, perhaps, be insensible to that small crackle. In civil life, however, the friend's laugh at us is the loudest of the danger signals to stop our course: and the very wealthy nobleman, who is known for not a fool, is kept from hearing it. Unless he does hear it, he can have no suspicion of its being about him: he cannot imagine such 'lese-majeste' in the subservient courtiers too prudent to betray a sign. So Fleetwood was unwarned; and his child-like unconsciousness of the boiling sentiments around, seasoned, pricked, and maddened his parasites under compression to invent, for a faint relief. He had his title for them, they their tales of him.

Dame Gossip would recount the tales. She is of the order of persons inclining to suspect the tittle of truth in prodigies of scandal. She is rustling and bustling to us of 'Carinthia Jane's run up to London to see Sarah Winch's grand new shop,' an eclipse of all existing grand London western shops; and of Rose Mackrell's account of her dance of proud delight in the shop, ending with a 'lovely cheese' just as my lord enters; and then a scene, wild beyond any conceivable 'for pathos and humour'—her pet pair of the dissimilar twins, both banging at us for tear-drops by different roads, through a common aperture:—and the earl has the Whitechapel baby boy plumped into his arms; and the countess fetches him a splendid bob-dip and rises out of a second cheese to twirl and fandango it; and, all serious on a sudden, request, whimperingly beseech, his thanks to her for the crowing successor she has presented him with: my lord ultimately, but carefully, depositing the infant on a basket of the last oranges of the season, fresh from the Azores, by delivery off my lord's own schooner-yacht in Southampton water; and escaping, leaving his gold-headed stick behind him—a trophy for the countess? a weapon, it may be.

Quick she tucks up her skirts, she is after him. Dame Gossip speaks amusingly enough of the chase, and many eye-witnesses to the earl's flight at top speed down the right side of the way along by the Green Park; and of a Prince of the Blood, a portly Royal Duke on foot, bumped by one or the other of them, she cannot precisely say which, but 'thinks it to have been Carinthia Jane,' because the exalted personage, his shock of surprise abating, turned and watched the chase, in much merriment. And it was called, we are informed, 'The Piccadilly Hare and Hound' from that day.

Some tradition of an extenuated nobleman pursued by a light-footed lady amid great excitement, there is; the Dame attaches importance also to verses of one of the ballads beginning to gain currency at the time (issuing ostensibly from London's poetic centre, the Seven Dials, which had, we are to conjecture, got the story by discolouring filtration through footmen retailing in public-houses the stock of anecdotes they gathered when stationed behind Rose Mackrell's chair, or Captain Abrane's, or Chumley 'Potts's), and would have the whole of it quoted:—

"'Tho' fair I be a powdered peruke,
And once was a gaping silly,
Your Whitechapel Countess will prove, Lord Duke,
She's a regular tiger-lily.
She'll fight you with cold steel or she'll run you off your legs
Down the length of Piccadilly!"

That will satisfy; and perhaps indicate the hand.

'Popular sympathy, of course, was all on the side of the Fair, as ever in those days when women had not forfeited it by stepping from their sanctuary seclusion.'

The Dame shall expose her confusions. She really would seem to fancy that the ballad verifies the main lines of the story, which is an impossible one. Carinthia had not the means to travel: she was moneyless. Every bill of her establishment was paid without stint by Mr. Howell Edwards, the earl's manager of mines; but she had not even the means for a journey to the Gowerland rocks she longed to see. She had none since she forced her brother to take the half of her share of their inheritance, L1400, and sent him the remainder.

Accepted by Chillon John as a loan, says Dame Gossip, and no sooner received than consumed by the pressing necessities of a husband with the Rose Beauty of England to support in the comforts and luxuries he deemed befitting.

Still the Dame leans to her opinion that 'Carinthia Jane' may have been seen about London: for 'where we have much smoke there must be fire.' And the countess never denying an imputation not brought against her in her hearing, the ballad was unchallenged and London's wags had it their own way. Among the reasons why they so persistently hunted the earl, his air of a smart correctness shadowed by this new absurdity invited them, as when a spot of mud on the trimmest of countenances arrests observation: Humour plucked at him the more for the good faith of his handsome look under the prolific little disfigurement. Besides, a wealthy despot, with no conception of any hum around him, will have the wags in his track as surely as the flexibles in front: they avenge his exactions.

Fleetwood was honestly unaware of ridicule in the condition of inventive mania at his heels. Scheming, and hesitating to do, one-half of his mind was absorbed with the problem of how now to treat the mother of his boy. Her behaviour in becoming a mother was acknowledged to be good: the production of a boy was good—considerate, he almost thought. He grew so far reconciled to her as to have intimations of a softness coming on; a wish to hear her speak of the trifling kindness done to the sister of Madge in reward of kindness done to her; wishes for looks he remembered, secret to him, more his own than any possessions. Dozens of men had wealth, some had beautiful wives; none could claim as his own that face of the look of sharp steel melting into the bridal flower, when she sprang from her bed to defend herself and recognized the intruder at her window; stood smitten:—'It is my, husband.' Moonlight gave the variation of her features.

And that did not appease the resentment tearing him from her, so justifiable then, as he forced himself to think, now hideous. Glimpses of the pictures his deeds painted of him since his first meeting with this woman had to be shunned. He threw them off; they were set down to the mystery men are. The degrading, utterly different, back view of them teaches that Life is an irony. If the teaching is not accepted, and we are to take the blame, can we bear to live? Therefore, either way the irony of Life is proved. Young men straining at thought, in the grip of their sensations, reach this logical conclusion. They will not begin by examining the ground they stand on, and questioning whether they have consciences at peace with the steps to rearward.

Having established Life as the coldly malignant element, which induces to what it chastises, a loathing of womanhood, the deputed Mother of Life, ensues, by natural sequence. And if there be one among women who disturbs the serenity we choose to think our due, she wears for us the sinister aspect of a confidential messenger between Nemesis and the Parcae. Fleetwood was thus compelled to regard Carinthia as both originally and successively the cause of his internal as well as his exterior discomfort; otherwise those glimpses would have burnt into perpetual stigmas. He had also to get his mind away from her. They pleaded against him volubly with the rising of her image into it.

His manager at the mines had sent word of ominous discontent down there. His presence might be required. Obviously, then, the threatened place was unfitting for the Countess of Fleetwood. He despatched a kind of order through Mr. Howell Edwards, that she should remove to Esslemont to escape annoyances. Esslemont was the preferable residence. She could there entertain her friends, could spend a pleasanter time there.

He waited for the reply; Edwards deferred it.

Were they to be in a struggle with her obstinate will once more?

Henrietta was preparing to leave London for her dismal, narrow, and, after an absence, desired love-nest. The earl called to say farewell, cool as a loyal wife could wish him to be, admiring perforce. Marriage and maternity withdrew nothing—added to the fair young woman's bloom.

She had gone to her room to pack and dress. Livia received him. In the midst of the casual commonplaces her memory was enlightened.

'Oh,' said she, and idly drew a letter out of a blottingpad, 'we have heard from Wales.' She handed it to him.

Before he knew the thing he did, he was reading:

'There is no rest foamy brother, and I cannot help; I am kept so poor I have not the smallest of sums. I do not wish to leave Wales—the people begin to love me; and can one be mistaken? I know if I am loved or hated. But if my lord will give me an allowance of money of some hundreds, I will do his bidding; I will leave England or I will go to Esslemont; I could say—to Mr. Woodseer, in that part of London. He would not permit. He thinks me blacked by it, like a sweepboy coming from a chimney; and that I have done injury to his title. No, Riette, to be a true sister, I must bargain with my lord before I submit. He has not cared to come and see his little son. His boy has not offended him. There may be some of me in this dear. I know whose features will soon show to defend the mother's good name. He is early my champion. He is not christened yet, and I hear it accuse me, and I am not to blame,—I still wait my lord's answer.'

'Don't be bothered to read the whole,' Livia had said, with her hand out, when his eyes were halfway down the page.

Fleetwood turned it, to read the signature: 'Janey.'

She seemed servile enough to some of her friends. 'Carinthia' would have had—a pleasanter sound. He folded the letter.

'Why give me this? Take it,'—said he.

She laid it on the open pad.

Henrietta entered and had it restored to her, Livia remarking: 'I found it in the blotter after all.'

She left them together, having to dress for the drive to the coach office with Henrietta.

'Poor amusement for you this time.' Fleetwood bowed, gently smiling.

'Oh!' cried Henrietta, 'balls, routs, dinners, music—as much music as I could desire, even I! What more could be asked? I am eternally grateful.'

'The world says, you are more beautiful than ever.'

'Happiness does it, then,—happiness owing to you, Lord Fleetwood.'

'Columelli pleases you?'

'His voice is heavenly! He carries me away from earth.'

'He is a gentleman, too-rare with those fellows.'

'A pretty manner. He will speak his compliments in his English.'

'You are seasoned to endure them in all languages. Pity another of your wounded: Brailstone has been hard hit at the tables.

'I cannot pity gamblers.—May I venture?—half a word?'

'Tomes! But just a little compassion for the devoted. He wouldn't play so madly—if, well, say a tenth dilution of the rapt hearing Columelli gets.'

'Signor Columelli sings divinely.'

'You don't dislike Brailstone?'

'He is one of the agreeable.'

'He must put his feelings into Italian song!'

'To put them aside will do.'

'We are not to have our feelings?'

'Yes, on the proviso that ours are respected. But, one instant, Lord Fleetwood, pray. She is—I have to speak of her as my sister. I am sure she regrets... She writes very nicely.'

'You have a letter from her?'

Henrietta sighed that it would not bear exposure to him: 'Yes.'

'Nicely worded?'

'Well, yes, it is.'

He paused, not expecting that the letter would be shown, but silence fired shots, and he had stopped the petition. 'We are to have you for a week's yachting. You prescribe your company. Only be merciful. Exclusion will mean death to some. Columelli will be touring in Switzerland. You shall have him in the house when my new bit of ground Northwest of London is open: very handy, ten miles out. We'll have the Opera troupe there, and you shall command the Opera.'

Her beauty sweetened to thank him.

If, as Livia said, his passion for her was unchanged, the generosity manifested in the considerate screen it wore over any physical betrayal of it, deserved the lustre of her eyes. It dwelt a moment, vivid with the heart close behind and remorseful for misreading of old his fine character. Here was a young man who could be the very kindest of friends to the woman rejecting him to wed another. Her smile wavered. How shall a loving wife express warmth of sentiment elsewhere, without the one beam too much, that plunges her on a tideway? His claim of nothing called for everything short of the proscribed. She gave him her beauty in fullest flower.

It had the appearance of a temptation; and he was not tempted, though he admired; his thought being, Husband of the thing!

But he admired. That condition awakened his unsatisfied past days to desire positive proof of her worthlessness. The past days writhed in him. The present were loveless, entirely cold. He had not even the wish to press her hand. The market held beautiful women of a like description. He wished simply to see her proved the thing he read her to be: and not proved as such by himself. He was unable to summon or imagine emotion enough for him to simulate the forms by which fair women are wooed to their perdition. For all he cared, any man on earth might try, succeed or fail, as long as he had visual assurance that she coveted, a slave to the pleasures commanded by the wealth once disdained by her. Till that time, he could not feel himself perfectly free.

Dame Gossip prefers to ejaculate. Young men are mysteries! and bowl us onward. No one ever did comprehend the Earl of Fleetwood, she says: he was bad, he was good; he was whimsical and stedfast; a splendid figure, a mark for ridicule; romantic and a close arithmetician; often a devil, sometimes the humanest of creatures.

In fine, he was a millionaire nobleman, owing to a considerable infusion of Welsh blood in the composition of him. Now, to the Cymry and to the pure Kelt, the past is at their elbows continually. The past of their lives has lost neither face nor voice behind the shroud; nor are the passions of the flesh, nor is the animate soul, wanting to it. Other races forfeit infancy, forfeit youth and manhood with their progression to the wisdom age may bestow. These have each stage always alive, quick at a word, a scent, a sound, to conjure up scenes, in spirit and in flame. Historically, they still march with Cadwallader, with Llewellyn, with Glendower; sing with Aneurin, Taliesin, old Llywarch: individually, they are in the heart of the injury done them thirty years back or thrilling to the glorious deed which strikes an empty buckler for most of the sons of Time. An old sea rises in them, rolling no phantom billows to break to spray against existing rocks of the shore. That is why, and even if they have a dose of the Teuton in them, they have often to feel themselves exiles when still in amicable community among the preponderating Saxon English.

Add to the single differentiation enormous wealth—we convulse the excellent Dame by terming it a chained hurricane, to launch in foul blasts or beneficent showers, according to the moods during youth—and the composite Lord Fleetwood comes nearer into our focus. Dame Gossip, with her jigging to be at the butterwoman's trot, when she is not violently interrupting, would suffer just punishment were we to digress upon the morality of a young man's legal possession of enormous wealth as well.

Wholly Cambrian Fleetwood was not. But he had to the full the Cambrian's reverential esteem for high qualities. His good-bye with Henrietta, and estimate of her, left a dusky mental, void requiring an orb of some sort for contemplation; and an idea of the totally contrary Carinthia, the woman he had avowedly wedded, usurped her place. Qualities were admitted. She was thrust away because she had offended: still more because he had offended. She bore the blame for forcing him to an examination of his conduct at this point and that, where an ancestral savage in his lineaments cocked a strange eye. Yet at the moment of the act of the deed he had known himself the veritable Fleetwood. He had now to vindicate himself by extinguishing her under the load of her unwomanliness: she was like sun-dried linen matched beside oriental silk: she was rough, crisp, unyielding. That was now the capital charge. Henrietta could never be guilty of the unfeminine. Which did he prefer?

It is of all questions the one causing young men to screw wry faces when they are asked; they do so love the feminine, the ultra-feminine, whom they hate for her inclination to the frail. His depths were sounded, and he answered independently of his will, that he must be up to the heroical pitch to decide. Carinthia stood near him then. The confession was a step, and fraught with consequences. Her unacknowledged influence expedited him to Sarah Winch's shop, for sight of one of earth's honest souls; from whom he had the latest of the two others down in Wales, and of an infant there.

He dined the host of his Ixionides, leaving them early for a drive at night Eastward, and a chat with old Mr. Woodseer over his punching and sewing of his bootleather. Another honest soul. Mr. Woodseer thankfully consented to mount his coach-box next day, and astonish Gower with a drop on his head from the skies about the time of the mid-day meal.

There we have our peep into Dame Gossip's young man mysterious.

BOOK IV

CHAPTER XXIX

CARINTHIA IN WALES

An August of gales and rains drove Atlantic air over the Welsh highlands. Carinthia's old father had impressed on her the rapture of 'smelling salt' when by chance he stood and threw up his nostrils to sniff largely over a bed of bracken, that reminded him of his element, and her fancy would be at strain to catch his once proud riding of the seas. She felt herself an elder daughter of the beloved old father, as she breathed it in full volume from the billowy West one morning early after sunrise and walked sisterly with the far-seen inexperienced little maid, whom she saw trotting beside him through the mountain forest, listening, storing his words, picturing the magnetic, veined great gloom of an untasted world.

This elder daughter had undergone a shipwreck; but clear proof that she had not been worsted was in the unclouded liveliness of the younger one gazing forward. Imaginative creatures who are courageous will never be lopped of the hopeful portion of their days by personal misfortune. Carinthia could animate both; it would have been a hurt done to a living human soul had she suffered the younger self to run overcast. Only, the gazing forward had become interdicted to her experienced self. Nor could she vision a future having any horizon for her child. She saw it in bleak squares, and snuggled him between dangers weathered and dangers apprehended.

The conviction that her husband hated her had sunk into her nature. Hating the mother, he would not love her boy. He was her boy, and strangely bestowed, not beautifully to be remembered rapturously or gratefully, and with deep love of the father. She felt the wound recollection dealt her. But the boy was her one treasure, and no treasure to her husband. They were burdens, and the heir of his House, child of a hated mother, was under perpetual menace from an unscrupulous tyrannical man. The dread and antagonism were first aroused by the birth of her child. She had not known while bearing him her present acute sensation of the hunted flying and at bay. Previously, she could say: I did wrong here; I did wrong there. Distrust had brought the state of war, which allows not of the wasting of our powers in confessions.

Her husband fed her and he clothed her; the limitation of his bounty was sharply outlined. Sure of her rectitude, a stranger to the world, she was not very sensible of dishonour done to her name. It happened at times that her father inquired of her how things were going with his little Carin; and then revolt sprang up and answered on his behalf rather fiercely. She was, however, prepared for any treaty including forgiveness, if she could be at peace in regard to her boy, and have an income of some help to her brother. Chillon was harassed on all sides; she stood incapable of aiding; so foolishly feeble in the shadow of her immense longing to strive for him, that she could think her husband had purposely lamed her with an infant. Her love of her brother, now the one man she loved, laid her insufficiency on the rack and tortured imbecile cries from it.

On the contrary, her strange husband had blest her with an infant. Everything was pardonable to him if he left her boy untouched in the mother's charge. Much alone as she was, she raised the dead to pet and cherish her boy. Chillon had seen him and praised him. Mrs. Owain Wythan, her neighbour over a hill, praised him above all babes on earth, poor childless woman!

She was about to cross the hill and breakfast with Mrs. Wythan. The time for the weaning of the babe approached, and had as prospect beyond it her dull fear that her husband would say the mother's work was done, and seize the pretext to separate them: and she could not claim a longer term to be giving milk, because her father had said: 'Not a quarter of a month more than nine for the milk of the mother'—or else the child would draw an unsustaining nourishment from the strongest breast. She could have argued her exceptional robustness against another than he. But the dead father wanting to build a great race of men and women ruled.

Carinthia knelt at the cradle of a princeling gone from the rich repast to his alternative kingdom.

'You will bring him over when he wakes,' she said to Madge. 'Mrs. Wythan would like to see him every day. Martha can walk now.'

'She can walk and hold a child in her two arms, my lady,' said Madge. 'She expects miners popping up out of the bare ground when she sees no goblins.'

'They!—they know him, they would not hurt him, they know my son,' her mistress answered.

The population of the mines in revolt had no alarms for her. The works were empty down below. Men sat by the wayside brooding or strolled in groups, now and then loudly exercising their tongues; or they stood in circle to sing hymns: melancholy chants of a melancholy time for all.

How would her father have acted by these men? He would have been among them. Dissensions in his mine were vapours of a day. Lords behaved differently. Carinthia fancied the people must regard their master as a foreign wizard, whose power they felt, without the chance of making their cry to him heard. She, too, dealt with a lord. It was now his wish for her to leave the place where she had found some shreds of a home in the thought of being useful. She was gathering the people's language; many of their songs she could sing, and please them by singing to them. They were not suspicious of her; at least, their women had open doors for her; the men, if shy, were civil. She had only to go below, she was greeted in the quick tones of their speech all along the street of the slate-roofs.

But none loved the castle, and she as little, saving the one room in it where her boy lay. The grey of Welsh history knew a real castle beside the roaring brook frequently a torrent. This was an eighteenth century castellated habitation on the verge of a small wood midway up the height, and it required a survey of numberless happy recollections to illumine its walls or drape its chambers. The permanently lighted hearth of a dear home, as in that forsaken unfavoured old white house of the wooded Austrian crags, it had not. Rather it seemed a place waiting for an ill deed to be done in it and stop all lighting of hearths thereafter.

Out on the turf of the shaven hills, her springy step dispersed any misty fancies. Her short-winged hive set to work in her head as usual, building scaffoldings of great things to be done by Chillon, present evils escaped. The rolling big bade hills with the riding clouds excited her as she mounted, and she was a figure of gladness on the ridge bending over to hospitable Plas Llwyn, where the Wythans lived, entertaining rich and poor alike.

They had led the neighbourhood to call on the discarded Countess of Fleetwood.

A warm strain of arms about her neck was Carinthia's welcome from Mrs. Wythan lying along the couch in her boudoir; an established invalid, who yearned sanely to life, and caught a spark of it from the guest eyed tenderly by her as they conversed.

'Our boy?—our Chillon Kirby till he has his baptism names; he is well? I am to see him?'

'He follows me. He sleeps almost through the night now.'

'Ah, my dear,' Mrs. Wythan sighed, imagining: 'It would disappoint me if he did not wake me.'

'I wake at his old time and watch him.'

Carinthia put on the baby's face in the soft mould of slumber.

'I see him!' Mrs. Wythan cried. 'He is part mine. He has taught Owain to love babies.'

A tray of breakfast was placed before the countess. 'Mr. Wythan is down among his men?' she said.

'Every morning, as long as this agitation lasts. I need not say good appetite to you after your walk. You have no fear of the men, I know. Owain's men are undisturbed; he has them in hand. Absentee masters can't expect continued harmony. Dear, he tells me Mr. Edwards awaits the earl.'

Drinking her tea, Carinthia's eyelids shut; she set down her cup, 'If he must come,' she said. 'He wishes me to leave. I am to go again where I have no friends, and no language to learn, and can be of no use. It is not for me that I dread his coming. He speaks to command. The men ask to be heard. He will have submission first. They do not trust him. His coming is a danger. For me, I should wish him to come. May I say...?'

'Your Rebecca bids you say, my darling.'

'It is, I am with the men because I am so like them. I beg to be heard. He commands obedience. He is a great nobleman, but I am the daughter of a greater man, and I have to say, that if those poor miners do harm, I will not stand by and see an anger against injustice punished. I wish his coming, for him to agree upon the Christian names of the boy. I feel his coming will do me, injury in making me offend him worse.

I would avoid that. Oh, dear soul! I may say it to you:—he cannot hurt me any more. I am spared loving him when I forgive him; and I do. The loving is the pain. That is gone by.'

Mrs. Wythan fondled and kissed Carinthia's hand.

'Let me say in my turn; I may help you, dear. You know I have my husband's love, as he mine. Am I, have I ever been a wife to him? Here I lie, a dead weight, to be carried up and down, all of a wife that Owain has had for years. I lie and pray to be taken, that my good man, my proved good man, may be free to choose a healthy young woman and be rewarded before his end by learning what a true marriage is. The big simpleton will otherwise be going to his grave, thinking he was married! I see him stepping about softly in my room, so contented if he does not disturb me, and he crushes me with a desire to laugh at him while I worship. I tricked him into marrying the prostrate invalid I am, and he can't discover the trick, he will think it's a wife he has, instead of a doctor's doll. Oh! you have a strange husband, it has been a strange marriage for you, but you have your invincible health, you have not to lie and feel the horror of being a deception to a guileless man, whose love blindfolds him. The bitter ache to me is, that I can give nothing. You abound in power to give.'

Carinthia lifted her open hands for sign of their emptiness.

'My brother would not want, if I could give. He may have to sell out of. the army, he thinks, fears; and I must look on. Our mother used to say she had done something for her country in giving a son like Chillon to the British army. Poor mother! Our bright opening days all seem to end in rain. We should turn to Mr. Wythan for a guide.'

'He calls you Morgan le Fay christianized.'

'What I am!' Carinthia raised and let fall her head. 'An example makes dwarfs of us. When Mr. Wythan does penance for temper by descending into his mine and working among his men for a day with the pick, seated, as he showed me down below, that is an example. If I did like that, I should have no firedamp in the breast, and not such a task to forgive, that when I succeed I kill my feelings.'

The entry of Madge and Martha, the nurse-girl, with the overflowing armful of baby, changed their converse into melodious exclamations.

'Kit Ines has arrived, my lady,' Madge said. 'I saw him on the road and stopped a minute.'

Mrs. Wythan studied Carinthia. Her sharp invalid's ears had caught the name. She beckoned. 'The man who—the fighting man?'

'It will be my child this time,' said Carinthia; 'I have no fear for myself.' She was trembling, though her features were hard for the war her lord had declared, as it seemed. 'Did he tell you his business here?' she asked of Madge.

'He says, to protect you, my lady, since you won't leave.'

'He stays at the castle?'

'He is to stay there, he says, as long as the Welsh are out.'

'The "Welsh" are misunderstood by Lord Fleetwood,'

Mrs. Wythan said to Carinthia. 'He should live among them. They will not hurt their lady. Protecting may be his intention; but we will have our baby safe here. Not?' she appealed. 'And baby's mother. How otherwise?'

'You read my wishes,' Carinthia rejoined. 'The man I do not think a bad man. He has a master. While I am bound to my child I must be restful, and with the man at the castle Martha's goblins would jump about me day and night. My boy makes a coward of his mother.'

'We merely take a precaution, and I have the pleasure of it,' said her hostess. 'Give orders to your maid not less than a fortnight. It will rejoice my husband so much.'

As with the warmly hospitable, few were the words. Madge was promised by her mistress plenty of opportunities daily for seeing Kit Ines, and her mouth screwed to one of women's dimples at a corner. She went off in a cart to fetch boxes, thinking: We are a hunted lot! So she was not mildly disposed for the company of Mr. Kit on her return to the castle.

England's champion light-weight thought it hard that his, coming down to protect the castle against the gibbering heathen Welsh should cause a clearing out, and solitariness for his portion.

'What's the good of innocence if you 're always going to suspect a man!' he put it, like a true son of the pirates turned traders. 'I've got a paytron, and a man in my profession must have a paytron, or where is he? Where's his money for a trial of skill? Say he saves and borrows and finds the lump to clap it down, and he's knocked out o' time. There he is, bankrup', and a devil of a licking into the bargain. That 's the cream of our profession, if a man has got no paytron.

No prize-ring can live without one. The odds are too hard on us. My lady ought to take into account I behaved respectful when I was obliged to do my lord's orders and remove her from our haunts, which wasn't to his taste. Here I'm like a cannon for defending the house, needs be, and all inside flies off scarified.'

'It strikes me, Kit Ines, a man with a paytron is no better than a tool of a man,' said Madge.

'And don't you go to be sneering at honest tools,' Ines retorted. 'When will women learn a bit of the world before they're made hags of by old Father Wear-and-Tear! A young woman in her prime, you Madge! be such a fool as not see I serve tool to stock our shop.'

'Your paytron bid you steal off with my lady's child, Kit Ines, you'd do it to stock your shop.'

Ines puffed. 'If you ain't a girl to wallop the wind! Fancy me at that game! Is that why my lady—but I can't be suspected that far? You make me break out at my pores. My paytron's a gentleman: he wouldn't ask and I couldn't act such a part. Dear Lord! it'd have to be stealing off, for my lady can use a stick; and put it to the choice between my lady and her child and any paytron living, paytron be damned, I'd say, rather'n go against my notions of honour. Have you forgot all our old talk about the prize-ring, the nursery of honour in Old England?'

'That was before you sold yourself to a paytron, Kit Ines.'

'Ah! Women wants mast-heading off and on, for 'em to have a bit of a look-out over life as it is. They go stewing over books of adventure and drop into frights about awful man. Take me, now; you had a no small admiration for my manly valour once, and you trusted yourself to me, and did you ever repent it?—owning you're not the young woman to tempt to t' other way.'

'You wouldn't have found me talking to you here if I had.'

'And here I'm left to defend an empty castle, am I?'

'Don't drink or you'll have your paytron on you. He's good use there.'

'I ask it, can I see my lady?'

'Drunk nor sober you won't. Serve a paytron, be a leper, you'll find, with all honest folk.'

Ines shook out an execrating leg at the foul word. 'Leper, you say? You say that? You say leper to me?'

'Strut your tallest, Kit Ines. It's the money rattles in your pocket says it.'

'It's my reputation for decent treatment of a woman lets you say it, Madge Winch.'

'Stick to that as long as your paytron consents. It's the one thing you've got left.'

'Benefit, you hussy, and mind you don't pull too stiff.'

'Be the woman and have the last word!'

His tongue was checked. He swallowed the exceeding sourness of a retort undelivered, together with the feeling that she beat him in the wrangle by dint of her being an unreasonable wench.

Madge huffed away to fill her boxes.

He stood by the cart, hands deep down his pockets, when she descended. She could have laughed at the spectacle of a champion prize-fighter out of employ, hulking idle, because he was dog to a paytron; but her contempt of him declined passing in small change.

'So you're off. What am I to tell my lord when he comes?' Kit growled. 'His yacht's fetching for a Welsh seaport.'

She counted it a piece of information gained, and jumped to her seat, bidding the driver start. To have pretty well lost her character for a hero changed into a patron's dog, was a thought that outweighed the show of incivility. Some little distance away, she reproached herself for not having been so civil as to inquire what day my lord was expected, by his appointment. The girl reflected on the strangeness of a body of discontented miners bringing my lord and my lady close, perhaps to meet.

CHAPTER XXX

The earl was looked for at the, chief office of the mines, and each day an expectation of him closed in disappointment, leaving it to be surmised that there were more serious reasons for his continued absence during a crisis than any discussed; whether indeed, as when a timepiece neglects to strike the hour which is, by the reckoning of natural impatience, past, the capital charge of 'crazy works' must not be brought against a nobleman hitherto precise upon business, of a just disposition, fairly humane. For though he was an absentee sucking the earth through a tube, in Ottoman ease, he had never omitted the duty of personally attending on the spot to grave cases under dispute. The son of the hardheaded father came out at a crisis; and not too highhandedly: he could hear an opposite argument to the end. Therefore, since he refused to comply without hearing, he was wanted on the spot imperatively, now.

Irony perusing History offers the beaten and indolent a sugary acid in the indication of the spites and the pranks, the whims and the tastes, at the springs of main events. It is, taken by itself, destructive nourishment. But those who labour in the field to shovel the clods of earth to History, would be wiser of their fellows for a minor dose of it. Mr. Howell Edwards consulting with Mr. Owain Wythan on the necessity, that the earl should instantly keep his promise to appear among the men and stop the fermentation, as in our younger days a lordly owner still might do by small concessions and the physical influence—the nerve-charm—could suppose him to be holding aloof for his pleasure or his pride; perhaps because of illness or inability to conceive the actual situation at a distance. He mentioned the presence of the countess, and Mr. Wythan mentioned it, neither of them thinking a rational man would so play the lunatic as to let men starve, and wreck precious mines, for the sake of avoiding her.

Sullen days went by. On these days of the slate-cloud or the leaden-winged, Carinthia walked over the hills to her staring or down-eyed silent people, admitted without a welcome at some doors, rejected at some. Her baskets from the castle were for the most part received as graciously. She continued to direct them for delivery where they were needed, and understood why a charity that supplied the place of justice was not thanked. She and her people here were one regarding the master, as she had said. They could not hurt her sensitiveness, she felt too warmly with them. And here it was not the squalid, flat, bricked east-corner of London at the close of her daily pilgrimage. Up from the solitary street of the slate-roofs, she mounted a big hill and had the life of high breathing. A perpetual escape out of the smoky, grimy city mazes was trumpeted to her in the winds up there: a recollected contrast lightened the skyless broad spaces overhead almost to sunniness. Having air of the hills and activity for her limbs, she made sunshine for herself. Regrets were at no time her nestlings.

Look backward only to correct an error of conduct for the next attempt, says one of her father's Maxims; as sharply bracing for women as for men. She did not look back to moan. Now that her hunger for the safety of her infant was momentarily quieted, she could see Kit Ines hanging about the lower ground, near the alehouse, and smile at Madge's comparison of him to a drummed-out soldier, who would like to be taken for a holiday pensioner.

He saluted; under the suspicion of his patron's lady his legs were hampered, he dared not approach her; though his innocence of a deed not proposed to him yet—and all to stock that girl Madge's shop, if done! knocked at his ribs with fury to vindicate himself before the lady and her maid. A gentleman met them and conducted them across the hills.

And two Taffy gentlemen would hardly be sufficient for the purpose, supposing an ill-used Englishman inclined to block their way!—What, and play footpad, Kit Ines? No, it's just a game in the head. But a true man hates to feel himself suspected. His refuge is the beer of the country.

Next day there were the two gentlemen to conduct the lady and her maid; and Taffy the first walks beside the countess; and that girl Madge trudges along with no other than my lord's Mr. Woodseer, chattering like a watering-can on a garden-bed: deuce a glance at Kit Ines. How can she keep it up and the gentleman no more than nodding? How does he enjoy playing second fiddle with the maid while Mr. tall brown-face Taffy violins it to her ladyship a stone's throw in front? Ines had less curiosity to know the object of Mr. Woodseer's appearance on the scene. Idle, unhandsomely treated, and a cave of the yawns, he merely commented on his observations.

'Yes, there he is, don't look at him,' Madge said to Gower; 'and whatever he's here for, he has a bad time of it, and rather more than it's pleasant for him to think over, if a slave to a "paytron" thinks at all. I won't judge him; my mistress is bitten with the fear for the child, worse than ever. And the earl, my lord, not coming, and he wanting her to move again, seems to her he durstn't do it here and intends to snap at the child on the road. She-'s forced to believe anything of such a husband and father. And why does he behave so? I can't spell it. He's kind to my Sally—you've seen the Piccadilly shop?—because she was... she did her best in love and duty for my lady. And behaves like a husband hating his wife's life on earth! Then he went down with good Mr. Woodseer, and called on Sally, pretending to inquire, after she was kidnapped by that Kit Ines acting to please his paytron, he must be shown up to the room where she slept, and stands at the door and peeps in, Sally's letter says, and asks if he may enter the room. He went to the window looking on the chimneys she used to see, and touched an ornament over the fireplace, called grandfather's pigtail case—he was a sailor; only a ridiculous piece of china, that made my lady laugh about the story of its holding a pigtail. But he turns it over because she did—Sally told him. He couldn't be pretending when he bought the beautiful shop and stocked it for Sally. He gets her lots of customers; and no rent to pay till next Michaelmas a year. She's a made woman through him. He said to her, he had heard from Mr. Woodseer the Countess of Fleetwood called her sister; he shook her hand.'

'The Countess of Fleetwood called both of you her sisters, I think,' said Gower.

'I'm her servant. I'd rather serve her than have a fortune.'

'You were born with a fortune one would like to have a nibble at, Madge.'

'I can't lay hand on it, then.'

'It's the capacity for giving, my dear.'

'Please, Mr. Gower, don't say that; you'll make me cry. He keeps his wife so poor she hasn't a shilling of her own; she wearies about her brother; she can't help. He can spend hundreds on my Sally for having been good to her, in our small way—it's a fairy tale; and he won't hear of money for his wife, except that she's never to want for anything it can buy.'

'You give what it can't buy.'

'Me. I'm "a pugilist's wench"—I've heard myself called. She was the first who gave me a lift; never mind me. Have you come to take her away? She'd trust herself and the child to you.'

'Take her?—reason with her as to the best we can do. He holds off from a meeting just now. I fancy he's wearing round to it. His keeping his wife without money passes comprehension. After serving him for a few months, I had a store invested to support me for years—as much as I need before I join the ranks of the pen. I was at my reading and writing and drowsing, and down he rushes: I 'm in harness again. I can't say it's dead waste of time; besides I pick up an independence for the days ahead. But I don't respect myself for doing the work. Here's the difference between us two servants, Madge: I think of myself, and you don't.'

'The difference is more like between the master and mistress we serve, Mr. Gower.'

'Well, I'd rather be the woman in this case.'

'You know the reputation I've got. And can only just read, and can't spell. My mistress teaches me bits of German and French on her walks.'

Gower took a new observation of this girl, whom he had not regarded as like himself, a pushing blade among the grasses. He proposed to continue her lessons, if she cared to learn; saying it could be done in letters.

'I won't be ashamed of writing, if you mean it,' said she. 'My mistress will have a usefuller servant. She had a strange honeymoon of a marriage, if ever was—and told me t' other day she was glad because it brought us together—she a born lady!'

'A fling-above born ladies. She's quick as light to hit on a jewel where there is one, whether it shines or not. She stands among the Verities of the world.'

'Yes,' Madge said, panting for more. 'Do speak of her. When you praise her, I feel she's not wasted. Mistress; and friend and wife—if he'd let her be; and mother; never mother like her. The boy 'll be a sturdy. She'll see he has every chance. He's a lucky little one to have that mother.'

'You think her handsome, Madge?'

Gower asked it, wishing to hear a devotee's confusion of qualities and looks.

The question was a drop on lower spheres, and it required definitions, to touch the exact nature of the form of beauty, and excuse a cooler tone on the commoner plane. These demanded language. She rounded the difficulty, saying: 'You see engravings of archery; that 's her figure—her real figure. I think her face... I can't describe... it flashes.'

'That's it,' said Gower, delighted with his perception of a bare mind at work and hitting the mark perforce of warmth. 'When it flashes, it's unequalled. There's the supremacy of irregular lines. People talk of perfect beauty: suitable for paintings and statues. Living faces, if they're to show the soul, which is the star on the peak of beauty, must lend themselves to commotion. Nature does it in a breezy tree or over ruffled waters. Repose has never such splendid reach as animation—I mean, in the living face. Artists prefer repose. Only Nature can express the uttermost beauty with her gathering and tuning of discords. Well, your mistress has that beauty. I remember my impression when I saw her first on her mountains abroad. Other beautiful faces of women go pale, grow stale. The diversified in the harmony of the flash are Nature's own, her radiant, made of her many notes, beyond our dreams to reproduce. We can't hope to have a true portrait of your mistress. Does Madge understand?'

The literary dose was a strong one for her; but she saw the index, and got a lift from the sound. Her bosom heaved. 'Oh, I do try, Mr. Gower. I think I do a little. I do more while you're talking. You are good to talk so to me. You should have seen her the night she went to meet my lord at those beastly Gardens Kit Ines told me he was going to. She was defending him. I've no words. You teach me what's meant by poetry. I couldn't understand that once.'

Their eyes were on the countess and her escort in advance. Gower's praises of her mistress's peculiar beauty set the girl compassionately musing. His eloquence upon the beauty was her clue.

Carinthia and Mr. Wythan started at a sharp trot in the direction of the pair of ponies driven by a groom along the curved decline of the narrow roadway. His whip was up for signal.

It concerned the house and the master of it. His groom drove rapidly down, while he hurried on the homeward way, as a man will do, with the dread upon him that his wife's last breath may have been yielded before he can enfold her.

Carinthia walked to be overtaken, not daring to fever her blood at a swifter pace; 'lamed with an infant,' the thought recurred.

'She is very ill, she has fainted, she lies insensible,' Madge heard from her of Mrs. Wythan. 'We were speaking of her when the groom appeared. It has happened twice. They fear the third. He fears it, though he laughs at a superstition. Now step, I know you like walking, Mr. Woodseer. Once I left you behind.'

'I have the whole scene of the angel and the cripple,' Gower replied.

'O that day!'

They 'were soon speculating on the unimpressionable house in its clump of wood midway below, which had no response for anxieties.

A maid-servant at the garden gate, by Mr. Wythan's orders, informed Carinthia that her mistress had opened her eyes: There was a hope of weathering the ominous third time. But the hope was a bird of short flight from bush to bush until the doctor should speak to confirm it. Even the child was under the shadow of the house. Carinthia had him in her arms, trusting to life as she hugged him, and seeing innumerable darts out of all regions assailing her treasure.

'She wishes to have you,' Mr. Wythan came and said to her. 'Almost her first word. The heart is quickening. She will live for me if she can.'

He whispered it. His features shot the sparkle.

Rebecca Wythan had strength to press Carinthia's hand faintly. She made herself heard: 'No pain.' Her husband sat upright, quite still, attentive for any sign. His look of quiet pleasure ready to show, sprightliness dwelt on her. She returned the look, unable to give it greeting. Past the sense of humour, she wanted to say: 'See the poor simple fellow who will think it a wife that he has!' She did but look.

Carinthia spoke his name, 'Mr. Wythan,' by chance, and Rebecca breathed heavily until she formed the words: 'Owain to me.'

'To me,' Owain added.

The three formed a chain of clasped hands.

It was in the mind of the sick lady to disburden herself of more than her weakness could utter, so far was she above earthly links. The desire in her was to be quit of the flesh, bearing a picture of her husband as having the dues of his merits.

Her recovered strength next day brought her nearer to our laws. 'You will call him Owain, Carinthia?' she said. 'He is not one to presume on familiarity. I must be going soon. I cannot leave him the wife I would choose. I can leave him the sister. He is a sure friend. He is the knightly man women dream of. I harp on it because I long for testimony that I leave him to have some reward. And this may be, between two so pure at heart as you two.'

'Dear soul friend, yes, and Owain, yes, I can say it,' Carinthia rejoined. 'Brother? I have only my Chillon. My life is now for him. I am punished for separating myself from the son of my father. I have no heart for a second brother. What I can give to my friend I will. I shall love you in him, if I am to lose you.'

'Not Owain—it was I was the wretch refused to call on the lonely lady at the castle until I heard she had done a romantic little bit of thing—hushed a lambkin's bleating. My loss! my loss! And I could afford it so poorly. Since then Carinthia has filled my days. I shudder to leave you and think of your going back to the English. Their sneer withers. They sent you down among us as a young woman to be shunned.'

'I did wildly, I was ungoverned, I had one idea,' said Carinthia. 'One idea is a bullet, good for the day of battle to beat the foe, father tells us. It was a madness in me. Now it has gone, I see all round. I see straight, too. With one idea, we see nothing—nothing but itself. Whizz! we go. I did. I shall no longer offend in that way. Mr. Gower Woodseer is here from my lord.'

'With him the child will be safe.'

'I am not alarmed. It is to request—they would have me gone, to prepare the way for my lord.'

'You have done, it; he has the castle to himself. I cannot-spare you. A tyrant ordering you to go should be defied. My Lord Fleetwood puts lightning into my slow veins.'

'We have talked: we shall be reproved by the husband and the doctor,' said Carinthia.

Sullen days continued and rolled over to night at the mines. Gower's mission was rendered absurd by the countess's withdrawal from the castle. He spoke of it to Mr. Wythan once, and the latter took a big breath and blew such a lord to the winds. 'Persuade our guest to leave us, that the air may not be tainted for her husband when he comes? He needn't call; he's not obliged to see her. She's offered Esslemont to live in? I believe her instinct's right—he has designs on the child. A little more and we shall have a mad dog in the fellow. He doubles my work by keeping his men out. If she were away we should hear of black doings. Twenty dozen of his pugilists wouldn't stop the burning.'

They agreed that persuasions need not be addressed to the countess. She was and would remain Mr. Wythan's guest. As for the earl, Gower inclined to plead hesitatingly, still to plead, on behalf of a nobleman owning his influence and very susceptible to his wisdom, whose echo of a pointed saying nearly equalled the satisfaction bestowed by print. The titled man affected the philosopher in that manner; or rather, the crude philosopher's relish of brilliant appreciation stripped him of his robe. For he was with Owain Wythan at heart to scorn titles which did not distinguish practical offices. A nation bowing to them has gone to pith, for him; he had to shake himself, that he might not similarly stick; he had to do it often. Objects elevated even by a decayed world have their magnetism for us unless we nerve the mind to wakeful repulsion. He protested he had reason to think the earl was humanizing, though he might be killing a woman in the process. 'Could she wish for better?' he asked, with at least the gravity of the undermining humourist; and he started Owain to course an idea when he remarked of Lord Fleetwood: 'Imagine a devil on his back on a river, flying a cherub.'

Owain sparkled from the vision of the thing to wrath with it.

'Ay, but while he's floating, his people are edging on starvation. And I've a personal grievance. I keep, you know, open hall, bread and cheese and beer, for poor mates. His men are favouring us with a call. We have to cart treble from the town. If I straighten the sticks he dies to bend, it'll be a grievance against me—and a fig for it! But I like to be at peace with my neighbours, and waft them "penillion" instead of dealing the "cleddyfal" of Llewellyn.'

At last the tension ceased; they had intelligence of the earl's arrival.

His countess was little moved by it; and the reason for that lay in her imagination being absorbed. Henrietta had posted her a journal telling of a deed of Chillon's: no great feat, but precious for its 'likeness to him,' as they phrased it; that is, for the light it cast on their conception of the man. Heading a squadron in a riotous Midland town, he stopped a charge, after fire of a shot from the mob, and galloped up the street to catch a staggering urchin to his saddle-bow, and place the mite in safety. Then it was a simple trot of the hussars ahead; way was made for him.

Now, to see what banquet there is for the big of heart in the world's hot stress, take the view of Carinthia, to whom her brother's thoughtful little act of gentleness at the moment of the red-of-the-powder smoke was divinest bread and wine, when calamity hung around, with the future an unfooted wilderness, her powers untried, her husband her enemy.

CHAPTER XXXI

WE HAVE AGAIN TO DEAL WITH THE EXAMPLES OF OUR YOUNGER MAN

The most urgent of Dames is working herself up to a grey squall in her detestation of imagerial epigrams. Otherwise Gower Woodseer's dash at the quintessential young man of wealth would prompt to the carrying of it further, and telling how the tethered flutterer above a 'devil on his back on a river' was beginning to pull if not drag his withholder and teaser.

Fleetwood had almost a desire to see the small dot of humanity which drew the breath from him;—and was indistinguishably the bubbly grin and gurgle of the nurses, he could swear. He kicked at the bondage to our common fleshly nature imposed on him by the mother of the little animal. But there had been a mother to his father: odd movements of a warmish curiosity brushed him when the cynic was not mounting guard. They were, it seemed, external—no part of him: like blasts of a wayside furnace across wintry air. They were, as it chanced, Nature's woman in him plucking at her separated partner, Custom's man; something of an oriental voluptuary on his isolated regal seat; and he would suck the pleasures without a descent into the stale old ruts where Life's convict couple walk linked to one another, to their issue more.

There was also a cold curiosity to see the male infant such a mother would have. The grandson of Old Lawless might turn out a rascal,—he would be no mean one, no coward.

That mother, too, who must have been a touch astonished to find herself a mother:—Fleetwood laughed a curt bark, and heard rebukes, and pleaded the marriage-trap to the man of his word; devil and cherub were at the tug, or say, dog and gentleman, a survival of the schoolboy—that mother, a girl of the mountains, perhaps wanted no more than smoothing by the world. 'It is my husband' sounded foolish, sounded freshish,—a new note. Would she repeat it? The bit of simplicity would bear repeating once. Gower Woodseer says the creature grows and studies to perfect herself. She's a good way off that, and may spoil herself in the process; but she has a certain power. Her donkey obstinacy in refusing compliance, and her pursuit of 'my husband,' and ability to drench him with ridicule, do not exhibit the ordinary young female. She stamps her impression on the people she meets. Her husband is shaken to confess it likewise, despite a disagreement between them.

He has owned he is her husband: he has not disavowed the consequence. That fellow, Gower Woodseer, might accuse the husband of virtually lying, if he by his conduct implied her distastefulness or worse. By heaven! as felon a deed as could be done. Argue the case anyhow, it should be undone. Let her but cease to madden. For whatever the rawness of the woman, she has qualities; and experience of the facile loves of London very sharply defines her qualities. Think of her as raw, she has the gift of rareness: forget the donkey obstinacy, her character grasps. In the grasp of her character, one inclines, and her husband inclines, to become her advocate. She has only to discontinue maddening.

The wealthy young noble prized any form of rareness wherever it was visible, having no thought of the purchase of it, except with worship. He could listen pleased to the talk of a Methodist minister sewing bootleather. He picked up a roadside tramp and made a friend of him, and valued the fellow's honesty, submitted to his lectures, pardoned his insolence. The sight of Carinthia's narrow bedroom and strip of bed over Sarah Winch's Whitechapel shop had gone a step to drown the bobbing Whitechapel Countess. At least, he had not been hunted by that gaunt chalk-quarry ghost since his peep into the room. Own it! she likewise has things to forgive. Women nurse their larvae of ideas about fair dealing. But observe the distinction: aid if women understood justice they would be the first to proclaim, that when two are tied together, the one who does the other serious injury is more naturally excused than the one who-tenfold abhorrent if a woman!—calls up the grotesque to extinguish both.

With this apology for himself, Lord Fleetwood grew tolerant of the person honourably avowed as his wife. So; therefore, the barrier between him and his thoughts of her was broken. The thoughts carrying red doses were selected. Finally, the taste to meet her sprouted. If agreeable, she could be wooed; if barely agreeable, tormented; if disagreeable, left as before.

Although it was the hazard of a die, he decided to follow his taste. Her stay at the castle had kept him long from the duties of his business; and he could imagine it a grievance if he pleased, but he put it aside. Alighting at his chief manager's office, he passed through the heated atmosphere of black-browed, wiry little rebels, who withheld the salute as they lounged: a posture often preceding the spring in compulsorily idle workers. He was aware of instinct abroad, an antagonism to the proprietor's rights. They roused him to stand by them, and were his own form of instinct, handsomely clothed. It behoved that he should examine them and the claims against them, to be sure of his ground. He and Mr. Howell Edwards debated the dispute for an hour; agreeing, partially differing. There was a weakness on the principle in Edwards. These fellows fixed to the spot are for compromise too much. An owner of mines has no steady reckoning of income if the rate of wage is perpetually to shift according to current, mostly ignorant, versions of the prosperity of the times. Are we so prosperous? It is far from certain. And if the rate ascends, the question of easing it down to suit the discontinuance of prosperity agitating our exchequer—whose demand is for fixity—perplexes us further.

However, that was preliminary. He and Howell Edwards would dine and wrangle it out. The earl knew himself a hot disputant after dinner. Incidentally he heard of Lady Fleetwood as a guest of Mrs. Wythan; and the circumstance was injurious to him because he stood against Mr. Wythan's pampering system with his men.

Ines up at the castle smelt of beer, and his eyelids were sottish. Nothing to do tries the virtue of the best. He sought his excuse in a heavy lamentation over my lady's unjust suspicion of him,—a known man of honour, though he did serve his paytron.

The cause of Lady Fleetwood's absence was exposed to her outraged lord, who had sent the man purely to protect her at this castle, where she insisted on staying. The suspicion cast on the dreary lusher was the wife's wild shot at her husband. One could understand a silly woman's passing terror. Her acting under the dictate of it struck the husband's ribbed breast as a positive clap of hostilities between them across a chasm.

His previous placable mood was immediately conceived by him to have been one of his fits of generosity; a step to a frightful dutiful embrace of an almost repulsive object. He flung the thought of her back on her Whitechapel. She returned from that place with smiles, dressed in a laundry white with a sprinkle of smuts, appearing to him as an adversary armed and able to strike. There was a blow, for he chewed resentments; and these were goaded by a remembered shyness of meeting her eyes when he rounded up the slope of the hill, in view of his castle, where he supposed she would be awaiting 'my husband.' The silence of her absence was lively mockery of that anticipation.

Gower came on him sauntering about the grounds.

'You're not very successful down here,' Fleetwood said, without greeting.

'The countess likes the air of this country,' said Gower, evasively, impertinently, and pointlessly; offensively to the despot employing him to be either subservient or smart.

'I wish her to leave it.'

'She wishes to see you first.'

'She takes queer measures. I start to-morrow for my yacht at Cardiff.' There the matter ended; for Fleetwood fell to talking of the mines. At dinner and after dinner it was the topic, and after Howell Edwards had departed.

When the man who has a heart will talk of nothing but what concerns his interests, and the heart is hurt, it may be perceived by a cognizant friend, that this is his proud mute way of petitioning to have the tenderer subject broached. Gower was sure of the heart, armoured or bandaged though it was,—a haunt of evil spirits as well,—and he began: 'Now to speak of me half a minute. You cajoled me out of my Surrey room, where I was writing, in the vein...'

'I've had the scene before me!' the earl interposed. 'Juniper dells and that tree of the flashing leaf, and that dear old boy, your father, young as you and me, and saying love of Nature gives us eternal youth. On with you.'

'I doubted whether I should be of use to you. I told you the amount of alloy in my motives. A year with you, I have subsistence for ten years assured to me.'

'Don't be a prosy dog, Gower Woodseer.'

'Will you come over to the Wythans before you go?'

'I will not.'

'You would lengthen your stride across a wounded beast?'

'I see no wound to the beast.'

'You can permit yourself to kick under cover of a metaphor.'

'Tell me what you drive at, Gower.'

'The request is, for you to spare pain by taking one step—an extra strain on the muscles of the leg. It 's only the leg wants moving.'

'The lady has legs to run away, let them bring her back.'

'Why have me with you, then? I'm useless. But you read us all, see everything, and wait only for the mood to do the right. You read me, and I'm not open to everybody. You read the crux of a man like me in my novel position. You read my admiration of a beautiful woman and effort to keep honest. You read my downright preference of what most people would call poverty, and my enjoyment of good cookery and good company. You enlist among the crew below as one of our tempters. You find I come round to the thing I like best. Therefore, you have your liking for me; and that's why you turn to me again, after your natural infidelities. So much for me. You read this priceless lady quite as clearly. You choose to cloud her with your moods. She was at a disadvantage, 'arriving in a strange country, next to friendless; and each new incident bred of a luckless beginning—I could say more.'

Fleetwood nodded. 'You are read without the words: You read in history, too, I suppose, that there are two sides to most cases. The loudest is not often the strongest. However, now the lady shows herself crazed. That's reading her charitably. Else she has to be taken for a spiteful shrew, who pretends to suspect anything that's villanous, because she can hit on no other way of striking.'

'Crazed, is a wide shot and hits half the world,' muttered Gower. 'Lady Fleetwood had a troubled period after her marriage. She suffered a sort of kidnapping when she was bearing her child. There's a book by an Edinburgh doctor might be serviceable to you. It enlightens me. She will have a distrust of you, as regards the child, until she understands you by living with you under one roof.'

'Such animals these women are!' Good Lord!' Fleetwood ejaculated. 'I marry one, and I 'm to take to reading medical books!' He yawned.

'You speak that of women and pretend to love Nature,' said Gower. 'You hate Nature unless you have it served on a dish by your own cook. That's the way to the madhouse or the monastery. There we expiate the sin of sins. A man finds the woman of all women fitted to stick him in the soil, and trim and point him to grow, and she's an animal for her pains! The secret of your malady is, you've not yet, though you're on a healthy leap for the practices of Nature, hopped to the primary conception of what Nature means. Women are in and of Nature. I've studied them here—had nothing to do but study them. That most noble of ladies' whole mind was knotted to preserve her child during her time of endurance up to her moment of trial. Think it over. It's your one chance of keeping sane.

And expect to hear flat stuff from me while you go on playing tyrant.'

'You certainly take liberties,' Fleetwood's mildest voice remarked.

'I told you I should try you, when you plucked me out of my Surrey nest.'

Fleetwood, passed from a meditative look to a malicious half-laugh. 'You seem to have studied the "most noble of ladies" latterly rather like a barrister with a brief for the defendant—plaintiff, if you like!'

'As to that, I'll help you to an insight of a particular weakness of mine,' said Gower. 'I require to have persons of even the highest value presented to me on a stage, or else I don't grasp them at all—they 're simply pictures. I saw the lady; admired, esteemed, sufficiently, I supposed, until her image appeared to me in the feelings of another. Then I saw fathoms. No doubt, it was from feeling warmer. I went through the blood of the other for my impression.'

'Name the other,' said the earl, and his features were sharp.

You can have the name,' Gower answered. 'It was the girl, Madge Winch.'

Fleetwood's hard stare melted to surprise and contemptuous amusement. 'You see the lady to be the "most noble of ladies" through the warming you get by passing into the feelings of Madge Winch?'

Sarcasm was in the tone, and beneath it a thrill of compassionateness traversed him and shot a remorseful sting with the vision of those two young women on the coach at the scene of the fight. He had sentience of their voices, nigh to hearing them. The forlorn bride's hand given to the anxious girl behind her gushed an image of the sisterhood binding women under the pangs they suffer from men. He craved a scourging that he might not be cursing himself; and he provoked it, for Gower was very sensitive to a cold breath on the weakness he had laid bare; and when Fleetwood said: 'You recommend a bath in the feelings of Madge Winch?' the retort came:—'It might stop you on the road to a cowl.'

Fleetwood put on the mask of cogitation to cover a shudder, 'How?'

'A question of the man or the monk with you, as I fancy I've told you more than once!'

'You may fancy committing any impertinence and be not much out.'

'The saving of you is that you digest it when you've stewed it down.'

'You try me!'

'I don't impose the connection.'

'No, I take the blame for that.'

They sat in dumbness, fidgeted, sprang to their feet, and lighted bedroom candles.

Mounting the stairs, Gower was moved to let fall a benevolent look on the worried son of fortune. 'I warned you I should try you. It ought to be done politely. If I have to speak a truth I 'm boorish. The divinely damnable naked truth won't wear ornaments. It's about the same as pitching a handful of earth.'

'You dirt your hands, hit or miss. Out of this corridor! Into my room, and spout your worst,' cried the earl.

Gower entered his dressing-room and was bidden to smoke there.

'You're a milder boor when you smoke. That day down in Surrey with the grand old bootmaker was one of our days, Gower Woodseer! There's no smell of the boor in him. Perhaps his religion helps him, more than Nature-worship: not the best for manners. You won't smoke your pipe?—a cigar? Lay on, then, as hard as you like.'

'You're asking for the debauchee's last luxury—not a correction,' said Gower, grimly thinking of how his whip might prove effective and punish the man who kept him fruitlessly out of his bed.

'I want stuff for a place in the memory,' said Fleetwood; and the late hour, with the profitless talk, made it a stinging taunt.

'You want me to flick your indecision.'

'That's half a hit.'

'I 'm to talk italics, for you to store a smart word or so.'

'True, I swear! And, please, begin.'

'You hang for the Fates to settle which is to be smothered in you, the man or the lord—and it ends in the monk, if you hang much longer.'

'A bit of a scorpion in his intention,' Fleetwood muttered on a stride. 'I'll tell you this, Gower Woodseer; when you lay on in earnest, your diction is not so choice. Do any of your remarks apply to Lady Fleetwood?'

'All should. I don't presume to allude to Lady Fleetwood.'

'She has not charged you to complain?'

'Lady Fleetwood is not the person to complain or condescend to speak of injuries.'

'She insults me with her insane suspicion.'

A swollen vein on the young nobleman's forehead went to confirm the idea at the Wythans' that he was capable of mischief. They were right; he was as capable of villany as of nobility. But he happened to be thanking Gower Woodseer's whip for the comfortable numbness he felt at Carinthia's behaviour, while detesting her for causing him to desire it and endure it, and exonerate his prosy castigator.

He was ignorant of the revenge he had on Gower, whose diction had not been particularly estimable. In the feebleness of a man vainly courting sleep, the disarmed philosopher tossed from one side to the other through the remaining hours of darkness, polishing sentences that were natural spouts of choicest diction; and still the earl's virulent small sneer rankled. He understood why, after a time. The fervour of advocacy, which inspires high diction, had been wanting. He had sought more to lash the earl with his personal disgust and partly to parade his contempt of a lucrative dependency—than he had felt for the countess. No wonder his diction was poor. It was a sample of limp thinness; a sort of tongue of a Master Slender:—flavourless, unsatisfactory, considering its object: measured to be condemned by its poor achievement. He had nevertheless a heart to feel for the dear lady, and heat the pleading for her, especially when it ran to its object, as along a shaft of the sun-rays, from the passionate devotedness of that girl Madge.

He brooded over it till it was like a fire beneath him to drive him from his bed and across the turfy roller of the hill to the Wythans', in the front of an autumnal sunrise—grand where the country is shorn of surface decoration, as here and there we find some unadorned human creature, whose bosom bears the ball of warmth.

CHAPTER XXXII

IN WHICH WE SEE CARINTHIA PUT IN PRACTICE ONE OF HER OLD FATHER'S LESSONS

Seated at his breakfast-table, the earl saw Gower stride in, and could have wagered he knew the destination of the fellow's morning walk. It concerned him little; he would be leaving the castle in less than an hour. She might choose to come or choose to keep away. The whims of animals do not affect men unless they are professionally tamers. Petty domestic dissensions are besides poor webs to the man pulling singlehanded at ropes with his revolted miners. On the topic of wages, too, he was Gower's master, and could hold forth: by which he taught himself to feel that practical affairs are the proper business of men, women and infants being remotely secondary; the picturesque and poetry, consequently, sheer nonsense.

'I suppose your waiting here is useless, to quote you,' he said. 'The countess can decide now to remain, if she pleases. Drive with me to Cardiff—I miss you if you 're absent a week. Or is it legs? Drop me a line of your stages on the road, and don't loiter much.'

Gower spoke of starting his legs next day, if he had to do the journey alone: and he clouded the yacht for Fleetwood with talk of the Wye and the Usk, Hereford and the Malvern Hills elliptical over the plains.

'Yes,' the earl acquiesced jealously; 'we ought to have seen—tramped every foot of our own country. That yacht of mine, there she is, and I said I would board her and have a fly with half a dozen fellows round the Scottish isles. We're never free to do as we like.'

'Legs are the only things that have a taste of freedom,' said Gower.

They strolled down to Howell Edwards' office at nine, Kit Ines beside the luggage cart to the rear.

Around the office and along to the street of the cottages crowds were chattering, gesticulating; Ines fancied the foreign jabberers inclined to threaten. Howell Edwards at the door of his office watched them calculatingly. The lord of their destinies passed in with him, leaving Gower to study the features of the men, and Ines to reckon the chance of a fray.

Fleetwood came out presently, saying to Edwards:

'That concession goes far enough. Because I have a neighbour who yields at every step? No, stick to the principle. I've said my final word. And here's the carriage. If the mines are closed, more's the pity: but I'm not responsible. You can let them know if you like, before I drive off; it doesn't matter to me.'

The carriage was ready. Gower cast a glance up the hill. Three female figures and a pannier-donkey were visible on the descent. He nodded to Edwards, who took the words out of his mouth. 'Her ladyship, my lord.'

She was distinctly seen, and looked formidable in definition against the cloud. Madge and the nurse-maid Martha were the two other young women. On they came, and the angry man seated in the carriage could not give the order to start. Nor could he quite shape an idea of annoyance, though he hung to it and faced at Gower a battery of the promise to pay him for this. Tattling observers were estimated at their small importance there, as everywhere, by one so high above them. But the appearance of the woman of the burlesque name and burlesque actions, and odd ascension out of the ludicrous into a form to cast a spell, so that she commanded serious recollections of her, disturbed him. He stepped from his carriage. Again he had his incomprehensible fit of shyness; and a vision of the complacent, jowled, redundant, blue-coated monarch aswing in imbecile merriment on the signboard of the Royal Sovereign inn; constitutionally his total opposite, yet instigating the sensation.

In that respect his countess and he had shifted characters. Carinthia came on at her bold mountain stride to within hail of him. Met by Gower, she talked, smiled, patted her donkey, clutched his ear, lifted a silken covering to show the child asleep; entirely at her ease and unhurried. These women get aid from their pride of maternity. And when they can boast a parson behind them, they are indecorous up to insolent in their ostentation of it.

She resumed her advance, with a slight abatement of her challengeing match, sedately; very collectedly erect; changed in the fulness of her figure and her poised calm bearing.

He heard her voice addressing Gower: 'Yes, they do; we noticed the slate-roofs, looking down on them. They do look like a council of rooks in the hollow; a parliament, you said. They look exceedingly like, when a peep of sunshine falls. Oh, no; not clergymen!'

She laughed at the suggestion.

She might be one of the actresses by nature.

Is the man unsympathetic with women a hater of Nature deductively? Most women are actresses. As to worshipping Nature, we go back to the state of heathen beast, Mr. Philosopher Gower could be answered....

Fleetwood drew in his argument. She stood before him. There was on his part an insular representation of old French court salute to the lady, and she replied to it in the exactest measure, as if an instructed proficient.

She stood unshadowed. 'We have come to bid you adieu, my lord,' she said, and no trouble of the bosom shook her mellow tones. Her face was not the chalk-quarry or the rosed rock; it was oddly individual, and, in a way, alluring, with some gentle contraction of her eyelids. But evidently she stood in full repose, mistress of herself.

Upon him, it appeared, the whole sensibility of the situation was to be thrown. He hardened.

'We have had to settle business here,' he said, speaking resonantly, to cover his gazing discomposedly, all but furtively.

The child was shown, still asleep. A cunning infant not a cry in him to excuse a father for preferring concord or silence or the bachelor's exemption.

'He is a strong boy,' the mother said. 'Our doctor promises he will ride over all the illnesses.'

Fleetwood's answer set off with an alarum of the throat, and dwindled to 'We 'll hope so. Seems to sleep well.'

She had her rocky brows. They were not barren crags, and her shape was Nature's ripeness, it was acknowledged: She stood like a lance in air-rather like an Amazon schooled by Athene, one might imagine. Hues of some going or coming flush hinted the magical trick of her visage. She spoke in modest manner, or it might be indifferently, without a flaunting of either.

'I wish to consult you, my lord. He is not baptized. His Christian names?'

'I have no choice.'

'I should wish him to bear one of my brother's names.'

'I have no knowledge of your brother's names.'

'Chillon is one.'

'Ah! Is it, should you think, suitable to our climate?'

'Another name of my brother's is John.'

'Bull.' The loutish derision passed her and rebounded on him. 'That would be quite at home.'

'You will allow one of your own names, my lord?'

'Oh, certainly, if you desire it, choose. There are four names you will find in a book of the Peerage or Directory or so. Up at the castle—or you might have written:—better than these questions on the public road. I don't demur. Let it be as you like.'

'I write empty letters to tell what I much want,' Carinthia said.

'You have only to write your plain request.'

'If, now I see you, I may speak another request, my lord.'

'Pray,' he said, with courteous patience, and stepped forward down to the street of the miners' cottages. She could there speak out-bawl the request, if it suited her to do so.

On the point of speaking, she gazed round.

'Perfectly safe! no harm possible,' said he, fretful under the burden of this her maniacal maternal anxiety.

'The men are all right, they would not hurt a child. What can rationally be suspected!'

'I know the men; they love their children,' she replied. 'I think my child would be precious to them. Mr. Woodseer and Mr. Edwards and Madge are there.'

'Is the one more request—I mean, a mother's anxiety does not run to the extent of suspecting everybody?'

'Some of the children are very pretty,' said Carinthia, and eyed the bands of them at their games in the roadway and at the cottage doors. 'Children of the poor have happy mothers.'

Her eyes were homely, morning over her face. They were open now to what that fellow Woodseer (who could speak to the point when he was not aiming at it) called the parlour, or social sitting-room; where we may have converse with the tame woman's mind, seeing the door to the clawing recesses temporarily shut.

'Forgive me if I say you talk like the bigger child,' Fleetwood said lightly, not ungenially; for the features he looked on were museful, a picture in their one expression.

Her answer chilled him. 'It is true, my lord. I will not detain you. I would beg to be supplied with money.'

He was like the leaves of a frosted plant, in his crisp curling inward:—he had been so genial.

'You have come to say good-bye, that an opportunity to—as you put it—beg for money. I am not sure of your having learnt yet the right disposal of money.'

'I beg, my lord, to have two thousand pounds a year allowed me.'

'Ten—and it's a task to spend the sum on a single household—shall be alloted to your expenditure at Esslemont;—stables, bills, et caetera. You can entertain. My steward Leddings will undertake the management. You will not be troubled with payings.'

Her head acknowledged the graciousness.—'I would have two thousand pounds and live where I please.'

'Pardon me: the two, for a lady living where she pleases, exceeds the required amount.'

'I will accept a smaller sum, my lord.'

'Money!-it seems a singular demand when all supplies are furnished.'

'I would have control of some money.'

'You are thinking of charities.'

'Not charities.'

'Edwards here has a provision for the hospital needs of the people. Mr. Woodseer applies to me in cases he can certify. Leddings will do the same at Esslemont.'

'I am glad, I am thankful. The money I would have is for my own use. It is for me.'

'Ah. Scarcely that, I fancy.'

The remark should have struck home. He had a thirst for the sign of her confessing to it. He looked. Something like a petrifaction of her wildest face was shown.

Carinthia's eyes were hard out on a scattered knot of children down the street.

She gathered up her skirts. Without a word to him, she ran, and running shouted to the little ones around and ahead: 'In! in! indoors, children! "Blant, i'r ty!" Mothers, mothers, ho! get them in. See the dog! "Ci! Ci!" In with them! "Blant, i'r ty! Vr ty!"'

A big black mongrel appeared worrying at one of two petticoated urchins on the ground.

She scurried her swiftest, with such warning Welsh as she had on the top of her mountain cry; and doors flew wide, there was a bang of doors when she darted by: first gust of terrible heavens that she seemed to the cottagers.

Other shouts behind her rent the air, gathering to a roar, from the breasts of men and women. 'Mad dog about' had been for days the rumour, crossing the hills over the line of village, hamlet, farm, from Cardiff port.

Dead hush succeeded the burst. Men and women stood off. The brute was at the lady.

Her arms were straight above her head; her figure overhanging, on a bend of the knees. Right and left, the fury of the slavering fangs shook her loose droop of gown; and a dull, prolonged growl, like the clamour of a far body of insurrectionary marching men, told of the rage.

Fleetwood hovered helpless as a leaf on a bough.

'Back—', I pray,' she said to him, and motioned it, her arms at high stretch.

He held no weapon. The sweat of his forehead half blinded him. And she waved him behind her, beckoned to the crowd to keep wide way, used her lifted hands as flappers; she had all her wits. There was not a wrinkle of a grimace. Nothing but her locked lips betrayed her vision of imminent doom. The shaking of her gown and the snarl in the undergrowl sounded insatiate.

The brute dropped hold. With a weariful jog of the head, it pursued its course at an awful even swinging pace: Death's own, Death's doer, his reaper,—he, the very Death of the Terrors.

Carinthia's cry rang for clear way to be kept on either side, and that accursed went the path through a sharp-edged mob, as it poured pell-mell and shrank back, closing for the chase to rear of it.

'Father taught me,' she said to the earl, not more discomposed than if she had taken a jump.

'It's over!' he groaned, savagely white, and bellowed for guns, any weapons. 'Your father? pray?' She was entreated to speak.

'Yes, it must be shot; it will be merciful to kill it,' she said. 'They have carried the child indoors. The others are safe. Mr. Woodseer, run to my nurse-girl, Martha. He goes,' she murmured, and resumed to the earl: 'Father told me women have a better chance than men with a biting dog. He put me before him and drilled me. He thought of everything. Usually the poor beast snaps—one angry bite, not more. My dress teased it.'

Fleetwood grinned civilly in his excitement; intending to yield patient hearing, to be interested by any mortal thing she might choose to say.

She was advised by recollection to let her father rest.

'No, dear girl, not hurt, no scratch,—only my gown torn,' she said to Madge; and Madge heaved and whimpered, and stooped to pin the frayed strips. 'Quite safe; you see it is easy for women to escape, Mr. Edwards.'

Carinthia's voice hummed over the girl's head

'Father made me practise it, in case. He forethought. Madge, you heard of this dog. I told you how to act. I was not feverish. Our babe will not feel it.'

She bade Madge open her hands. 'A scratch would kill. Never mind the tearings; I will hold my dress. Oh! there is that one child bitten. Mr. Edwards, mount a man for the doctor. I will go in to the child. He was bitten. Lose not one minute, Mr. Edwards. I see you go.'

He bowed and hastened.

The child's mother was red eyes at her door for ease of her heart to the lady. Carinthia stepped into the room, where the little creature was fetching sobs after the spout of screams.

'God in heaven! she can't be going to suck the bite?' Fleetwood cried to Madge, whose answer was disquieting 'If it's to save life, my mistress won't stop at anything.'

His heart sprang with a lighted comprehension of Gower Woodseer's meaning. This girl's fervour opened portals to new views of her mistress, or opened eyes.

CHAPTER XXXIII

A FRIGHTFUL DEBATE

Pushing through a swarm into the cot, Fleetwood saw Carinthia on a knee beside a girl's lap, where the stripped child lay. Its mother held a basin for the dabbing at raw red spots.

A sting of pain touched the memory of its fright, and brought further screams, then the sobs. Carinthia hummed a Styrian cradle-song as the wailing lulled

She glanced up; she said to the earl: 'The bite was deep; it was in the blood. We may have time. Get me an interpreter. I must ask the mother. I know not many words.'

'What now?' said he, at the looming of new vexations.

'We have no choice. Has a man gone? Dr. Griffiths would hurry fast. An hour may be too late. The poison travels: Father advised it:—Fifty years for one brave minute! This child should be helped to live.'

'We 'll do our best. Why an interpreter?'

'A poker in the fire. The interpreter—whether the mother will bear to have it done.'

'Burn, do you mean?'

'It should be burnt.'

'Not by you?'

'Quick! Quick!'

'But will you—could you? No, I say!'

'If there is no one else.'

'You forget your own child.'

'He is near the end of his mother.'

'The doctor will soon arrive.'

'The poison travels. It cannot be overtaken unless we start nearly equal, father said.'

'Work like that wants an experienced hand.'

'A steady one. I would not quake—not tremble.'

'I cannot permit it.'

'Mr. Wythan would know!—he would know!

'Do you hear, Lady Fleetwood—the dog may not be mad!'

'Signs! He ran heavy, he foamed.'

'Foam 's no sign.'

'Go; order to me a speaker of English and Welsh.'

The earl spun round, sensible of the novelty of his being commanded, and submitting; but no sooner had he turned than he fell into her view of the urgency, and he went, much like the boy we see at school, with a strong hand on his collar running him in.

Madge entered, and said: 'Mr. Woodseer has seen baby and Martha and the donkey all safe.'

'He is kind,' said Carinthia. 'Do we right to bathe the wound? It seems right to wash it. Little things that seem right may be exactly wrong after all, when we are ignorant. I know burning the wound is right.'

Madge asked: 'But, my lady, who is to do it?'

'You would do it, dear, if I shrank,' her mistress replied.

'Oh, my lady, I don't know, I can't say. Burning a child! And there's our baby.'

'He has had me nearly his time.'

'Oh, my dear lady! Would the mother consent?'

'My Madge! I have so few of their words yet. You would hold the child to save it from a dreadful end.'

'God help me, my lady—I would, as long as I live I will.... Oh! poor infant, we do need our courage now.'

Seeing that her mistress had not a tear or a tremor, the girl blinked and schooled her quailing heart, still under the wicked hope that the mother would not consent; in a wonderment at this lady, who was womanly, and who could hold the red iron at living flesh, to save the poor infant from a dreadful end. Her flow of love to this dear lady felt the slicing of a cut; was half revulsion, half worship; uttermost worship in estrangement, with the further throbbing of her pulses.

The cottage door was pushed open for Lord Fleetwood and Howell Edwards, whom his master had prepared to stand against immediate operations. A mounted messenger had been despatched. But it was true, the doctor might not be at home. Assuming it to be a bite of rabies, minutes lost meant the terrible: Edwards bowed his head to that. On the other hand, he foresaw the closest of personal reasons for hesitating to be in agreement with the lady wholly. The countess was not so much a persuasive lady as she was, in her breath and gaze, a sweeping and a wafting power. After a short argument, he had the sense of hanging like a bank detached to fatality of motion by the crack of a landslip, and that he would speedily be on his manhood to volunteer for the terrible work.

He addressed the mother. Her eyes whitened from their red at his first word of laying hot iron on the child: she ran out with the wild woman's howl to her neighbours.

'Poor mother!' Carinthia sighed. 'It may last a year in the child's body, and one day he shudders at water. Father saw a bitten man die. I could fear death with the thought of that poison in me. I pray Dr. Griffiths may come.'

Fleetwood shuffled a step. 'He will come, he will come.'

The mother and some women now packed the room.

A gabble arose between them and Edwards. They fired sharp snatches of speech, and they darted looks at the lady and her lord.

'They do not know!' said Carinthia.

Gower brought her news that the dog had been killed; Martha and her precious burden were outside, a mob of men, too. He was not alarmed; but she went to the door and took her babe in her arms, and when the women observed the lady holding her own little one, their looks were softened. At a hint of explanation from Edwards, the guttural gabble rattled up to the shrill vowels.

Fleetwood's endurance broke short. The packed small room, the caged-monkey lingo, the wailful child, and the past and apprehended debate upon the burning of flesh, composed an intolerable torture. He said to Edwards: 'Go to the men; settle it with them. We have to follow that man Wythan; no peace otherwise. Tell the men the body of the dog must be secured for analysis. Mad or not, it's the same. These Welsh mothers and grandmothers won't allow cautery at any price. Hark at them!'

He turned to Carinthia: 'Your ladyship will let Mr. Edwards or Mr. Woodseer conduct you to the house where you are residing. You don't know these excitable people. I wish you to leave.'

She replied softly: 'I stay for the doctor's coming.'

'Impossible for me to wait, and I can't permit you to be here.'

'It is life and death, and I must not be commanded.'

'You may be proposing gratuitous agony.'

'I would do it to my own child.'

The earl attacked Gower: 'Add your voice to persuade Lady Fleetwood.'

Gower said: 'What if I think with Lady Fleetwood?'

'You would see her do it?'

'Do it myself, if there was no one else'

'This dog-all of you have gone mad,' the earl cried.

'Griffiths may keep his head; it's the only chance. Take my word, these Welshwomen just listen to them won't have it. You 'll find yourself in a nest of Furies. It may be right to do, it's folly to propose it, madness to attempt it. And I shall be bitten if I stop here a minute longer; I'm gone; I can neither command nor influence. I should have thought Gower Woodseer would have kept his wits.'

Fleetwood's look fell on Madge amid the group. Gower's perception of her mistress through the girl's devotion to her moved him. He took Madge by the hand, and the sensation came that it was the next thing to pressing his wife's. 'You're a loyal girl. You have a mistress it 's an honour to serve. You bind me. By the way, Ines shall run down for a minute before I go.'

'Let him stay where he is,' Madge said, having bobbed her curtsey.

'Oh, if he's not to get a welcome!' said the earl; and he could now fix a steadier look on his countess, who would have animated him with either a hostile face or a tender. She had no expression of a feeling. He bent to her formally.

Carinthia's words were: 'Adieu, my lord.'

'I have only to say, that Esslemont is ready to receive you,' he remarked, bowed more curtly, and walked out...

Gower followed him. They might as well have been silent, for any effect from what was uttered between them. They spoke opinions held by each of them—adverse mainly; speaking for no other purpose than to hold their positions.

'Oh, she has courage, no doubt; no one doubted it,' Fleetwood said, out of all relation to the foregoing.

Courage to grapple with his pride and open his heart was wanting in him.

Had that been done, even to the hint of it, instead of the lordly indifference shown, Gower might have ventured on a suggestion, that the priceless woman he could call wife was fast slipping away from him and withering in her allegiance. He did allude to his personal sentiment. 'One takes aim at Philosophy; Lady Fleetwood pulls us up to pay tribute to our debts.' But this was vague, and his hearer needed a present thunder and lightning to shake and pierce him.

'I pledged myself to that yacht,' said Fleetwood, by way of reply, 'or you and I would tramp it, as we did once-jolly old days! I shall have you in mind. Now turn back. Do the best you can.'

They parted midway up the street, Gower bearing away a sharp contrast of the earl and his countess; for, until their senses are dulled, impressionable young men, however precociously philosophical, are mastered by appearances; and they have to reflect under new lights before vision of the linked eye and mind is given them.

Fleetwood jumped into his carriage and ordered the coachman to drive smartly. He could not have admitted the feeling small; he felt the having been diminished, and his requiring a rapid transportation from these parts for him to regain his proper stature. Had he misconducted himself at the moment of danger? It is a ghastly thought, that the craven impulse may overcome us. But no, he could reassure his repute for manliness. He had done as much as a man could do in such a situation.

At the same time, he had done less than the woman.

Needed she to have gone so far? Why precipitate herself into the jaws of the beast?

Now she, proposes to burn the child's wound And she will do it if they let her. One, sees her at the work,—pale, flinty; no faces; trebly the terrific woman in her mild way of doing the work. All because her old father recommended it. Because she thinks it a duty, we will say; that is juster. This young woman is a very sword in the hand of her idea of duty. She can be feminine, too,—there is one who knows. She can be particularly distant, too. If in timidity, she has a modest view of herself—or an enormous conception of the magi that married her. Will she take the world's polish a little?

Fleetwood asked with the simplicity of the superior being who will consequently perhaps bestow the debt he owes...

But his was not the surface nature which can put a question of the sort and pass it. As soon as it had been formed, a vision of the elemental creature calling him husband smote to shivers the shell we walk on, and caught him down among the lower forces, up amid the higher; an infernal and a celestial contest for the extinction of the one or the other of them, if it was not for their union. She wrestled with him where the darknesses roll their snake-eyed torrents over between jagged horns of the netherworld. She stood him in the white ray of the primal vital heat, to bear unwithering beside her the test of light. They flew, they chased, battled, embraced, disjoined, adventured apart, brought back the count of their deeds, compared them,—and name the one crushed! It was the one weighted to shame, thrust into the cellar-corner of his own disgust, by his having asked whether that starry warrior spirit in the woman's frame would 'take polish a little.'

Why should it be a contention between them? For this reason: he was reduced to admire her act; and if he admired, he could not admire without respecting; if he respected, perforce he reverenced; if he reverenced, he worshipped. Therefore she had him at her feet. At the feet of any woman, except for the trifling object! But at the feet of 'It is my husband!' That would be a reversal of things.

Are not things reversed when the name Carinthia sounds in the thought of him who laughed at the name not less angelically martial than Feltre's adored silver trumpets of his Papal procession; sweeter of the new morning for the husband of the woman; if he will but consent to the worshipper's posture? Yes, and when Gower Woodseer's 'Malady of the Wealthy,' as he terms the pivotting of the whole marching and wheeling world upon the favoured of Fortune's habits and tastes, promises to quit its fell clutch on him?

Another voice in the young nobleman cried: Pooh, dolt and dupe! and surrounded her for half a league with reek of burnt flesh and shrieks of a tortured child; giving her the aspect of a sister of the Parcw. But it was not the ascendant' voice. It growled underneath, much like the deadly beast at Carinthia's gown while she stood:—an image of her to dominate the princeliest of men.

The princeliest must have won his title to the place before he can yield other than complimentary station to a woman without violation of his dignity; and vast wealth is not the title; worldly honours are not; deeds only are the title. Fleetwood consented to tell himself that he had not yet performed the deeds.

Therefore, for him to be dominated was to be obscured, eclipsed. A man may outrun us; it is the fortune of war. Eclipsed behind the skirts of a woman waving her upraised hands, with, 'Back, pray!'—no, that ignominy is too horribly abominable! Be sure, the situation will certainly recur in some form; will constantly recur. She will usurp the lead; she will play the man.

Let matters go on as they are. We know our personal worth.

Arrived at this point in the perpetual round of the conflict Carinthia had implanted, Fleetwood entered anew the ranks of the ordinary men of wealth and a coronet, and he hugged himself. He enjoyed repose; knowing it might be but a truce. Matters might go on as they were. Still, he wished her away from those Wythans, residing at Esslemont. There she might come eventually to a better knowledge of his personal worth:—'the gold mine we carry in our bosoms till it is threshed out of us in sweat,' that fellow Gower Woodseex says; adding, that we are the richer for not exploring it. Philosophical cynicism is inconclusive. Fleetwood knew his large capacities; he had proved them and could again. In case a certain half foreseen calamity should happen:—imagine it a fact, imagine him seized, besides admiring her character, with a taste for her person! Why, then, he would have to impress his own mysteriously deep character on her portion of understanding. The battle for domination would then begin.

Anticipation of the possibility of it hewed division between the young man's pride of being and his warmer feelings. Had he been free of the dread of subjection, he would have sunk to kiss the feet of the statuesque young woman, arms in air, firm-fronted over the hideous death that tore at her skirts.

CHAPTER XXXIV

A SURVEY OF THE RIDE OF THE WELSH CAVALIERS ESCORTING THE COUNTESS OF FLEETWOOD TO KENTISH ESSLEMONT

A formal notification from the earl, addressed to the Countess of Fleetwood in the third person, that Esslemont stood ready to receive her, autocratically concealed her lord's impatience to have her there; and by the careful precision with which the stages of her journey were marked, as places where the servants despatched to convey their lady would find preparations for her comfort, again alarmed the disordered mother's mind on behalf of the child she deemed an object of the father's hatred, second to his hatred of the mother. But the mother could defend herself, the child was prey the child of a detested wife was heir to his title and estates. His look at the child, his hasty one look down at her innocent, was conjured before her as resembling a kick at a stone in his path. His indifference to the child's Christian names pointed darkly over its future.

The distempered wilfulness of a bruised young woman directed her thoughts. She spoke them in the tone of reason to her invalid friend Rebecca Wythan, who saw with her, felt with her, yearned to retain her till breath was gone. Owain Wythan had his doubts of the tyrant guilty of maltreating this woman of women. 'But when you do leave Wales,' he said, 'you shall be guarded up to your haven.'

Carinthia was not awake to his meaning then. She sent a short letter of reply, imitating the style of her lord; very baldly stating, that she was unable to leave Wales because of her friend's illness and her part as nurse. Regrets were unmentioned.

Meanwhile Rebecca Wythan was passing to death. Not cheerlessly, more and more faintly, her thread of life ran to pause, resembling a rill of the drought; and the thinner-it grew, the shrewder were her murmurs for Carinthia's ears in commending 'the most real of husbands of an unreal wife' to her friendly care of him when he would no longer see the shadow he had wedded. She had the privilege of a soul beyond our minor rules and restrainings to speak her wishes to the true wife of a mock husband-no husband; less a husband than this shadow of a woman a wife, she said; and spoke them without adjuring the bowed head beside her to record a promise or seem to show the far willingness, but merely that the wishes should be heard on earth in her last breath, for a good man's remaining one chance of happiness. On the theme touching her husband Owain, it was verily to hear a soul speak, and have knowledge of the broader range, the rich interflowings of the tuned discords, a spirit past the flesh can find. Her mind was at the same time alive to our worldly conventions when other people came under its light; she sketched them and their views in her brief words between the gasps, with perspicuous, humorous bluntness, as vividly as her twitched eyebrows indicated the laugh. Gower Woodseer she read startlingly, if correctly.

Carinthia could not leave her. Attendance upon this dying woman was a drinking at the springs of life.

Rebecca Wythan under earth, the earl was briefly informed of Lady Fleetwood's consent to quit Wales, obedient to a summons two months old,—and that she would be properly escorted; for the which her lord had made provision. Consequently the tyrant swallowed his wrath, little conceiving the monstrous blow she was about to strike.

In peril of fresh floods from our Dame, who should be satisfied with the inspiring of these pages, it is owned that her story of 'the four and twenty squires of Glamorgan and Caermarthen in their brass-buttoned green coats and buckskins, mounted and armed, an escort of the Countess of Fleetwood across the swollen Severn, along midwinter roads, up to the Kentish gates of Esslemont,' has a foundation, though the story is not the more credible for her flourish of documentary old ballad-sheets, printed when London's wags had ears on cock to any whisper of the doings. of their favourite Whitechapel Countess; and indeed hardly depended on whispers.

Enthusiasm sufficient to troop forth four and twenty and more hundreds of Cambrian gentlemen, and still more of the common folk, as far as they could journey afoot, was over the two halves of the Principality, to give the countess a reputable and gallant body-guard. London had intimations of kindling circumstances concerning her, and magnified them in the interests of the national humour: which is the English way of exalting to criticize, criticizing to depreciate, and depreciating to restore, ultimately to cherish, in reward for the amusement furnished by an eccentric person, not devoid of merit.

These little tales of her, pricking cool blood to some activity, were furze-fires among the Welsh. But where the latter heard Bardic strings inviting a chorus, the former as unanimously obeyed the stroke of their humorous conductor's baton for an outburst from the ribs or below. And it was really funny to hear of Whitechapel's titled heroine roaming Taffyland at her old pranks.

Catching a maddened bull by the horns in the marketplace, and hanging to the infuriate beast, a wild whirl of clouts, till he is reduced to be a subject for steaks, that is no common feat.

Her performances down mines were things of the underworld. England clapped hands, merely objecting to her not having changed her garb for the picador's or matador's, before she seized the bull. Wales adopted and was proud of her in any costume. Welshmen North and South, united for the nonce, now propose her gallantry as a theme to the rival Bards at the next Eisteddfod. She is to sit throned in full assembly, oak leaves and mistletoe interwoven on her head, a white robe and green sash to clothe her, and the vanquished beast's horns on a gilded pole behind the dais; hearing the eulogies respectively interpreted to her by Colonel Fluellen Wythan at one ear, and Captain Agincourt Gower at the other. A splendid scene; she might well insist to be present.

There, however, we are at the pitch of burlesque beyond her illustrious lord's capacity to stand. Peremptory orders from England arrive, commanding her return. She temporizes, postpones, and supplicates to have the period extended up to the close of the Eisteddfod. My lord's orders are imperatively repeated, and very blunt. He will not have her 'continue playing the fool down there.' She holds her ground from August into February, and then sets forth, to undergo the further process of her taming at Esslemont in England; with Llewellyn and Vaughan and Cadwallader, and Watkyn and Shenkyn and the remains of the race of Owen Tudor, attending her; vowed to extract a receipt from the earl her lord's responsible servitors for the safe delivery of their heroine's person at the gates of Esslemont; ich dien their trumpeted motto.

Counting the number at four and twenty, it wears the look of an invasion. But the said number is a ballad number, and has been since the antique time. There was, at a lesser number, enough of a challenge about it for squires of England, never in those days backward to pick up a glove or give the ringing rejoinder for a thumb-bite, to ride out and tilt compliments with the Whitechapel Countess's green cavaliers, rally their sprites and entertain them exactly according to their degrees of dignity, as exhibited by their 'haviour under something of a trial; and satisfy also such temporary appetites as might be excited in them by (among other matters left to the luck of events) a metropolitan play upon the Saxon tongue, hard of understanding to the leeky cocks until their ready store of native pepper seasons it; which may require a corresponding English condiment to rectify the flavour of the stew.

Now the number of Saxe-Normans riding out to meet and greet the Welshmen is declared to have not exceeded nine. So much pretends to be historic, in opposition to the poetic version. They would, we may be sure, have made it a point of honour to meet and greet their invading guests in precisely similar numbers a larger would have overshot the mark of courtesy; and doubtless a smaller have fallen deplorably short of it. Therefore, an acquaintance with her chivalrous, if less impulsive, countrymen compels to the dismissing of the Dame's ballad authorities. She has every right to quote them for her own good pleasure, and may create in others an enjoyment of what has been called 'the Mackrell fry.'

Her notion of a ballad is, that it grows like mushrooms from a scuffle of feet on grass overnight, and is a sort of forest mother of the pied infant reared and trimmed by historians to show the world its fatherly antecedent steps. The hand of Rose Mackrell is at least suggested in more than one of the ballads. Here the Welsh irruption is a Chevy Chase; next we have the countess for a disputed Helen.

The lady's lord is not a shining figure. How can an undecided one be a dispenser of light? Poetry could never allow him to say with her:

'Where'er I go I make a name,
And leave a song to follow.'

Yet he was the master of her fortunes at the time; all the material power was his. Even doggerel verse (it is worth while to brood on the fact) denies a surviving pre-eminence to the potent moody, reverses the position between the driven and the driver. Poetry, however erratic, is less a servant of the bully Present, or pomlious Past, than History. The Muse of History has neither the same divination of the intrinsic nor the devotion to it, though truly, she has possession of all the positive matter and holds us faster by the crediting senses.

Nine English cavaliers, then, left London early on a January or February morning in a Southerly direction, bearing East; and they were the Earl of Fleetwood's intimates, of the half-dependent order; so we may suppose them to have gone at his bidding. That they met the procession of the Welsh, and claimed to take charge of the countess's carriage, near the Kentish border-line, is an assertion supported by testimony fairly acceptable.

Intelligence of the advancing party had reached the earl by courier, from the date of the first gathering on the bridge of Pont-y-pridd; and from Gloucester, along to the Thames at Reading; thence away to the Mole, from Mickleham, where the Surrey chalk runs its final turfy spine North-eastward to the slope upon Kentish soil.

Greatly to the astonishment of the Welsh cavaliers, a mounted footman, clad in the green and scarlet facings of Lord Fleetwood's livery, rode up to them a mile outside the principal towns and named the inn where the earl had ordered preparations for the reception of them. England's hospitality was offered on a princely scale. Cleverer fencing could not be.

The meeting, in no sense an encounter, occurred close by a thirty-acre meadow, famous over the county; and was remarkable for the punctilious exchange of ceremonial speech, danger being present; as we see powder-magazines protected by their walls and fosses and covered alleys. Notwithstanding which, there was a scintillation of sparks.

Lord Brailstone, spokesman of the welcoming party, expressed comic regrets that they had not an interpreter with them.

Mr. Owain Wythan, in the name of the Cambrian chivalry, assured him of their comprehension and appreciation of English slang.

Both gentlemen kept their heads uncovered in a suspense; they might for a word or two more of that savour have turned into the conveniently spacious meadow. They were induced, on the contrary, to enter the channel of English humour, by hearing Chumley Potts exclaim: 'His nob!' and all of them laughed at the condensed description of a good hit back, at the English party's cost.

Laughter, let it be but genuine, is of a common nationality, indeed a common fireside; and profound disagreement is not easy after it. The Dame professes to believe that 'Carinthia Jane' had to intervene as peacemaker, before the united races took the table in Esslemont's dining-hall for a memorable night of it, and a contest nearer the mark of veracity than that shown in another of the ballads she would have us follow. Whatever happened, they sat down at table together, and the point of honour for them each and every was, not to be first to rise from it. Once more the pure Briton and the mixed if not fused English engaged, Bacchus for instrument this time, Bacchus for arbiter of the fray.

You may imagine! says the Dame. She cites the old butler at Esslemont, 'as having been much questioned on the subject by her family relative, Dr. Glossop, and others interested to know the smallest items of the facts,'—and he is her authority for the declaration that the Welsh gentlemen and the English gentlemen, 'whatever their united number,' consumed the number of nine dozen and a half of old Esslemont wine before they rose, or as possibly sank, at the festive board at the hour of five of the morning.

Years later, this butler, Joshua Queeney, 'a much enfeebled old man,' retold and enlarged the tale of the enormous consumption of his best wine; with a sacred oath to confirm it, and a tear expressive of elegiacal feelings.

'They bled me twelve dozen, not a bottle less,' she quotes him, after a minute description of his countenance and scrupulously brushed black suit, pensioner though he had become. He had grown, during the interval, to be more communicative as to particulars. The wines were four. Sherry led off the parade pace, Hock the trot into the merry canter, Champagne the racing gallop, Burgundy the grand trial of constitutional endurance for the enforced finish. All these wines, except the sparkling, had their date of birth in the precedent century. 'They went like water.'

Questioned anxiously by Dr. Glossop, Queeney maintained an impartial attitude, and said there was no victor, no vanquished. They did not sit in blocks. The tactics for preserving peace intermingled them. Each English gentleman had a Welsh gentleman beside him; they both sat firm; both fell together. The bottles or decanters were not stationary for the guest to fill his glass, they circulated, returning to an empty glass. All drank equally. Often the voices were high, the talk was loud. The gentlemen were too serious to sing.

At one moment of the evening Queeney confidently anticipated a 'fracassy,' he said. One of the foreign party—and they all spoke English, after five dozen bottles had gone the round, as correct as the English themselves—remarked on the seventy-years Old Brown Sherry, that 'it had a Madeira flavour.' He spoke it approvingly. Thereupon Lord Simon Pitscrew calls to Queeney, asking him 'why Madeira had been supplied instead of Esslemont's renowned old Sherry?' A second Welsh gentleman gave his assurances that his friend had not said it was Madeira. But Lord Brailstone accused them of the worse unkindness to a venerable Old Brown Sherry, in attributing a Madeira flavour to it. Then another Welsh gentleman briskly and emphatically stated his opinion, that the attribution of Madeira flavour to it was a compliment. At this, which smelt strongly, he said, of insult, Captain Abrane called on the name of their absent host to warrant the demand of an apology to the Old Brown Sherry, for the imputation denying it an individual distinction. Chumley Potts offered generally to bet that he would distinguish blindfold at a single sip any Madeira from any first-class Sherry, Old Brown or Pale. 'Single sip or smell!' Ambrose Mallard cried, either for himself or his comrade, Queeney could not say which.

Of all Lord Fleetwood's following, Mr. Potts and Mr. Mallard were, the Dame informs us, Queeney's favourites, because they were so genial; and he remembered most of what they said and did, being moved to it by 'poor young Mr. Mallard's melancholy end and Mr. Potts's grief!'

The Welsh gentlemen, after paying their devoirs to the countess next morning, rode on in fresh health and spirits at mid-day to Barlings, the seat of Mr. Mason Fennell, a friend of Mr. Owain Wythan's. They shouted, in an unseemly way, Queeney thought, at their breakfast-table, to hear that three of the English party, namely, Captain Abrane, Mr. Mallard, and Mr. Potts, had rung for tea and toast in bed. Lord Simon Pitscrew, Lord Brailstone, and the rest of the English were sore about it; for it certainly wore a look of constitutional inferiority on the English side, which could boast of indubitably stouter muscles. The frenzied spirits of the Welsh gentlemen, when riding off, let it be known what their opinion was. Under the protection of the countess's presence, they were so cheery as to seem triumphantly ironical; they sent messages of condolence to the three in bed.

With an undisguised reluctance, the countess, holding Mr. Owain Wythan's hand longer than was publicly decent, calling him by his Christian name, consented to their departure. As they left, they defiled before her; the vow was uttered by each, that at the instant of her summons he would mount and devote himself to her service, individually or collectively. She waved her hand to them. They ranged in line and saluted. She kissed her hand. Sweeping the cavaliers' obeisance, gallantest of bows, they rode away.

A striking scene, Dame Gossip says; but raises a wind over the clipped adventure, and is for recounting what London believed about it. Enough has been conceded for the stoppage of her intrusion; she is left in the likeness of a full-charged pistol capless to the clapping trigger.

That which London believed, or affected to believe about it, would fill chapters. There was during many months an impression of Lord Fleetwood's countess as of a tenacious, dread, prevailing young woman, both intrepid and astute, who had, by an exercise of various arts, legitimate in open war of husband and wife, gathered the pick of the Principality to storm and carry another of her husband's houses. The certification that her cavaliers were Welsh gentlemen of wealth and position required a broader sneer at the Welsh than was warranted by later and more intimate acquaintance, if it could be made to redound to her discredit. So, therefore, added to the national liking for a plucky woman, she gained the respect for power. Whitechapel was round her like London's one street's length extension of smoky haze, reminder of the morning's fog under novel sunbeams.

Simultaneously, strange to say, her connubial antagonist, far from being overshadowed, grew to be proportionately respected, and on the strength of his deserts, apart from his title and his wealth. He defended himself, as he was bound to do, by welcoming the picked Welsh squires with hospitable embrace, providing ceremonies, receptions, and most comfortable arrangements for them, along the route. But in thus gravely entering into the knightly burlesque of the procession, and assisting to swell the same, he not only drew the venom from it, he stood forth as England's deputed representative, equal to her invasive challengeing guests at all points, comic, tragic, or cordial. He saw that it had to be treated as a national affair; and he parried the imputation which would have injured his country's name for courtly breeding, had they been ill-received, while he rescued his own good name from derision by joining the extravagance.

He was well inspired. It was popularly felt to be the supreme of clever-nay, noble-fencing. Really noble, though the cleverness was conspicuous. A defensive stroke, protecting him against his fair one's violent charge of horse, warded off an implied attack upon Old England, in Old England's best-humoured easy manner.

Supposing the earl to have acted otherwise, his countess would virtually have ridden over him, and wild Wales have cast a shadow on the chivalry of magisterial England. He and his country stood to meet the issue together the moment the Countess of Fleetwood and her escort crossed the Welsh border; when it became a question between the hot-hearted, at their impetuous gallop, and the sedatively minded, in an unfortified camp of arm-chairs. The earl's adroitness, averting a collision fatal or discomforting to both, disengaged him from an incumbent odium, of which, it need hardly be stated, neither the lady nor her attendant cavaliers had any notion at the hour of the assembly for the start for England on the bridge of Pont-y-pridd. The hungry mother had the safety of her babe in thought. The hotheaded Welshmen were sworn to guard their heroine.

That is the case presented by the Dame's papers, when the incredible is excised. She claims the being a good friend to fiction in feeding popular voracity with all her stores. But the Old Buccaneer, no professed friend to it, is a sounder guide in the maxim, where he says: Deliver yourself by permit of your cheque on the 'Bank of Reason, and your account is increased instead of lessened.

Our account with credulity, he would signify.

The Dame does not like the shaking for a sifting. Romance, however, is not a mountain made of gold, but a vein running some way through; and it must be engineered, else either we are filled with wind from swallowing indigestible substance, or we consent to a debasing of the currency, which means her to-morrow's bankruptcy; and the spectacle of Romance in the bankruptcy court degrades us (who believe we are allied to her) as cruelly as it appals. It gives the cynic licence to bark day and night for an entire generation.

Surely the Countess of Fleetwood's drive from the Welsh borders to Esslemont, accompanied by the chosen of the land, followed by the vivats of the whole Principality, and England gaping to hear the stages of her progress, may be held sufficiently romantic without stuffing of surprises and conflicts, adventures at inns, alarms at midnight, windings of a horn over hilly verges of black heaths, and the rape of the child, the pursuit, the recovery of the child, after a new set of heroine performances on the part of a strung-wire mother, whose outcry in a waste country district, as she clasps her boy to her bosom again: 'There's a farm I see for milk for him!' the Dame repeats, having begun with an admission that the tale has been contradicted, and is not produced on authority. The end in design is to win the ear by making a fuss, and roll event upon event for the braining of common intelligence, until her narrative resembles dusty troopings along a road to the races.

Carinthia and her babe reached Esslemont, no matter what impediments. There, like a stopped runner whose pantings lengthen to the longer breath, her alarms over the infant subsided, ceasing for as long as she clasped it or was in the room with it. Walking behind the precious donkey-basket round the park, she went armed, and she soon won a fearful name at Kentish cottage-hearths, though she 'was not black to see, nor old. No, she was very young. But she did all the things that soldiers do,—was a bit of a foreigner;—she brought a reputation up from the Welsh land, and it had a raven's croak and a glow-worm's drapery and a goblin's origin.

Something was hinted of her having agitated London once. Somebody dropped word of her and that old Lord Levellier up at Croridge. She stalked park and country at night. Stories, one or two near the truth, were told of a restless and a very decided lady down these parts as well; and the earl her husband daren't come nigh in his dread of her, so that he runs as if to save his life out of every place she enters. And he's not one to run for a trifle. His pride is pretty well a match for princes and princesses.

All the same, he shakes in his shoes before her, durst hardly spy at Esslemont again while she's in occupation. His managing gentleman comes down from him, and goes up from her; that's how they communicate. One week she's quite solitary; another week the house is brimful as can be. She 's the great lady entertaining then. Yet they say it 's a fact, she has not a shilling of her own to fling at a beggar. She 'll stock a cottage wanting it with provision for a fortnight or more, and she'll order the doctor in, and she'll call and see the right things done for illness. 'But no money; no one's to expect money of her. The shots you hear in Esslemont grounds out of season are she and her maid, always alongside her, at it before a target on a bank, trying that old Lord Levellier's gunpowder out of his mill; and he's got no money either; not for his workmen, they say, until they congregate, and a threatening to blow him up brings forth half their pay, on account. But he 's a known miser. She's not that. She's a pleasant-faced lady for the poor. She has the voice poor people like. It's only her enemy, maybe her husband, she can be terrible to. She'd drive a hole through a robber stopping her on the road, as soon as look at him.

This was Esslemont's atmosphere working its way to the earl, not so very long after the establishment of his countess there. She could lay hold of the English, too, it seemed. Did she call any gentleman of the district by his Christian name? Lord Simon Pitscrew reported her doing so in the case of one of the Welshmen. Those Welshmen! Apparently they are making a push for importance in the kingdom!

CHAPTER XXXV

IN WHICH CERTAIN CHANGES MAY BE DISCERNED

Behind his white plaster of composure, Lord Fleetwood had alternately raged and wondered during the passage of the Welsh cavalcade up Eastward: a gigantic burlesque, that would have swept any husband of their heroine off the scene had he failed to encounter it deferentially, preserving his countenance and ostensibly his temper. An idiot of a woman, incurable in her lunacy, suspects the father of the infant as guilty of designs done to death in romances; and so she manages to set going solemnly a bigger blazing Tom Fool's show than any known or written romance gives word of! And that fellow, Gower Woodseer, pleads, in apology, for her husband's confusion, physiologically, that it comes of her having been carried off and kept a prisoner when she was bearing the child and knitting her whole mind to ensure the child. But what sheer animals these women are, if they take impressions in such a manner! And Mr. Philosopher argues that the abusing of women proves the hating of Nature; names it 'the commonest insanity, and the deadliest,' and men are 'planted in the bog of their unclean animal condition until they do proper homage to the animal Nature makes the woman be.' Oh, pish, sir!—as Meeson Corby had the habit of exclaiming when Abrane's 'fiddler' argues him into a corner. The fellow can fiddle fine things and occasionally clear sense:—'Men hating Nature are insane. Women and Nature are close. If it is rather general to hate Nature and maltreat women, we begin to see why the world is a mad world.' That is the tune of the fiddler's fiddling. As for him, something protects him. He was the slave of Countess Livia; like Abrane, Mallard, Corby, St. Ombre, young Cressett, and the dozens. He is now her master. Can a man like that be foolish, in saying of the Countess Carinthia, she is 'not only quick to understand, she is in the quick of understanding'? Gower Woodseer said it of her in Wales, and again on the day of his walk up to London from Esslemont, after pedestrian exercise, which may heat the frame, but cools the mind. She stamped that idea on a thoughtful fellow.

He's a Welshman. They are all excitable,—have heads on hound's legs for a flying figure in front. Still, they must have an object, definitely seen by them—definite to them if dim to their neighbours; and it will run in the poetic direction: and the woman to win them, win all classes of them, within so short a term, is a toss above extraordinary. She is named Carinthia—suitable name for the Welsh pantomimic procession. Or cry out the word in an amphitheatre of Alpine crags,—it sounds at home.

She is a daughter of the mountains,—should never have left them. She is also a daughter of the Old Buccaneer—no poor specimen of the fighting Englishman of his day. According to Rose Mackrell, he, this Old Buccaneer, it was, who, by strange adventures, brought the great Welsh mines into the family! He would not be ashamed in spying through his nautical glass, up or down, at his daughter's doings. She has not yet developed a taste for the mother's tricks:—the mother, said to have been a kindler. That Countess of Cressett was a romantic little fly-away bird. Both parents were brave: the daughter would inherit gallantry. She inherits a kind of thwarted beauty. Or it needs the situation seen in Wales: her arms up and her unaffrighted eyes over the unappeasable growl. She had then the beauty coming from the fathom depths, with the torch of Life in the jaws of Death to light her: beauty of the nether kingdom mounting to an upper place in the higher. Her beauty recognized, the name of the man who married her is not Longears—not to himself, is the main point; nor will it be to the world when he shows that it is not so to himself.

Suppose he went to her, would she be trying at domination? The woman's pitch above woman's beauty was perceived to be no intermittent beam, but so living as to take the stamp of permanence. More than to say it was hers, it was she. What a deadly peril brought into view was her character-soul, some call it: generally a thing rather distasteful in women, or chilling to the masculine temperament. Here it attracts. Here, strange to say, it is the decided attraction, in a woman of a splendid figure and a known softness. By rights, she should have more understanding than to suspect the husband as guilty of designs done to death in romances. However, she is not a craven who compliments him by rearing him, and he might prove that there is no need for fear. But she would be expecting explanations before the reconcilement. The bosom of these women will keep on at its quick heaving until they have heard certain formal words, oaths to boot. How speak them?

His old road of the ladder appeared to Fleetwood an excellent one for obviating explanations and effecting the reconcilement without any temporary seeming forfeit of the native male superiority. For there she is at Esslemont now; any night the window could be scaled. 'It is my husband.' The soul was in her voice when she said it.

He remembered that it had not ennobled her to him then; had not endeared; was taken for a foreign example of the childish artless, imperfectly suited to our English clime.' The tone of adorable utterances, however much desired, is never for repetition; nor is the cast of divine sweet looks; nor are the particular deeds-once pardonable, fitly pleaded. A second scaling of her window—no, night's black hills girdle the scene with hoarse echoes; the moon rushes out of her clouds grimacing. Even Fleetwood's devil, much addicted to cape and sword and ladder, the vulpine and the gryphine, rejected it.

For she had, by singular transformation since, and in spite of a deluging grotesque that was antecedently incredible, she had become a personage, counting her adherents; she could put half the world in motion on her side. Yell those Welshmen to scorn, they were on a plane finding native ground with as large a body of these English. His baser mind bowed to the fact. Her aspect was entirely different; her attitude toward him as well: insomuch that he had to chain her to her original features by the conjuring of recollected phrases memorable for the vivid portraiture of her foregone simplicity and her devotion to 'my husband.'

Yes, there she was at Essleinont, securely there, near him, to be seen any day; worth claiming, too; a combatant figure, provocative of the fight and the capture rather than repellent. The respect enforced by her attitude awakened in him his inherited keen old relish for our intersexual strife and the indubitable victory of the stronger, with the prospect of slavish charms, fawning submission, marrowy spoil. Or perhaps, preferably, a sullen submission, reluctant charms; far more marrowy. Or who can say?—the creature is a rocket of the shot into the fiery garland of stars; she may personate any new marvel, be an unimagined terror, an overwhelming bewitchment: for she carries the unexpected in her bosom. And does it look like such indubitable victory, when the man, the woman's husband, divided from her, toothsome to the sex, acknowledges within himself and lets the world know his utter dislike of other women's charms, to the degree that herbal anchorites positively could not be colder, could not be chaster: and he no forest bird, but having the garden of the variety of fairest flowers at nod and blush about him! That was the truth. Even Henrietta's beauty had the effect of a princess's birthday doll admired on show by a contemptuous boy.

Wherefore, then, did the devil in him seek to pervert this loveliest of young women and feed on her humiliation for one flashing minute? The taste had gone, the desire of the vengeance was extinct, personal gratification could not exist. He spied into himself, and set it down to one among the many mysteries.

Men uninstructed in analysis of motives arrive at this dangerous conclusion, which spares their pride and caresses their indolence, while it flatters the sense of internal vastness, and invites to headlong intoxication. It allows them to think they are of such a compound, and must necessarily act in that manner. They are not taught at the schools or by the books of the honoured places in the libraries, to examine and see the simplicity of these mysteries, which it would be here and there a saving grace for them to see; as the minstrel, dutifully inclining to the prosy in their behalf and morality's, should exhibit; he should arrest all the characters of his drama to spring it to vision and strike perchance the chord primarily if not continually moving them, that readers might learn the why and how of a germ of evil, its flourishing under rebuke, the persistency of it after the fell creative energy has expired and pleasure sunk to be a phlegmatic dislike, almost a loathing.

This would here be done, but for signs of a barometric dead fall in Dame Gossip's chaps, already heavily pendent. She would be off with us on one of her whirling cyclones or elemental mad waltzes, if a step were taken to the lecturing-desk. We are so far in her hands that we have to keep her quiet. She will not hear of the reasons and the change of reasons for one thing and the other. Things were so: narrate them, and let readers do their reflections for themselves, she says, denouncing our conscientious method as the direct road downward to the dreadful modern appeal to the senses and assault on them for testimony to the veracity of everything described; to the extent that, at the mention of a vile smell, it shall be blown into the reader's nostrils, and corking-pins attack the comfortable seat of him simultaneously with a development of surprises. 'Thither your conscientiousness leads.'

It is not perfectly visible. And she would gain information of the singular nature of the young of the male sex in listening to the wrangle between Lord Fleetwood and Gower Woodseer on the subject of pocket-money for the needs of the Countess Carinthia. For it was a long and an angry one, and it brought out both of them, exposing, of course, the more complex creature the most. They were near a rupture, so scathing was Gower's tone of irate professor to shirky scholar—or it might be put, German professor to English scuffleshoe.

She is for the scene of 'Chillon John's' attempt to restore the respiration of his bank-book by wager; to wit, that he would walk a mile, run a mile, ride a mile, and jump ten hurdles, then score five rifle-shots at a three hundred yards' distant target within a count of minutes; twenty-five, she says; and vows it to have been one of the most exciting of scenes ever witnessed on green turf in the land of wagers; and that he was accomplishing it quite certainly when, at the first of the hurdles, a treacherous unfolding and waving of a white flag caused his horse to swerve and the loss of one minute, seven and twenty seconds, before he cleared the hurdles; after which, he had to fire his shots hurriedly, and the last counted blank, for being outside the circle of the stated time.

So he was beaten. But a terrific uproar over the field proclaimed the popular dissatisfaction. Presently there was a cleavage of the mob, and behold a chase at the heels of the fellow to rival the very captain himself for fleetness. He escaped, leaving his pole with the sheet nailed to it, by way of flag, in proof of foul play; or a proof, as the other side declared, of an innocently premature signalizing of the captain's victory.

However that might be, he ran. Seeing him spin his legs at a hound's pace, half a mile away, four countrymen attempted to stop him. All four were laid on their backs in turn with stupefying celerity; and on rising to their feet, and for the remainder of their natural lives, they swore that no man but a Champion could have floored them so. This again may have been due to the sturdy island pride of four good men knocked over by one. We are unable to decide. Wickedness there was, the Dame says; and she counsels the world to 'put and put together,' for, at any rate, 'a partial elucidation of a most mysterious incident.' As to the wager-money, the umpires dissented; a famous quarrel, that does not concern us here, sprang out of the dispute; which was eventually, after great disturbance 'of the country, referred to three leading sportsmen in the metropolitan sphere, who pronounced the wager 'off,' being two to one. Hence arose the dissatisfied third party, and the letters of this minority to the newspapers, exciting, if not actually dividing, all England for several months.

Now the month of December was the month of the Dame's mysterious incident. From the date of January, as Madge Winch knew, Christopher Ines had ceased to be in the service of the Earl of Fleetwood. At Esslemont Park gates, one winter afternoon of a North-east wind blowing 'rum-shrub into men for a stand against rheumatics,' as he remarked, Ines met the girl by appointment, and informing her that he had money, and that Lord Fleetwood was 'a black nobleman,' he proposed immediate marriage. The hymeneal invitation, wafted to her on the breath of rum-shrub, obtained no response from Madge until she had received evasive answers as to why the earl dismissed him, and whence the stock of money came.

Lord Fleetwood, he repeated, was a black nobleman. She brought him to say of his knowledge, that Lord Fleetwood hated, and had reason to hate, Captain Levellier. 'Shouldn't I hate the man took my sweetheart from me and popped me into the noose with his sister instead?' Madge was now advised to be overcome by the smell of rum-shrub:—a mere fancy drink tossed off by heroes in their idle moments, before they settle down to the serious business of real drinking, Kit protested. He simulated envious admiration of known heroes, who meant business, and scorned any of the weak stuff under brandy, and went at it till the bottles were the first to give in. For why? They had to stomach an injury from the world or their young woman, and half-way on they shoved that young person and all enemies aside, trampled 'em. That was what Old O'Devy signified; and many's the man driven to his consolation by a cat of a girl, who's like the elements in their puffs and spits at a gallant ship, that rides the tighter and the tighter for all they can do to capsize. 'Tighter than ever I was tight I'll be to-night, if you can't behave.'

They fell upon the smack of words. Kit hitched and huffed away, threatening bottles. Whatever he had done, it was to establish the petticoated hornet in the dignity of matron of a champion light-weight's wholesome retreat of a public-house. A spell of his larkish hilarity was for the punishment of the girl devoted to his heroical performances, as he still considered her to be, though women are notoriously volatile, and her language was mounting a stage above the kitchen.

Madge had little sorrow for him. She was the girl of the fiery heart, not the large heart; she could never be devoted to more than one at a time, and her mistress had all her heart. In relation to Kit, the thought of her having sacrificed her good name to him, flung her on her pride of chastity, without the reckoning of it as a merit. It was the inward assurance of her independence: the young spinster's planting of the standard of her proud secret knowledge of what she is, let it be a thing of worth or what you will, or the world think as it may. That was her thought.

Her feeling, the much livelier animation, was bitter grief, because her mistress, unlike herself, had been betrayed by her ignorance of the man into calling him husband. Just some knowledge of the man! The warning to the rescue might be there. For nothing did the dear lady weep except for her brother's evil fortune. The day when she had intelligence from Mrs. Levellier of her brother's defeat, she wept over the letter on her knees long hours. 'Me, my child, my brother!' she cried more than once. She had her suspicion of the earl then, and instantly, as her loving servant had. The suspicion was now no dark light, but a clear day-beam to Madge. She adopted Kit's word of Lord Fleetwood. 'A black nobleman he is! he is!' Her mistress had written like a creature begging him for money. He did not deign a reply. To her! When he had seen good proof she was the bravest woman on earth; and she rushed at death to save a child, a common child; as people say. And who knows but she saved that husband of hers, too, from bites might have sent him out of the world barking, and all his wealth not able to stop him!

They were in the month of March. Her dear mistress had been begging my lord through Mr. Woodseer constantly of late for an allowance of money; on her knees to him, as it seemed; and Mr. Woodseer was expected at Esslemont. Her mistress was looking for him eagerly. Something her heart was in depended on it, and only her brother could be the object, for now she loved only him of these men; though a gentleman coming over from Barlings pretty often would pour mines of money into her lap for half a word.

Carinthia had walked up to Croridge in the morning to meet her brother at Lekkatts. Madge was left guardian of the child. She liked a stroll any day round Esslemont Park, where her mistress was beginning to strike roots; as she soon did wherever she was planted, despite a tone of pity for artificial waters and gardeners' arts. Madge respected them. She knew nothing of the grandeur of wildness. Her native English veneration for the smoothing hand of wealth led her to think Esslemont the home of all homes for a lady with her husband beside her. And without him, too, if he were wafted over seas and away: if there would but come a wind to do that!

The wild North-easter tore the budded beeches. Master John Edward Russett lay in the cradling-basket drawn by his docile donkey, Martha and Madge to right and left of him; a speechless rustic, graduating in footman's livery, to rear.

At slow march round by the wrinkled water, Madge saw the park gates flung wide. A coach drove up the road along on the farther rim of the circle, direct for the house. It stopped, the team turned leisurely and came at a smart pace toward the carriage-basket. Lord Fleetwood was recognized.

He alighted, bidding one of his grooms drive to stables. Madge performed her reverence, aware that she did it in clumsy style; his presence had startled her instincts and set them travelling.

'Coldish for the youngster,' he said. 'All well, Madge?'

'Baby sleeps in the air, my lord,' she replied. 'My lady has gone to Croridge.'

'Sharp air for a child, isn't it?'

'My lady teaches him to breathe with his mouth shut, like her father taught her when she was little. Our baby never catches colds.'

Madge displayed the child's face.

The father dropped a glance on it from the height of skies.

'Croridge, you said?'

'Her uncle, Lord Levellier's.'

'You say, never catches cold?'

'Not our baby, my lord.'

Probably good management on the part of the mother. But the wife's absence disappointed the husband strung to meet her, and an obtrusion of her practical motherhood blurred the prospect demanded by his present step.

'When do you expect her to return, Madge?'

'Before nightfall, my lord.'

'She walks?'

'Oh yes, my lady is fond of walking.'

'I suppose she could defend herself?'

'My lady walks with a good stick.'

Fleetwood weighed the chances; beheld her figure attacked, Amazonian.

'And tell me, my dear—Kit?'

I don't see more of Kit Ines.'

'What has the fellow done?'

'I'd like him to let me know why he was dismissed.'

'Ah. He kept silent on that point.'

'He let out enough.'

'You've punished him, if he's to lose a bonny sweetheart, poor devil! Your sister Sally sends you messages?'

'We're both of us grateful, my lord.'

He lifted the thin veil from John Edward Russett's face with a loveless hand.

'You remember the child bitten by a dog down in Wales. I have word from my manager there. Poor little wretch has died—died raving.'

Madge's bosom went shivering up and sank. 'My lady was right. She's not often wrong.'

'She's looking well?' said the earl, impatient with her moral merits:—and this communication from Wales had been the decisive motive agent in hurrying him at last to Esslemont. The next moment he heard coolly of the lady's looking well. He wanted fervid eulogy of his wife's looks, if he was to hear any.

The girl was counselled by the tremor of her instincts to forbear to speak of the minor circumstance, that her mistress had, besides a good stick, a good companion on the road to Croridge: and she rejoiced to think her mistress had him, because it seemed an intimation of justice returning upon earth. She was combative, a born rebel against tyranny. She weighed the powers, she felt to the worth of the persons coming into her range of touch: she set her mistress and my lord fronting for a wrestle, and my lord's wealth went to thin vapour, and her mistress's character threw him. More dimly, my lord and the Welsh gentleman were put to the trial: a tough one for these two men. She did not proclaim the winner, but a momentary flutter of pity in the direction of Lord Fleetwood did as much. She pitied him; for his presence at Esslemont betrayed an inclination; he was ignorant of his lady's character, of how firm she could be to defy him and all the world, in her gratitude to the gentleman she thought of as her true friend, smiled at for his open nature,—called by his Christian name.

The idea of a piece of information stinging Lord Fleetwood, the desire to sting, so as to be an instrument of retribution (one of female human nature's ecstasies); and her, abstaining, that she, might not pain the lord who had been generous to her sister Sally, made the force in Madge's breast which urges to the gambling for the undeveloped, entitled prophecy. She kept it low and felt it thrill.

Lord Fleetwood, chatted; Madge had him wincing. He might pull the cover off the child's face carelessly—he looked at the child. His look at the child was a thought of the mother. If he thought of the mother, he would be wanting to see her. If he heard her call a gentleman by his Christian name, and heard the gentleman say 'Carinthia' my lord would begin to shiver at changes. Women have to do unusual things when they would bring that outer set to human behaviour. Perhaps my lord would mount the coach-box and whip his horses away, adieu forever. His lady would not weep. He might, perhaps, command her to keep her mouth shut from gentlemen's Christian names, all except his own. His lady would not obey. He had to learn something of changes that had come to others as well as to himself. Ah, and then would he dare hint, as base men will? He may blow foul smoke on her, she will shine out of it. He has to learn what she is, that is his lesson; and let him pray all night and work hard all day for it not to be too late. Let him try to be a little like Mr. Woodseer, who worships the countess, and is hearty with the gentleman she treats as her best of friends. There is the real nobleman.

Fleetwood chatted on airily. His instincts were duller than those of the black-browed girl, at whom he gazed for idle satisfaction of eye from time to time while she replied demurely and maintained her drama of, the featureless but well-distinguished actors within her bosom,—a round, plump bust, good wharfage and harbourage, he was thinking. Excellent harbourage, supposing the arms out in pure good-will. A girl to hold her voyager fast and safe! Men of her class had really a capital choice in a girl like this. Men of another class as well, possibly, for temporary anchorage out midchannel. No?—possibly not. Here and there a girl is a Tartar. Ines talked of her as if she were a kind of religious edifice and a doubt were sacrilege. She could impress the rascal: girls have their arts for reaching the holy end, and still they may have a welcome for a foreign ship.

The earl said humorously: 'You will grant me permission to lunch at your mistress's table in her absence?' And she said: 'My lord!' And he resumed, to waken her interest with a personal question: 'You like our quiet country round Esslemont?' She said: 'I do,' and gave him plain look for look. Her eye was undefended: he went into it, finding neither shallow nor depth, simply the look, always the look;

whereby he knew that no story of man was there, and not the shyest of remote responsive invitations from Nature's wakened and detected rogue. The bed of an unmarried young woman's eye yields her secret of past and present to the intrepid diver, if he can get his plunge; he holds her for the tenth of a minute, that is the revealment. Jewel or oyster-shell, it is ours. She cannot withhold it, he knew right well. This girl, then, was, he could believe, one of the rarely exampled innocent in knowledge. He was practised to judge.

Invitation or challenge or response from the handsomest he would have scorned just then. His native devilry suffered a stir at sight of an innocent in knowledge and spotless after experiences. By a sudden singular twist, rather unfairly, naturally, as it happened, he attributed it to an influence issuing from her mistress, to whom the girl was devoted, whom consequently she copied; might physically, and also morally, at a distance, resemble.

'Well, you've been a faithful servant to your lady, my dear; I hope you'll be comfortable here,' he said. 'She likes the mountains.'

'My lady would be quite contented if she could pass two months of the year in the mountains,' Madge answered.

'Look at me. They say people living together get a likeness to one another. What's your opinion? Upon my word, your eyebrows remind me, though they're not the colour—they have a bend!'

'You've seen my lady in danger, my lord.'

'Yes; well, there 's no one to resemble her there, she has her mark—kind of superhuman business. We're none of us "fifty feet high, with phosphorus heads," as your friend Mr. Gower Woodseer says of the prodigiosities. Lady Fleetwood is back—when?'

'Before dark, she should be.'

He ran up the steps to the house.

At Lekkatts beneath Croridge a lean midday meal was being finished hard on the commencement by a silent company of three. When eating is choking to the younger members of the repast, bread and cold mutton-bone serve the turn as conclusively as the Frenchman's buffet-dishes. Carinthia's face of unshed tears dashed what small appetite Chillon had. Lord Levellier plied his fork in his right hand ruminating, his back an arch across his plate.

Riddles to the thwarted young, these old people will not consent to be read by sensations. Carinthia watched his jaws at their work of eating under his victim's eye-knowing Chillon to be no longer an officer in the English service; knowing that her beloved had sold out for the mere money to pay debts and support his Henrietta; knowing, as he must know, that Chillon's act struck a knife to pierce his mother's breast through her coffin-boards! This old man could eat, and he could withhold the means due to his dead sister's son. Could he look on Chillon and not feel that the mother's heart was beating in her son's fortunes? Half the money due to Chillon would have saved him from ruin.

Lord Levellier laid his fork on the plate. He munched his grievance with his bit of meat. The nephew and niece here present feeding on him were not so considerate as the Welsh gentleman, a total stranger, who had walked up to Lekkatts with the Countess of Fleetwood, and expressed the preference to feed at an inn. Relatives are cormorants.

His fork on his plate released the couple. Barely half a dozen words, before the sitting to that niggard restoration, had informed Carinthia of the step taken by her brother. She beckoned him to follow her.

'The worst is done now, Chillon. I am silent. Uncle is a rock. You say we must not offend. I have given him my whole mind. Say where Riette is to live.'

'Her headquarters will be here, at a furnished house. She's, with her cousin, the Dowager.'

'Yes. She should be with me.'

'She wants music. She wants—poor girl! let her have what comes to her.'

Their thoughts beneath their speech were like fish darting under shadow of the traffic bridge.

'She loves music,' said Carinthia; 'it is almost life to her, like fresh air to me. Next month I am in London; Lady Arpington is kind. She will give me as much of their polish as I can take. I dare say I should feel the need of it if I were an enlightened person.'

'For instance, did I hear "Owain," when your Welsh friend was leaving?' Chillon asked.

'It was his dying wife's wish, brother.'

'Keep to the rules, dear.'

'They have been broken, Chillon.'

'Mend them.'

'That would be a step backward.'

'"The right one for defence!" father says.'

'Father says, "The habit of the defensive paralyzes will."'

'"Womanizes," he says, Carin. You quote him falsely, to shield the sex. Quite right. But my sister must not be tricky. Keep to the rules. You're an exceptional woman, and it would be a good argument, if you were not in an exceptional position.'

'Owain is the exceptional man, brother.'

'My dear, after all, you have a husband.'

'I have a brother, I have a friend, I have no—I am a man's wife and the mother of his child; I am free, or husband would mean dungeon. Does my brother want an oath from me? That I can give him.'

'Conduct, yes; I couldn't doubt you,' said Chillon. 'But "the world's a flood at a dyke for women, and they must keep watch," you've read.'

'But Owain is not our enemy,' said Carinthia, in her deeper tones, expressive of conviction, and not thereby assuring to hear. 'He is a man with men, a child with women. His Rebecca could describe him; I laugh now at some of her sayings of him; I see her mouth, so tenderly comical over her big "simpleton," she called him, and loved him so.'

The gentleman appeared on the waste land above the house. His very loose black suit and a peculiar roll of his gait likened him to a mourning boatswain who was jolly. In Lord Levellier's workshop his remarks were to the point. Chillon's powders for guns and blasting interested him, and he proposed to ride over from Barlings to witness a test of them.

'You are staying at Barlings?' Chillon said.

'Yes; now Carinthia is at Esslemont,' he replied, astoundingly the simpleton.

His conversation was practical and shrewd on the walk with Chillon and Carinthia down to Esslemont evidently he was a man well armed to encounter the world; social usages might be taught him. Chillon gained a round view of the worthy simple fellow, unlikely to turn out impracticable, for he talked such good sense upon matters of business.

Carinthia saw her brother tickled and interested. A feather moved her. Full of tears though she was, her, heart lay open to the heavens and their kind, small, wholesome gifts. Her happiness in the walk with her brother and her friend—the pair of them united by her companionship, both of them showing they counted her their comrade—was the nearest to the radiant day before she landed on an island, and imagined happiness grew here, and found it to be gilt thorns, loud mockery. A shaving North-easter tore the scream from hedges and the roar from copses under a faceless breadth of sky, and she said, as they turned into Esslemont Park lane: 'We have had one of our old walks to-day, Chillon!'

'You used to walk together long walks over in your own country,' said Mr. Wythan.

'Yes, Owain, we did, and my brother never knew me tired.'

'Never knew you confess to it,' said Chillon, as he swallowed the name on her lips.

'Walking was flying over there, brother.'

'Say once or twice in Wales, too,' Mr. Wythan begged of her.

'Wales reminded. Yes,.. Owain, I shall not forget Wales, Welsh people. Mr. Woodseer says they have the three-stringed harp in their breasts, and one string is always humming, whether you pull it or no.'

'That 's love of country! that 's their love of wild Wales, Carinthia.'

There was a quiet interrogation in Chillon's turn of the head at this fervent simpleton.

'I love them for that hum,' said she. 'It joins one in me.'

'Call to them any day, they are up, ready to march!'

'Oh, dear souls!' Carinthia said.

Her breath drew in.

The three were dumb. They saw Lord Fleetwood standing in the park gateway.

CHAPTER XXXVII

BETWEEN CARINTHIA AND HER LORD

The earl's easy grace of manner was a ceremonial mantle on him as he grasped the situation in a look. He bent with deferential familiarity to his countess, exactly toning the degree of difference which befitted a salute to the two gentlemen, amiable or hostile.

'There and back?' he said, and conveyed a compliment to Carinthia's pedestrian vigour in the wary smile which can be recalled for a snub.

She replied: 'We have walked the distance, my lord.'

Her smile was the braced one of an untired stepper.

'A cold wind for you.'

'We walked fast.'

She compelled him to take her in the plural, though he addressed her separately, but her tones had their music.

'Your brother, Captain Kirby-Levellier, I believe?'

'My brother is not of the army now, my lord.'

She waved her hand for Madge to conduct donkey and baby to the house. He noticed. He was unruffled.

The form of amenity expected from her, in relation to her brother, was not exhibited. She might perhaps be feeling herself awkward at introductions, and had to be excused.

'I beg,' he said, and motioned to Chillon the way of welcome into the park, saw the fixed figure, and passed over the unspoken refusal, with a remark to Mr. Wythan: 'At Barlings, I presume?'

'My tent is pitched there,' was the answer.

'Good-bye, my brother,' said Carinthia.

Chillon folded his arms round her. 'God bless you, dear love. Let me see you soon.' He murmured:

'You can protect yourself.'

'Fear nothing for me, dearest.'

She kissed her brother's cheek. The strain of her spread fingers on his shoulder signified no dread at her being left behind.

Strangers observing their embrace would have vowed that the pair were brother and sister, and of a notable stock.

'I will walk with you to Croridge again when you send word you are willing to go; and so, good-bye, Owain,' she said.

She gave her hand; frankly she pressed the Welshman's, he not a whit behind her in frankness.

Fleetwood had a skimming sense of a drop upon a funny, whirly world. He kept from giddiness, though the whirl had lasted since he beheld the form of a wild forest girl, dancing, as it struck him now, over an abyss, on the plumed shoot of a stumpy tree.

Ay, and she danced at the ducal schloss;—she mounted his coach like a witch of the Alps up crags;—she was beside him pelting to the vale under a leaden Southwester;—she sat solitary by the fireside in the room of the inn.

Veil it. He consented to the veil he could not lift. He had not even power to try, and his heart thumped.

London's Whitechapel Countess glided before him like a candle in the fog.

He had accused her as the creature destroying Romance. Was it gold in place of gilding, absolute upper human life that the ridiculous object at his heels over London proposed instead of delirious brilliancies, drunken gallops, poison-syrups,—puffs of a young man's vapours?

There was Madge and the donkey basket-trap ahead on the road to the house, bearing proof of the veiled had-been: signification of a might-have-been. Why not a possible might-be? Still the might-be might be. Looking on this shaven earth and sky of March with the wrathful wind at work, we know that it is not the end: a day follows for the world. But looking on those blown black funeral sprays, and the wrinkled chill waters, and the stare of the Esslemont house-windows, it has an appearance of the last lines of our written volume: dead Finis. Not death; fouler, the man alive seeing himself stretched helpless for the altering of his deeds; a coffin carrying him; the fatal whiteheaded sacerdotal official intoning his aims on the march to front, the drear craped files of the liveried, salaried mourners over his failure, trooping at his heels.

Frontward was the small lake's grey water, rearward an avenue of limes.

But the man alive, if but an inch alive, can so take his life in his clutch, that he does alter, cleanse, recast his deeds:—it is known; priests proclaim it, philosophers admit it.

Can he lay his clutch on another's life, and wring out the tears shed, the stains of the bruises, recollection of the wrongs?

Contemplate the wounded creature as a woman. Then, what sort of woman is she? She was once under a fascination—ludicrously, painfully, intensely like a sort of tipsy poor puss, the trapped hare tossed to her serpent; and thoroughly reassured for a few caresses, quite at home, caged and at home; and all abloom with pretty ways, modest pranks, innocent fondlings. Gobbled, my dear!

It is the doom of the innocents, a natural fate. Smother the creature with kindness again, show we are a point in the scale above that old coiler snake—which broke no bones, bit not so very deep;—she will be, she ought to be, the woman she was. That is, if she was then sincere, a dose of kindness should operate happily to restore the honeymoony fancies, hopes, trusts, dreams, all back, as before the honeymoon showed the silver crook and shadowy hag's back of a decaying crescent. And true enough, the poor girl's young crescent of a honeymoon went down sickly-yellow rather early. It can be renewed. She really was at that time rather romantic. She became absurd. Romance is in her, nevertheless. She is a woman of mettle: she is probably expecting to be wooed. One makes a hash of yesterday's left dish, but she may know no better. 'Add a pickle,' as Chummy Potts used to say. The dish is rendered savoury by a slight expenditure of attentions, just a dab of intimated soft stuff.

'Pleasant to see you established here, if you find the place agreeable,' he said.

She was kissing her hand to her brother, all her eyes for him—or for the couple; and they were hidden by the park lodge before she replied: 'It is an admired, beautiful place.'

'I came,' said he, 'to have your assurance that it suits you.'

'I thank you, my lord.'

'"My lord" would like a short rest, Carinthia.'

She seemed placidly acquiescing. 'You have seen the boy?'

'Twice to-day. We were having a conversation just now.'

'We think him very intelligent.'

'Lady Arpington tells me you do the honours here excellently.'

'She is good to me.'

'Praises the mother's management of the young one. John Edward: Edward for call-name. Madge boasts his power for sleeping.'

'He gives little trouble.'

'And babes repay us! We learn from small things. Out of the mouth of babes wisdom? Well, their habits show the wisdom of the mother. A good mother! There's no higher title. A lady of my acquaintance bids fair to win it, they say.'

Carinthia looked in simplicity, saw herself, and said 'If a mother may rear her boy till he must go to school, she is rewarded for all she does.'

'Ah,' said he, nodding over her mania of the perpetual suspicion. 'Leddings, Queeney, the servants here, run smoothly?'

'They do: they are happy in serving.'

'You see, we English are not such bad fellows when we're known. The climate to-day, for example, is rather trying.'

'I miss colours most in England,' said Carinthia. 'I like the winds. Now and then we have a day to remember.'

'We 're to be "the artist of the day," Gower Woodseer says, and we get an attachment to the dreariest; we are to study "small variations of the commonplace"—dear me! But he may be right. The "sky of lead and scraped lead" over those lines, he points out; and it's not a bad trick for reconciling us to gloomy English weather. You take lessons from him?'

'I can always learn from him,' said Carinthia.

Fleetwood depicted his plodding Gower at the tussle with account-books. She was earnest in sympathy; not awake to the comical; dull as the clouds, dull as the discourse. Yet he throbbed for being near her took impression of her figure, the play of her features, the carriage of her body.

He was shut from her eyes. The clear brown eyes gave exchange of looks; less of admission than her honest maid's.

Madge and the miracle infant awaited them on the terrace. For so foreign did the mother make herself to him, that the appearance of the child, their own child, here between them, was next to miraculous; and the mother, who might well have been the most astonished, had transparently not an idea beyond the verified palpable lump of young life she lifted in her arms out of the arms of Madge, maternally at home with its presence on earth.

Demonstrably a fine specimen, a promising youngster. The father was allowed to inspect him. This was his heir: a little fellow of smiles, features, puckered brows of inquiry; seeming a thing made already, and active on his own account.

'Do people see likenesses?' he asked.

'Some do,' said the mother.

'You?'

She was constrained to give answer. 'There is a likeness to my father, I have thought.'

There's a dotage of idolatrous daughters, he could have retorted; and his gaze was a polite offer to humdrum reconcilement, if it pleased her.

She sent the child up the steps.

'Do you come in, my lord?'

'The house is yours, my lady.'

'I cannot feel it mine.'

'You are the mistress to invite or exclude.'

'I am ready to go in a few hours for a small income of money, for my child and me.'

'—Our child.'

'Yes.'

'It is our child.'

'It is.'

'Any sum you choose to name. But where would you live?'

'Near my brother I would live.'

'Three thousand a year for pin-money, or more, are at your disposal. Stay here, I beg. You have only to notify your wants. And we'll talk familiarly now, as we're together. Can I be of aid to your brother? Tell me, pray. I am disposed in every way to subscribe to your wishes. Pray, speak, speak out.'

So the earl said. He had to force his familiar tone against the rebuke of her grandeur of stature; and he was for inducing her to deliver her mind, that the mountain girl's feebleness in speech might reinstate him. She rejoined unhesitatingly: 'My brother would not accept aid from you, my lord. I will take no money more than for my needs.'

'You spoke of certain sums down in Wales.'

'I did then.' Her voice was dead.

'Ah! You must be feeling the cold North-wind here.'

'I do not. You may feel the cold, my lord. Will you enter the house?'

'Do you invite me?'

'The house is your own.'

'Will the mistress of the house honour me so far?'

'I am not the mistress of the house, my lord.'

'You refuse, Carinthia?'

'I would keep from using those words. I have no right to refuse the entry of the house to you.'

'If I come in?'

'I guard my rooms.'

She had been awake, then, to the thrusting and parrying behind masked language.

'Good. You are quite decided, I may suppose.'

'I will leave them when I have a little money, or when I know of how I may earn some.'

'The Countess of Fleetwood earning a little money?'

'I can put aside your title, my lord.'

'No, you can't put it aside while the man with the title lives, not even if you're running off in earnest, under a dozen Welsh names. Why should you desire to do it? The title entitles you to the command of half my possessions. As to the house; don't be alarmed; you will not have to guard your rooms. The extraordinary wild animal you—the impression may have been produced; I see, I see. If I were in the house, I should not be rageing at your doors; and it is not my intention to enter the house. That is, not by right of ownership. You have my word.'

He bowed to her, and walked to the stables.

She had the art of extracting his word from him. The word given, she went off with it, disengaged mistress of Esslemont. And she might have the place for residence, but a decent courtesy required that she should remain at the portico until he was out of sight. She was the first out of sight, rather insolently.

She returned him without comment the spell he had cast on her, and he was left to estimate the value of a dirited piece of metal not in the currency, stamped false coin. An odd sense of impoverishment chilled him. Chilly weather was afflicting the whole country, he was reminded, and he paced about hurriedly until his horses were in the shafts. After all, his driving away would be much more expected of him than a stay at the house where the Whitechapel Countess resided, chill, dry, talking the language of early Exercises in English, suitable to her Welshmen. Did she 'Owain' them every one?

As he whipped along the drive and left that glassy stare of Esslemont behind him, there came a slap of a reflection:—here, on the box of this coach, the bride just bursting her sheath sat, and was like warm wax to take impressions. She was like hard stone to retain them, pretty evidently. Like women the world over, she thinks only of her side of the case. Men disdain to plead theirs. Now money is offered her, she declines it. Formerly, she made it the principal subject of her conversation.

Turn the mind to something brighter. Fleetwood strung himself to do so, and became agitated by the question whether the bride sat to left or to right of him when the South-wester blew-a wind altogether preferable to the chill North-east. Women, when they are no longer warm, are colder than the deadliest catarrh wind scything across these islands. Of course she sat to left of him. In the line of the main road, he remembered a look he dropped on her, a look over his left shoulder.

She never had a wooing: she wanted it, had a kind of right to it, or the show of it. How to begin? But was she worth an effort? Turn to something brighter. Religion is the one refuge from women, Feltre says: his Roman Catholic recipe. The old shoemaker, Mr. Woodseer, hauls women into his religion, and purifies them by the process,—fancies he does. He gets them to wear an air. Old Gower, too, has his Religion of Nature, with free admission for women, whom he worships in similes, running away from them, leering sheepishly. No, Feltre's' rigid monastic system is the sole haven. And what a world, where we have no safety except in renouncing it! The two sexes created to devour one another must abjure their sex before they gain 'The Peace,' as Feltre says, impressively, if absurdly. He will end a monk if he has the courage of his logic. A queer spectacle—an English nobleman a shaven monk!

Fleetwood shuddered. We are twisted face about to discover our being saved by women from that horror—the joining the ranks of the nasal friars. By what women? Bacchante, clearly, if the wife we have is a North-easter to wither us, blood, bone, and soul.

He was hungry; he waxed furious with the woman who had flung him out upon the roads. He was thirsty as well. The brightest something to refresh his thoughts grew and glowed in the form of a shiny table, bearing tasty dishes, old wines; at an inn or anywhere. But, out of London, an English inn to furnish the dishes and the wines for a civilized and self-respecting man is hard to seek, as difficult to find as a perfect skeleton of an extinct species. The earl's breast howled derision of his pursuit when he drew up at the sign of the Royal Sovereign, in the dusky hour, and handed himself desperately to Mrs. Rundles' mercy.

He could not wait for a dinner, so his eating was cold meat. Warned by a sip, that his drinking, if he drank, was to be an excursion in chemical acids, the virtues of an abstainer served for his consolation. Tolerant of tobacco, although he did not smoke, he fronted the fire, envying Gower Woodseer the contemplative pipe, which for half a dozen puffs wafted him to bracing deserts, or primaeval forests, or old highways with the swallow thoughts above him, down the Past, into the Future. A pipe is pleasant dreams at command. A pipe is the concrete form of philosophy. Why, then, a pipe is the alternative of a friar's frock for an escape from women. But if one does not smoke!... Here and there a man is visibly in the eyes of all men cursed: let him be blest by Fortune; let him be handsome, healthy, wealthy, courted, he is cursed.

Fleetwood lay that night beneath the roof of the Royal Sovereign. Sleep is life's legitimate mate. It will treat us at times as the faithless wife, who becomes a harrying beast, behaves to her lord. He had no sleep. Having put out his candle, an idea took hold of him, and he jumped up to light it again and verify the idea that this room... He left the bed and strode round it, going in the guise of an urgent somnambulist, or ghost bearing burden of an imperfectly remembered mission. This was the room.

Reason and cold together overcame his illogical scruples to lie down on that bed soliciting the sleep desired. He lay and groaned, lay and rolled. All night the Naval Monarch with the loose cheeks and jelly smile of the swinging sign-board creaked. Flaws of the North-easter swung and banged him. He creaked high, in complaint,—low, in some partial contentment. There was piping of his boatswain, shrill piping—shrieks of the whistle. How many nights had that most ill-fated of brides lain listening to the idiotic uproar! It excused a touch of craziness. But how many? Not one, not two, ten, twenty:—count, count to the exact number of nights the unhappy girl must have heard those mad colloquies of the hurricane boatswain and the chirpy king. By heaven! Whitechapel, after one night of it, beckons as a haven of grace.

CHAPTER XXXVIII

A DIP INTO THE SPRING'S WATERS

The night Lord Fleetwood had passed cured him of the wound Carinthia dealt, with her blunt, defensive phrase and her Welshman. Seated on his coach-box, he turned for a look the back way leading to Esslemont, and saw rosed crag and mountain forest rather than the soft undulations of parkland pushing green meadows or brown copse up the slopes under his eye. She had never been courted: she deserved a siege. She was a daughter of the racy highlands. And she, who could say to her husband, 'I guard my rooms,' without sign of the stage-face of scorn or defiance or flinging of the glove, she would have to be captured by siege, it was clear. She wore an aspect of the confident fortress, which neither challenges nor cries to treat, but commands respect. How did she accomplish this miracle of commanding respect after such a string of somersaults before the London world?

He had to drive North-westward: his word was pledged to one of his donkey Ixionides—Abrane, he recollected—to be a witness at some contemptible exhibition of the fellow's muscular skill: a match to punt against a Thames waterman: this time. Odd how it should come about that the giving of his word forced him now to drive away from the woman once causing him to curse his luck as the prisoner of his word! However, there was to be an end of it soon—a change; change as remarkable as Harry Monmouth's at the touching of his crown. Though in these days, in our jog-trot Old England, half a step on the road to greatness is the utmost we can hop; and all England jeers at the man attempting it. He caps himself with this or that one of their titles. For it is not the popular thing among Englishmen. Their hero, when they have done their fighting, is the wealthy patron of Sport. What sort of creatures are his comrades? But he cannot have comrades unless he is on the level of them. Yet let him be never so high above them, they charge him and point him as a piece of cannon; assenting to the flatteries they puff into him, he is their engine, 'The idol of the hour is the mob's wooden puppet, and the doing of the popular thing seed of no harvest,' Gower Woodseer says, moderately well, snuffing incense of his happy delivery. Not to be the idol, to have an aim of our own, there lies the truer pride, if we intend respect of ourselves.

The Mr. Pulpit young men have in them, until their habits have fretted him out, was directing Lord Fleetwood's meditations upon the errors of the general man, as a cover for lateral references to his hitherto erratic career: not much worse than a swerving from the right line, which now seemed the desirable road for him, and had previously seemed so stale, so repulsive. He was, of course, only half-conscious of his pulpitizing; he fancied the serious vein of his thoughts attributable to a tumbled night. Nevertheless, he had the question whether that woman—poor girl!—was influencing his thoughts. For in a moment, the very word 'respect' pitched him upon her character; to see it a character that emerged beneath obstacles, and overcame ridicule, won suffrages, won a reluctant husband's admiration, pricked him from distaste to what might really be taste for her companionship, or something more alarming to contemplate in the possibilities,—thirst for it. He was driving away, and he longed to turn back. He did respect her character: a character angular as her features were, and similarly harmonious, splendid in action.

Respect seems a coolish form of tribute from a man who admires. He had to say that he did not vastly respect beautiful women. Have they all the poetry? Know them well, and where is it?

The pupil of Gower Woodseer asked himself to specify the poetry of woman. She is weak and inferior, but she has it; civilized men acknowledge it; and it is independent, or may be beside her gift of beauty. She has more of it than we have. Then name it.

Well, the flowers of the field are frail things. Pluck one, and you have in your hand the frailest of things. But reach through the charm of colour and the tale of its beneficence in frailty to the poetry of the flower, and secret of the myriad stars will fail to tell you more than does that poetry of your little flower. Lord Feltre, at the heels of St. Francis, agrees in that.

Well, then, much so with the flowers of the two hands and feet. We do homage to those ungathered, and reserve our supremacy; the gathered, no longer courted, are the test of men. When the embraced woman breathes respect into us, she wings a beast. We have from her the poetry of the tasted life; excelling any garden-gate or threshold lyrics called forth by purest early bloom. Respect for her person, for her bearing, for her character that is in the sum a beauty plastic to the civilized young man's needs and cravings, as queenly physical loveliness has never so fully been to him along the walks of life, and as ideal worships cannot be for our nerving contentment. She brings us to the union of body and soul; as good as to say, earth and heaven. Secret of all human aspirations, the ripeness of the creeds, is there; and the passion for the woman desired has no poetry equalling that of the embraced respected woman.

Something of this went reeling through Fleetwood; positively to this end; accompanied the while with flashes of Carinthia, her figure across the varied scenes. Ridicule vanished. Could it ever have existed? If London had witnessed the scene down in Wales, London never again would laugh at the Whitechapel Countess.

He laughed amicably at himself for the citizen sobriety of these views, on the part of a nobleman whose airy pleasure it had been to flout your sober citizens, with their toad-at-the-hop notions, their walled conceptions, their drab propriety; and felt a petted familiar within him dub all pulpitizing, poetizing drivellers with one of those detested titles, invented by the English as a corrective of their maladies or the excesses of their higher moods. But, reflection telling him that he had done injury to Carinthia—had inflicted the sorest of the wounds a young woman a new bride can endure, he nodded acquiescence to the charge of misbehaviour, and muzzled the cynic.

As a consequence, the truisms flooded him and he lost his guard against our native prosiness. Must we be prosy if we are profoundly, uncynically sincere? Do but listen to the stuff we are maundering! Extracts of poetry, if one could hit upon the right, would serve for a relief and a lift when we are in this ditch of the serious vein. Gower Woodseer would have any number handy to spout. Or Felter:—your convinced and fervent Catholic has quotations of images and Latin hymns to his Madonna or one of his Catherines, by the dozen, to suit an enthusiastic fit of the worship of some fair woman, and elude the prosy in commending her. Feltre is enviable there. As he says, it is natural to worship, and only the Catholics can prostrate themselves with dignity. That is matter for thought. Stir us to the depths, it will be found that we are poor soupy stuff. For estimable language, and the preservation of self-respect in prostration, we want ritual, ceremonial elevation of the visible object for the soul's adoring through the eye. So may we escape our foul or empty selves.

Lord Feltre seemed to Fleetwood at the moment a more serviceable friend than Gower Woodseer preaching 'Nature'—an abstraction, not inspiring to the devout poetic or giving us the tongue above our native prosy. He was raised and refreshed by recollected lines of a Gregorian chant he and Feltre had heard together under the roof of that Alpine monastery.

The Dame collapses. There is little doubt of her having the world to back her in protest against all fine filmy work of the exploration of a young man's intricacies or cavities. Let her not forget the fact she has frequently impressed upon us, that he was 'the very wealthiest nobleman of his time,' instructive to touch inside as well as out. He had his share of brains, too. And also she should be mindful of an alteration of English taste likely of occurrence in the remote posterity she vows she is for addressing after she has exhausted our present hungry generation. The posterity signified will, it is calculable, it is next to certain, have studied a developed human nature so far as to know the composition of it a not unequal mixture of the philosophic and the romantic, and that credible realism is to be produced solely by an involvement of those two elements. Or else, she may be sure, her story once out of the mouth, goes off dead as the spirits of a vapour that has performed the stroke of energy. She holds a surprising event in the history of 'the wealthiest nobleman of his time,' and she would launch it upon readers unprepared, with the reference to our mysterious and unfathomable nature for an explanation of the stunning crack on the skull.

This may do now. It will not do ten centuries hence. For the English, too, are a changeable people in the sight of ulterior Time.

One of the good pieces of work Lord Fleetwood could suppose he had performed was recalled to him near the turning to his mews by the handsome Piccadilly fruit-shop. He jumped to the pavement, merely to gratify. Sarah Winch with a word of Madge; and being emotional just then, he spoke of Lady Fleetwood's attachment to Madge; and he looked at Sarah straight, he dropped his voice: 'She said, you remember, you were sisters to her.'

Sarah remembered that he had spoken of it before. Two brilliant drops from the deepest of woman's ready well stood in her eyes.

He carried the light of them away. They were such pure jewels of tribute to the Carinthia now seen by him as worshipping souls of devotees offer to their Madonna for her most glorious adornment.

BOOK V

CHAPTER XXXIX

THE RED WARNING FROM A SON OF VAPOUR

Desiring loneliness or else Lord Feltre's company, Fleetwood had to grant a deferred audience at home to various tradesmen, absurdly fussy about having the house of his leased estate of Calesford furnished complete and habitable on the very day stipulated by his peremptory orders that the place should be both habitable and hospitable. They were right, they were excused; grand entertainments of London had been projected, and he fell into the weariful business with them, thinking of Henrietta's insatiable appetite for the pleasures. He had taken the lease of this burdensome Calesford, at an eight-miles' drive from the Northwest of town, to gratify the devouring woman's taste which was, to have all the luxuries of the town in a framework of country scenery.

Gower Woodseer and he were dining together in the evening. The circumstance was just endurable, but Gower would play the secretary, and doggedly subjected him to hear a statement of the woeful plight of Countess Livia's affairs. Gower, commissioned to examine them, remarked: 'If we have all the figures!'

'If we could stop the bleeding!' Fleetwood replied. 'Come to the Opera to-night; I promised. I promised Abrane for to-morrow. There's no end to it. This gambling mania's a flux. Not one of them except your old enemy, Corby, keeps clear of it; and they're at him for subsidies, as they are at me, and would be at you or any passenger on the suspected of a purse. Corby shines among them.'

That was heavy judgement enough, Gower thought. No allusion to Esslemont ensued. The earl ate sparely, and silently for the most part.

He was warmed a little at the Opera by hearing Henrietta's honest raptures over her Columelli in the Pirata. But Lord Brailstone sat behind her, and their exchange of ecstasies upon the tattered pathos of

E il mio tradito amor,

—was not moderately offensive.

His countenance in Henrietta's presence had to be studied and interpreted by Livia. Why did it darken? The demurest of fuliginous intriguers argued that Brail stone was but doing the spiriting required of him, and would have to pay the penalty unrewarded, let him Italianize as much as he pleased. Not many months longer, and there would be the bit of an outburst, the whiff of scandal, perhaps a shot, and the rupture of an improvident alliance, followed by Henrietta's free hand to the moody young earl, who would then have possession of the only woman he could ever love: and at no cost. Jealousy of a man like Brailstone, however infatuated the man, was too foolish. He must perceive how matters were tending? The die-away acid eyeballs-at-the-ceiling of a pair of fanatics per la musica might irritate a husband, but the lover should read and know. Giddy as the beautiful creature deprived of her natural aliment seems in her excuseable hunger for it, she has learnt her lesson, she is not a reeling libertine.

Brailstone peered through his eyelashes at the same shadow of a frown where no frown sat on his friend's brows. Displeasure was manifest, and why? Fleetwood had given him the dispossessing shrug of the man out of the run, and the hint of the tip for winning, with the aid of operatic arias; and though he was in Fleetwood's books ever since the prize-fight, neither Fleetwood nor the husband nor any skittishness of a timorous wife could stop the pursuer bent to capture the fairest and most inflaming woman of her day.

'I prefer your stage Columelli,' Fleetwood said.

'I come from exile!' said Henrietta; and her plea in excuse of ecstatics wrote her down as confessedly treasonable to the place quitted.

Ambrose Mallard entered the box, beholding only his goddess Livia. Their eyebrows and inaudible lips conversed eloquently. He retired like a trumped card on the appearance of M. de St. Ombre. The courtly Frenchman won the ladies to join him in whipping the cream of the world for five minutes, and passed out before his flavour was exhausted. Brailstone took his lesson and departed, to spy at them from other boxes and heave an inflated shirt-front. Young Cressett, the bottle of effervescence, dashed in, and for him Livia's face was motherly. He rattled a tale of the highway robbery of Sir Meeson Corby on one of his Yorkshire moors. The picture of the little baronet arose upon the narration, and it amused. Chumley Potts came to 'confirm every item,' as he said. 'Plucked Corby clean. Pistol at his head. Quite old style. Time, ten P.M. Suspects Great Britain, King, Lords and Commons, and buttons twenty times tighter. Brosey Mallard down on him for a few fighting men. Perfect answer to Brosey.'

'Mr. Mallard did not mention the robbery,' Henrietta remarked.

'Feared to shock: Corby such a favoured swain,' Potts accounted for the omission.

'Brosey spilling last night?' Fleetwood asked.

'At the palazzo, we were,' said Potts. 'Luck pretty fair first off. Brosey did his trick, and away and away and away went he! More old Brosey wins, the wiser he gets. I stayed.' He swung to Gower: 'Don't drink dry Sillery after two A.M. You read me?'

'Egyptian, but decipherable,' said Gower.

The rising of the curtain drew his habitual groan from Potts, and he fled to collogue with the goodly number of honest fellows in the house of music who detested 'squallery.' Most of these afflicted pilgrims to the London conservatory were engaged upon the business of the Goddess richly inspiring the Heliconian choir, but rendering the fountain-waters heady. Here they had to be, if they would enjoy the spectacle of London's biggest and choicest bouquet: and in them, too, there was an unattached air during Potts' cooling discourse of turf and tables, except when he tossed them a morsel of tragedy, or the latest joke, not yet past the full gallop on its course. Their sparkle was transient; woman had them fast. Compelled to think of them as not serious members of our group, he assisted at the crush-room exit, and the happy riddance of the beautiful cousins dedicated to the merry London midnights' further pastures.

Fleetwood's word was extracted, that he would visit the 'palazzo' within a couple of hours.

Potts exclaimed: 'Good. You promise. Hang me, if I don't think it 's the only certain thing a man can depend upon in this world.'

He left the earl and Gower Woodseer to their lunatic talk. He still had his ideas about the association of the pair. 'Hard-headed player of his own game, that Woodseer, spite of his Mumbo-Jumbo-oracle kind of talk.'

Mallard's turn of luck downward to the deadly drop had come under Potts' first inspection of the table. Admiring his friend's audacity, deploring his rashness, reproving his persistency, Potts allowed his verdict to go by results; for it was clear that Mallard and Fortune were in opposition. Something like real awe of the tremendous encounter kept him from a plunge or a bet. Mallard had got the vertigo, he reported the gambler's launch on dementedness to the earl. Gower's less experienced optics perceived it. The plainly doomed duellist with the insensible Black Goddess offered her all the advantages of the Immortals challenged by flesh. His effort to smile was a line cut awry in wood; his big eyes were those of a cat for sociability; he looked cursed, and still he wore the smile. In this condition, the gambler runs to emptiness of everything he has, his money, his heart, his brains, like a coal-truck on the incline of the rails to a collier.

Mallard applied to the earl for a loan of fifty guineas. He had them and lost them, and he came, not begging, blustering for a second supply; quite in the wrong tone, Potts knew. Fleetwood said: 'Back it with pistols, Brosey'; and, as Potts related subsequently, 'Old Brosey had the look of a staked horse.'

Fortune and he having now closed the struggle, perforce of his total disarmament, he regained the wits we forfeit when we engage her. He said to his friend Chummy: 'Abrane tomorrow? Ah, yes, punts a Thames waterman. Start of—how many yards? Sunbury-Walton: good reach. Course of two miles: Braney in good training. Straight business? I mayn't be there. But you, Chummy, you mind, old Chums, all cases of the kind, safest back the professional. Unless—you understand!'

Fleetwood could not persuade Gower to join the party. The philosopher's pretext of much occupation masked a bashfully sentimental dislike of the flooding of quiet country places by the city's hordes. 'You're right, right,' said Fleetwood, in sympathy, resigned to the prospect of despising his associates without a handy helper. He named Esslemont once, shot up a look at the sky, and glanced it Eastward.

Three coaches were bound for Sunbury from a common starting-point at nine of the morning. Lord Fleetwood, Lord Brailstone, and Lord Simon Pitscrew were the whips. Two hours in advance of them, the earl's famous purveyors of picnic feasts bowled along to pitch the riverside tent and spread the tables. Our upper and lower London world reported the earl as out on another of his expeditions: and, say what we will, we must think kindly of a wealthy nobleman ever to the front to enliven the town's dusty eyes and increase Old England's reputation for pre-eminence in the Sports.

He is the husband of the Whitechapel Countess—got himself into that mess; but whatever he does, he puts the stamp of style on it. He and the thing he sets his hand to, they're neat, they're finished, they're fitted to trot together, and they've a shining polish, natural, like a lily of the fields; or say Nature and Art, like the coat of a thoroughbred led into the paddock by his groom, if you're of that mind.

Present at the start in Piccadilly, Gower took note of Lord Fleetwood's military promptitude to do the work he had no taste for, and envied the self-compression which could assume so pleasant an air. He heard here and there crisp comments on his lordship's coach and horses and personal smartness; the word 'style,' which reflects handsomely on the connoisseur conferring it, and the question whether one of the ladies up there was the countess. His task of unearthing and disentangling the monetary affairs of 'one of the ladies' compelled the wish to belong to the party soon to be towering out of the grasp of bricks, and delightfully gay, spirited, quick for fun. A fellow, he thought, may brood upon Nature, but the real children of Nature—or she loves them best—are those who have the careless chatter, the ready laugh, bright welcome for a holiday. In catching the hour, we are surely the bloom of the hour? Why, yes, and no need to lose the rosy wisdom of the children when we wrap ourselves in the patched old cloak of the man's.

On he went to his conclusions; but the Dame will have none of them, though here was a creature bent on masonry-work in his act of thinking, to build a traveller's-rest for thinkers behind him; while the volatile were simply breaking their bubbles.

He was discontented all day, both with himself and the sentences he coined. A small street-boy at his run along the pavement nowhither, distanced him altogether in the race for the great Secret; precipitating the thought, that the conscious are too heavily handicapped. The unburdened unconscious win the goal. Ay, but they leave no legacy. So we must fret and stew, and look into ourselves, and seize the brute and scourge him, just to make one serviceable step forward: that is, utter a single sentence worth the pondering for guidance.

Gower imagined the fun upon middle Thames: the vulcan face of Captain Abrane; the cries of his backers, the smiles of the ladies, Lord Fleetwood's happy style in the teeth of tattlean Aurora's chariot for overriding it. One might hope, might almost see, that he was coming to his better senses on a certain subject. As for style overriding the worst of indignities, has not Scotia given her poet to the slack dependant of the gallows-tree, who so rantingly played his jig and wheeled it round in the shadow of that institution? Style was his, he hit on the right style to top the situation, and perpetually will he slip his head out of the noose to dance the poet's verse.

In fact, style is the mantle of greatness; and say that the greatness is beyond our reach, we may at least pray to have the mantle.

Strangest of fancies, most unphilosophically, Gower conceived a woman's love as that which would bestow the gift upon a man so bare of it as he. Where was the woman? He embraced the idea of the sex, and found it resolving to a form of one. He stood humbly before the one, and she waned into swarms of her sisters. So did she charge him with the loving of her sex, not her. And could it be denied, if he wanted a woman's love just to give him a style? No, not that, but to make him feel proud of himself. That was the heart's way of telling him a secret in owning to a weakness. Within it the one he had thought of forthwith obtained her lodgement. He discovered this truth, in this roundabout way, and knew it a truth by the warm fireside glow the contemplation of her cast over him.

Dining alone, as he usually had to do, he was astonished to see the earl enter his room.

'Ah, you always make the right choice!' Fleetwood said, and requested him to come to the library when he had done eating.

Gower imagined an accident. A metallic ring was in the earl's voice.

One further mouthful finished dinner, for Gower was anxious concerning the ladies. He joined the earl and asked.

'Safe. Oh yes. We managed to keep it from them,' said Fleetwood. 'Nothing particular, perhaps you'll think. Poor devil of a fellow! Father and mother alive, too! He did it out of hearing, that 'a one merit. Mallard: Ambrose Mallard. He has blown his brains out.'

Seated plunged in the armchair, with stretched legs and eyes at the black fire-grate, Fleetwood told of the gathering under the tent, and Mallard seen, seen drinking champagne; Mallard no longer seen, not missed.

'He killed himself three fields off. He must have been careful to deaden the sound. Small pocket-pistol hardly big enough to—but anything serves. Couple of brats came running up to Chummy Potts:— "Gentleman's body bloody in a ditch." Chummy came to me, and we went. Clean dead;—in the mouth, pointed up; hole through the top of the skull. We're crockery! crockery! I had to keep Chummy standing. I couldn't bring him back to our party. We got help at a farm; the body lies there. And that's not the worst. We found a letter to me in his pocket pencilled his last five minutes. I don't see what he could have done except to go. I can't tell you more. I had to keep my face, rowing and driving back. "But where is Mr. Potts? Where can Mr. Mallard be?" Queer sensation, to hear the ladies ask! Give me your hand.'

The earl squeezed Gower's hand an instant; and it was an act unknown for him to touch or bear a touch; it said a great deal.

Late at night he mounted to Gower's room. The funeral of the day's impressions had not been shaken off. He kicked at it and sunk under it as his talk rambled. 'Add five thousand,' he commented, on the spread of Livia's papers over the table. 'I've been having an hour with her. Two thousand more, she says. Better multiply by two and a half for a woman's confession. We have to trust to her for some of the debts of honour. See her in the morning. No one masters her but you. Mind, the first to be clear of must be St. Ombre. I like the fellow; but these Frenchmen—they don't spare women. Ambrose,'—the earl's eyelids quivered. 'Jealousy fired that shot. Quite groundless. She 's cool as a marble Venus, as you said. Go straight from her house to Esslemont. I don't plead a case. Make the best account you can of it. Say—you may say my eyes are opened. I respect her. If you think that says little, say more. It can't mean more. Whatever the Countess of Fleetwood may think due to her, let her name it. Say my view of life, way of life, everything in me, has changed. I shall follow you. I don't expect to march over the ground. She has a heap to forgive. Her father owns or boasts, in that book of his Rose Mackrell lent me, he never forgave an injury.'

Gower helped the quotation, rubbing his hands over it, for cover of his glee at the words he had been hearing. 'Never forgave an injury without a return blow for it. The blow forgives. Good for the enemy to get it. He called his hearty old Pagan custom "an action of the lungs" with him. And it's not in nature for injuries to digest in us. They poison the blood, if we try. But then, there's a manner of hitting back. It is not to go an inch beyond the exact measure, Captain Kirby warns us.'

Fleetwood sighed down to a low groan.

'Lord Feltre would have an answer for you. She's a wife; and a wife hitting back is not a pleasant—well, petticoats make the difference. If she's for amends, she shall exact them; and she may be hard to satisfy, she shall have her full revenge. Call it by any other term you like. I did her a wrong. I don't defend myself; it 's not yet in the Law Courts. I beg to wipe it out, rectify it—choose your phrase—to the very fullest. I look for the alliance with her to...'

He sprang up and traversed the room: 'We're all guilty of mistakes at starting: I speak of men. Women are protected; and if they're not, there's the convent for them, Feltre says. But a man has to live it on before the world; and this life, with these flies of fellows... I fell into it in some way. Absolutely like the first bird I shot as a youngster, and stood over the battered head and bloody feathers, wondering! There was Ambrose Mallard—the same splintered bones—blood—come to his end; and for a woman; that woman the lady bearing the title of half-mother to me. God help me! What are my sins? She feels nothing, or about as much as the mortuary paragraph of the newspapers, for the dead man; and I have Ambrose Mallard's look at her and St. Ombre talking together, before he left the tent to cross the fields. Borrow, beg, or steal for money to play for her! and not a glimpse of the winning post.

St. Ombre 's a cool player; that 's at the bottom of the story. He's cool because play doesn't bite him, as it did Ambrose. I should say the other passion has never bitten him. And he's alive and presentable; Ambrose under a sheet, with Chummy Potts to watch. Chummy cried like a brat in the street for his lost mammy. I left him crying and sobbing. They have their feelings, these "children of vapour," as you call them. But how did I fall into the line with a set I despised? She had my opinion of her gamblers, and retorted that young Cressett's turn for the fling is my doing. I can't swear it's not. There's one of my sins. What's to wipe them out! She has a tender feeling for the boy; confessed she wanted governing. Why; she's young, in a way. She has that particular vice of play. She might be managed. Here's a lesson for her! Don't you think she might? The right man,—the man she can respect, fancy incorruptible! He must let her see he has an eye for tricks. She's not responsible for—his mad passion was the cause, cause of everything he did. The kind of woman to send the shaft. You called her "Diana seated." You said, "She doesn't hunt, she sits and lets fly her arrow." Well, she showed feeling for young Cressett, and her hit at me was an answer. It struck me on the mouth. But she's an eternal anxiety. A man she respects! A man to govern her!'

Fleetwood hurried his paces. 'I couldn't have allowed poor Ambrose. Besides, he had not a chance— never had in anything. It wants a head, wants the man who can say no to her. "The Reveller's Aurora," you called her. She has her beauty, yes. She respects you. I should be relieved—a load off me! Tell her, all debts paid; fifty thousand invested, in her name and her husband's. Tell her, speak it, there's my consent—if only the man to govern her! She has it from me, but repeat it, as from me. That sum and her portion would make a fair income for the two. Relieved? By heaven, what a relief! Go early. Coach to Esslemont at eleven. Do my work there. I haven't to repeat my directions. I shall present myself two days after. I wish Lady Fleetwood to do the part of hostess at Calesford. Tell her I depute you to kiss my son for me. Now I leave you. Good-night. I shan't sleep. I remember your saying, "bad visions come under the eyelids." I shall keep mine open and read—read her father's book of the Maxims; I generally find two or three at a dip to stimulate. No wonder she venerates him. That sort of progenitor is your "permanent aristocracy." Hard enemy. She must have some of her mother in her, too. Abuse me to her, admit the justice of reproaches, but say, reason, good feeling—I needn't grind at it. Say I respect her. Advise her to swallow the injury—not intended for insult. I don't believe anything higher than respect can be offered to a woman. No defence of me to her, but I'll tell you, that when I undertook to keep my word with her, I plainly said—never mind; good-night. If we meet in the morning, let this business rest until it 's done. I must drive to help poor Chums and see about the Inquest.'

Fleetwood nodded from the doorway. Gower was left with humming ears

CHAPTER XL

RECORD OF MINOR INCIDENTS

They went to their beds doomed to lie and roam as the solitaries of a sleepless night. They met next day like a couple emerging from sirocco deserts, indisposed for conversation or even short companionship, much of the night's dry turmoil in their heads. Each would have preferred the sight of an enemy; and it was hardly concealed by them, for they inclined to regard one another as the author of their infernal passage through the drear night's wilderness.

Fleetwood was the civiller; his immediate prospective duties being clear, however abhorrent. But he had inflicted a monstrous disturbance on the man he meant in his rash, decisive way to elevate, if not benefit. Gower's imagination, foreign to his desires and his projects, was playing juggler's tricks with him, dramatizing upon hypotheses, which mounted in stages and could pretend to be soberly conceivable, assuming that the earl's wild hints overnight were a credible basis. He transported himself to his first view of the Countess Livia, the fountain of similes born of his prostrate adoration, close upon the invasion and capture of him by the combined liqueurs in the giddy Batlen lights; and joining the Arabian magic in his breast at the time with the more magical reality now proposed as a sequel to it, he entered the land where dreams confess they are outstripped by revelations.

Yet it startled him to hear the earl say: 'You'll get audience at ten; I've arranged; make the most of the situation to her. I refuse to help. I foresee it 's the only way of solving this precious puzzle. You do me and every one of us a service past paying. Not a man of her set worth.... She—but you'll stop it; no one else can. Of course, you've had your breakfast. Off, and walk yourself into a talkative mood, as you tell me you do.'

'One of the things I do when I've nobody to hear,' said Gower, speculating whether the black sprite in this young nobleman was for sending him as a rod to scourge the lady: an ingenious device, that smelt of mediaeval Courts and tickled his humour.

'Will she listen?' he said gravely.

'She will listen; she has not to learn you admire. You admit she has helped to trim and polish, and the rest. She declares you're incorruptible. There's the ground open. I fling no single sovereign more into that quicksand, and I want not one word further on the subject. I follow you to Esslemont. Pray, go.'

Fleetwood pushed into the hall. A footman was ordered to pack and deposit Mr. Woodseer's portmanteau at the coach-office.

'The principal point is to make sure we have all the obligations,' Gower said.

'You know the principal point,' said the earl. 'Relieve me.'

He faced to the opening street door. Lord Feltre stood in the framing of it—a welcome sight. The 'monastic man of fashion,' of Gower's phrase for him, entered, crooning condolences, with a stretched waxen hand for his friend, a partial nod for Nature's worshipper—inefficient at any serious issue of our human affairs, as the earl would now discover.

Gower left the two young noblemen to their greetings. Happily for him, philosophy, in the present instance, after a round of profundities, turned her lantern upon the comic aspect of his errand. Considering the Countess Livia, and himself, and the tyrant, who benevolently and providentially, or sardonically, hurled them to their interview, the situation was comic, certainly, in the sense of its being an illumination of this life's odd developments. For thus had things come about, that if it were possible even to think of the lady's condescending, he, thanks to the fair one he would see before evening, was armed and proof against his old infatuation or any renewal of it. And he had been taught to read through the beautiful twilighted woman, as if she were burnt paper held at the fire consuming her. His hopes hung elsewhere. Nevertheless, an intellectual demon-imp very lively in his head urged him to speculate on such a contest between them, and weigh the engaging forces. Difficulties were perceived, the scornful laughter on her side was plainly heard; but his feeling of savage mastery, far from beaten down, swelled so as to become irritable for the trial; and when he was near her house he held a review of every personal disadvantage he could summon, incited by an array of limping deficiencies that flattered their arrogant leader with ideas of the power he had in spite of them.

In fact, his emancipation from sentiment inspired the genial mood to tease. Women, having to encounter a male adept at the weapon for the purpose, must be either voluble or supportingly proud to keep the skin from shrinking: which is a commencement of the retrogression; and that has frequently been the beginning of a rout. Now the Countess Livia was a lady of queenly pose and the servitorial conventional speech likely at a push to prove beggarly. When once on a common platform with a man of agile tongue instigated by his intellectual demon to pursue inquiries into her moral resources, after a ruthless exposure of the wrecked material, she would have to be, after the various fashions, defiant, if she was to hold her own against pressure; and seeing, as she must, the road of prudence point to conciliation, it was calculable that she would take it. Hence a string of possible events, astounding to mankind, but equally calculable, should one care to give imagination headway. Gower looked signally Captain Abrane's 'fiddler' while he waited at Livia's house door. A studious intimacy with such a lady was rather like the exposure of the silver moon to the astronomer's telescope.

The Dame will have nought of an interview and colloquy not found mentioned in her collection of ballads, concerning a person quite secondary in Dr. Glossop's voluminous papers. She as vehemently prohibits a narration of Gower Woodseer's proposal some hours later, for the hand of the Countess of Fleetwood's transfixed maid Madge, because of the insignificance of the couple; and though it was a quaint idyll of an affection slowly formed, rationally based while seeming preposterous, tending to bluntly funny utterances on both sides. The girl was a creature of the enthusiasms, and had lifted that passion of her constitution into higher than the worship of sheer physical bravery. She had pitied Mr. Gower Woodseer for his apparently extreme, albeit reverential, devotion to her mistress. The plainly worded terms of his asking a young woman of her position and her reputation to marry him came on her like an intrusion of dazzling day upon the closed eyelids of the night, requiring time, and her mistress's consent, and his father's expressed approval, before she could yield him an answer that might appear a forgetfulness of her station, her ignorance, her damaged character. Gower protested himself, with truth, a spotted pard, an ignoramus, and an outcast of all established classes, as the worshipper of Nature cannot well avoid being.

'But what is it you like me for, Mr. Gower?' Madge longed to know, that she might see a way in the strange land where he had planted her after a whirl; and he replied: 'I 've thought of you till I can say I love you because you have naturally everything I shoot at.'

The vastness of the compliment drove her to think herself empty of anything.

He named courage, and its offspring, honesty, and devotedness, constancy. Her bosom rose at the word.

'Yes, constancy,' he repeated; and 'growing girls have to "turn corners," as you told me once.'

'I did?' said she, reddening under a memory, and abashed by his recollection of a moment she knew to have been weak with her, or noisy of herself.

Madge went straightway to her mistress and related her great event, in the tone of a confession of crime. Her mistress's approbation was timidly suggested rather than besought.

It came on a flood. Carinthia's eyes filled; she exclaimed: 'Oh, that good man!—he chooses my Madge for wife. She said it, Rebecca said it. Mrs. Wythan saw and said Mr. Woodseer loved my Madge. I hear her saying it. Then yes, and yes, from me for both your sakes, dear girl. He will have the faithfullest, he will have the kindest—Oh! and I shall know there can be a happy marriage in England.'

She summoned Gower; she clasped his hand, to thank him for appreciating her servant and sister, and for the happiness she had in hearing it; and she gazed at him and the laden brows of her Madge alternately, encouraging him to repeat his recital of his pecuniary means, for the poetry of the fact it verified, feasting on the sketch of a four-roomed cottage and an agricultural labourer's widow for cook and housemaid; Madge to listen to his compositions of the day in the evening; Madge to praise him, Madge to correct his vanity.

Love was out of the count, but Carinthia's leaping sympathy decorated the baldness of the sketch and spied his features through the daubed mask he chose to wear as a member of the order of husbands, without taking it for his fun. Dry material statements presented the reality she doated to think of. Moreover, the marriage of these two renewed her belief in true marriages, and their intention to unite was evidence of love.

'My journey to England was worth all troubles for the meeting Madge,' she said. 'I can look with pleasure to that day of my meeting her first—the day, it was then!'

She stopped. Madge felt the quivering upward of a whimper to a sob in her breast. She slipped away.

'It's a day that has come round to be repaired, Lady Fleetwood,' said Gower. 'If you will. Will you not? He has had a blow—the death of a friend, violent death. It has broken him. He wants a month or so in your mountains. I have thought him hard to deal with; he is humane. His enormous wealth has been his tempter. Madge and I will owe him our means of livelihood, enough for cottagers, until I carve my way. His feelings are much more independent of his rank than those of most noblemen. He will repeat your kind words to Madge and me; I am sure of it. He has had heavy burdens; he is young, hardly formed yet. He needs a helper; I mean, one allied to him. You forgive me? I left him with a Catholic lord for comforter, who regards my prescript of the study of Nature, when we're in grief, as about the same as an offer of a dish of cold boiled greens. Silver and ivory images are more consoling. Neither he nor I can offer the right thing for Lord Fleetwood. It will be found here. And then your mountains. More than I, nearly as much as you, he has a poet's ardour for mountain land. He and Mr. Wythan would soon learn to understand one another on that head, if not as to management of mines.'

The pleading was crafty, and it was penetrative in the avoidance of stress. Carinthia shook herself to feel moved. The endeavour chilled her to a notion that she was but half alive. She let the question approach her, whether Chillon could pardon Lord Fleetwood. She, with no idea of benignness, might speak pardon's word to him, on a late autumn evening years hence, perhaps, or to his friends to-morrow, if he would considerately keep distant. She was upheld by the thought of her brother's more honourable likeness to their father, in the certainty of his refusal to speak pardon's empty word or touch an offending hand, without their father's warrant for the injury wiped out; and as she had no wish for that to be done, she could anticipate his withholding of the word.

For her brother at wrestle with his fallen fortunes was now the beating heart of Carinthia's mind. Her husband was a shadow there. He did obscure it, and he might annoy, he was unable to set it in motion. He sat there somewhat like Youth's apprehension of Death:—the dark spot seen mistily at times through people's tears, or visioned as in an ambush beyond the hills; occasionally challenged to stimulate recklessness; oftener overlooked, acknowledged for the undesired remote of life's conditions, life's evil, fatal, ill-assorted yoke-fellow; and if it was in his power to burst out of his corner and be terrible to her, she could bring up a force unnamed and unmeasured, that being the blood of her father in her veins. Having done her utmost to guard her babe, she said her prayers; she stood for peace or the struggle.

'Does Lord Fleetwood speak of coming here?' she said.

'To-morrow.'

'I go to Croridge to-morrow.'

'Your ladyship returns?'

'Yes, I return Mr. Gower, you have fifty minutes before you dress for dinner.'

He thought only of the exceeding charity of the intimation; and he may be excused for his not seeing the feminine full answer it was, in an implied, unmeditated contrast. He went gladly to find his new comrade, his flower among grass-blades, the wonderful creature astonishing him and surcharging his world by setting her face at him, opening her breast to him, breathing a young man's word of words from a woman's mouth. His flower among grass-blades for a head looking studiously down, she was his fountain of wisdom as well, in the assurance she gave him of the wisdom of his choice.

But Madge had put up the 'prize-fighter's lass,' by way of dolly defence, to cover her amazed confusion when the proposal of this well-liked gentleman to a girl such as she sounded churchy. He knocked it over easily; it left, however, a bee at his ear and an itch to transfer the buzzer's attentions and tease his darling; for she had betrayed herself as right good game. Nor is there happier promise of life-long domestic enlivenment for a prescient man of Letters than he has in the contemplation of a pretty face showing the sensitiveness to the sting, which is not allowed to poison her temper, and is short of fetching tears. The dear innocent girl gave this pleasing promise; moreover, she could be twisted-to laugh at herself, just a little. Now, the young woman who can do that has already jumped the hedge into the highroad of philosophy, and may become a philosopher's mate in its by-ways, where the minute discoveries are the notable treasures.

They had their ramble, agreeable to both, despite the admonitory dose administered to one of them. They might have been espied at a point or two from across the parkpalings; their laughter would have caught an outside pedestrian's hearing. Whatever the case, Owain Wythan, riding down off Croridge, big with news of her brother for the countess, dined at her table, and walking up the lane to the Esslemont Arms on a moonless night, to mount his horse, pitched against an active and, as it was deemed by Gower's observation of his eyes, a scientific fist. The design to black them finely was attributable to the dyeing accuracy of the stroke. A single blow had done it. Mr. Wythan's watch and purse were untouched; and a second look at the swollen blind peepers led Gower to surmise that they were, in the calculation of the striker, his own.

He walked next day to the Royal Sovereign inn. There he came upon the earl driving his phaeton. Fleetwood jumped down, and Gower told of the mysterious incident, as the chief thing he had to tell, not rendering it so mysterious in his narrative style. He had the art of indicating darkly.

'Ines, you mean?' Fleetwood cried, and he appeared as nauseated and perplexed as he felt. Why should Ines assault Mr. Wythan? It happened that the pugilist's patron had, within the last fifteen minutes, driven past a certain thirty-acre meadow, sight of which on his way to Carinthia had stirred him. He had even then an idea of his old deeds dogging him to bind him, every one of them, the smallest.

'But you've nothing to go by,' he said. 'Why guess at this rascal more than another?'

Gower quoted Mrs. Rundles and the ostler for witnesses to Kit's visit yesterday to the Royal Sovereign, though Kit shunned the bar of the Esslemont Arms.

'I guess pretty clearly, because I suspect he was hanging about and saw me and Madge together.'

'Consolations for failures in town?—by the way, you are complimented, and I don't think you deserved it. However, there was just the chance to stop a run to perdition. But, Madge? Madge? I'd swear to the girl!'

'Not so hard as I,' said Gower, and spoke of the oath to come between the girl and him.

Fleetwood's dive into the girl's eyes drew her before him. He checked a spirt of exclamations.

'You fancy the brute had a crack for revenge and mistook his man?'

'That's what I want her ladyship to know,' said Gower.

'How could you let her hear of it?'

'Nothing can be concealed from her.'

The earl was impressionable to the remark, in his disgust at the incident. It added a touch of a new kind of power to her image.

'She's aware of my coming?'

'To-day or to-morrow.'

They scaled the phaeton and drove.

'You undervalue Lord Feltre. You avoid your adversaries,' Fleetwood now rebuked his hearer. 'It 's an easy way to have the pull of them in your own mind. You might learn from him. He's willing for controversy. Nature-worship—or "aboriginal genuflexion," he calls it; Anglicanism, Methodism; he stands to engage them. It can't be doubted, that in days of trouble he has a faith "stout as a rock, with an oracle in it," as he says; and he's right, "men who go into battle require a rock to back them or a staff to lean on." You have your "secret," you think; as far as I can see, it's to keep you from going into any form of battle.'

The new influence at work on the young nobleman was evident, if only in the language used.

Gower answered mildly: 'That can hardly be said of a man who's going to marry.'

'Perhaps not. Lady Fleetwood is aware?'

'Lady Fleetwood does me the honour to approve my choice.'

'You mean, you're dead on to it with this girl?'

'For a year or more.'

'Fond of her?'

'All my heart.'

'In love!'

'Yes, in love. The proof of it is, I 've asked her now I can support her as a cottager leaning on the Three Per Cents.'

'Well, it helps you to a human kind of talk. It carries out your theories. I never disbelieved in your honesty. The wisdom's another matter. Did you ever tell any one, that there's not an act of a man's life lies dead behind him, but it is blessing or cursing him every step he takes?'

'By that,' rejoined Gower, 'I can say Lord Feltre proves there's wisdom in the truisms of devoutness.'

He thought the Catholic lord had gone a step or two to catch an eel.

Fleetwood was looking on the backward of his days, beholding a melancholy sunset, with a grimace in it.

'Lord Feltre might show you the "leanness of Philosophy";—you would learn from hearing him:—"an old gnawed bone for the dog that chooses to be no better than a dog."'

'The vertiginous roast haunch is recommended,' Gower said.

'See a higher than your own head, good sir. But, hang the man! he manages to hit on the thing he wants.' Fleetwood set his face at Gower with cutting heartiness. 'In love, you say, and Madge: and mean it to be the holy business! Well, poor old Chummy always gave you credit for knowing how to play your game. She has given proof she 's a good girl. I don't see why it shouldn't end well. That attack on the Welshman's the bad lookout. Explained, if you like, but women's impressions won't get explained away. We must down on our knees or they. Her ladyship attentive at all to affairs of the house?'

'Every day with Queeney; at intervals with Leddings.'

'Excellent! You speak like a fellow recording the devout observances of a great dame with her minor and superior, ecclesiastical comforters. Regular at church?'

'Her ladyship goes.'

'A woman without religion, Gower Woodseer, is a weed on the water, or she's hard as nails. We shall see. Generally, Madge and the youngster parade the park at this hour. I drive round to the stables. Go in and offer your version of that rascally dog's trick. It seems the nearest we can come at. He's a sot, and drunken dogs 'll do anything. I've had him on my hands, and I've got the stain of him.'

They trotted through Esslemont Park gates. 'I've got that place, Calesford, on my hands, too,' the earl said, suddenly moved to a liking for his Kentish home.

He and Gower were struck by a common thought of the extraordinary burdens his indulgence in impulses drew upon him. Present circumstances pictured to Gower the opposing weighed and matured good reason for his choosing Madge, and he complimented himself in his pity for the earl. But Fleetwood, as he reviewed a body of acquaintances perfectly free from the wretched run in harness, though they had their fits and their whims, was pushed to the conclusion that fatalism marked his particular course through life. He could not hint at such an idea to the unsympathetic fellow, or rather, the burly antagonist to anything of the sort, beside him. Lord Feltre would have understood and appreciated it instantly. Where is aid to be had if we have the Fates against us? Feltre knew the Power, he said; was an example of 'the efficacy of supplications'; he had been 'fatally driven to find the Power,' and had found it—on the road to Rome, of course: not a delectable road for an English nobleman, except that the noise of another convert in pilgrimage on it would deal our English world a lively smack, the very stroke that heavy body wants. But the figure of a 'monastic man of fashion' was antipathetic to the earl, and he flouted an English Protestant mass merely because of his being highly individual, and therefore revolutionary for the minority.

He cast his bitter cud aside. 'My man should have arrived. Lady Fleetwood at home?'

Gower spoke of her having gone to Croridge in the morning.

'Has she taken the child?'

'She has, yes. For the air of the heights.'

'For greater security. Lady Arpington praises the thoughtful mother. I rather expected to see the child.'

'They can't be much later,' Gower supposed.

'You don't feel your long separation from "the object"?'

Letting him have his cushion for pins, Gower said 'It needs all my philosophy:

He was pricked and probed for the next five minutes; not bad rallying, the earl could be smart when he smarted. Then they descended the terrace to meet Lady Fleetwood driving her pony-trap. She gave a brief single nod to the salute of her lord, quite in the town-lady's manner, surprisingly.

CHAPTER XLI

The home of husband and wife was under one roof at last. Fleetwood went, like one deported, to his wing of the house, physically sensible, in the back turned to his wife's along the corridor, that our ordinary comparison for the division of a wedded twain is correct. She was Arctic, and Antarctic he had to be, perforce of the distance she put between them. A removal of either of them from life—or from 'the act of breathing,' as Gower Woodseer's contempt of the talk about death would call it—was an imaginable way of making it a wider division. Ambrose Mallard was far enough from his fatal lady now— farther than the Poles asunder. Ambrose, if the clergy will allow him, has found his peace.. But the road and the means he chose were a madman's.

The blotting of our character, to close our troubles, is the final proof of our being 'sons of vapour,' according to Gower Woodseer's heartless term for poor Ambrose and the lot. They have their souls; and above philosophy, 'natural' or unnatural, they may find a shelter. They can show in their desperation that they are made of blood, as philosophers rather fail of doing. An insignificant brainless creature like Feltre had wits, by the aid of his religion, to help or be charitable to his fellows, particularly the sinners, in the crisis of life, surpassing any philosopher's.

Information of her ladyship's having inspected the apartments, to see to the minutest of his customary luxuries, cut at him all round. His valet had it from the footmen and maids; and their speaking of it meant a liking for their mistress; and that liking, added to her official solicitude on his behalf, touched a soft place in him and blew an icy wind; he was frozen where he was warmed. Here was evidence of her intending the division to be a fixed gap. She had entered this room and looked about her. He was here to feel her presence in her absence.

Some one or something had schooled her, too. Her large-eyed directness of gaze was the same as at that inn and in Wales, but her easy sedateness was novel, her English, almost the tone of the English world: he gathered it, at least, from the few remarks below stairs.

His desire to be with her was the desire to escape the phantasm of the woman haunting to subjugate him when they were separate. He could kill illusion by magnifying and clawing at her visible angles and audible false notes; and he did it until his recollections joined to the sight of her, when a clash of the thought of what she had been and the thought of what she was had the effect of conjuring a bitter sweet image that was a more seductive illusion. Strange to think, this woman once loved the man who was not half the value of the man she no longer loved. He took a shot at cynicism, but hit no mark. This woman protected her whole sex.

They sat at the dinner-table alone, thanks to a handsome wench's attractions for a philosopher. Married, and parents of a lusty son, this was their first sitting at table together. The mouth that said 'I guard my rooms' was not obtruded; she talked passingly of her brother, much of Lady Arpington and of old Mr. Woodseer; and, though she reserved a smile, there was no look of a lock on her face. She seemed pleased to be treated very courteously; she returned the stately politeness in exactest measure; very simply, as well. Her face had now an air of homeliness, well suited to an English household interior.

She could chat. Any pauses occurring, he was the one guilty of them; she did not allow them to be barrier chasms, or 'strids' for the leap with effort; she crossed them like the mountain maid over a gorge's plank—kept her tones perfectly. Her Madge and Mr. Gower Woodseer made a conversible topic. She was inquisitive for accounts of Spanish history and the land of Spain.

They passed into the drawing-room. She had heard of the fate of the poor child in Wales, she said, without a comment.

'I see now, I ought to have backed your proposal,' he confessed, and was near on shivering. She kept silent, proudly or regretfully.

Open on her workbasket was a Spanish guide-book and a map attached to it. She listened to descriptions of Cadiz, Malaga, Seville, Granada. Her curiosity was chiefly for detailed accounts of Catalonia and the Pyrenees.

'Hardly the place for you; there's a perpetual heaving of Carlism in those mountains; your own are quieter for travellers,' he remarked; and for a moment her lips moved to some likeness of a smile; a dimple in a flowing thought.

He remarked the come and go of it.

He regretted his inability to add to her knowledge of the Spanish Pyrenees.

Books helped her at present, she said.

Feeling acutely that hostility would have brought them closer than her uninviting civility, he spoke of the assault on Mr. Wythan, and Gower Woodseer's conjecture, and of his having long since discharged the rascal Ines.

To which her unreproachful answer, 'You made use of those men, my lord,' sent a cry ringing through him, recalling Feltre's words, as to the grip men progressively are held in by their deeds done.

'Oh, quite true, we change our views and ways of life,' he said, thinking she might set her considerations on other points of his character. But this reflection was a piece of humility not yet in his particular estimate of his character, and he spurned it: an act of pride that drove his mind, for occupation, to contemplate hers; which speedily became an embrace of her character, until he was asking whether the woman he called wife and dared not clasp was one of those rarest, who can be idealized by virtue of their being known. For the young man embracing a character loses grasp of his own, is plucked out of himself and passes into it, to see the creature he is with the other's eyes, and feel for the other as a very self. Such is the privilege and the chastisement of the young.

Gower Woodseer's engagement with the girl Madge was a happier subject for expatiation and agreement. Her deeper tones threw a light on Gower, and where she saw goodness, he could at least behold the natural philosopher practically philosophizing.

'The girl shall have a dowry from me,' he said; and the sum named was large. Her head bent acknowledgingly; money had small weight with her now. His perception of it stripped him and lamed him.

He wished her ladyship good-night. She stood up and performed a semi-ceremonious obeisance, neatly adapted to their mutual position. She had a well-bred mother.

Probably she would sleep. No such expectation could soothe the friend, and some might be thinking misleader, of Ambrose Mallard, before he had ocular proof that the body lay underground. His promise was given to follow it to the grave, a grave in consecrated earth. Ambrose died of the accidental shot of a pocket-pistol he customarily carried loaded. Two intimate associates of the dead man swore to that habit of his. They lied to get him undisputed Christian burial. Aha! The earl laughed outright at Chummy Potts's nursery qualms. The old fellow had to do it, and he lied like a man for the sake of Ambrose Mallard's family. So much is owing to our friend.

Can ecclesiastical casuists decide upon cases of conscience affecting men of the world?

A council sat upon the case the whole night long. A committee of the worldly held argumentation in a lower chamber.

These are nights that weaken us to below the level of women. A shuttle worked in Fleetwood's head. He defended the men of the world. Lord Feltre oiled them, damned them, kindled them to a terrific expiatory blaze, and extinguishingly salved and wafted aloft the released essence of them. Maniacal for argument, Fleetwood rejected the forgiveness of sins, if sins they be. Prove them sins, and the suffering is of necessity everlasting, his insomnia logic insisted. Whichever side he took, his wife was against him; not in speech, but in her look. She was a dumb figure among the wranglers, clouded up to the neck. Her look said she knew more of him than they knew.

He departed next day for London, after kissing his child; and he would have done wisely to abstain from his exhibition of the paternal. Knowing it a step to conciliation, he checked his impulsive warmth, under the apprehension that the mother would take it for a piece of acting to propitiate—and his lips pecked the baby's cheek. Its mother held arms for it immediately.

Not without reason did his heart denounce her as a mere mother, with little of a mind to see.

The recent series of feverishly sleepless nights disposed him to snappish irritability or the thirst for tenderness. Gower had singular experiences of him on the drive North-westward. He scarcely spoke; he said once: 'If you mean to marry, you'll be wanting to marry soon, of course,' and his curt nod before the reply was formulated appeared to signify, the sooner the better, and deliverance for both of us. Honest though he might, be sometimes deep and sometimes picturesque, the philosopher's day had come to an end. How can Philosophy minister to raw wounds, when we are in a raging gale of the vexations, battered to right and left! Religion has a nourishing breast: Philosophy is breastless. Religion condones offences: Philosophy has no forgiveness, is an untenanted confessional: 'wide air to a cry in anguish,' Feltre says.

All the way to London Fleetwood endured his companion, letting him talk when he would.

He spent the greater part of the night discussing human affairs and spiritual with Lord Feltre, whose dialectical exhortations and insinuations were of the feeblest, but to an isolated young man, yearning for the tenderness of a woman thinking but of her grievances, the ointment brought comfort.

It soothed him during his march to and away from Ambrose Mallard's grave; where it seemed to him curious and even pitiable that Chumley Potts should be so inconsolably shaken. Well, and if the priests have the secret of strengthening the backbone for a bend of the knee in calamity, why not go to the priests, Chummy? Potts's hearing was not addressed; nor was the chief person in the meditation affected by a question that merely jumped out of his perturbed interior.

Business at Calesford kept Fleetwood hanging about London several days further; and his hatred of a place he wasted time and money to decorate grew immeasurable. It distorted the features of the beautiful woman for whose pleasure the grand entertainments to be held there had, somewhere or other—when felon spectres were abroad over earth—been conceived.

He could then return to Esslemont. Gower was told kindly, with intentional coldness, that he could take a seat in the phaeton if he liked; and he liked, and took it. Anything to get to that girl of his!

Whatever the earl's inferiors did, their inferior station was not suffered to discolour it for his judgement. But an increasing antagonism to Woodseer's philosophy—which the fellow carried through with perpetual scorings of satisfaction—caused him to set a hard eye on the damsel under the grisly spotting shadow of the sottish bruiser, of whom, after once touching the beast, he could not rub his hands clean; and he chose to consider the winning of the prize-fighter's lass the final triumph or flag on the apex of the now despised philosophy. Vain to ask how he had come to be mixed up with the lot, or why the stolidly conceited, pretentious fellow had seat here, as by right, beside him! We sow and we reap; 'plant for sugar and taste the cane,' some one says—this Woodseer, probably; he can, when it suits him, tickle the ears of the worldlings. And there is worthier stuff to remember; stuff to nourish: Feltre's 'wisdom of our fathers,' rightly named Religion.

More in the country, when he traversed sweep and rise of open land, Carinthia's image began to shine, and she threw some of her light on Madge, who made Woodseer appear tolerable, sagacious, absurdly enviable, as when we have the fit to wish we were some four-foot. The fellow's philosophy wore a look of practical craft.

He was going to the girl he liked, and she was, one could swear, an honest girl; and she was a comely girl, a girl to stick to a man. Her throwing over a sot was creditable. Her mistress loved her. That said much for any mortal creature. Man or woman loved by Carinthia could not be cowardly, could not be vile, must have high qualities. Next to Religion, she stood for a test of us. Had she any strong sense of Religion, in addition to the formal trooping to one of their pallid Protestant churches? Lord Feltre might prove useful to her. For merely the comprehension of the signification of Religion steadies us. It had done that for him, the earl owned.

He broke a prolonged silence by remarking to Gower 'You haven't much to say to-day'; and the answer was 'Very little. When I'm walking, I'm picking up; and when I'm driving, I'm putting together.'

Gower was rallied on the pursuit of the personal object in both cases. He pointed at sheep, shepherd, farmer, over the hedge, all similarly occupied; and admitted shamelessly, that he had not a thought for company, scarce a word to fling. 'Ideas in gestation are the dullest matter you can have.'

'There I quite agree with you,' said Fleetwood. Abrane, Chummy Potts, Brailstone, little Corby, were brighter comrades. And these were his Ixionides! Hitherto his carving of a way in the world had been sufficiently ill-considered. Was it preferable to be a loutish philosopher? Since the death of Ambrose

Mallard, he felt Woodseer's title for that crew grind harshly; and he tried to provoke a repetition of it, that he might burst out in wrathful defence of his friends—to be named friends when they were vilified: defence of poor Ambrose at least, the sinner who, or one as bad, might have reached to pardon through the priesthood.

Gower offered him no chance..

Entering Esslemont air, Fleetwood tossed his black mood to the winds. She breathed it. She was a mountain girl, and found it hard to forgive our lowlands. She would learn tolerance, taking her flights at seasons. The yacht, if she is anything of a sailor, may give her a taste of England's pleasures. She will have a special allowance for distribution among old Mr. Woodseer's people. As to the rest of the Countess of Fleetwood's wishes, her family ranks with her husband's in claims of any kind on him. There would be—she would require and had a right to demand—say, a warm half-hour of explanations: he knew the tone for them, and so little did he revolve it apprehensively, that his mind sprang beyond, to the hearing from her mouth of her not intending further to 'guard her rooms.' How quietly the words were spoken! There was a charm in the retrospect of her mouth and manner. One of the rare women who never pout or attitudinize, she could fling her glove gracefully—one might add, capturingly under every aspect, she was a handsome belligerent. The words he had to combat pleased his memory. Some good friend, Lady Arpington probably, had instructed her in the art of dressing to match her colour.

Concerning himself, he made no stipulation, but he reflected on Lord Feltre's likely estimate of her as a bit of a heathen. And it might be to her advantage, were she and Feltre to have some conversations. Whatever the faith, a faith should exist, for without the sentiment of religion, a woman, he says, is where she was when she left the gates of Eden. A man is not much farther. Feltre might have saved Ambrose Mallard. He is, however, right in saying, that the woman with the sentiment of religion in her bosom is a box of holy incense distinguishing her from all other women. Empty of it, she is devil's bait. At best, she is a creature who cannot overlook an injury, or must be exacting God knows what humiliations before she signs the treaty.

Informed at the house that her ladyship had been staying up on Croridge for the last two days, Fleetwood sent his hardest shot of the eyes at Gower. Let her be absent: it was equal to the first move of war, and absolved him from contemplated proposals to make amends. But the enforced solitary companionship with this ruminator of a fellow set him asking whether the godless dog he had picked up by the wayside was not incarnate another of the sins he had to expiate. Day after day, almost hourly, some new stroke fell on him. Why? Was he selected for persecution because he was wealthy? The Fates were driving him in one direction, no doubt of that.

This further black mood evaporated, and like a cessation of English storm-weather bequeathed him gloom. Ashamed of the mood, he was nevertheless directed by its final shadows to see the ruminating tramp in Gower, and in Madge the prize-fighter's jilt: and round about Esslemont a world eyeing an Earl of Fleetwood, who painted himself the man he was, or was held to be, by getting together such a collection, from the daughter of the Old Buccaneer to the ghastly corpse of Ambrose Mallard. Why, clearly, wealth was the sole origin and agent of the mischief. With somewhat less of it, he might have walked in his place among the nation's elect, the 'herd of the gilt horns,' untroubled by ambitions and ideas.

Arriving thus far, he chanced to behold Gower and Madge walking over the grounds near the western plantation, and he regretted the disappearance of them, with the fellow talking hard into the girl's ear.

Those two could think he had been of some use. The man pretending to philosophical depth was at any rate honest; one could swear to the honesty of the girl, though she had been a reckless hussy. Their humble little hopes and means to come to union approached, after a fashion, hymning at his ears. Those two were pleasanter to look on than amorous lords and great ladies, who are interesting only when they are wicked.

Four days of desolate wanderings over the estate were occupied chiefly in his decreeing the fall of timber that obstructed views, and was the more imperatively doomed for his bailiff's intercession. 'Sound wood' the trees might be: they had to assist in defraying the expense of separate establishments. A messenger to Queeney from Croridge then announced the Countess's return 'for a couple of hours.' Queeney said it was the day when her ladyship examined the weekly bills of the household. That was in the early morning. The post brought my lord a letter from Countess Livia, a most infrequent writer. She had his word to pay her debts; what next was she for asking? He shrugged, opened the letter, and stared at the half dozen lines. The signification of them rapped on his consciousness of another heavy blow before he was perfectly intelligent.

All possible anticipation seemed here outdone: insomuch that he held palpable evidence of the Fates at work to harass and drive him. She was married to the young Earl of Cressett!'

Fleetwood printed the lines on his eyeballs. They were the politely flowing feminine of a statement of the fact, which might have been in one line. They flourished wantonly: they were deadly blunt. And of all men, this youngster, who struck at him through her lips with the reproach, that he had sped the good-looking little beast upon his road to ruin:—perhaps to Ambrose Mallard's end!

CHAPTER XLII

THE RETARDED COURTSHIP

Carinthia reached Esslemont near noon. She came on foot, and had come unaccompanied, stick in hand, her dress looped for the roads. Madge bustled her shorter steps up the park beside her; Fleetwood met her on the terrace.

'No one can be spared at Croridge,' she said. 'I go back before dark.' Apology was not thought of; she seemed wound to the pitch.

He bowed; he led into the morning-room. 'The boy is at Croridge?'

'With me. He has his nurse. Madge was at home here more than there.'

'Why do you go back?'

'I am of use to my brother.'

'Forgive me—in what way?'

'He has enemies about him. They are the workmen of Lord Levellier. They attacked Lekkatts the other night, and my uncle fired at them out of a window and wounded a man. They have sworn they will be revenged. Mr. Wythan is with my brother to protect him.'

'Two men, very well; they don't want, if there's danger, a woman's aid in protecting him?'

She smiled, and her smile was like the hint of the steel blade an inch out of sheath.

'My brother does not count me a weak woman.'

'Oh no! No one would think that,' Fleetwood said hurriedly and heartily. 'Least of all men, I, Carinthia. But you might be rash.'

'My brother knows me cautious.'

'Chillon?'

'It is my brother's name.'

'You used to call him by his name.

'I love his name.'

'Ah, well! I may be pardoned for wishing to hear what part you play there.'

'I go the rounds with my brother.'

'Armed?'

'We carry arms.'

'Queer sight to see in England. But there are rascals in this country, too.'

She was guilty of saying, though not pointedly: 'We do not hire defenders.'

'In civilized lands...' he began and stopped 'You have Mr. Wythan?'

'Yes, we are three.'

'You call him, I think, Owain?'

'I do.'

'In your brother's hearing?'

'Yes, my lord; it would be in your hearing if you were near.'

'No harm, no doubt.'

'There is none.'

'But you will not call your brother Chillon to me.'

'You dislike the name.'

'I learn to like everything you do and say; and every person you like.'

'It is by Mr. Wythan's dead wife's request that I call him by his name. He is our friend. He is a man to trust.'

'The situation...' Fleetwood hung swaying between the worldly view of it and the white light of this woman's nature flashed on his emotion into his mind. 'You shall be trusted for judging. If he is your friend, he is my friend. I have missed the sight of our boy. You heard I was at Esslemont?'

'I heard from Madge!'

'It is positive you must return to Croridge?'

'I must be with my brother, yes.'

'Your ladyship will permit me to conduct you.'

Her head assented. There was nothing to complain of, but he had not gained a step.

The rule is, that when we have yielded initiative to a woman, we are unable to recover it without uncivil bluster. So, therefore, women dealing with gentlemen are allowed unreasonable advantages. He had never granted it in colloquy or act to any woman but this one. Consequently, he was to see, that if the gentleman in him was not put aside, the lady would continue moving on lines of the independence he had likewise yielded, or rather flung, to her. Unless, as a result, he besieged and wooed his wife, his wife would hold on a course inclining constantly farther from the union he desired. Yet how could he begin to woo her if he saw no spark of womanly tenderness? He asked himself, because the beginning of the wooing might be checked by the call on him for words of repentance only just possible to conceive. Imagine them uttered, and she has the initiative for life.

She would not have it, certainly, with a downright brute. But he was not that. In an extremity of bitterness, he fished up a drowned old thought, of all his torments being due to the impulsive half-brute he was. And between the good and the bad in him, the sole point of strength was a pride likely, as the smooth simplicity of her indifference showed him, soon to be going down prostrate beneath her feet. Wholly a brute—well? He had to say, that playing the perfect brute with any other woman he would have his mastery. The summoning of an idea of personal power to match this woman in a contest was an effort exhausting the idea.

They passed out of Esslemont gates together at that hour of the late afternoon when South-westerly breezes, after a summer gale, drive their huge white flocks over blue fields fresh as morning, on the march to pile the crown of the sphere, and end a troubled day with grandeur. Up the lane by the park they had open land to the heights of Croridge.

'Splendid clouds,' Fleetwood remarked.

She looked up, thinking of the happy long day's walk with her brother to the Styrian Baths. Pleasure in the sight made her face shine superbly. 'A flying Switzerland, Mr. Woodseer says,' she replied. 'England is beautiful on days like these.—For walking, I think the English climate very good.'

He dropped a murmur: 'It should suit so good a walker,' and burned to compliment—her spirited easy stepping, and scorned himself for the sycophancy it would be before they were on the common ground of a restored understanding. But an approval of any of her acts threatened him with enthusiasm for the whole of them, her person included; and a dam in his breast had to keep back the flood.

'You quote Woodseer to me, Carinthia. I wish you knew Lord Feltre. He can tell you of every cathedral, convent, and monastery in Europe and Syria. Nature is well enough; she is, as he says, a savage. Men's works, acting under divine direction to escape from that tangle, are better worthy of study, perhaps. If one has done wrong, for example.'

'I could listen to him,' she said.

'You would not need—except, yes, one thing. Your father's book speaks of not forgiving an injury.'

'My father does. He thinks it weakness to forgive an injury. Women do, and are disgraced, they are thought slavish. My brother is much stronger than I am. He is my father alive in that.'

'It is anti-Christian, some would think.'

'Let offending people go. He would not punish them. They may go where they will be forgiven. For them our religion is a happy retreat; we are glad they have it. My father and my brother say that injury forbids us to be friends again. My father was injured by the English Admiralty: he never forgave it; but he would have fought one of their ships and offered his blood any day, if his country called to battle.'

'You have the same feeling, you mean.'

'I am a woman. I follow my brother, whatever he decides. It is not to say he is the enemy of persons offending him; only that they have put the division.'

'They repent?'

'If they do, they do well for themselves.'

'You would see them in sackcloth and ashes?'

'I would pray to be spared seeing them.'

'You can entirely forget—well, other moments, other feelings?'

'They may heighten the injury.'

'Carinthia, I should wish to speak plainly, if I could, and tell you....'

'You speak quite plainly, my lord.'

'You and I cannot be strangers or enemies.'

'We cannot be, I would not be. To be friends, we should be separate.'

'You say you are a woman; you have a heart, then?'—for, if not, what have you? was added in the tone.

'My heart is my brother's,' she said.

'All your heart?'

'My heart is my brother's until one of us drops.'

'There is not another on earth beside your brother Chillon?'

'There is my child.'

The dwarf square tower of Croridge village church fronted them against the sky, seen of both.

'You remember it,' he said; and she answered: 'I was married there.'

'You have not forgotten that injury, Carinthia?'

'I am a mother.'

'By all the saints! you hit hard. Justly. Not you. Our deeds are the hard hitters. We learn when they begin to flagellate, stroke upon stroke! Suppose we hold a costly thing in the hand and dash it to the ground—no recovery of it, none! That must be what your father meant. I can't regret you are a mother. We have a son, a bond. How can I describe the man I was!' he muttered,—'possessed! sort of werewolf! You are my wife?'

'I was married to you, my lord.'

'It's a tie of a kind.'

'It binds me.'

'Obey, you said.'

'Obey it. I do.'

'You consider it holy?'

'My father and my mother spoke to me of the marriage-tie. I read the service before I stood at the altar. It is holy. It is dreadful. I will be true to it.'

'To your husband?'

'To his name, to his honour.'

'To the vow to live with him?'

'My husband broke that for me.'

'Carinthia, if he bids you, begs you to renew it? God knows what you may save me from!'

'Pray to God. Do not beg of me, my lord. I have my brother and my little son. No more of husband for me! God has given me a friend, too,—a man of humble heart, my brother's friend, my dear Rebecca's husband. He can take them from me: no one but God. See the splendid sky we have.'

With those words she barred the gates on him; at the same time she bestowed the frank look of an amiable face brilliant in the lively red of her exercise, in its bent-bow curve along the forehead, out of the line of beauty, touching, as her voice was, to make an undertone of anguish swell an ecstasy. So he felt it, for his mood was now the lover's. A torture smote him, to find himself transported by that voice at his ear to the scene of the young bride in thirty-acre meadow.

'I propose to call on Captain Kirby-Levellier tomorrow, Carinthia,' he said. 'The name of his house?'

'My brother is not now any more in the English army,' she replied. 'He has hired a furnished house named Stoneridge.'

'He will receive me, I presume?'

'My brother is a courteous gentleman, my lord.'

'Here is the church, and here we have to part for today. Do we?'

'Good-bye to you, my lord,' she said.

He took her hand and dropped the dead thing.

'Your idea is, to return to Esslemont some day or other?'

'For the present,' was her strange answer.

She bowed, she stepped on. On she sped, leaving him at the stammered beginning of his appeal to her.

Their parting by the graveyard of the church that had united them was what the world would class as curious. To him it was a further and a well-marked stroke of the fatality pursuing him. He sauntered by the graveyard wall until her figure slipped out of sight. It went like a puffed candle, and still it haunted the corner where last seen. Her vanishing seemed to say, that less of her belonged to him than the phantom his eyes retained behind them somewhere.

There was in his pocket a memento of Ambrose Mallard, that the family had given him at his request. He felt the lump. It had an answer for all perplexities. It had been charged and emptied since it was in his possession; and it could be charged again. The thing was a volume as big as the world to study. For the touch of a finger, one could have its entirely satisfying contents, and fly and be a raven of that night wherein poor Ambrose wanders lost, but cured of human wounds.

He leaned on the churchyard wall, having the graves to the front of eyes bent inward. They were Protestant graves, not so impressive to him as the wreathed and gilt of those under dedication to Feltre's Madonna. But whatever they were, they had ceased to nurse an injury or feel the pain for having inflicted it. Their wrinkles had gone from them, whether of anger or suffering. Ambrose Mallard lay as peaceful in consecrated ground: and Chumley Potts would be unlikely to think that the helping to lay Ambrose in his quiet last home would cost him a roasting until priestly intercession availed. So Chummy continues a Protestant; dull consciences can! But this is incomprehensible, that she, nursing her injury, should be perfectly civil. She is a woman without emotion. She is a woman full of emotion, one man knows. She ties him to her, to make him feel the lash of his remorse. He feels it because of her casting him from her—and so civilly. If this were a Catholic church, one might go in and give the stained soul free way to get a cleansing. As it is, here are the graves; the dead everywhere have their sanctity, even the heathen.

Fleetwood read the name of the family of Meek on several boards at the head of the graves. Jonathan Meek died at the age of ninety-five. A female Meek had eighty-nine years in this life. Ezra Meek gave up the ghost prematurely, with a couplet, at eighty-one. A healthy spot, Croridge, or there were virtues in the Meek family, he reflected, and had a shudder that he did not trace to its cause, beyond an acknowledgement of a desire for the warm smell of incense.

CHAPTER XLIII

ON THE ROAD TO THE ACT OF PENANCE

His customary wrestle with the night drove Lord Fleetwood in the stillness of the hour after matins from his hated empty Esslemont up again to the village of the long-lived people, enjoying the moist earthiness of the air off the ironstone. He rode fasting, a good preparatory state for the simple pleasures, which are virtually the Great Nourisher's teats to her young. The earl was relieved of his dejection by a sudden filling of his nostrils. Fat Esslemont underneath had no such air. Except on the mornings of his walk over the Salzkammergut and Black Forest regions, he had never consciously drawn that deep breath of the satisfied rapture, charging the whole breast with thankfulness. Huntsmen would know it, if the chase were not urgent to pull them at the tail of the running beast. Once or twice on board his yacht he might have known something like it, but the salt sea-breeze could not be disconnected from his companion Lord Feltre, and a thought of Feltre swung vapour of incense all about him. Breathing this air of the young sun's kiss of earth, his invigoration repelled the seductions of the burnt Oriental gums.

Besides, as he had told his friend, it was the sincerity of the Catholic religion, not the seductiveness, that won him to a form of homage—the bend of the head of a foreign observer at a midnight mass. Asceticism, though it may not justify error, is a truth in itself, it is the essence extracted of the scourge, flesh vanquished; and it stands apart from controversy. Those monks of the forested mountain heights, rambling for their herbs, know the blessedness to be found in mere breathing: a neighbour readiness to yield the breath inspires it the more. For when we do not dread our end, the sense of a free existence comes back to us: we have the prized gift to infancy under the piloting of manhood. But before we taste that happiness we must perform our penance; 'No living happiness can be for the unclean,' as the holy father preached to his flock of the monastery dispersing at matins.

Ay, but penance? penance? Is there not such a thing as the doing of penance out of the Church, in the manly fashion? So to regain the right to be numbered among the captains of the world's fighting men, incontestably the best of comrades, whether or no they led away on a cataract leap at the gates of life. Boldly to say we did a wrong will clear our sky for a few shattering peals.

The penitential act means, youth put behind us, and a steady course ahead. But, for the keeping of a steady course, men made of blood in the walks of the world must be steadied. Say it plainly—mated. There is the humiliating point of our human condition. We must have beside us and close beside us the woman we have learned to respect; supposing ourselves lucky enough to have found her; 'that required other scale of the human balance,' as Woodseer calls her now he has got her, wiser than Lord Feltre in reference to men and women. We get no balance without her. That is apparently the positive law; and by reason of men's wretched enslavement, it is the dance to dissolution when we have not honourable union with women. Feltre's view of women sees the devilish or the angelical; and to most men women are knaves or ninnies. Hence do we behold rascals or imbeciles in the offspring of most men.

He embraced the respected woman's character, with the usual effect:—to see with her sight; and she beheld a speckled creature of the intermittent whims and moods and spites; the universal Patron, whose ambition to be leader of his world made him handle foul brutes—corrupt and cause their damnation, they retort, with curses, in their pangs. She was expected to pardon the husband, who had not abstained from his revenge on her for keeping him to the pledge of his word. And what a revenge!— he had flung the world at her. She is consequently to be the young bride she was on the memorable morning of the drive off these heights of Croridge down to thirty-acre meadow! It must be a saint to forgive such offences; and she is not one, she is deliciously not one, neither a Genevieve nor a Griselda. He handed her the rod to chastise him. Her exchange of Christian names with the Welshman would not do it; she was too transparently sisterly, provincially simple; she was, in fact, respected. Any whipping from her was child's play to him, on whom, if he was to be made to suffer, the vision of the intense felicity of austerest asceticism brought the sensation as bracingly as the Boreal morning animates men of high blood in ice regions. She could but gently sting, even if vindictive.

Along the heights, outside the village, some way below a turn of the road to Lekkatts, a gentleman waved hand. The earl saluted with his whip, and waited for him.

'Nothing wrong, Mr. Wythan?'

'Nothing to fear, my lord.'

'I get a trifle uneasy.'

'The countess will not leave her brother.'

A glow of his countess's friendliness for this open-faced, prompt-speaking, good fellow of the faintly inky eyelids, and possibly sheepish inclinations, melted Fleetwood. Our downright repentance of misconduct toward a woman binds us at least to the tolerant recognition of what poor scraps of consolement she may have picked up between then and now—when we can stretch fist in flame to defy it on the oath of her being a woman of honour.

The earl alighted and said: 'Her brother, I suspect, is the key of the position.'

'He's worth it—she loves her brother,' said Mr. Wythan, betraying a feature of his quick race, with whom the reflection upon a statement is its lightning in advance.

Gratified by the instant apprehension of his meaning, Fleetwood interpreted the Welshman's. 'I have to see the brother worthy of her love. Can you tell me the hour likely to be convenient?'.....

Mr. Wythan thought an appointment unnecessary which conveyed the sufficient assurance of audience granted.

'You know her brother well, Mr. Wythan?'

'Know him as if I had known him for years. They both come to the mind as faith comes—no saying how; one swears by them.'

Fleetwood eyed the Welsh gentleman, with an idea that he might readily do the same by him.

Mr. Wythan's quarters were at the small village inn, whither he was on his way to breakfast. The earl slipped an arm through the bridle reins and walked beside him, listening to an account of the situation at Lekkatts. It was that extraordinary complication of moves and checks which presents in the main a knot, for the powers above to cut. A miserly old lord withholds arrears of wages; his workmen strike at a critical moment; his nephew, moved by common humanity, draws upon crippled resources to supply their extremer needs, though they are ruining his interests. They made one night a demonstration of the terrorizing sort round Lekkatts, to give him a chorus; and the old lord fired at them out of window and wounded a man. For that they vowed vengeance. All the new gunpowder milled in Surrey was, for some purpose of his own, stored by Lord Levellier on the alder island of the pond near his workshops, a quarter of a mile below the house. They refused, whatever their object, to let a pound of it be moved, at a time when at last the Government had undertaken to submit it to experiments. And there they stood on ground too strong for 'the Captain,' as they called him, to force, because of the quantity stored at Lekkatts being largely beyond the amount under cover of Lord Levellier's licence. The old lord was very ill, and he declined to see a doctor, but obstinately kept from dying. His nephew had to guard him and at the same time support an enemy having just cause of complaint. This, however, his narrow means would not much longer permit him to do. The alternative was then offered him of either siding arbitrarily against the men and his conscience or of taking a course 'imprudent on the part of a presumptive heir,' Mr. Wythan said hurriedly at the little inn's doorsteps.

'You make one of his lordship's guard?' said Fleetwood.

'The countess, her brother, and I, yes'

'Danger at all?'

'Not so much to fear while the countess is with us.'

'Fear is not a word for Carinthia.'

Her name on the earl's lips drew a keen shot of the eye from Mr. Wythan, and he read the signification of the spoken name. 'You know what every Cambrian living thinks of her, my lord.'

'She shall not have one friend the less for me.'

Fleetwood's hand was out for a good-bye, and the hand was grasped by one who looked happy in doing it. He understood and trusted the man after that, warmed in thinking how politic his impulses could be.

His intention of riding up to Croridge at noon to request his interview with Mr. Kirby-Levellier was then stated.

'The key of the position, as you said,' Mr. Wythan remarked, not proffering an opinion of it more than was expressed by a hearty, rosy countenance, that had to win its way with the earl before excuse was found for the venturesome repetition of his phrase.

Cantering back to that home of the loves of Gower Woodseer and Madge Winch, the thought of his first act of penance done, without his feeling the poorer for it, reconciled Fleetwood to the aspect of the hollow place.

He could not stay beneath the roof. His task of breakfasting done, he was off before the morning's delivery of letters, riding round the country under Croridge, soon up there again. And Henrietta might be at home, he was reminded by hearing band-music as he followed the directions to the house named Stoneridge. The band consisted of eight wind instruments; they played astonishingly well for itinerant musicians. By curious chance, they were playing a selection from the Pirata; presently he heard the notes to 'il mio tradito amor.' They had hit upon Henrietta's favourite piece!

At the close of it he dismounted, flung the reins to his groom, and, addressing a compliment to the leader, was deferentially saluted with a 'my lord.' Henrietta stood at the window, a servant held the door open for him to enter; he went in, and the beautiful young woman welcomed him: 'Oh, my dear lord, you have given me such true delight! How very generous of you!' He protested ignorance. She had seen him speak to the conductor and receive the patron's homage; and who but he knew her adored of operas, or would have had the benevolent impulse to think of solacing her exile from music in the manner so sure of her taste! She was at her loveliest: her features were one sweet bloom, as of the sunny flower garden; and, touched to the heart by the music and the kindness, she looked the look that kisses; innocently, he felt, feeling himself on the same good ground while he could own he admired the honey creature, much as an amateur may admire one of the pictures belonging to the nation.

'And you have come...?' she said. 'We are to believe in happy endings?'

He shrugged, as the modest man should, who says:

'If it depends on me'; but the words were firmly spoken and could be credited.

'Janey is with her brother down at Lekkatts. Things are at a deadlock. A spice of danger, enough to relieve the dulness; and where there is danger Janey's at home.' Henrietta mimicked her Janey. 'Parades with her brother at night; old military cap on her head; firearms primed; sings her Austrian mountain songs or the Light Cavalry call, till it rings all day in my ears—she has a thrilling contralto. You are not to think her wild, my lord. She's for adventure or domesticity, "whichever the Fates decree." She really is coming to the perfect tone.'

'Speak of her,' said the earl. 'She can't yet overlook…?'

'It's in the family. She will overlook anything her brother excuses.'

'I'm here to see him.'

'I heard it from Mr. Wythan.'

'"Owain," I believe?'

Henrietta sketched apologies, with a sidled head, soft pout, wavy hand. 'He belongs to the order of primitive people. His wife—the same pattern, one supposes—pledged them to their Christian names. The man is a simpleton, but a gentleman; and Janey holds his dying wife's wish sacred. We are all indebted to him.'

'Whatever she thinks right!' said Fleetwood.

The fair young woman's warm nature flew out to him on a sparkle of grateful tenderness in return for his magnanimity, oblivious of the inflamer it was: and her heart thanked him more warmly, without the perilous show of emotion, when she found herself secure.

She was beautiful, she was tempting, and probably the weakest of players in the ancient game of two; and clearly she was not disposed to the outlaw game; was only a creature of ardour. That he could see, seeing the misinterpretation a fellow like Brailstone would put upon a temporary flush of the feminine, and the advantage he would take of it, perhaps not unsuccessfully—the dog! He committed the absurdity of casting a mental imprecation at the cunning tricksters of emotional women, and yelled at himself in the worn old surplice of the converted rake. But letting his mind run this way, the tradito amor of the band outside the lady's window was instantly traced to Lord Brailstone; so convincingly, that he now became a very counsel for an injured husband in denunciation of the seductive compliment.

Henrietta prepared to conduct him to Lekkatts; her bonnet was brought. She drew forth a letter from a silken work-bag, and raised it,—Livia's handwriting. 'I 've written my opinion,' he said.

'Not too severe, pray.'

'Posted.'

'Livia wanted a protector.'

'And chose—what on earth are you saying!'

Livia and her boyish lord were abandoned on the spot, though Henrietta could have affirmed stoutly that there was much to be pleaded, if a female advocate dared it, and a man would but hear.

His fingers were at the leaves of a Spanish dictionary.

'Oh yes, and here we have a book of Travels in Spain,' she said. 'Everything Spanish for Janey now. You are aware?—no?'

He was unaware and desired to be told.

'Janey's latest idea; only she would have conceived the notion. You solve our puzzle, my lord.'

She renewed the thanks she persisted in offering for the military music now just ceasing: vexatiously, considering that it was bad policy for him to be unmasking Brailstone to her. At the same time, the blindness which rendered her unconscious of Brailstone's hand in sending members of a military band to play selections from the favourite opera they had jointly drunk of to ecstasy, was creditable; touching, when one thought of the pursuer's many devices, not omitting some treason on the part of her present friend.

'Tell me—I solve?' he said....

Henrietta spied the donkey-basket bearing the two little ones.

'Yes, I hope so—on our way down,' she made answer. 'I want you to see the pair of love-birds in a nest.'

The boy and girl were seen lying side by side, both fast asleep; fair-haired girl, dark-haired boy, faced to one another.

'Temper?' said Fleetwood, when he had taken observation of them.

'Very imperious—Mr. Boy!' she replied, straightening her back under a pretty frown, to convey the humour of the infant tyrant.

The father's mind ran swiftly on a comparison of the destinies of the two children, from his estimate of their parents; many of Gower Woodseer's dicta converging to reawaken thoughts upon Nature's laws, which a knowledge of his own nature blackened. He had to persuade himself that this child of his was issue of a loving union; he had to do it violently, conjuring a vivid picture of the mother in bud, and his recognition of her young charm; the pain of keeping to his resolve to quit her, lest she should subjugate him and despoil him of his wrath; the fatalism in his coming and going; the romantic freak it had been,—a situation then so clearly wrought, now blurred past comprehension. But there must have been love, or some love on his part. Otherwise he was bound to pray for the mother to predominate in the child, all but excluding its father.

Carinthia's image, as a result, ascended sovereignty, and he hung to it.

For if we are human creatures with consciences, nothing is more certain than that we make our taskmasters of those to whom we have done a wrong, the philosopher says. Between Lord Feltre and Gower Woodseer, influenced pretty equally by each of them, this young nobleman was wakening to the claims of others—Youth's infant conscience. Fleetwood now conceived the verbal supplication for his wife's forgiveness involved in the act of penance; and verbal meant abject; with him, going so far, it would mean naked, precise, no slurring. That he knew, and a tremor went over him. Women, then, are really the half of the world in power as much as in their number, if men pretend to a step above the savage. Or, well, his wife was a power.

He had forgotten the puzzle spoken of by Henrietta, when she used the word again and expressed her happiness in the prospect before them—caused by his presence, of course.

'You are aware, my dear lord, Janey worships her brother. He was defeated, by some dastardly contrivance, in a wager to do wonderful feats—for money! money! money! a large stake. How we come off our high horses! I hadn't an idea of money before I was married. I think of little else. My husband has notions of honour; he engaged himself to pay a legacy of debts; his uncle would not pay debts long due to him. He was reduced to the shift of wagering on his great strength and skill. He could have done it. His enemy managed—enemy there was! He had to sell out of the army in consequence. I shall never have Janey's face of suffering away from my sight. He is a soldier above all things. It seems hard on me, but I cannot blame him for snatching at an opportunity to win military distinction. He is in treaty for the post of aide to the Colonel—the General of the English contingent bound for Spain, for the cause of the Queen. My husband will undertake to be at the orders of his chief as soon as he can leave this place. Janey goes with him, according to present arrangements.'

Passing through a turnstile, that led from the road across a meadow-slope to the broken land below, Henrietta had view of the earl's hard white face, and she hastened to say: 'You have altered that, my lord. She is devoted to her brother; and her brother running dangers... and danger in itself is an attraction to her. But her husband will have the first claim. She has her good sense. She will never insist on going, if you oppose. She will be ready to fill her station. It will be-her pride and her pleasure.'

Henrietta continued in the vein of these assurances; and Carinthia's character was shooting lightnings through him, withering that of the woman who referred to his wife's good sense and her station; and certainly would not have betrayed herself by such drawlings if she had been very positive that Carinthia's disposition toward wealth and luxury resembled hers. She knew the reverse; or so his contemptuously generous effort to frame an apology for the stuff he was hearing considered it. His wife was lost to him. That fact smote on his breast the moment he heard of her desire to go with her brother.

Wildest of enterprises! But a criminal saw himself guilty of a large part in the disaster the two heroical souls were striving desperately to repair. If her Chillon went, Carinthia would go—sure as flame is drawn to air. The exceeding splendour in the character of a young woman, injured as she had been, soft to love, as he knew her, and giving her husband no other rival than a beloved brother, no ground of complaint save her devotion to her brother, pervaded him, without illuminating or lifting; rather with an indication of a foul contrast, that prostrated him.

Half of our funny heathen lives we are bent double to gather things we have tossed away! was one of the numbers of apposite sayings that hummed about him, for a chorus of the world's old wisdom in derision, when he descended the heathy path and had sight of Carinthia beside her Chillon. Would it be the same thing if he had it in hand again? Did he wish it to be the same? Was not he another man? By the leap of his heart to the woman standing down there, he was a better man.

But recent spiritual exercises brought him to see superstitiously how by that sign she was lost to him; for everlastingly in this life the better pays for the worse; thus is the better a proved thing.

Both Chillon and Carinthia, it is probable, might have been stirred to deeper than compassion, had the proud young nobleman taken them into his breast to the scouring of it; exposing the grounds of his former brutality, his gradual enlightenment, his ultimate acknowledgement of the pricelessness of the woman he had won to lose her. An imploring of forgiveness would not have been necessary with those two, however great their—or the woman's—astonishment at the revelation of an abysmal male humanity. A complete exposure of past meanness is the deed of present courage certain of its reward without as well as within; for then we show our fellows that the slough is cast. But life is a continuous fight; and members of the social world display its degree of civilization by fighting in armour; most of them are born in it; and their armour is more sensitive than their skins. It was Fleetwood's instinct of his inability to fling it off utterly which warned him of his loss of the wife, whose enthusiasm to wait on her brother in danger might have subsided into the channel of duty, even tenderness, had he been able resolutely to strip himself bare. This was the further impossible to him, because of a belief he now imposed upon himself, to cover the cowardly shrinking from so extreme a penitential act, that such confessions are due from men to the priest only, and that he could confess wholly and absolutely to the priest—to heaven, therefore, under seal, and in safety, but with perfect repentance.

So, compelled to keep his inner self unknown, he fronted Chillon; courteously, in the somewhat lofty seeming of a guarded manner, he requested audience for a few minutes; observing the princely figure of the once hated man, and understanding Henrietta's sheer womanly choice of him; Carinthia's idolatry, too, as soon as he had spoken. The man was in his voice.

Chillon said: 'It concerns my sister, I have to think. In that case, her wish is to be present. Your lordship will shorten the number of minutes for the interview by permitting it.'

Fleetwood encountered Carinthia's eyes. They did not entreat or defy. They seconded her brother, and were a civil shining naught on her husband. He bowed his head, constrained, feeling heavily the two to one.

She replied to the look: 'My brother and I have a single mind. We save time by speaking three together, my lord.'

He was led into the long room of the workshop, where various patterns of muskets, rifles, pistols, and swords were stars, crosses, wedges, over the walls, and a varnished wooden model of a piece of cannon occupied the middle place, on a block.

Contempt of military weapons and ridicule of the art of war were common on those days among a people beginning to sit with habitual snugness at the festive board provided for them by the valour of their fathers. Fleetwood had not been on the side of the banqueting citizens, though his country's journals and her feasted popular wits made a powerful current to whelm opposition. But the appearance of the woman, his wife, here, her head surrounded by destructive engines in the form of trophy, and the knowledge that this woman bearing his name designed to be out at the heels of a foreign army or tag-rag of uniformed rascals, inspired him to reprobate men's bad old game as heartily as good sense does in the abstract, and as derisively as it is the way with comfortable islanders before the midnight trumpet-notes of panic have tumbled them to their legs. He took his chair; sickened.

He was the next moment taking Carinthia's impression of Chillon, compelled to it by an admiration that men and women have alike for shapes of strength in the mould of grace, over whose firm build a flicker of agility seems to run. For the young soldier's figure was visibly in its repose prompt to action as the mind's movement. This was her brother; her enthusiasm for her brother was explained to him. No sooner did he have the conception of it than it plucked at him painfully; and, feeling himself physically eclipsed by the object of Carinthia's enthusiasm, his pride of the rival counselled him to preserve the mask on what was going on within, lest it should be seen that he was also morally beaten at the outset. A trained observation told him, moreover, that her Chillon's correctly handsome features, despite their conventional urbanity, could knit to smite, and held less of the reserves of mercy behind them than Carinthia's glorious barbaric ruggedness. Her eyes, each time she looked at her brother, had, without doating, the light as of the rise of happy tears to the underlids as they had on a certain day at the altar, when 'my lord' was 'my husband,'—more shyly then. He would have said, as beautifully, but for envy of the frank, pellucid worship in that look on her proved hero. It was the jewel of all the earth to win back to himself; and it subjected him, through his desire for it, to a measurement with her idol, in character, quality, strength, hardness. He heard the couple pronouncing sentence of his loss by anticipation.

Why had she primed her brother to propose the council of three? Addressing them separately, he could have been his better or truer self. The sensation of the check imposed on him was instructive as to her craft and the direction of her wishes. She preferred the braving of hazards and horrors beside her brother, in scorn of the advantages he could offer; and he yearned to her for despising by comparison the bribe he proposed in the hope that he might win her to him. She was with religion to let him know the meanness of wealth.

Thus, at the edge of the debate, or contest, the young lord's essential nobility disarmed him; and the revealing of it, which would have appealed to Carinthia and Chillon both, was forbidden by its constituent pride, which helped him to live and stood obstructing explanatory speech.

CHAPTER XLIV

BETWEEN THE EARL, THE COUNTESS AND HER BROTHER, AND OF A SILVER CROSS

Carinthia was pleased by hearing Lord Fleetwood say to her: 'Your Madge and my Gower are waiting to have the day named for them.'

She said: 'I respect him so much for his choice of Madge. They shall not wait, if I am to decide.'

'Old Mr. Woodseer has undertaken to join them.'

'It is in Whitechapel they will be married.'

The blow that struck was not intended, and Fleetwood passed it, under her brother's judicial eye. Any small chance word may carry a sting for the neophyte in penitence.

'My lawyers will send down the settlement on her, to be read to them to-day or to-morrow. With the interest on that and the sum he tells me he has in the Funds, they keep the wolf from the door—a cottage door. They have their cottage. There's an old song of love in a cottage. His liking for it makes him seem wiser than his clever sayings. He'll work in that cottage.'

'They have a good friend to them in you, my lord. It will not be poverty for their simple wants. I hear of the little cottage in Surrey where they are to lodge at first, before they take one of their own.'

'We will visit them.'

'When I am in England I shall visit them often.'

He submitted.

'The man up here wounded is recovering?'

'Yes, my lord. I am learning to nurse the wounded, with the surgeon to direct me.'

'Matters are sobering down?—The workmen?'

'They listen to reason so willingly when we speak personally, we find.'

The earl addressed Chillon. 'Your project of a Spanish expedition reminds me of favourable reports of your chief.'

'Thoroughly able and up to the work,' Chillon answered.

'Queer people to meddle with.'

'We 're on the right side on the dispute.'

'It counts, Napoleon says. A Spanish civil war promises bloody doings.'

'Any war does that.'

'In the Peninsula it's war to the knife, a merciless business.'

'Good schooling for the profession.'

Fleetwood glanced: she was collected and attentive. 'I hear from Mrs. Levellier that Carinthia would like to be your companion.'

'My sister has the making of a serviceable hospital nurse.'

'You hear the chatter of London!'

'I have heard it.'

'You encourage her, Mr. Levellier?'

'She will be useful—better there than here, my lord.'

'I claim a part in the consultation.'

'There 's no consultation; she determines to go.'

'We can advise her of all the risks.'

'She has weighed them, every one.'

'In the event of accidents, the responsibility for having persuaded her would rest on you.'

'My brother has not persuaded me,' Carinthia's belltones intervened. 'I proposed it. The persuasion was mine. It is my happiness to be near him, helping, if I can.'

'Lady Fleetwood, I am entitled to think that your brother yielded to a request urged in ignorance of the nature of the risks a woman runs.'

'My brother does not yield to a request without examining it all round, my lord, and I do not. I know the risks. An evil that we should not endure,—life may go. There can be no fear for me.'

She spoke plain truth. The soul of this woman came out in its radiance to subdue him, as her visage sometimes did; and her voice enlarged her words. She was a warrior woman, Life her sword, Death her target, never to be put to shame, unconquerable. No such symbolical image smote him, but he had an impression, the prose of it. As in the scene of the miners' cottares, her lord could have knelt to her: and for an unprotesting longer space now. He choked a sigh, shrugged, and said, in the world's patient manner with mad people: 'You have set your mind on it; you see it rose-coloured. You would not fear, no, but your friends would have good reason to fear. It's a menagerie in revolt over there. It is not really the place for you. Abandon the thought, I beg.'

'I shall, if my brother does not go,' said Carinthia.

Laughter of spite at a remark either silly or slyly defiant was checked in Fleetwood by the horror of the feeling that she had gone, was ankle-deep in bloody mire, captive, prey of a rabble soldiery, meditating the shot or stab of the blessed end out of woman's half of our human muddle.

He said to Chillon: 'Pardon me, war is a detestable game. Women in the thick of it add a touch to the brutal hideousness of the whole thing.'

Chillon said: 'We are all of that opinion. Men have to play the game; women serving in hospital make it humaner.'

'Their hospitals are not safe.'

'Well! Safety!'

For safety is nowhere to be had. But the earl pleaded: 'At least in our country.'

'In our country women are safe?'

'They are, we may say, protected.'

'Laws and constables are poor protection for them.'

'The women we name ladies are pretty safe, as a rule.'

'My sister, then, was the exception.'

After a burning half minute the earl said: 'I have to hear it from you, Mr. Levellier. You see me here.'

That was handsomely spoken. But Lord Fleetwood had been judged and put aside. His opening of an old case to hint at repentance for brutality annoyed the man who had let him go scathless for a sister's sake.

'The grounds of your coming, my lord, are not seen; my time is short.'

'I must, I repeat, be consulted with regard to Lady Fleetwood's movements.'

'My sister does not acknowledge your claim.'

'The Countess of Fleetwood's acts involve her husband.'

'One has to listen at times to what old sailors call Caribbee!' Chillon exclaimed impatiently, half aloud. 'My sister received your title; she has to support it. She did not receive the treatment of a wife:—or lady, or woman, or domestic animal. The bond is broken, as far as it bears on her subjection. She holds to the rite, thinks it sacred. You can be at rest as to her behaviour. In other respects, your lordship does not exist for her.'

'The father of her child must exist for her.'

'You raise that curtain, my lord!'

In the presence of three it would not bear a shaking.

Carinthia said, in pity of his torture:—

'I have my freedom, and am thankful for it, to follow my brother, to share his dangers with him. That is more to me than luxury and the married state. I take only my freedom.'

'Our boy? You take the boy?'

'My child is with my sister Henrietta!

'Where?'

'We none know yet.'

'You still mistrust me?'

Her eyes were on a man that she had put from her peaceably; and she replied, with sweetness in his ears, with shocks to a sinking heart, 'My lord, you may learn to be a gentle father to the child. I pray you may. My brother and I will go. If it is death for us, I pray my child may have his father, and God directing his father.'

Her speech had the clang of the final.

'Yes, I hope—if it be the worst happening, I pray, too,' said he, and drooped and brightened desperately: 'But you, too, Carinthia, you could aid by staying, by being with the boy and me. Carinthia!' he clasped her name, the vapour left to him of her: 'I have learnt learnt what I am, what you are; I have to climb a height to win back the wife I threw away. She was unknown to me; I to myself nearly as much. I sent a warning of the kind of husband for you—a poor kind; I just knew myself well enough for that. You claimed my word—the blessing of my life, if I had known it! We were married; I played—I see the beast I played. Money is power, they say. I see the means it is to damn the soul, unless we—unless a man does what I do now.'

Fleetwood stopped. He had never spoken such words—arterial words, as they were, though the commonest, and with moist brows, dry lips, he could have resumed, have said more, have taken this woman, this dream of the former bride, the present stranger, into his chamber of the brave aims and sentenced deeds. Her brother in the room was the barrier; and she sat mute, large-eyed, expressionless. He had plunged low in the man's hearing; the air of his lungs was thick, hard to breathe, for shame of a degradation so extreme.

Chillon imagined him to be sighing. He had to listen further. 'Soul' had been an uttered word. When the dishonouring and mishandling brute of a young nobleman stuttered a compliment to Carinthia on her 'faith in God's assistance and the efficacy of prayer,' he jumped to his legs, not to be shouting 'Hound!' at him. He said, under control: 'God's name shall be left to the Church. My sister need not be further troubled. She has shown she is not persuaded by me. Matters arranged here quickly,—we start. If I am asked whether I think she does wisely to run the risks in an insurrectionary country rather than remain at home exposed to the honours and amusements your lordship offers, I think so; she is acting in her best interests. She has the choice of being abroad with me or staying here unguarded by me. She has had her experience. She chooses rightly. Paint the risks she runs, you lay the colours on those she escapes.' She thanks the treatment she has undergone for her freedom to choose. I am responsible for nothing but the not having stood against her most wretched marriage. It might have been foreseen. Out there in the war she is protected. Here she is with—I spare your lordship the name.'

Fleetwood would have heard harsher had he not been Carinthia's husband. He withheld his reply. The language moved him to proud hostility: but the speaker was Carinthia's brother.

He said to her: 'You won't forget Gower and Madge?'

She gave him a smile in saying: 'It shall be settled for a day after next week.'

The forms of courtesy were exchanged.

At the closing of the door on him, Chillon said: 'He did send a message: I gathered it—without the words—from our Uncle Griphard. I thought him in honour bound to you—and it suited me that I should.'

'I was a blindfold girl, dearest; no warning would have given me sight,' said Carinthia. 'That was my treachery to the love of my brother.. I dream of father and mother reproaching me.'

The misery of her time in England had darkened her mind's picture of the early hour with Chillon on the heights above the forsaken old home; and the enthusiasm of her renewed devotion to her brother giving it again, as no light of a lost Eden, as the brilliant step she was taking with him from their morning Eastern Alps to smoky-crimson Pyrenees and Spanish Sierras; she could imagine the cavernous interval her punishment for having abandoned a sister's duties in the quest of personal happiness.

But simultaneously, the growing force of her mind's intelligence, wherein was no enthusiasm to misdirect by overcolouring, enabled her to gather more than a suspicion of comparative feebleness in the man stripped of his terrors. She penetrated the discrowned tyrant's nature some distance, deep enough to be quit of her foregoing alarms. These, combined with his assured high style, had woven him the magical coat, threadbare to quiet scrutiny. She matched him beside her brother. The dwarfed object was then observed; and it was not for a woman to measure herself beside him. She came, however, of a powerful blood, and he was pressing her back on her resources: without the measurement or a thought of it, she did that which is the most ordinary and the least noticed of our daily acts in civilized intercourse, she subjected him to the trial of the elements composing him, by collision with what she felt of her own; and it was because she felt them strongly, aware of her feeling them, but unaware of any conflict, that the wrestle occurred. She flung him, pitied him, and passed on along her path elsewhere. This can be done when love is gone. It is done more or less at any meeting of men and men; and men and women who love not are perpetually doing it, unconsciously or sensibly. Even in their love, a time for the trial arrives among certain of them; and the leadership is assumed, and submission ensues, tacitly; nothing of the contention being spoken, perhaps, nothing definitely known.

In Carinthia's case, her revived enthusiasm for her brother drove to the penetration of the husband pleading to thwart its course. His offer was wealth: that is, luxury, amusement, ease. The sub-audible 'himself' into the bargain was disregarded, not counting with one who was an upward rush of fire at the thought that she was called to share her brother's dangers.

Chillon cordially believed the earl to be the pestilent half madman, junction with whom is a constant trepidation for the wife, when it is not a screaming plight. He said so, and Carinthia let him retain his opinion. She would have said it herself to support her scheme, though 'mad' applied to a man moving in the world with other men was not understood by her.

With Henrietta for the earl's advocate, she was patient as the deaf rock-wall enthusiasm can be against entreaties to change its direction or bid it disperse: The 'private band of picked musicians' at the disposal of the Countess of Fleetwood, and Opera singers (Henrietta mentioned resonant names) hired for wonderful nights at Esslemont and Calesford or on board the earl's beautiful schooner yacht, were no temptation. Nor did Henrietta's allusions to his broken appearance move his wife, except in her saying regretfully: 'He changes.'

On the hall table at Esslemont, a letter from his bankers informed the earl of a considerable sum of money paid in to his account in the name of Lord Brailstone. Chumley Potts, hanging at him like a dog without a master since the death of his friend Ambrose, had journeyed down: 'Anxious about you,' he said. Anxious about or attracted by the possessor of Ambrose Mallard's 'clean sweeper,' the silver-mounted small pistol; sight of which he begged to have; and to lengthened his jaw on hearing it was loaded. A loaded pistol, this dark little one to the right of the earl's blotting-pad and pens, had the look of a fearful link with his fallen chaps and fishy hue. Potts maundered moralities upon 'life,' holding the thing in his hand, weighing it, eyeing the muzzle. He 'couldn't help thinking of what is going to happen to us after it all': and 'Brosey knows now!' was followed by a twitch of one cheek and the ejaculation 'Forever!' Fleetwood alive and Ambrose dead were plucking the startled worldling to a peep over the verge into our abyss; and the young lord's evident doing of the same commanded Chumley Potts' imitation of him under the cloud Ambrose had become for both of them.

He was recommended to see Lord Feltre, if he had a desire to be instructed on the subject of the mitigation of our pains in the regions below. Potts affirmed that he meant to die a Protestant Christian. Thereupon, carrying a leaden burden of unlaughed laughable stuff in his breast, and Chummy's concluding remark to speed him: 'Damn it, no, we'll stick to our religion!' Fleetwood strode off to his library, and with the names of the Ixionides of his acquaintance ringing round his head, proceeded to strike one of them off the number privileged at the moment to intrude on him. Others would follow; this one must be the first to go. He wrote the famous letter to Lord Brailstone, which debarred the wily pursuer from any pretext to be running down into Mrs. Levellier's neighbourhood, and also precluded the chance of his meeting the fair lady at Calesford. With the brevity equivalent to the flick of a glove on the cheek, Lord Brailstone was given to understand by Lord Fleetwood that relations were at an end between them. No explanation was added; a single sentence executed the work, and in the third person. He did not once reflect on the outcry in the ear of London coming from the receiver of such a letter upon payment of a debt.

The letter posted and flying, Lord Fleetwood was kinder to Chumley Potts; he had a friendly word for Gower Woodseer; though both were heathens, after their diverse fashions, neither of them likely ever to set out upon the grand old road of Rome: Lord Feltre's 'Appian Way of the Saints and Comforters.'

Chummy was pardoned when they separated at night for his reiterated allusions to the temptation of poor Ambrose Mallard's conclusive little weapon lying on the library table within reach of a man's arm-chair: in its case, and the case locked, yes, but easily opened, 'provoking every damnable sort of mortal curiosity!' The soundest men among us have their fits of the blues, Fleetwood was told. 'Not wholesome!' Chummy shook his head resolutely, and made himself comprehensibly mysterious. He meant well. He begged his old friend to promise he would unload and keep it unloaded. 'For I know the infernal worry you have—deuced deal worse than a night's bad luck!' said he; and Fleetwood smiled sourly at the world's total ignorance of causes. His wretchedness was due now to the fact that the aforetime huntress refused to be captured. He took a silver cross from a table-drawer and laid it on the pistol-case. 'There, Chummy,' he said; that was all; not sermonizing or proselytizing. He was partly comprehended by Chumley Potts, fully a week later. The unsuspecting fellow, soon to be despatched in the suite of Brailstone, bore away an unwontedly affectionate dismissal to his bed, and spoke some rather squeamish words himself, as he recollected with disgust when he ran about over London repeating his executioner's.

The Cross on the pistol-case may have conduced to Lord Fleetwood's thought, that his days among unrepentant ephemeral Protestant sinners must have their immediate termination. These old friends were the plague-infected clothes he flung off his body. But the Cross where it lay, forbidding a movement of the hand to that box, was authoritative to decree his passage through a present torture, by the agency of the hand he held back from the solution of his perplexity, at the cost which his belief in the Eternal would pay. Henrietta had mentioned her husband's defeat, by some dastardly contrivance. He had to communicate, for the disburdening of his soul, not only that he was guilty, but the meanest of criminals, in being no more than half guilty. His training told him of the contempt women entertain toward the midway or cripple sinner, when they have no special desire to think him innocent. How write, or even how phrase his having merely breathed in his ruffian's hearing the wish that he might hear of her husband's defeat! And with what object? Here, too, a woman might, years hence, if not forgive, bend her head resignedly over the man's vile nature, supposing strong passion his motive. But the name for the actual motive? It would not bear writing, or any phrasing round it. An unsceptred despot bidden take a fair woman's eyes into his breast, saw and shrank. And now the eyes were Carinthia's: he saw a savage bridegroom, and a black ladder-climber, and the sweetest of pardoning brides, and the devil in him still insatiate for revenge upon her who held him to his word.

He wrote, read, tore the page, trimmed the lamp, and wrote again. He remembered Gower Woodseer's having warned him he would finish his career a monk. Not, like Feltre, an oily convert, but under the hood, yes, and extracting a chartreuse from his ramble through woods richer far than the philosopher's milk of Mother Nature's bosom. There flamed the burning signal of release from his torments; there his absolving refuge, instead of his writing fruitless, intricate, impossible stuff to a woman. The letter was renounced and shredded: the dedicated ascetic contemplated a hooded shape, washed of every earthly fleck. It proved how men may by power of grip squeeze raptures out of pain.

CHAPTER XLV

CONTAINS A RECORD OF WHAT WAS FEARED, WHAT WAS HOPED, AND WHAT HAPPENED

The Dame is at her thumps for attention to be called to 'the strangeness of it,' that a poor, small, sparse village, hardly above a hamlet, on the most unproductive of Kentish heights, part of old forest land, should at this period become 'the cynosure of a city beautifully named by the poet Great Augusta, and truly indeed the world's metropolis.'

Put aside her artful pother to rouse excitement at stages of a narrative, London's general eye upon little Croridge was but another instance of the extraordinary and not so wonderful. Lady Arpington, equal to a Parliament in herself, spoke of the place and the countess courted by her repentant lord. Brailstone and Chumley Potts were town criers of the executioner letter each had received from the earl; Potts with his chatter of a suicide's pistol kept loaded in a case under a two-inch-long silver Cross, and with sundry dramatic taps on the forehead, Jottings over the breast, and awful grimace of devoutness. There was no mistaking him. The young nobleman of the millions was watched; the town spyglass had him in its orbit. Tales of the ancestral Fleetwoods ran beside rumours of a Papist priest at the bedside of the Foredoomed to Error's dying mother. His wealth was counted, multiplied by the ready naughts of those who know little and dread much. Sir Meeson Corby referred to an argument Lord Fleetwood had held on an occasion hotly against the logical consistency of the Protestant faith; and to his alarm lest some day 'all that immense amount of money should slip away from us to favour the machinations of Roman Catholicism!' The Countess of Cressett, Livia, anticipated her no surprise at anything Lord Fleetwood might do: she knew him.

So thereupon, with the whirr of a covey on wing before the fowler, our crested three of immemorial antiquity and a presumptive immortality, the Ladies Endor, Eldritch, and Cowry, shot up again, hooting across the dormant chief city Old England's fell word of the scarlet shimmer above the nether pit-flames, Rome. An ancient horror in the blood of the population, conceiving the word to signify, beak, fang, and claw, the fiendish ancient enemy of the roasting day of yore, heard and echoed. Sleepless at the work of the sapper, in preparation for the tiger's leap, Rome is keen to spy the foothold of English stability, and her clasp of a pillar of the structure sends tremors to our foundations.

The coupling of Rome and England's wealthiest nobleman struck a match to terrorize the Fire Insurance of Smithfield. That meteoric, intractable, perhaps wicked, but popular, reputedly clever; manifestly evil-starred, enormously wealthy, young Earl of Fleetwood, wedded to an adventuress, and a target for the scandals emanating from the woman, was daily, without omission of a day, seen walking Piccadilly pavement in company once more with the pervert, the Jesuit agent, that crafty Catesby of a Lord Feltre, arm in arm the pair of them, and uninterruptedly conversing, utterly unlike Englishmen. Mr. Rose Mackrell passed them, and his breezy salutation of the earl was unobserved in my lord's vacant glass optics, as he sketched the scene. London had report of the sinister tempter and the imperilled young probationer undisguisedly entering the Roman Catholic chapel of a fashionable district-chapel erected on pervert's legacies, down a small street at the corner of a grandee square, by tolerance or connivance of our constabulary,—entering it linked; and linked they issued, their heads bent; for the operation of the tonsure, you would say. Two English noblemen! But is there no legislation to stop the disease? Our female government asks it vixenly of our impotent male; which pretends, beneath an air of sympathy, that we should abstain from any compulsory action upon the law to interfere, though the situation is confessedly grave; and the aspect men assume is correspondingly, to the last degree provokingly, grave-half alive that they are, or void of patriotism, or Babylonian at heart!

Lord Fleetwood's yet undocked old associates vowed he 'smelt strong' of the fumes of the whirled silver censer-balls. His disfavour had caused a stoppage of supplies, causing vociferous abomination of their successful rivals, the Romish priests. Captain Abrane sniffed, loud as a horse, condemnatory as a cat, in speaking of him. He said: 'By George, it comes to this; we shall have to turn Catholics for a loan!' Watchdogs of the three repeated the gigantic gambler's melancholy roar. And, see what gap, cried the ratiocination of alarm, see the landslip it is in our body, national and religious, when exalted personages go that way to Rome!

As you and the world have reflected in your sager moods, an ordinary pebble may roll where it likes, for individualism of the multitudinously obscure little affects us. Not so the costly jewel, which is a congregation of ourselves, in our envies and longings and genuflexions thick about its lustres. The lapses of precious things must needs carry us, both by weight and example, and it will ceaselessly be, that we are possessed by the treasure we possess, we hang on it. A still, small voice of England's mind under panic sent up these truisms containing admonitions to the governing Ladies. They, the most conservative of earthly bodies, clamoured in return, like cloud-scud witches that have caught fire at their skirts from the torches of marsh-fire radicals. They cited for his arrest the titled millionaire who made a slide for the idiots of the kingdom; they stigmatized our liberty as a sophistry, unless we have in it the sustaining element of justice; and where is the justice that punishes his country for any fatal course a mad young Croesus may take! They shackled the hands of testators, who endangered the salvation of coroneted boys by having sanction to bequeath vast wealth in bulk. They said, in truth, that it was the liberty to be un-Christian. Finally, they screeched a petitioning of Parliament to devote a night to a sitting, and empower the Lord Chancellor to lay an embargo on the personal as well as the real estate of wealthy perverts; in common prudence depriving Rome of the coveted means to turn our religious weapons against us.

The three guardian ladies and their strings of followers headed over the fevered and benighted town, as the records of the period attest, windpiping these and similar Solan notes from the undigested cropful of alarms Lord Fleetwood's expected conduct crammed into them. They and all the world traced his present madness to the act foregoing: that marriage! They reviewed it to deplore it, every known incident and the numbers imagined; yet merely to deplore: frightful comparisons of then with now rendered the historical shock to the marriage market matter for a sick smile. Evil genius of some sort beside him the wealthy young nobleman is sure to have. He has got rid of one to take up with a viler. First, a sluttish trollop of German origin is foisted on him for life; next, he is misled to abjure the faith of his fathers for Rome. But patently, desperation in the husband of such a wife weakened his resistance to the Roman Catholic pervert's insinuations. There we punctuate the full stop to our inquiries; we have the secret.

And upon that, suddenly comes a cyclonic gust; and gossip twirls, whines, and falls to the twanging of an entirely new set of notes, that furnish a tolerably agreeable tune, on the whole. O hear! The Marchioness of Arpington proclaims not merely acquaintanceship with Lord Fleetwood's countess, she professes esteem for the young person. She has been heard to say, that if the Principality of Wales were not a royal title, a dignity of the kind would be conferred by the people of those mountains on the Countess of Fleetwood: such unbounded enthusiasm there was for her character when she sojourned down there. As it is, they do speak of her in their Welsh by some title. Their bards are offered prizes to celebrate her deeds. You remember the regiment of mounted Welsh gentlemen escorting her to her Kentish seat, with their band of the three-stringed harps! She is well-born, educated, handsome, a perfectly honest woman, and a sound Protestant. Quite the reverse of Lord Fleetwood's seeking to escape her, it is she who flies; she cannot forgive him his cruelties and infidelities: and that is the reason why he threatens to commit the act of despair. Only she can save him! She has flown for refuge to her uncle, Lord Levellier's house at a place named Croridge—not in the gazetteer—hard of access and a home of poachers, where shooting goes on hourly; but most picturesque and romantic, as she herself is! Lady Arpington found her there, nursing one of the wounded, and her uncle on his death-bed; obdurate all round against her husband, but pensive when supplicated to consider her country endangered by Rome. She is a fervent patriot. The tales of her Whitechapel origin, and heading mobs wielding bludgeons, are absolutely false, traceable to scandalizing anecdotists like Mr. Rose Mackrell. She is the beautiful example of an injured wife doing honour to her sex in the punishment of a faithless husband, yet so little cherishing her natural right to deal him retribution, that we dare hope she will listen to her patriotic duty in consenting to the reconcilement, which is Lord Fleetwood's alternative: his wife or Rome! They say she has an incommunicable charm, accounting for the price he puts on her now she holds aloof and he misses it. Let her but rescue him from England's most vigilant of her deadly enemies, she will be entitled to the nation's lasting gratitude. She has her opportunity for winning the Anglican English, as formerly she won the Dissenter Welsh. She may yet be the means of leading back the latter to our fold.

A notation of the cries in air at a time of surgent public excitement can hardly yield us music; and the wording of them, by the aid of compounds and transplants, metaphors and similes only just within range of the arrows of Phoebus' bow (i.e. the farthest flight known), would, while it might imitate the latent poetry, expose venturesome writers to the wrath of a people commendably believing their language a perfected instrument when they prefer the request for a plateful, and commissioning their literary police to brain audacious experimenters who enlarge or wing it beyond the downright aim at that mark. The gossip of the time must therefore appear commonplace, in resemblance to the panting venue a terre of the toad, instead of the fiery steed's; although we have documentary evidence that our country's heart was moved;—in no common degree, Dr. Glossop's lucid English has it, at the head of a broadsheet ballad discovered by him, wherein the connubially inclined young earl and the nation in turn beseech the countess to resume her place at Esslemont, and so save both from a terrific dragon's jaw, scarlet as the infernal flames; described as fascinating—

'The classes with the crests,
And the lining to their vests,
Till down they jump, and empty leave
A headless trunk that rests.'

These ballads, burlesque to present reading, mainly intended for burlesque by the wits who dogged without much enlivening an anxious period of our history, when corner-stones were falling the way the young lord of the millions threatened to go, did, there is little doubt, according to another part of their design (Rose Mackrell boasts it indirectly in his Memoirs), interpret public opinion, that is, the English humour of it—the half laugh in their passing and not simulated shudder.

Carinthia had a study of the humours of English character in the person of the wounded man she nursed on little Croridge, imagining it the most unobserved of English homes, and herself as unimportant an object. Daniel Charner took his wound, as he took his medicine and his posset from her hand, kindly, and seemed to have a charitable understanding of Lord Levellier now that the old nobleman had driven a pellet of lead into him and laid him flat. It pleased him to assure her that his mates were men of their word, and had promised to pay the old lord with a 'rouse' for it, nothing worse. Her father used to speak of the 'clean hearts of the English' as to the husbanding of revenge; that is, the 'no spot of bad blood' to vitiate them. Captain John Peter seconded all good-humoured fighters 'for the long account': they will surely win; and it was one of his maxims: 'My foe can spoil my face; he beats me if he spoils my temper.'

Recalling the scene of her bridal day—the two strong Englishmen at the shake of hands, that had spoiled one another's faces, she was enlightened with a comprehension of her father's love for the people; seeing the spiritual of the gross ugly picture, as not every man can do, and but a warrior Joan among women. Chillon shall teach the Spanish people English heartiness, she thought. Lord Fleetwood's remarks on the expedition would have sufficed to stamp it righteous with her; that was her logic of the low valuation of him. She fancied herself absolutely released at his departure. Neither her sister Riette nor her friend Owain, administering sentiment and common sense to her by turns, could conceive how the passion for the recovery of her brother's military name fed the hope that she might aid in it, how the hope fed the passion. She had besides her hunger to be at the work she could do; her Chillon's glory for morning sky above it.

Such was the mind Lady Arpington brought the world's wisdom to bear upon; deeming it in the end female only in its wildness and obstinacy. Carinthia's answers were few, barely varied. Her repetition of 'my brother' irritated the great lady, whose argument was directed to make her see that these duties toward her brother were primarily owing to her husband, the man she would reclaim and could guide. And the Countess of Fleetwood's position, her duty to society, her dispensing of splendid hospitality, the strengthening of her husband to do his duty to the nation, the saving of him from a fatal step-from Rome; these were considerations for a reasonable woman to weigh before she threw up all to be off on the maddest of adventures. 'Inconceivable, my dear child!' Lady Arpington proceeded until she heard herself as droning.

Carinthia's unmoved aspect of courteous attention appeared to invoke the prolongation of the sermon it criticized. It had an air of reversing their positions while she listened to the charge of folly, and incidentally replied.

Her reason for not fearing Roman Catholic encroachments was, she said, her having known good Catholics in the country she came from. For herself, she should die professing the faith of her father and mother. Behind her correct demeanour a rustic intelligence was exhibited. She appreciated her duty to her marriage oath: 'My husband's honour is quite safe with me.' Neither England nor religion, nor woman's proper devotion to a husband's temporal and spiritual welfare, had claims rivalling her devotion to her brother. She could not explain a devotion that instigated her to an insensate course. It seemed a kind of enthusiasm; and it was coldly spoken; in the tone referring to 'her husband's honour.' Her brother's enterprise had her approval because 'her mother's prayer was for him to serve in the English army.' By running over to take a side in a Spanish squabble? she was asked and answered: 'He will learn war; my Chillon will show his value; he will come back a tried soldier.'

She counted on his coming back? She did.

'I cannot take a step forward without counting on success. We know the chances we are to meet. My father has written of death. We do not fear it, so it is nothing to us. We shall go together; we shall not have to weep for one another.'

The strange young woman's avoidance of any popular sniffle of the pathetic had a recognized merit.

'Tell me,' Lady Arpington said abruptly; 'this maid of yours, who is to marry the secretary, or whatever he was—you are satisfied with her?'

'She is my dear servant Madge.' A cloud opened as Carinthia spoke the name. 'She will be a true wife to him. They will always be my friends!'

Nothing against the earl in that direction, apparently; unless his countess was blest with the density of frigidity.

Society's emissary sketched its perils for unprotected beautiful woman; an outline of the London quadrille Henrietta danced in; and she glanced at Carinthia and asked: 'Have you thought of it?'

Carinthia's eyes were on the great lady's. Their meaning was, 'You hit my chief thought.' They were read as her farthest thought. For the hint of Henrietta's weakness deadened her feelings with a reminder of warm and continued solicitations rebutted; the beautiful creature's tortures at the idea of her exile from England. An outwearied hopelessness expressed a passive sentiment very like indifference in the clear wide gaze. She replied: 'I have. My proposal to her was Cadiz, with both our young ones. She will not.'

And there is an end to that part of the question! Lady Arpington interpreted it, by the gaze more than the words, under subjection of the young woman's character. Nevertheless, she bore away Carinthia's consent to a final meeting with the earl at her house in London, as soon as things were settled at Croridge. Chillon, whom she saw, was just as hard, unforgiving, careless of his country's dearest interests; brother and sister were one heart of their one blood. She mentioned the general impression in town, that the countess and only she could save the earl from Rome. A flash of polite laughter was Chillon's response. But after her inspection of the elegant athlete, she did fancy it possible for a young wife, even for Henrietta, to bear his name proudly in his absence—if that was worth a moment's consideration beside the serious issues involved in her appeal to the countess; especially when the suggestion regarding young wives left unprotected, delicately conveyed to the husband, had failed of its purpose. The handsome husband's brows fluttered an interrogation, as if her clear-obscure should be further lighted; and it could not be done. He weighed the wife by the measure of the sister, perhaps; or his military head had no room for either. His callousness to the danger of his country's disintegration, from the incessant, becoming overt, attacks of a foreign priesthood might—an indignant great lady's precipitation to prophecy said would—bring chastisement on him. She said it, and she liked Henrietta, vowing to defeat her forecast as well as she could in a land seeming forsaken by stable principles; its nobles breaking up its national church, going over to Rome, embracing the faith of the impostor Mahomet.

Gossip fed to the starvation bone of Lady Arpington's report, until one late afternoon, memorable for the breeding heat in the van of elemental artillery, newsboys waved damp sheets of fresh print through the streets, and society's guardians were brought to confess, in shame and gladness, that they had been growing sceptical of the active assistance of Providence. At first the 'Terrible explosion of gunpowder at Croridge' alarmed them lest the timely Power should have done too much. A day later the general agitation was pacified; Lady Arpington circulated the word 'safe,' and the world knew the disaster had not engulphed Lady Fleetwood's valuable life. She had the news by word of mouth from the lovely Mrs. Kirby-Levellier, sister-in-law to the countess. We are convinced we have proof of Providence intervening when some terrific event of the number at its disposal accomplishes the thing and no more than the thing desired. Pitiful though it may seem for a miserly old lord to be blown up in his bed, it is necessarily a subject of congratulation if the life, or poor remnant of a life, sacrificed was an impediment to our righteous wishes. But this is a theme for the Dame, who would full surely have committed another breach of the treaty, had there not been allusion to her sisterhood's view of the government of human affairs.

On the day preceding the catastrophe, Chillon's men returned to work. He and Carinthia and Mr. Wythan lunched with Henrietta at Stoneridge. Walking down to Lekkatts, they were astounded to see the figure of the spectral old lord on the plank to the powder store, clad in his long black cloak, erect. He was crossing, he told them, to count his barrels; a dream had disturbed him. Chillon fell to rapid talk upon various points of business, and dispersed Lord Levellier's memory relating to his errand. Leaning on Carinthia's arm, he went back to the house, where he was put to bed in peace of mind. His resuscitated physical vigour blocked all speculation for the young people assembled at Stoneridge that night. They hardly spoke; they strangled thoughts forming as larvae of wishes. Henrietta would be away to Lady Arpington's next day, Mr. Wythan to Wales. The two voyagers were sadder by sympathy than the two whom they were leaving to the clock's round of desert sameness. About ten at night Chillon and Mr. Wythan escorted Carinthia, for the night's watch beside her uncle, down to Lekkatts. It was midway that the knocks on air, as of a muffled mallet at a door and at farther doors of caverns, smote their ears and shook the ground.

After an instant of the silence following a shock, Carinthia touched her brother's arm; and Chillon said:

'Not my powder!'

They ran till they had Lekkatts in sight. A half moon showed the house; it stood. Fifty paces below, a column of opal smoke had begun to wreathe and stretch a languid flag. The 'rouse' promised to Lord Levellier by Daniel Charner's humorous mates had hit beyond its aim. Intended to give him a start—or 'One-er in return,' it surpassed his angry shot at the body of them in effect.

Carinthia entered his room and saw that he was lying stretched restfully. She whispered of this to Chillon, and began upon her watch, reading her Spanish phrasebook; and she could have wept, if she had been a woman for tears. Her duty to stay in England with Chillon's fair wife crossed the beckoning pages like a black smoke. Her passion to go and share her brother's dangers left the question of its righteousness at each fall of the big breath.

Her uncle's grey head on his pillow was like a flintstone in chalk under her look by light of dawn; the chin had dropped.

CHAPTER XLVI

A CHAPTER OF UNDERCURRENTS AND SOME SURFACE FLASHES

Thus a round and a good old English practical repartee, worthy a place in England's book of her historical popular jests; conceived ingeniously, no bit murderously, even humanely, if Englishmen are to be allowed indulgence of a jolly hit back for an injury—more a feint than a real stroke—gave the miserly veteran his final quake and cut Chillon's knot.

Lord Levellier dead of the joke detracted from the funny idea there had been in the anticipation of his hearing the libertine explosion of his grand new powder, and coming out cloaked to see what walls remained upright. Its cleverness, however, was magnified by the shades into which it had despatched him. The man who started the 'rouse for old Griphard' was named: nor did he shuffle his honours off. Chillon accused him, and he regretfully grinned; he would have owned to it eloquently, excited by the extreme ingenuity, but humour at the criminal bar is an abject thing, that has to borrow from metaphysics for the expository words. He lacked them entirely, and as he could not, fronting his master, supply the defect with oaths, he drew up and let out on the dead old lord, who wanted a few pounds of blasting powder, like anything else in everybody's way. Chillon expected the lowest of his countrymen to show some degree of chivalry upon occasions like the present. He was too young to perceive how it is, that a block of our speech in the needed direction drives it storming in another, not the one closely expressing us. Carinthia liked the man; she was grieved to hear of his having got the sack summarily, when he might have had a further month of service or a month's pay. Had not the workmen's forbearance been much tried? And they had not stolen, they had bought the powder, only intending to startle.

She touched her brother's native sense of fairness and vexed him with his cowardly devil of impatience, which kicked at a simply stupid common man, and behaved to a lordly offender, smelling rascal, civilly. Just as her father would have—treated the matter, she said: 'Are we sorry for what has happened, Chillon?' The man had gone, the injustice was done; the master was left to reflect on the part played by his inheritance of the half share of ninety thousand pounds in his proper respect for Lord Levellier's memory. Harsh to an inferior is a horrible charge. But the position of debtor to a titled cur brings a worse for endurance. Knowing a part of Lord Fleetwood's message to Lord Levellier suppressed, the bride's brother, her chief guardian, had treated the omission as of no importance, and had all the while understood that he ought to give her his full guess at the reading of it: or so his racked mind understood it now. His old father had said: A dumb tongue can be a heavy liar; and, Lies are usurers' coin we pay for ten thousand per cent. His harshness in the past hour to a workman who had suffered with him and had not intended serious mischief was Chillon's unsounded motive for the resolution to be out of debt to the man he loathed. There is a Muse that smiles aloft surveying our acts from the well-springs.

Carinthia heard her brother's fuller version of the earl's communication to her uncle before the wild day of her marriage. 'Not particularly fitted for the married state,' Chillon phrased it, saying: 'He seems to have known himself, he was honest so far.' She was advised to think it over, that the man was her husband.

She had her brother's heart in her breast, she could not misread him. She thought it over, and felt a slight drag of compassion for the reluctant bridegroom. That was a stretch long leagues distant from love with her; the sort of feeling one has for strange animals hurt and she had in her childish blindness done him a hurt, and he had bitten her. He was a weak young nobleman; he had wealth for a likeness of strength; he had no glory about his head. Why had he not chosen a woman to sit beside him who would have fancied his coronet a glory and his luxury a kindness? But the poor young nobleman did not choose! The sadly comic of his keeping to the pledge of his word—his real wife—the tyrant of the tyrant—clothed him; the vision of him at the altar, and on the coach, and at the Royal Sovereign Inn, and into the dimness where a placidly smiling recollection met a curtain and lost the smile.

Suppose that her duty condemned her to stay in England on guard over Chillon's treasure! The perpetual struggle with a weak young nobleman of aimless tempers and rightabout changes, pretending to the part of husband, would, she foresaw, raise another figure of duty, enchaining a weak young woman. The world supported his pretension; and her passion to serve as Chillon's comrade sank at a damping because it was flame. Chillon had done that; Lady Arpington, to some extent; Henrietta more. A little incident, pointing in no direction, had left a shadow of a cloud, consequent upon Lady Arpington's mention of Henrietta's unprotectedness. Stepping up the hill to meet her sister, on the morning of Henrietta's departure for London under the convoy of Mr. Wythan, Carinthia's long sight spied Kit Ines, or a man like him, in the meadow between Lekkatts and Croridge. He stood before Henrietta, and vanished light-legged at a gesture. Henrietta was descending to take her leave of her busied husband; her cheeks were flushed; she would not speak of the fellow, except to reply, 'oh, a beggar,' and kept asking whether she ought not to stay at Stoneridge. And if she did she would lose the last of the Opera in London! How could she help to investigate the cause of an explosion so considerate to them? She sang snatches of melodies, clung to her husband, protested her inability to leave him, and went, appearing torn away. As well bid healthy children lie abed on a bright summer morning, as think of holding this fair young woman bound to the circle of safety when she has her view of pleasure sparkling like the shore-sea mermaid's mirror.

Suspicions were not of the brood Carinthia's bosom harboured. Suspicion of Chillon's wife Carinthia could not feel. An uncaptained vessel in the winds on high seas was imagined without a picturing of it. The apparition of Ives, if it was he, would not fit with any conjecture. She sent a warning to Madge, and at the same time named the girl's wedding day for her; pained in doing it. She had given the dear girl her word that she would be present at this of all marriages. But a day or two days or more would have to be spent away from Chillon; and her hunger for every hour beside her brother confessed to the war going on within her, as to which was her holier duty, the one on the line of her inclinations, or that one pointing to luxury-choice between a battle-horse and a cushioned-chair; between companionship with her glorious brother facing death, and submission to a weak young nobleman claiming his husband's rights over her. She had submitted, had forgotten his icy strangeness, had thought him love; and hers was a breast for love, it was owned by the sobbing rise of her breast at the thought. And she might submit again—in honour? scorning the husband? Chillon scorned him. Yet Chillon left the decision to her, specified his excuses. And Henrietta and Owain, Lady Arpington, Gower Woodseer, all the world—Carinthia shuddered at the world's blank eye on what it directs for the acquiescence of the woman. That shred of herself she would become, she felt herself becoming it when the view of her career beside her brother waned. The dead Rebecca living in her heart was the only soul among her friends whose voice was her own against the world's.

But there came a turn where she and Rebecca separated. Rebecca's insurgent wishes taking shape of prophecy, robbed her of her friend Owain, to present her an impossible object, that her mind could not compass or figure. She bade Rebecca rest and let her keep the fancy of Owain as her good ghost of a sun in the mist of a frosty morning; sweeter to her than an image of love, though it were the very love, the love of maidens' dreams, bursting the bud of romance, issuing its flower. Delusive love drove away with a credulous maiden, under an English heaven, on a coach and four, from a windy hill-top, to a crash below, and a stunned recovery in the street of small shops, mud, rain, gloom, language like musket-fire and the wailing wounded.

No regrets, her father had said; they unman the heart we want for to-morrow. She kept her look forward at the dead wall Chillon had thrown up. He did not reject her company; his prospect of it had clouded; and there were allusions to Henrietta's loneliness. 'His Carin could do her service by staying, if she decided that way.' Her enthusiasm dropped to the level of life's common ground. With her sustainment gone, she beheld herself a titled doll, and had sternly to shut her eyes on the behind scenes, bar any shadowy approaches of womanly softness; thinking her father's daughter dishonoured in the submissive wife of the weak young nobleman Chillon despised as below the title of man.

Madge and Gower came to Stoneridge on their road to London three days before their union. Madge had no fear of Ines, but said: 'I never let Mr. Gower out of my sight.' Perforce of studying him with the thirsty wonder consequent upon his proposal to her, she had got fast hold of the skirts of his character; she 'knew he was happy because he was always making her laugh at herself.' Her manner of saying, 'She hoped to give him a comfortable home, so that he might never be sorry for what he had done,' was toned as in a church, beautiful to her mistress. Speaking of my lord's great kindness, her eyes yearned for a second and fell humbly. She said of Kit Ives, 'He's found a new "paytron," Sarah says Mr. Woodseer tells her, my lady. It's another nobleman, Lord Brailstone, has come into money lately and hired him for his pugilist when it's not horseracing.' Gower spoke of thanks to Lord Fleetwood for the independence allowing him to take a wife and settle to work in his little Surrey home. He, too, showed he could have said more and was advised not to push at a shut gate. My lord would attend their wedding as well as my lady, Carinthia heard from Madge; counting it a pity that wealthy noblemen had no professions to hinder the doing of unprofitable things.

Her sensibility was warmer on the wedding-day of these two dear ones. He graced the scene, she admitted, when reassured by his perfect reserve toward her personally. He was the born nobleman in his friendliness with the bridal pair and respectfulness to Mr. Woodseer. High social breeding is an exquisite performance on the instrument we are, and his behaviour to her left her mind at liberty for appreciation of it. Condescension was not seen, his voice had no false note. During the ceremony his eyelids blinked rapidly. At the close, he congratulated the united couple, praising them each for the wisdom of their choice. He said to his countess:

'This is one of the hopeful marriages; chiefly of your making.'

She replied: 'My prayers will be for them always.'

'They are fortunate who have your prayers,' he said, and turned to Sarah Winch. She was to let him know when she also had found her 'great philosopher.' Sarah was like a fish on a bank, taking gasps at the marvel of it all; she blushed the pale pink of her complexion, and murmured of 'happiness.' Gower had gone headlong into happiness, where philosophers are smirkers and mouthers of ordinary stuff. His brightest remark was to put the question to his father: 'The three good things of the Isle of Britain?' and treble the name of Madge Woodseer for a richer triad than the Glamorgan man could summon. Pardonably foolish; but mindful of a past condition of indiscipline, Nature's philosopher said to the old minister: 'Your example saved me for this day at a turn of my road, sir.' Nature's poor wild scholar paid that tribute to the regimental sectarian. Enough for proud philosophy to have done the thing demonstrably right, Gower's look at his Madge and the world said. That 'European rose of the coal-black order,' as one of his numerous pictures of her painted the girl, was a torch in a cavern for dusky redness at her cheeks. Her responses beneath the book Mr. Woodseer held open had flashed a distant scene through Lord Fleetwood. Quaint to notice was her reverence for the husband she set on a towering monument, and her friendly, wifely; whispered jogs at the unpractical creature's forgetfulness of his wraps, his books; his writing-desk—on this tremendous occasion, his pipe. Again the earl could have sworn, that despite her antecedents, she brought her husband honest dower, as surely as she gave the lucky Pagan a whole heart; and had a remarkably fine bust to house the organ, too; and a clarionet of a voice, curiously like her, mistress's. And not a bad fellow, but a heathen dog, a worshipper of Nature, walked off with the girl, whose voice had the ring of Carinthia's. The Powers do not explain their dispensations.

These two now one by united good-will for the junction Lord Fleetwood himself drove through Loudon to the hills, where another carriage awaited them by his orders, in the town of London's race-course. As soon as they were seated he nodded to them curtly from his box, and drove back, leaving them puzzled. But his countess had not so very coldly seen him start his horses to convey the modest bridal pair. His impulses to kindness could be politic. Before quitting Whitechapel, she went with Sarah to look at the old shop of the fruits and vegetables. They found it shut, untenanted; Mr. Woodseer told them that the earl was owner of it by recent purchase, and would not lease it. He had to say why; for the countess was dull to the notion of a sentimental desecration in the occupying of her bedchamber by poor tradespeople. She was little flattered. The great nobleman of her imagination when she lay there dwindled to a whimsy infant, despot of his nursery, capricious with his toys; likely to damage himself, if left to himself.

How it might occur, she heard hourly from her hostess, Lady Arpington; from Henrietta as well, in different terms. He seemed to her no longer the stationed nobleman, but one of other idle men, and the saddest of young men. His weakness cast a net on her. Worse than that drag of compassion, she foresaw the chance of his having experience of her own weakness, if she was to be one among idle women: she might drop to the love of him again. Chillon's damping of her enthusiasm sank her to a mere breathing body, miserably an animal body, no comrade for a valiant brother; this young man's feeble consort, perhaps: and a creature thirsting for pleasure, disposed to sigh in the prospect of caresses. Enthusiasm gone, her spirited imagination of active work on the field of danger beside her brother flapped a broken wing.

She fell too low in her esteem to charge it upon Henrietta that she stood hesitating, leaning on the hated side of the debate; though she could almost have blamed Chillon for refusing her his positive counsel, and not ordering his wife to follow him. Once Lady Arpington, reasoning with her on behalf of the husband who sought reconciliation, sneered at her brother's project, condemned it the more for his resolve to carry it out now that he had means. The front of a shower sprang to Carinthia's eyelids. Now that her brother had means, he from whom she might be divided was alert to keep his engagement and study war on the field, as his father had done in foreign service, offering England a trained soldier, should his country subsequently need him. The contrast of her heroic brother and a luxurious idle lord scattering blood of bird or stag, and despising the soldier's profession, had a singular bitter effect, consequent on her scorn of words to defend the man her heart idolized. This last of young women for weeping wept in the lady's presence.

The feminine trick was pardoned to her because her unaccustomed betrayal of that form of enervation was desired. It was read as woman's act of self-pity over her perplexity: which is a melting act with the woman when there is no man to be dissolved by it. So far Lady Arpington judged rightly; Carinthia's tears, shed at the thought of her brother under the world's false judgement of him, left her spiritless to resist her husband's advocates. Unusual as they were, almost unknown, they were thunder-drops and shook her.

All for the vivid surface, the Dame frets at stresses laid on undercurrents. There is no bridling her unless the tale be here told of how Lord Brailstone in his frenzy of the disconcerted rival boasted over town the counterstroke he had dealt Lord Fleetwood, by sending Mrs. Levellier a statement of the latter nobleman's base plot to thwart her husband's wager, with his foul agent, the repentant and well-paid ruffian in person, to verify every written word. The town's conception of the necessity for the reunion of the earl and countess was too intense to let exciting scandal prosper. Moreover, the town's bright anticipation of its concluding festivity on the domain of Calesford argued such tattle down to a baffled adorer's malice. The Countess of Cressett, having her cousin, the beautiful Mrs. Kirby-Levellier, in her house, has denied Lord Brailstone admission at her door, we can affirm. He has written to her vehemently, has called a second time, has vowed publicly that Mrs. Levellier shall have warning against Lord Fleetwood. The madness of jealousy was exhibited. Lady Arpington pronounced him in his conduct unworthy the name of gentleman. And how foolish the scandal he circulates! Lord Fleetwood's one aim is to persuade his offended wife to take her place beside him. He expresses regret everywhere, that the death of her uncle Lord Levellier withholds her presence from Calesford during her term of mourning; and that he has given his word for the fete on a particular day, before London runs quite dry. His pledge of his word is notoriously inviolate. The Countess of Cressett—an extraordinary instance of a thrice married woman corrected in her addiction to play by her alliance with a rakish juvenile—declares she performs the part of hostess at the request of the Countess of Fleetwood. Perfectly convincing. The more so (if you have the gossips' keen scent of a deduction) since Lord Fleetwood and young Lord Cressett and the Jesuit Lord Feltre have been seen confabulating with very sacerdotal countenances indeed. Three English noblemen! not counting eighty years for the whole three! And dear Lady Cressett fears she may be called on to rescue her boy-husband from a worse enemy than the green tables, if Lady Fleetwood should unhappily prove unyielding, as it shames the gentle sex to imagine she will be. In fact, we know through Mrs. Levellier, the meeting of reconciliation between the earl and the countess comes off at Lady Arpington's, by her express arrangement, to-morrow: 'none too soon,' the expectant world of London declared it.

The meeting came to pass three days before the great day at Calesford. Carinthia and her lord were alone together. This had been his burning wish at Croridge, where he could have poured his heart to her and might have moved the wife's. But she had formed her estimate of him there: she had, in the comparison or clash of forces with him, grown to contemplate the young man of wealth and rank, who had once been impatient of an allusion to her father, and sought now to part her from her brother—stop her breathing of fresh air. Sensationally, too, her ardour for the exercise of her inherited gifts attributed it to him that her father's daughter had lived the mean existence in England, pursuing a husband, hounded by a mother's terrors. The influences environing her and pressing her to submission sharpened her perusal of the small object largely endowed by circumstances to demand it. She stood calmly discoursing, with a tempered smile: no longer a novice in the social manner. An equal whom he had injured waited for his remarks, gave ready replies; and he, bowing to the visible equality, chafed at a sense of inferiority following his acknowledgement of it. He was alone with her, and next to dumb; she froze a full heart. As for his heart, it could not speak at all, it was a swinging lump. The rational view of the situation was exposed to her; and she listened to that favourably, or at least attentively; but with an edge to her civil smile when he hinted of entertainments, voyages, travels, an excursion to her native mountain land. Her brother would then be facing death. The rational view, she admitted, was one to be considered. Yes, they were married; they had a son; they were bound to sink misunderstandings, in the interests of their little son. He ventured to say that the child was a link uniting them; and she looked at him. He blinked rapidly, as she had seen him do of late, but kept his eyes on her through the nervous flutter of the lids; his pride making a determined stand for physical mastery, though her look was but a look. Had there been reproach in it, he would have found the voice to speak out. Her look was a cold sky above a hungering man. She froze his heart from the marble of her own.

And because she was for adventuring with her brother at bloody work of civil war in the pay of a foreign government!—he found a short refuge in that mute sneer, and was hurled from it by an apparition of the Welsh scene of the bitten infant, and Carinthia volunteering to do the bloody work which would have saved it; which he had contested, ridiculed. Right then, her insanity now conjured the wretched figure of him opposing the martyr her splendid humaneness had offered her to be, and dominated his reason, subjected him to admire—on to worship of the woman, whatever she might do. Just such a feeling for a woman he had dreamed of in his younger time, doubting that he would ever meet the fleshly woman to impose it. His heart broke the frost she breathed. Yet, if he gave way to the run of speech, he knew himself unmanned, and the fatal habit of superiority stopped his tongue after he had uttered the name he loved to speak, as nearest to the embrace of her.

'Carinthia—so I think, as I said, we both see the common sense of the position. I regret over and over again—we'll discuss all that when we meet after this Calesford affair. I shall have things to say. You will overlook, I am sure—well, men are men!—or try to. Perhaps I'm not worse than—we'll say, some. You will, I know,—I have learnt it,—be of great service, help to me; double my value, I believe; more than double it. You will receive me—here? Or at Croridge or Esslemont; and alone together, as now, I beg.'

That was what he said. Having said it, his escape from high tragics in the comfortable worldly tone rejoiced him; to some extent also the courteous audience she gave him. And her hand was not refused. Judging by her aspect, the plain common-sense ground of their situation was accepted for the best opening step to their union; though she must have had her feelings beneath it, and God knew that he had! Her hand was friendly. He could have thanked her for yielding her hand without a stage scene; she had fine breeding by nature. The gracefullest of trained ladies could not have passed through such an interview so perfectly in the right key; and this was the woman he had seen at the wrestle with hideous death to save a muddy street-child! She touched the gentleman in him. Hard as it was while he held the hand of the wife, his little son's mother, who might be called his bride, and drew him by the contact of their blood to a memory, seeming impossible, some other world's attested reality,—she the angel, he the demon of it,—unimaginable, yet present, palpable, a fact beyond his mind, he let her hand fall scarce pressed. Did she expect more than the common sense of it to be said? The 'more' was due to her, and should partly be said at their next meeting for the no further separating; or else he would vow in his heart to spread it out over a whole life's course of wakeful devotion, with here and there a hint of his younger black nature. Better that except for a desire seizing him to make sacrifice of the demon he had been, offer him up hideously naked to her mercy. But it was a thing to be done by hints, by fits, by small doses. She could only gradually be brought to the comprehension of how the man or demon found indemnification under his yoke of marriage in snatching her, to torment, perhaps betray; and solace for the hurt to his pride in spreading a snare for the beautiful Henrietta. A confession! It could be to none but the priest.

Knowledge of Carinthia would have urged him to the confession straightway. In spite of horror, the task of helping to wash a black soul white would have been her compensation for loss of companionship with her soldier brother. She would have held hot iron to the rabid wound and come to a love of the rescued sufferer.

It seemed to please her when he spoke of Mr. Rose Mackrell's applications to get back his volume of her father's Book of Maxims.

'There is mine,' she said.

For the sake of winning her quick gleam at any word of the bridal couple, he conjured a picture of her Madge and his Gower, saying: 'That marriage—as you will learn—proves him honest from head to foot; as she is in her way, too.'

'Oh, she is,' was the answer.

'We shall be driving down to them very soon, Carinthia.'

'It will delight them to see either of us, my lord.'

'My lady, adieu until I am over with this Calesford,' he gestured, as in fetters.

She spared him the my lording as she said adieu, sensitive as she was, and to his perception now.

Lady Arpington had a satisfactory two minutes with him before he left the house. London town, on the great day at Calesford, interchanged communications, to the comforting effect, that the Countess of Fleetwood would reign over the next entertainment.

CHAPTER XLVII

THE LAST: WITH A CONCLUDING WORD BY THE DAME

It is of seemingly good augury for the cause of a suppliant man, however little for the man himself, when she who has much to pardon can depict him in a manner that almost smiles, not unlike a dandling nurse the miniature man-child sobbing off to sleep after a frenzy; an example of a genus framed for excuses, and he more than others. Chillon was amused up to inquisitive surprise by Carinthia's novel idea of her formerly dreaded riddle of a husband. As she sketched the very rational alliance proposed to her, and his kick at the fetters of Calesford, a shadowy dash for an image of the solicitous tyrant was added perforce to complete the scene; following which, her head moved sharply, the subject was flung over her shoulder.

She was developing; she might hold her ground with the husband, if the alliance should be resumed; and she would be a companion for Henrietta in England: she was now independent, as to money, and she could break an intolerable yoke without suffering privation. He kept his wrath under, determined not to use his influence either way, sure though he was of her old father's voting for her to quit the man and enter the field where qualities would be serviceable. The man probably feared a scandal more than the loss of his wife in her going. He had never been thrashed—the sole apology Chillon discovered for him, in a flushed review of the unavenged list of injuries Carinthia had sustained. His wise old father insisted on the value of an early thrashing to trim and shape the growth of most young men. There was no proof of Lord Fleetwood's having schemed to thwart his wager, so he put that accusation by: thinking for an instant, that if the man desired to have his wife with him, and she left the country with her brother, his own act would recoil; or if she stayed to hear of a villany, Carinthia's show of scorn could lash. Henrietta praised my lord's kindness. He had been one of the adorers—as what man would not be!—and upon her at least (he could hardly love her husband) he had not wreaked his disappointment. A young man of huge wealth, having nothing to do but fatten his whims, is the monster a rich country breeds under the blessing of peace. His wife, if a match for him, has her work traced out:—mean work for the child of their father, Chillon thought. She might be doing braver, more suitable to the blood in her veins. But women have to be considered as women, not as possible heroines; and supposing she held her own with this husband of hers, which meant, judging by the view of their unfolded characters at present, a certain command of the freakish beast; she, whatever her task, would not be the one set trotting. He came to his opinion through the estimate he had recently formed of Lord Fleetwood, and a study of his changed sister.

Her brows gloomed at a recurrence to that subject. Their business of the expedition absorbed her, each detail, all the remarks he quoted of his chief, hopeful or weariful; for difficulties with the Spanish Government, and with the English too, started up at every turn; and the rank and file of the contingent were mostly a rough lot, where they were rather better than soaked weeds. A small body of trained soldiers had sprung to the call to arms; here and there an officer could wheel a regiment.

Carinthia breasted discouragement. 'English learn from blows, Chillon.'

'He might have added, they lose half their number by having to learn from blows, Carin.'

'He said, "Let me lead Britons!"'

'When the canteen's fifty leagues to the rear, yes!'

'Yes, it is a wine country,' she sighed. 'But would the Spaniards have sent for us if their experience told them they could not trust us?'

Chillon brightened rigorously: 'Yes, yes; there's just a something about our men at their best, hard to find elsewhere. We're right in thinking that. And our chief 's the right man.'

'He is Owain's friend and countryman,' said Carinthia, and pleased, her brother for talking like a girl, in the midst of methodical calculations of the cost of this and that, to purchase the supplies he would need. She had an organizing head. On her way down from London she had drawn on instructions from a

London physician of old Peninsula experience to pencil a list of the medical and surgical stores required by a campaigning army; she had gained information of the London shops where they were to be procured; she had learned to read medical prescriptions for the composition of drugs. She was at her Spanish still, not behind him in the ordinary dialogue, and able to correct him on points of Spanish history relating to fortresses, especially the Basque. A French bookseller had supplied her with the Vicomte d'Eschargue's recently published volume of a Travels in Catalonia. Chillon saw paragraphs marked, pages dog-eared, for reference. At the same time, the question of Henrietta touched her anxiously. Lady Arpington's hints had sunk into them both.

'I have thought of St. Jean de Luz, Chillon, if Riette would consent to settle there. French people are friendly. You expect most of your work in and round the Spanish Pyrenees.'

'Riette alone there?' said he, and drew her by her love of him into his altered mind; for he did not object to his wife's loneliness at Cadiz when their plan was new.

London had taught her that a young woman in the giddy heyday of her beauty has to be guarded; her belonging to us is the proud burden involving sacrifices. But at St. Jean de Luz, if Riette would consent to reside there, Lord Fleetwood's absence and the neighbourhood of the war were reckoned on to preserve his yokefellow from any fit of the abominated softness which she had felt in one premonitory tremor during their late interview, and deemed it vile compared with the life of action and service beside, almost beside, her brother, sharing his dangers at least. She would have had Chillon speak peremptorily to his wife regarding the residence on the Spanish borders, adding, in a despair: 'And me with her to protect her!'

'Unfair to Riette, if she can't decide voluntarily,' he said.

All he refrained from was, the persuading her to stay in England and live reconciled with the gaoler of the dungeon, as her feelings pictured it.

Chillon and Carinthia journeyed to London for purchases and a visit to lawyer, banker, and tradesmen, on their way to meet his chief and Owain Wythan at Southampton. They lunched with Livia. The morrow was the great Calesford day; Henrietta carolled of it. Lady Arpington had been afflictingly demure on the theme of her presence at Calesford within her term of mourning. 'But I don't mourn, and I'm not related to the defunct, and I can't be denied the pleasure invented for my personal gratification,' Henrietta's happy flippancy pouted at the prudish objections. Moreover, the adored Columelli was to be her slave of song. The termination of the London season had been postponed a whole week for Calesford: the utmost possible strain; and her presence was understood to represent the Countess of Fleetwood, temporarily in decorous retirement. Chillon was assured by her that the earl had expressed himself satisfied with his wife's reasonableness. 'The rest will follow.' Pleading on the earl's behalf was a vain effort, but she had her grounds for painting Lord Fleetwood's present mood to his countess in warm colours. 'Nothing short of devotion, Chillon!' London's extreme anxiety to see them united, and the cause of it, the immense good Janey could do to her country, should certainly be considered by her, Henrietta said. She spoke feverishly. A mention of St. Jean de Luz for a residence inflicted, it appeared, a more violent toothache than she had suffered from the proposal of quarters in Cadiz. And now her husband had money?... she suggested his reinstatement in the English army. Chillon hushed that: his chief had his word. Besides, he wanted schooling in war. Why had he married! His love for her was the answer; and her beauty argued for the love. But possessing her, he was bound to win her a name. So his reasoning ran to an accord with his military instincts and ambition. Nevertheless, the mournful strange fact she recalled, that they had never waltzed together since they were made one, troubled his countenance in the mirror of hers. Instead of the waltz, grief, low worries, dulness, an eclipse of her, had been the beautiful creature's portion.

It established mighty claims to a young husband's indulgence. She hummed a few bars of his favourite old Viennese waltz, with 'Chillon!' invitingly and reproachfully. His loathing of Lord Fleetwood had to withstand an envious jump at the legs in his vison of her partner on the morrow. He said: 'You'll think of some one absent.'

'You really do wish me to go, my darling? It is Chillon's wish?' She begged for the words; she had them, and then her feverishness abated to a simple sparkling composure.

Carinthia had observed her. She was heart-sick under pressure of thoughts the heavier for being formless. They signified in the sum her doom to see her brother leave England for the war, and herself crumble to pieces from the imagined figure of herself beside him on or near the field. They could not be phrased, for they accused the beloved brother of a weakness in the excessive sense of obligation to the beautiful woman who had wedded him. Driving down to Southampton by the night-coach, her tenderness toward Henrietta held other thoughts unshaped, except one, that moved in its twilight, murmuring of how the love of pleasure keeps us blind children. And how the innocents are pushed by it to snap at wicked bait, which the wealthy angle with, pointed a charitable index on some of our social story. The Countess Livia, not an innocent like Henrietta had escaped the poisoned tongues by contracting a third marriage—'in time!' Lady Arpington said; and the knotty question was presented to a young mind: Why are the innocents tempted to their ruin, and the darker natures allowed an escape? Any street-boy could have told her of the virtue in quick wits. But her unexercised reflectiveness was on the highroad of accepted doctrines, with their chorus of the moans of gossips for supernatural intervention to give us justice. She had not learnt that those innocents, pushed by an excessive love of pleasure, are for the term lower in the scale than their wary darker cousins, and must come to the diviner light of intelligence through suffering.

However, the result of her meditations was to show her she was directed to be Henrietta's guardian. After that, she had no thoughts; travelling beside Chillon, she was sheer sore feeling, as of a body aching for its heart plucked out. The bitterness of the separation to come between them prophesied a tragedy. She touched his hand. It was warm now.

During six days of travels from port to port along the Southern and Western coasts, she joined in the inspection of the English contingent about to be shipped. They and their chief and her brother were plain to sight, like sample print of a book's first page, blank sheets for the rest of the volume. If she might have been one among them, she would have dared the reckless forecast. Her sensations were those of a bird that has flown into a room, and beats wings against the ceiling and the window-panes. A close, hard sky, a transparent prison wall, narrowed her powers, mocked her soul. She spoke little; what she said impressed Chillon's chief, Owain Wythan was glad to tell her. The good friend had gone counter to the tide of her breast by showing satisfaction with the prospect that she would take her rightful place in the world. Her concentrated mind regarded the good friend as a phantom of a man, the world's echo. His dead Rebecca would have understood her passion to be her brother's comrade, her abasement in the staying at home to guard his butterfly. Owain had never favoured her project; he could not now perceive the special dangers Chillon would be exposed to in her separation from him. She had no means of explaining what she felt intensely, that dangers, death, were nothing to either of them, if they shared the fate together.

Her rejected petition to her husband for an allowance of money, on the day in Wales, became the vivid memory which brings out motives in its glow. Her husband hated her brother; and why? But the answer was lighted fierily down another avenue. A true husband, a lord of wealth, would have rejoiced to help the brother of his wife. He was the cause of Chillon's ruin and this adventure to restore his fortunes. Could she endure a close alliance with the man while her brother's life was imperilled? Carinthia rebuked her drowsy head for not having seen his reason for refusing at the time. 'How long I am before I see anything that does not stare in my face!' She was a married woman, whose order of mind rendered her singularly subject to the holiness of the tie; and she was a weak woman, she feared. Already, at intervals, now that action on a foreign field of the thunders and lightnings was denied, imagination revealed her dissolving to the union with her husband, and cried her comment on herself as the world's basest of women for submitting to it while Chillon's life ran risks; until finally she said: 'Not before I have my brother home safe!' an exclamation equal to a vow.

That being settled, some appearance of equanimity returned; she talked of the scarlet business as one she participated in as a distant spectator. Chillon's chief was hurrying the embarkation of his troops; within ten days the whole expedition would be afloat. She was to post to London for further purchases, he following to take leave of his wife and babe. Curiously, but hardly remarked on during the bustle of work, Livia had been the one to send her short account of the great day at Calesford; Henrietta, the born correspondent, pencilling a couple of lines; she was well, dreadfully fatigued, rather a fright from a trip of her foot and fall over a low wire fence. Her message of love thrice underlined the repeated word.

Henrietta was the last person Carinthia would have expected to meet midway on the London road. Her name was called from a carriage as she drove up to the door of the Winchester hostlery, and in the lady, over whose right eye and cheek a covering fold of silk concealed a bandage, the voice was her sister Riette's. With her were two babes and their nursemaids.

'Chillon is down there—you have left him there?' Henrietta greeted her, saw the reply, and stepped out of her carriage. 'You shall kiss the children afterwards; come into one of the rooms, Janey.'

Alone together, before an embrace, she said, in the voice of tears hardening to the world's business, 'Chillon must not enter London. You see the figure I am. My character's in as bad case up there—thanks to those men! My husband has lost his "golden Riette." When you see beneath the bandage! He will have the right to put me away. His "beauty of beauties"! I'm fit only to dress as a page-boy and run at his heels. My hero! my poor dear! He thinking I cared for nothing but amusement, flattery. Was ever a punishment so cruel to the noblest of generous husbands! Because I know he will overlook it, make light of it, never reproach his Riette. And the rose he married comes to him a shrivelled leaf of a potpourri heap. You haven't seen me yet. I was their "beautiful woman." I feel for my husband most.'

She took breath. Carinthia pressed her lips on the cheek sensible to a hiss, and Henrietta pursued, in words liker to sobs: 'Anywhere, Cadiz, St. Jean de Luz, hospital work either, anywhere my husband likes, anything! I want to work, or I'll sit and rock the children. I'm awake at last. Janey, we're lambs to vultures with those men. I don't pretend I was the perfect fool. I thought myself so safe. I let one of them squeeze my hand one day, he swears. You know what a passion is; you have it for mountains and battles, I for music. I do remember, one morning before sunrise, driving back to town out of Windsor,— a dance, the officers of the Guards,—and my lord's trumpeter at the back of the coach blowing notes to melt a stone, I found a man's hand had mine. I remember Lord Fleetwood looking over his shoulder and smiling hard and lashing his horses. But listen—yes, at Calesford it happened. He—oh, hear the name, then; Chillon must never hear it;—Lord Brailstone was denied the right to step on Lord Fleetwood's grounds. The Opera company had finished selections from my Pirata. I went out for cool air; little Sir Meeson beside me. I had a folded gauze veil over my head, tied at the chin in a bow. Some one ran up to me—Lord Brailstone. He poured forth their poetry. They suppose it the wine for their "beautiful woman." I dare say I laughed or told him to go, and he began a tirade against Lord Fleetwood. There's no mighty difference between one beast of prey and another. Let me get away from them all! Though now! they would not lift an eyelid. This is my husband's treasure returning to him. We have to be burnt to come to our senses. Janey—oh! you do well!—it was fiendish; old ballads, melodrama plays, I see they were built on men's deeds. Janey, I could not believe it, I have to believe, it is forced down my throat;—that man, your husband, because he could not forgive my choosing Chillon, schemed for Chillon's ruin. I could not believe it until I saw in the glass this disfigured wretch he has made of me. Livia serves him, she hates him for the tyrant he is; she has opened my eyes. And not for himself, no, for his revenge on me, for my name to be as my face is. He tossed me to his dogs; fair game for them! You do well, Janey; he is capable of any villany. And has been calling at Livia's door twice a day, inquiring anxiously; begs the first appointment possible. He has no shame; he is accustomed to buy men and women; he thinks his money will buy my pardon, give my face a new skin, perhaps. A woman swears to you, Janey, by all she holds holy on earth, it is not the loss of her beauty—there will be a wrinkled patch on the cheek for life, the surgeon says; I am to bear a brown spot, like a bruised peach they sell at the fruit-shops cheap. Chillon's Riette! I think of that, the miserable wife I am for him without the beauty he loved so! I think of myself as guilty, a really guilty woman, when I compare my loss with my husband's.'

'Your accident, dearest Riette—how it happened?' Carinthia said, enfolding her.

'Because, Janey, what have I ever been to Chillon but the good-looking thing he was proud of? It's gone. Oh, the accident. Brailstone had pushed little Corby away; he held my hand, kept imploring, he wanted the usual two minutes, and all to warn me against—I've told you; and he saw Lord Fleetwood coming. I got my hand free, and stepped back, my head spinning; and I fell. That I recollect, and a sight of flames, like the end of the world. I fell on one of the oil-lamps bordering the grass; my veil lighted; I had fainted; those two men saw nothing but one another; and little Sir Meeson was no help; young Lord Cressett dashed out the flames. They brought me to my senses for a second swoon. Livia says I woke moaning to be taken away from that hated Calesford. It was, oh! never to see that husband of yours again. Forgive him, if you can. Not I. I carry the mark of him to my grave. I have called myself "Skin-deep" ever since, day and night—the name I deserve.'

'We will return to Chillon together, my own,' said Carinthia. 'It may not be so bad.' And in the hope that her lovely sister exaggerated a defacement leaving not much worse than a small scar, her heart threw off its load of the recent perplexities, daylight broke through her dark wood. Henrietta brought her liberty. How far guilty her husband might be, she was absolved from considering; sufficiently guilty to release her. Upon that conclusion, pity for the awakened Riette shed purer tear-drops through the gratitude she could not restrain, could hardly conceal, on her sister's behalf and her own. Henrietta's prompt despatch to Croridge to fetch the babes, her journey down out of a sick-room to stop Chillon's visit to London, proved her an awakened woman, well paid for the stain on her face, though the stain were lasting. Never had she loved Henrietta, never shown her so much love, as on the road to the deepening colours of the West. Her sisterly warmth surprised the woeful spotted beauty with a reflection that this martial Janey was after all a woman of feeling, one whom her husband, if he came to know it and the depth of it, the rich sound of it, would mourn in sackcloth to have lost.

And he did, the Dame interposes for the final word, he mourned his loss of Carinthia Jane in sackcloth and ashes, notwithstanding that he had the world's affectionate condolences about him to comfort him, by reason of his ungovernable countess's misbehaviour once more, according to the report, in running away with a young officer to take part in a foreign insurrection; and when he was most the idol of his countrymen and countrywomen, which it was once his immoderate aim to be, he mourned her day and night, knowing her spotless, however wild a follower of her father's MAXIMS FOR MEN. He believed—some have said his belief was not in error—that the woman to aid and make him man and be the star in human form to him, was miraculously revealed on the day of his walk through the foreign pine forest, and his proposal to her at the ducal ball was an inspiration of his Good Genius, continuing to his marriage morn, and then running downwards, like an overstrained reel, under the leadership of his Bad. From turning to turning of that descent, he saw himself advised to retrieve the fatal steps, at each point attempting it just too late; until too late by an hour, he reached the seaport where his wife had embarked; and her brother, Chillon John, cruelly, it was the common opinion, refused him audience. No syllable of the place whither she fled abroad was vouchsafed to him; and his confessions of sins and repentance of them were breathed to empty air. The wealthiest nobleman of all England stood on the pier, watching the regiments of that doomed expedition mount ship, ready with the bribe of the greater part of his possessions for a single word to tell him of his wife's destination. Lord Feltre, his companion, has done us the service to make his emotions known. He describes them, true, as the Papist who sees every incident contribute to precipitate sinners into the bosom of his Church. But this, we have warrant for saying, did not occur before the earl had visited and strolled in the woods with his former secretary, Mr. Gower Woodseer, of whom so much has been told, and he little better than an infidel, declaring his aim to be at contentedness in life. Lord Fleetwood might envy for a while, he could not be satisfied with Nature.

Within six months of Carinthia Jane's disappearance, people had begun to talk of strange doings at Calesford; and some would have it, that it was the rehearsal of a play, in which friars were prominent characters, for there the frocked gentry were seen flitting across the ground. Then the world learnt too surely that the dreaded evil had happened, its wealthiest nobleman had gone over to the Church of Rome! carrying all his personal and unentailed estate to squander it on images and a dogma. Calesford was attacked by the mob;—one of the notorious riots in our history was a result of the Amazing Marriage, and roused the talk of it again over Great Britain. When Carinthia Jane, after two years of adventures and perils rarely encountered by women, returned to these shores, she was, they say, most anxious for news of her husband; and then, indeed, it has been conjectured, they might have been united to walk henceforward as one for life, but for the sad fact that the Earl of Fleetwood had two months and some days previously abjured his rank, his remaining property, and his title, to become, there is one report, the Brother Russett of the mountain monastery he visited in simple curiosity once with his betraying friend, Lord Feltre. Or some say, and so it may truly be, it was an amateur monastery established by him down among his Welsh mountains, in which he served as a simple brother, without any authority over the priests or what not he paid to act as his superiors. Monk of some sort he would be. He was never the man to stop at anything half way.

Mr. Rose Mackrell, in his Memoirs, was the first who revealed to the world, that the Mademoiselle de Levellier of the French Count fighting with the Carlists—falsely claimed by him as a Frenchwoman—was, in very truth, Carinthia Jane, the Countess of Fleetwood, to whom Carlists and Legitimises alike were indebted for tender care of them on the field and in hospital; and who rode from one camp through the other up to the tent of the Pretender to the throne of Spain, bearing her petition for her brother's release; which was granted, in acknowledgement of her 'renowned humanity to both conflicting armies,' as the words translated by Dr. Glossop run. Certain it is she brought her wounded brother safe home to England, and prisoners in that war usually had short shrift. For three years longer she was the Countess of Fleetwood, 'widow of a living suicide,' Mr. Rose Mackrell describes the state of the Marriage at that period. No whisper of divorce did she tolerate.

Six months after it was proved that Brother Russett had perished of his austerities, or his heart, we learn she said to the beseeching applicant for her hand, Mr. Owain Wythan, with the gift of it, in compassion: 'Rebecca could foretell events.' Carinthia Jane had ever been ashamed of second marriages, and the union with her friend Rebecca's faithful simpleton gave it, one supposes, a natural air, for he as little as she had previously known the wedded state. She married him, Henrietta has written, because of his wooing her with dog's eyes instead of words. The once famous beauty carried a wrinkled spot on her cheek to her grave; a saving disfigurement, and the mark of changes in the story told you enough to make us think it a providential intervention for such ends as were in view.

So much I can say: the facts related, with some regretted omissions, by which my story has so skeleton a look, are those that led to the lamentable conclusion. But the melancholy, the pathos of it, the heart of all England stirred by it, have been—and the panting excitement it was to every listener—sacrificed in the vain effort to render events as consequent to your understanding as a piece of logic, through an exposure of character! Character must ever be a mystery, only to be explained in some degree by conduct; and that is very dependent upon accident: and unless we have a perpetual whipping of the tender part of the reader's mind, interest in invisible persons must needs flag. For it is an infant we address, and the storyteller whose art excites an infant to serious attention succeeds best; with English people assuredly, I rejoice to think, though I have to pray their patience here while that philosophy and exposure of character block the course along a road inviting to traffic of the most animated kind.

George Meredith – A Concise Bibliography

Novels
The Shaving of Shagpat (1856)
Farina (1857)
The Ordeal of Richard Feverel (1859)
Evan Harrington (1861)
Emilia in England (1864), republished as Sandra Belloni in 1887
Rhoda Fleming (1865)
Vittoria (1867)
The Adventures of Harry Richmond (1871)
Beauchamp's Career (1875)
The House on the Beach (1877)
The Case of General Ople and Lady Camper (1877)
The Tale of Chloe (1879)
The Egoist (1879)
The Tragic Comedians (1880)
Diana of the Crossways (1885)
One of our Conquerors (1891)
Lord Ormont and his Aminta (1894)
The Amazing Marriage (1895)
Celt and Saxon (1910)

www.ingramcontent.com/pod-product-compliance
Lightning Source LLC
Chambersburg PA
CBHW060529260626
47161CB00003B/823